Steve Cockayne was awarded a certificate of commendation by the National Book League for a story he wrote at the age of four. Following this, he took a forty-year sabbatical from literature to concentrate on a career in television as cameraman, manager, teacher and freelance consultant. He also managed to find time for some involvement in fringe theatre, music, puppetry and hypnotherapy. He lives in Leicestershire.

Find out more about Steve Cockayne and other Orbit authors by registering for the free monthly newsletter at www.orbitbooks.co.uk

By Steve Cockayne

Legends of the Land
Wanderers and Islanders
The Iron Chain

THE IRON CHAIN

LEGENDS OF THE LAND: BOOK TWO

STEVE COCKAYNE

www.orbitbooks.co.uk

An *Orbit* Book

First published in Great Britain by Orbit 2003
This edition published by Orbit 2004

Copyright © MetaVentures 2003

The moral right of the author has been asserted.

A CIP catalogue record for this book is available from the
British Library.

ISBN 1 84149 215 9

Typeset in Bembo by
Palimpsest Book Production Limited, Polmont, Stirlingshire
Printed and bound in Great Britain by
Mackays of Chatham plc, Chatham, Kent

Orbit
An imprint of
Time Warner Books UK
Brettenham House
Lancaster Place
London WC2E 7EN

Many people have helped, both directly and indirectly, in the writing of this book. I would especially like to mention Pauline Cockayne, and also Nick Austin, Kirsteen Brace, Stephanie Carpenter, Michael Cook, Anne Dewe, Martin Dow, Tim Holman, Ken Major, Liz Manners, Neeleigh Sparks, Lesley Starr and Julie Steele.

And apologies to anyone I have left out.

S.V.C.

Contents

Prologue:
CODES OF CONDUCT

The Pie Shop

'When is the new magician coming, Ruthie?'

Geoffrey Slater knew that Ruth was having one of her unhelpful days, so he hadn't really expected an answer to his question, but somehow he couldn't quite stop himself from asking her again. The reply was predictably curt.

'For heaven's sake, Geoff. I didn't know this morning, and I still don't know now. Why don't you just be quiet and eat your pie?'

They were seated at one of the tables, the one with the wobbly leg, at the back of the pie shop, and Ruth was staring absently towards the door, watching a group of apprentices tumbling out into the weak sunlight and making their way back towards the Palace. The midday rest period was nearly over and most of the tables in the shop were now unoccupied. The clattering sound of dishes in the sink drifted through from the kitchen, and the pie man had pulled the shutters almost all of the way across the hatch, leaving only the smallest crack. From time to time he peered through the narrow opening, anxious to close up for the afternoon.

With a sigh, Geoffrey pushed his dish away. Ruth's abruptness seemed to have taken away his appetite for his food. As usual, it had been mutton and parsnip pie, and Geoffrey had been looking forward to it. He always ordered exactly the same meal, and he always ordered his coffee with plenty of milk and sugar. Ruth preferred her coffee strong and black, and usually she didn't eat anything at all, preferring to smoke two or three of her nasty-smelling cigarettes. Now she stubbed the last one out.

'Come on,' she snapped. 'Let's get back. Put your cap on.'

Reluctantly, Geoffrey picked up his cap from the bench beside him, plonked it on his head and tried vaguely to pull it into shape. In common with many of the apprentices, he disliked wearing the traditional garb of cap, tunic and hose, but was reluctant to brave the wrath of the Brotherhood of Magicians by being seen without it. Ruth suffered from no such qualms, and had stopped wearing her cap the moment the old magician had gone away.

Geoffrey was desperately self-conscious about his appearance. With his stubby legs and wispy beard, he cut a ridiculous figure next to Ruth. She stood a full head taller than he did, and her long legs were as strong as a man's and looked quite splendid in the black hose of the Brotherhood. Without the cap, her long, untidy black hair framed her stern face impressively, and her small wire-framed spectacles made her look more clever and capable than he could ever hope to be. Geoffrey worshipped Ruth with a forlorn longing, and he wished that she could find something, anything, to admire in him.

Glumly, he followed her to the door of the shop, and together they walked the short distance along the ring road to the foot of Beggars' Row, where they took a sharp left turn into the steep, cobbled lane that twisted its way up to the service door at the rear of the Palace. Ruth strode quickly ahead, while Geoffrey stumbled along behind her, trying to keep up. There were only two or three listless-looking beggars sitting on the cobbles today, and as usual Ruth swept past them with a scathing disregard. Geoffrey felt a bit sorry for the beggars, but he was reluctant to part with what few coins he had left in his purse, because he knew that until the new magician arrived there would be no more money for him to spend.

Without a pause, they passed by the dozing sentry and followed their customary route through the maze of service corridors, inhaling lungfuls of carbolic-scented steam from the Palace laundry, zigzagging around the stacks of lumber outside the joiner's workshop, heaving themselves up the fraying rope banister of the winding rear staircase, until at last they arrived at the sturdy oak door of the magician's quarters. They no longer carried the heavy iron key, for they had stopped bothering to lock the door, as there was little inside that anyone was likely to steal.

Once inside, they picked their way across the obstacle course of the antechamber, ducked through the low connecting doorway into the gloom of the main room, and retired to their usual places at opposite corners. Geoffrey went to the cage where his furnace and anvils were installed, and Ruth went to her alcove with its stacks of books and scrolls. Then both of them flung themselves down on their mattresses and heaved their boots off. Geoffrey placed his neatly side by side, Ruth tossed hers carelessly in opposite directions. Then they both closed their eyes. In the absence of any instruction to the contrary, they had taken to having a little nap after their midday meal.

After an hour or so, the silence was broken by Ruth's voice, echoing down the length of the room.

'You know it'll all change when the new magician comes.'

'How will it change, Ruthie?'

Geoffrey sighed happily, relieved to find Ruth once again in a talkative mood. He knew that she had been thinking about what was going to happen to them, and he was eager to know what new ideas might have come to her.

'Well, I suppose we'll have to start eating in the Great Hall again. And I'll only be able to smoke on Fridays.'

'Can we ask him about the pie shop, Ruthie?'

'I suppose we can ask. But I wouldn't hold out too much hope.'

Both of them, for different reasons, enjoyed their trips to the pie shop, Geoffrey for the simple pleasure of his mutton and parsnip pies, Ruth because it was one of the few places where her cigarettes were tolerated.

The old magician, before his sudden disappearance, had always insisted that they take their daily meals in the formal setting of the Great Hall. This was not done in any spirit of small-mindedness, but simply in accordance with royal decree. None of the three had liked the arrangement, since the king, although a brave, wise and gifted man in his way, showed little interest in the affairs of the table, preferring to direct his energies towards the maintenance of courtly formality. Because of this predilection, mealtimes had tended to consist of lengthy stretches of ritual observance, grudgingly interspersed with undersized portions of unpalatable food. Fortunately, however, at some long-forgotten time, the royal counsellors and magicians and their apprentices and assistants had been granted special leave to dine at a place of their own choosing each Friday, and while the old magician and Ruth had taken the opportunity to languish in the ale-soaked atmosphere of the Crier's Rest, Geoffrey had preferred to mingle with his fellow apprentices at the pie shop. It was not until the day of the old magician's unexpected disappearance that Ruth had fallen into the habit of accompanying Geoffrey. Sitting proudly beside her at the table, Geoffrey had felt twice as tall as usual and only half as fat, and he had secretly revelled in the furtive glances of the other apprentices. All the same, it still rather felt to him as though Ruth didn't really want to be there.

Later in the afternoon, they took up their separate activities. Geoffrey prowled around his cage, laying out his metalworking tools and priming the forge. He was planning to add a few new links to the chain he was making. He was proud of his chains, and this was an extra-special chain of his own design. Its links were not oval, like those of ordinary chains, but square. With intense concentration, Geoffrey gave several sharp blasts on the bellows and grunted with satisfaction as the sparks began to jump and fly. As he bent to his task, his round, anxious face slowly relaxed into a smile.

Ruth drew the curtain across her alcove, lit the candle in its niche, and climbed up on a stool to pull down a scroll from the top of the stack. She was writing her diary, and she certainly didn't want Geoffrey or anyone else to see it. For most of the afternoon, the silence was broken only by the scratching of her quill and by occasional outbursts of hammering from Geoffrey. From time to time, the sharp scent of Ruth's cigarettes drifted across the vaulted space. Then, shortly before teatime, the peace was interrupted by a tap at the door.

'Hello?' called a diffident voice. 'Are these the magician's quarters? Who's that inside? My name is

Leonardo Pegasus. I suppose I should be known as Master Pegasus. Apparently I'm the new magician.'

The New Magician

He was much younger than they had expected, probably only four or five years older than Ruthie. He was tall, perhaps half a head taller even than she was, but he was already starting to show the beginnings of a stoop. His beard was small and neat, and his features reminded Geoffrey of one of the kestrels that used to nest in the old towers up on the battlements of the Palace. His robe and hat looked very new. He stared at the two of them, clearly disconcerted by their presence.

'Who are you?' he demanded finally. 'I hadn't really expected anyone to be here.'

'We come with the quarters,' Ruth replied quickly. 'We were indentured to your predecessor, the old magician. My name's Ruth, and I have four more years to serve.' She ushered him through the antechamber and into the main room. 'I can soon show you where everything is. And if you need any other help, finding your way about the city, places to get a drink, that sort of thing, just ask me. Oh, and this is Geoffrey. He's got another seven years to go.' While she was speaking, she had edged in front of Geoffrey, and he had to peer round the side of her to catch a glimpse of the magician.

'Well, Ruth, er, Geoffrey, I'm very pleased to meet you,' said the magician with a reluctant half-smile. 'I'm sure we shall get along splendidly. Perhaps I could start by having a look around the quarters? And, yes, some coffee would be nice. I assume you have a coffee engine here?'

'Not actually here in the quarters,' Ruth replied. 'The old fellow had some funny ideas about coffee. You definitely won't want to hear about them. But there's quite a good place just round the corner. Geoff, why don't you go out and get a big flask of coffee? And Master Pegasus, would you like to come over here and sit down while we're waiting? I'm afraid there aren't any chairs, but we've got these mattresses, they're a bit old but we make do. That's right, make yourself at home. And let me get a bit of light into the place.'

Leonardo Pegasus eased himself into a comfortable position and gazed at Ruth as she strode around the room throwing open the pairs of long, tattered curtains one after another. As the daylight began to seep reluctantly through the dirty lattice windows, the room and its contents came bit by bit into view. It was a long, high-ceilinged room with stone columns supporting a vaulted roof and with a disconcertingly uneven stone floor. Here and there, sullen-looking weeds sprouted from the cracks between the flagstones. The magician found himself wondering what type of vegetation such a place could support.

The rank-smelling mattress on which he was now slumped was situated in a narrow curtained alcove in which it took up most of the floor space. The walls of the alcove were completely obscured by racks of crumbling, dusty scrolls. At the far end of the room, in the opposite corner, stood what appeared to be a cage, looking for all the world like the lair of some degenerate beast. On the floor of the cage, surrounded by various pieces of ancient, bulky equipment, a second mattress was just visible, looking as if it might be a close rival in pungency to the one on which the magician was sitting. Around the walls of the room, heavy, stained workbenches were arranged at intervals, interspersed with tall, tottering cabinets stacked with glass jars, mostly containing small quantities of gloomily coloured chemicals. Some of them had noxious-looking sediments at the bottom. Tottering over the edge of every horizontal surface stood tangled structures of complicated-looking apparatus, incorporating oddly shaped vessels and retorts of various sizes, all connected together by curly tubes and angular tubes and straight tubes, and supported by forests of what looked like miniature scaffolding. The magician's predecessor had clearly been a practitioner of the alchemical school of magic, that sad, outdated system of belief that had fallen into such disrepute in recent decades. Things would certainly have to change before Leonardo could start any serious work.

Scattered around the room and amongst the benches and shelves, Leonardo also detected signs of recent, but probably not too highly civilised, human occupancy. Items of soiled clothing, both male and female, were heaped randomly in odd corners. Crusts of bread, pieces of mouldering fruit and overturned mugs were in evidence here and there. A chamber pot peeked shyly at him from beneath one of the benches. Peculiar aromas emanated from each of these items, and together with the fetid reek of the straw mattresses, the astringent tang of the chemicals, and of course the putrescence of the piles of laundry, they had combined to produce a vile-smelling miasma that draped the air in almost visible folds. Suddenly, Leonardo found himself gasping for breath.

'This place stinks,' he blurted out. 'Can't you open some of the windows?'

'Oh, sorry,' replied Ruth. 'I guess we've stopped noticing it.'

With some approval, Leonardo took in her tall, athletic form as she clambered down from the bench on which she had been straining to reach the skylight. She was slightly flushed and was breathing hard.

'The old chap never opened the windows,' she gasped. 'They're probably stuck, but I could have another go if you like.'

'Oh, don't worry now,' said Leonardo. 'Why don't you come and sit down here for a minute?'

But just then the creak of the main door, followed by a clatter and a splash, announced that Geoffrey had returned with the coffee.

* * *

'It doesn't seem right, somehow,' mused Master Pegasus. 'I mean, I've got this quite nice apartment over in the Western Suburb, and I can go home at night to my own bed, while you two have to sleep here on those ghastly mattresses. And having to live with that awful smell, as well. I think you apprentices get an awfully raw deal. I'd really like you to have places of your own one day.'

'I like it here,' said Geoffrey. 'I can be near my tools and things.'

'I hate it,' countered Ruth. 'I think everyone deserves a decent place to sleep. Is your apartment nice? I'd love to see it. What sort of things have you got there?'

The last few weeks had been busy, as, one by one, the old benches and jars and pieces of apparatus had been heaved out through the main door of the magician's quarters and piled in the corridor, where they would now form a three-dimensional kinetic obstacle course for passers-by until such time as the Palace labourers eventually arrived to remove them. The quarters had been swept and washed down, the walls had been painted, and men with crowbars and hammers and oil cans had eased open the windows. Other men had installed lengths of the heavy, snaking cable that would eventually carry the electrical power that the magician said he needed for his new apparatus. And crates had been delivered, crates containing inscrutable mirrors and winking lenses, tense coils of wire, cryptic-looking headphones and meters and rheostats, all packed in sawdust like the contents of some nightmarish bran tub.

Now another week was over, and the three of them were huddled around their usual table in the pie shop. Although Master Pegasus was, at least in principle, in favour of courtly protocol and appreciated the necessity of dining periodically in the Great Hall, Ruth had persuaded him, on four days of the week at least, to follow the example set by his predecessor and indulge in a less formal mode of refreshment.

'My apartment? Yes, of course, you can come and visit whenever you like, Ruth,' the magician was saying. 'I need some help anyway, to bring all my scrolls and plans and things across. And perhaps you could help me with the curtains while you're there. I somehow can't get them to hang straight. And you too, Geoffrey,' he added as an afterthought. 'You may as well come if you want.' He took a gulp of his coffee, shuddered violently for one terrifying moment, then subsided into a tentative smile.

'Yes. Not bad at all. But how did we get on to accommodation? I really wanted to talk about the new equipment I shall be introducing. In fact, I was trying to explain the notion of the empathy engine, wasn't I?' The two apprentices nodded, eager to learn about their master's plans. 'Of course, it's an entirely different principle from all those old chemicals and things,' Leonardo went on. 'It has to do with inducing in the operator a compelling personal experience derived directly from the imagination. It makes use of many of the new sciences – optics, magnetism and so on. It probably hasn't been done here before, so I've more or less come to the conclusion that we'll have to build one from scratch. Actually, it still hasn't really, I mean entirely, been invented yet.' He lapsed into silence for a few moments, seemingly lost in thought. Then he abruptly pulled himself together and continued, 'At any rate, I'll have to get a cabinet made for it, and then there's all the electrical and optical bits, I can do most of that myself. And you, Ruth, you'll need to get all those plans and diagrams in order. And there are lots of fiddly little parts that will need a special touch. And Geoffrey, there will be some metal parts that you can make up for me. And the nameplates, of course. Everything must have my name on it. I think brass would be nice, don't you?'

Grunting, Geoffrey wiped his dish clean with a hunk of bread. Ruth drained the last of her sour black coffee. And the new magician stared into unseen distances while his lobster and bean pie grew slowly cold in front of him.

Hanging the Curtains

Slumped on his mattress, Geoffrey was once again counting the links of his special chain. He enjoyed the heaviness of the chain as it passed to and fro through his hands, he enjoyed the oiled smoothness of each facet, he enjoyed the insolent angularity of the links, he enjoyed their reassuring similarities and, especially, he enjoyed their small, secret differences. He was spending a great deal of time with his chains these days, because, he had slowly come to realise, there wasn't much else for him to do.

Geoffrey had been generally quite happy with his life until Master Pegasus had arrived and started to turn everything upside down and to throw the old familiar things away. He hadn't minded too much about the benches and the chemicals, but he hadn't liked it much when some of the strange new engines had started to appear, and he hadn't liked it at all when the men came with their crowbars and forced open the windows. The gusts of clean, sharp air had blown away all the comfortable old smells, and the place now shivered under a harsh, hostile, unsettling atmosphere that confused him and made him feel restless and unhappy in a way he couldn't understand at all.

And then there was Ruthie. Ruthie didn't talk to him the way she used to. Ruthie actually didn't talk to him much at all these days. He wouldn't even have minded if she'd been bad-tempered and cross like she used to be, but she just didn't really seem to notice him any more.

The chain slipped through Geoffrey's stumpy fingers and rattled unnoticed into an angular heap on the floor. Geoffrey stared forlornly up into the far corner of the ceiling and tried to goad his sluggish brain into action. And, after a time, a glimmer of understanding began to kindle itself in a dim corner of Geoffrey's mind. All of Ruthie's strange behaviour, he realised, was because of Master Pegasus. Ever since the new magician had arrived, Ruthie had been completely taken up with doing things for him. She didn't want to do anything with Geoffrey any more.

Geoffrey tried to remember what things had actually been like before the old magician went away, but all he could remember was that everything had felt comfortable and he had always known what he was supposed to be doing. Now he really didn't know what anyone wanted of him any more. Master Pegasus had given him a few unimportant jobs, some brackets to make up and a few nameplates to engrave, but after that there had been nothing. He had asked Ruthie once, but it had been one of her unhelpful days, so that hadn't done much good, and he didn't like to ask Master Pegasus because most of the time he seemed too remote and important. So now Geoffrey just stopped out of the way in his cage, waiting for the next mealtime, hoping that he would be noticed again before long. Perhaps Master Pegasus and Ruthie were planning a special job for him. Yes, perhaps that was it.

Because Master Pegasus and Ruthie were always doing everything together now, and Geoffrey had been left out of things. They had even made him take his meals on his own. He had had to go to the pie shop by himself the last few days, while the others had gone to the Crier's Rest. That was where they were now. Geoffrey realised that he didn't really want them to come back. He sniffed loudly and a tear trickled down his cheek.

It must have been around the middle of the afternoon when the door finally burst open and Geoffrey heard their laughter spilling through from the antechamber. They always seemed to come back in a good mood, and that made Geoffrey feel more miserable than ever. He didn't even want them to notice him today. Pressing himself down flat against his mattress, peering furtively between the bars of the cage, Geoffrey watched as the two of them stumbled into the room. The magician was hanging on to Ruthie's arm – he seemed to be rather unsteady on his feet – and she was holding him up. She whispered something into his ear, something that Geoffrey couldn't hear. But the magician's reply was clearly audible.

'No, no, we don't need to go all the way over there, it's too far to walk now,' he shouted, and his voice seemed to tremble. 'Why don't we just go in your alcove? We could shut the curtains. But I don't think whatsisname's here anyway. I can't see him. And come to think of it, what does he do all day? We need to give him a bit of a sorting-out.'

There was more laughter as they staggered across the room. Geoffrey couldn't see what happened next, because his view was obscured by some bulky item of Master Pegasus's new equipment, but he could make out the sound of the curtain being pulled across the alcove.

After that, there were other sounds that sounded a bit like a game and a bit like a fight. Geoffrey couldn't understand what was going on, but he sensed that there was no place in it for him. Sadly, he began to finger his chain again.

Things went on in this way for some weeks. Nothing much ever seemed to get done after the midday rest period, but in the mornings, as more heavy cases were delivered and unpacked, the magician's equipment began bit by bit to take shape. Ruth would help Master Pegasus to assemble the delicate components and to fit the intricate structures into the heavy mahogany cabinets that continued to arrive at odd intervals from the joiner's workshop. Geoffrey was allowed to clear away the rubbish and the empty packing cases, and was occasionally ordered to make up a fishplate or a trunnion or to engrave another nameplate. When the midday chimes rang out from the Institute of Calibration, Ruth would accompany the magician to the Crier's Rest, while Geoffrey would make his solitary way to the pie shop, where he would be forced yet again to endure the derision of the other apprentices as he sat alone at his table. After the rest period, he was generally left to his own devices. Sometimes the others came back late and made their giggling way into the alcove. And sometimes they didn't come back at all.

Geoffrey had never been a sound sleeper, and he knew that Ruth was a restless soul too. At night, he would often find himself lying awake in his cage, straining to get a glimpse of her as she prowled about the room in her nightclothes, smoking one cigarette after another. So when she stopped coming back to the quarters at night he had known at once, and he understood that something must be very badly wrong indeed. One day he plucked up the courage to ask her where she went in the afternoons, and she had given him a look of withering contempt and told him not to be stupid. Sadly, he realised that he probably was stupid, and that there were a lot of things he would never understand.

'I've been helping Master Pegasus to hang the curtains in his apartment,' Ruth explained irritably. 'It's very complicated. It takes a long time. Sometimes it's too late to come back here, so he lets me stop the night.'

Geoffrey was baffled by all this.

'Can't he hang his own curtains?'

'They're very hard to get right.' Now she spoke slowly and patiently, as if talking to a small child. 'You just wouldn't understand, Geoffrey.'

And with that, Geoffrey had had to be content.

And then things changed once again. One morning, Geoffrey was checking a batch of hinges that he had made, counting them for the seventh time, when Ruth burst into the room on her own. She seemed very agitated about something, and her face looked white.

'He wants to talk to both of us,' she blurted out. 'He's coming in now.'

Moments later, the magician called them both into the antechamber.

'I've been checking your progress.' He seemed less friendly even than usual. 'There's a lot of work still to be done, so things have got to speed up from now on. Geoffrey, I've got enough hooks and brackets to last me the rest of my life. I need you to help me get some of these big engines into position. And the electricty has to be connected up. Do you know how to do that? And I need somewhere secure to store the portable equipment, so I want you to clear all the things out of the cage.' Geoffrey's face must have betrayed utter consternation, for the magician seemed to soften for an instant.

'Oh well, I suppose you can carry on sleeping in there if there's room.' He was becoming excited again. 'And Ruth, the antechamber still looks like a pigsty. I shall be receiving visitors before long, important visitors, perhaps even the King. I want that entranceway to look, to look, well, to look more welcoming, I suppose. It looks like a junk shop at the moment. Throw all that rubbish out into the corridor. Put a picture on the wall. Get some flowers or something. And where's your cap? You apprentices are a disgrace. What will the King think if you're not even wearing the proper garb?'

Sheepishly, Geoffrey and Ruth began to shuffle towards the door.

'No, wait a minute, I haven't finished. I want coffee. Why do we have to send out for it? I want a coffee engine installed in here by the end of the week. And I want some mugs. Blue and white striped ones, if you can find any. Do you understand?'

They had never seen him this angry before. For a moment, neither of them moved.

'Well, what are you waiting for? There's plenty to do. Will you just leave me alone and get on with it?'

So, for the rest of the day, and for several more days after that, each one of them worked at their own task in their own corner of the room, and nobody spoke to anyone else unless they really needed to.

In the Cage

Shortly after this episode, Geoffrey was awoken one night by a soft footfall at the entrance to his cage. As his sleepy eyes became accustomed to the gloom, he was surprised to make out Ruth's long-limbed figure slouched against the bars by the doorway. Even before she spoke a word, Geoffrey could tell that something was wrong. She had lost all of her sharpness and seemed somehow dull and unhappy.

There was a long silence. Then she took a step towards him.

'Oh, Geoff,' she said finally. 'I've been horrid to you lately, and I'm so sorry. Can I come and sit with you for a bit?' Her voice sounded small and sad and a bit

shaky, as if she had been crying, and before Geoffrey
could reply, she had thrown herself down on the
mattress and pulled the covers over the two of them.

'We used to get on all right, didn't we?' she said
mournfully. 'Until just lately. And now I've been spending all my time with Master Pegasus, and I've not had
a word to say to my Geoffrey. So if I promise to be
nice to you again, will you forgive me? Please say yes,
Geoffrey, please do.'

She started to sob, and Geoffrey, inexperienced in
such situations, found himself insinuating a tentative
arm around her sagging shoulders. A few minutes ago,
in his misery and loneliness, he would have been quite
happy if she had never come near to him again, but
now, now that she had started to tell him what was
the matter, he found that he desperately wanted the
two of them to be friends again.

'Of course I'll forgive you, Ruthie,' he replied.
'Won't you tell me what's wrong?'

'Oh, I don't know.' She sniffed loudly and snug-
gled down closer to him. 'Sometimes things just
happen and I let myself get carried along by them,
and then it all goes wrong. And now I realise that I've
been a silly girl and I just want things to be like they
used to be again. Can you understand that, Geoffrey?
Yes, that's nice. Can we lie here for a little while
longer?'

With a sense of baffled wonderment, Geoffrey held
her tighter, his nostrils tickled by the acrid scent of
her cigarettes, and a neglected corner of his mind also

finding itself tickled by another scent, a puzzling, musky aroma that wove its way furtively in and out of the tobacco smell. Geoffrey's heart had begun to pound, and he could feel a strange tightening in the region of his abdomen. He noticed that Ruth had begun to draw small circles with a speculative finger on his flabby chest.

'Can I show you a little trick, Geoffrey?' Her voice was tiny, but somehow she had begun to sound more certain of herself. 'A little trick I learned when I was younger? It's nothing much, but it might just make both of us feel a bit better.'

Slowly she sat up in bed. Then, with a sudden movement, she pulled her nightdress inside out over her head and tossed it away. It landed with a rustle against the bars on the far side of the cage. Underneath it, to Geoffrey's amazement, she was wearing nothing.

And then with a loud groan she threw herself down on her back on the mattress, reached out with her long arms, and pulled Geoffrey towards her.

It was still early when they awoke the next day, and the first thing Geoffrey saw was Ruth's face, staring at him from the other side of the mattress. Before he had time to collect his thoughts, Ruth leaned across to him and whispered fiercely in his ear.

'Master Pegasus will be here soon, Geoffrey, and he's not to know anything about this, and neither is anybody else. Do you understand that? It's got to be our little secret, you see. We can do it again, quite soon if you like, but only if you promise never, never to tell anyone. Will you promise me that, Geoffrey?'

'Yes, of course, Ruthie. I know how to keep a secret, of course I do.' He looked at her with alarm. 'But how soon will Master Pegasus be here?'

Just then, as if in answer to his question, the chimes of the Institute of Calibration rang out their morning peal. Ruth frowned at Geoffrey, then seemed to relent.

'I don't know. Maybe not for an hour or so yet. I suppose I've got time to show you something else.'

So, for the next few weeks, Geoffrey found himself in a happy daze, scarcely able to believe his good fortune. He wanted to shout to the whole city about what was happening to him, but he had to remind himself that he had promised Ruthie to keep it a secret. He didn't want to risk upsetting Ruthie, and he certainly didn't want to risk upsetting Master Pegasus, so Geoffrey took his promise seriously and remained silent. But, at last, Geoffrey was beginning to understand some of the unfathomable things that the other apprentices talked about in the pie shop. Although he still held himself back from joining in their ribald talk, he found that he could now at least sit back quietly and listen to them with a superior smile. Each night, after the magician had gone home, his Ruthie would come to him in his cage, each night she would show him another new trick, and each morning she would creep back to her own corner before the magician returned, leaving Geoffrey to assemble his scattered wits as best he could.

During the day, work in the magician's quarters continued to proceed in a reasonably orderly fashion. The magician was not particularly friendly to his apprentices, but on the other hand he didn't lose his temper with them again, and they all managed to carry out their allotted tasks without too much chatter and without too much fuss.

One day, when the new engines were nearly ready to be tried out, Master Pegasus called Geoffrey over to him.

'I've got an important job that needs doing, Geoff,' he said in a voice that sounded a bit kinder than usual. 'I do like those nameplates you've made me for the engines. They're good, very good. They really make all the difference. Would you like to do me a special one?'

Geoffrey was very excited at this suggestion, and drew himself up proudly, so that his tunic rose slightly above his plump knees.

'Of course, Master Pegasus. It will be an honour.'

The magician gave him a sidelong glance which displayed only the merest token quantity of suspicion.

'Well, I need a nameplate to go in the corridor. I think it should probably be attached to the main door. And it needs to be big, as big as you can make it, and it needs to tell everyone who I am and what I do. I've written down the details here.' He reached into one of the pockets of his robe and handed Geoffrey a scrap of parchment.

'I want it in an ornamental script, quite fancy, you know, so that it makes me look important. Yes, fancy and important, that's it. But not too fancy,' he added hurriedly, 'because people have still got to be able to read it and understand it. Do you think you can do that?'

Slowly and carefully, Geoffrey read through the words on the scroll. He was a bit disappointed that his own name did not feature on it, but he was still very proud that Master Pegasus had asked him to do the job.

That afternoon, Geoffrey began his task by carefully measuring the top panel of the heavy oak door with a length of knotted string. He counted the number of knots, both across and down, made a careful note on the writing tablet that hung at his waist, then made his way over to his cage and unearthed a suitably sized sheet of heavy brass, as well as an appropriate selection of hacksaws, files, drills, screwdrivers, bradawls and engraving irons. He marked up the outline of the plate, not at the corner of the sheet as he would usually do, but right in the middle, and then, with some help from Ruth, he fitted it into his vice, sawed it to size and burnished the edges with his files until they shone. Then, at suitable positions near the corners, he drilled and countersunk four holes that would just fit the supporting screws. Then, with his smallest engraving iron, he set out the construction lines for the rows of characters and, referring to one of his pattern books, roughed in the letters, making sure that they were evenly spaced and took up precisely the full length of each line. And then he started to engrave the words. As the engraving iron bit into the brass, and the long shiny spirals of swarf corkscrewed their way to the floor, Geoffrey found that he was enjoying the work more than he had enjoyed any of his work for as long as he could remember. For the remaining hours of that day, he found himself completely engrossed in it.

And then it was night-time again, and time for him to learn another trick from Ruthie. Geoffrey had never been happier.

Towards the end of the week, Geoffrey dragged a stool out into the corridor and, again with Ruth's help, heaved the plate up into position to mark out the pilot holes for the thick brass screws. When he had marked the holes, he drilled them out with his brace and bit, being especially careful not to drill through to the other side of the door. Then he called out again for Ruth, and she helped him to support the plate again while this time he finally fixed it to the door. For this task, he used his favourite screwdriver, the big one with the smooth wooden handle that had once been split and repaired. The deep crack in the wood and the rough iron staples that had been used to mend it had a warm, reassuring feel under his fingers. Finally, still balanced on the stool, he dropped his tools with a clatter on to the stone floor, took a deep breath, and inspected his handiwork. The plate looked truly imposing, and every passing eye would surely be drawn to it. In elegant cursive script, it bore the following legend:

> *THEATRE OF MAGIC:*
> *LEONARDO PEGASUS,*
> *CHIEF MAGICIAN TO THE KING.*
> *Please Ring for Attention*

'Isn't it fine, Ruthie?'

For a few moments more he balanced on the stool, continuing to admire the results of his labours. Ruth shifted from one foot to the other, but said nothing.

'I suppose he'll want us to make a bell, now,' Geoffrey continued. 'So that people can ring for attention. But don't you think it looks good?' He looked down, momentarily disconcerted to find himself for once taller than she. However, Ruth's upturned face was directed not, as he had expected, towards the nameplate, but towards Geoffrey himself. Slowly he became aware of an anxious look on her features.

'What's the matter, Ruthie?' Geoffrey asked, concerned now that he might have spelled a word incorrectly or perhaps hung the sign crooked. 'Don't you like it?'

'Yes, I suppose it's all right,' she replied absently. 'But the thing is, well, it's not the sign, Geoffrey, it's just that, well, I think I'm going to have a baby.' And she burst into tears.

'A baby?' Geoffrey was dumbfounded. 'Why are you going to have a baby?'

'Oh, you're so stupid,' she continued between sobs. 'You really haven't got a clue, have you? So just listen to me. I'm going to have a baby, and we're not going to be able to keep it a secret for ever. People are bound to find out about it before long. So I think we're going to have to tell Master Pegasus. I don't see what else we can do.'

The Principle of Chastity

'A baby?' The magician looked at them blankly. 'I'm not sure I can remember there being anything about babies in the lectures at the academy. It's not the sort of thing magicians usually concern themselves with. I suppose I could look it up for you sometime, if it's really important. I haven't unpacked all my books yet.'

The chairs still hadn't arrived, so the three of them were sprawled uncomfortably on the stone floor around the new coffee engine. This vital piece of equipment had been delivered only the previous day, and a certain amount of fine-tuning of its sensitive mechanism had yet to take place. At unpredictable intervals, therefore, it emitted, in unexpected directions, scalding streams of coffee or hissing jets of steam.

The magician, clearly anxious to return to work, took a tentative sip from his blue and white striped mug and frowned towards the empathy engine. Ruth moved to restrain him

'Actually, I think it may really be quite urgent.' She had caught hold of the sleeve of his robe to prevent him from standing up. 'Isn't there a code of conduct for the magical profession? Something about celibacy? People are going to notice a baby, aren't they? We're not going to be able to hide it for ever. And when people hear it crying, well, they're going to draw the obvious conclusion. Isn't that right, Geoffrey?'

Geoffrey, polishing the nameplate for the empathy engine, hadn't been listening.

'Geoffrey?'

Reluctantly, he transferred his attention towards the others.

'Yes. Yes, I suppose so, Ruthie.'

'Oh, he's useless. But seriously, Master Pegasus, we've simply got to do something before anyone finds out. I think you need to look it up in the book straight away.'

'All right, then.' Resignedly, Leonardo abandoned all hope of getting the empathy engine working that day. 'We'll probably end up having to unpack all the books, though. The one you need is bound to be right at the bottom.' He had risen to his feet and passed through the low doorway, and his words now echoed more faintly from the antechamber. 'And now you come to mention it, I think there may actually have been some instruction about celibacy. But I'm pretty sure it only applied to magicians, not to assistants or apprentices. Geoffrey, you'd better bring some tools, a hammer or a chisel or something.'

With much puffing and straining and swearing, they succeeded in prising open the large, square crate that contained all the books and scrolls and parchments that Master Pegasus had amassed during his under-graduate years at the Academy of Magic. Everything was packed in sawdust, and the crate was so heavy that when it first arrived it had required the efforts of four men to manoeuvre it through the door. Coughing at the eruption of dust, the magician pulled out a scroll at random, squinted at it, then tossed it towards the door of one of the adjoining storerooms. It missed its target by several feet and cartwheeled to a halt against the skirting board. By the time it came to rest, the magician had pulled out and inspected a couple more scrolls.

'I don't think I'll be needing any of these papers for now,' he concluded after a short interval. 'Let's just chuck them over there, and we can tidy them up out of the way later. I'd guess what you want will be some-where in one of the big books. And, as I said, I think they got packed down at the bottom of the crate. For stability, presumably.' He paused for a moment, consid-ering the mechanics of this proposition. Ruth coughed politely. 'Oh, yes, sorry,' continued the magician. 'I suppose we may as well get them sorted out while we're doing it. Geoff, you'll need to order some wood and build shelves for them in one of the alcoves.' He started to rummage doubtfully in the sawdust.

Eventually, the books were sorted into three categories. The largest category, arranged in two piles, consisted of a new-looking matching set of forty-six weighty volumes, enveloped in the rich scent of leather, and nearly all with their pages still uncut. The title of the set, embossed in gold letters on the heavily ridged spines, was *Codes of Conduct for the Magical and Counselling Professions.* The right-hand pile consisted of Volumes I to XXVII, and the left-hand pile consisted of Volumes XXIX to XLVII. Leonardo was not sure whether he had ever actually owned Volume XXVIII, but noted in passing that its absence had, thus far, not inconvenienced him unduly.

The second largest category of books consisted of eleven volumes of varying size, age and appearance. The titles, where they were decipherable, mainly concerned official rituals and procedures, including one, which somehow reached out and caught Geoffrey's eye, entitled *Modes of Refreshment, Section I {Courtly Protocol for Breakfast, Elevenses and Luncheon}.* Although the pages of this document appeared extremely well thumbed, Geoffrey could not recall anyone ever having mentioned a code of conduct for elevenses, not even the old magician, who had usually been a bit of a stickler for such things.

The third and final category consisted of one very battered cloth-bound octavo volume entitled *Fundamental Principles of Magic* and one very tattered paper-covered demi-octavo pamphlet entitled *Magic for Novices: How to Perplex Your Friends*, which the magician swiftly and surreptitiously thrust, without comment, into an inner pocket of his robe.

They then turned their attention back towards the two large piles of matching volumes, which Ruth had had the forethought to arrange in numerical order as they proceeded. The magician craned his head to one side and squinted at the shiny gold letters.

'*Affirmation* to *Backgammon*, no, that's not it, *Bastinado* to *Catastrophe*, ah, here we are, it should be here in Volume III. IIIrd from the bottom, unfortunately.' With some more puffing and straining and swearing, the volume in question was extracted from the pile, and the pile, largely due to the immediate proximity of Geoffrey's solid bulk, saved from collapse. With a flourish, the magician produced a paperknife from his robe and sliced open a few speculative pages.

'Celibacy, Celibacy, Celibacy, Celibacy,' he muttered as he rummaged through them. Eventually, with a groan, he sat back. 'No, it's not here. What are we going to do now?' Ruth frowned.

'Perhaps it's under Sexuality, or Marriage, or Virginity. We'll just have to keep looking. It's got to be in there somewhere. I just hope it wasn't in Volume XXVIII.'

Three-quarters of an hour later, the two piles of books had been thoroughly demolished, and the books were littered all over the floor of the antechamber, most of them sprawled on their stomachs, cracked open at one hopeless entry or another, their pristine pages streaked with grime from the floorboards. In the far corner, Geoffrey was also sprawled on his stomach, engrossed in *Modes of Refreshment, Section II {Courtly Protocol for Afternoon Tea, Dinner and Supper}*, while Ruth and the magician were on their knees, still searching intently through the remaining volumes.

'Here it is,' Ruth shouted triumphantly at last. 'Right back where we started from. Not Celibacy, but Chastity. It's even on the same page.'

'Let's see,' said the magician.

Together the two of them studied the paragraph in question, while Geoffrey remained happily absorbed in the arcane intricacies of The Incantation for the Offering Up of The Damson Jelly.

'It's pretty uncompromising,' Ruth concluded. 'Read it again. Aloud this time. And Geoffrey, pay attention. It does concern you as well.'

The magician coughed two or three times, then read aloud.

6.41: The Principle of Chastity

The carrying out of the duties of a Royal Counsellor, Soothsayer or Magician requires the dedicated service of single persons of unblemished record. Persons seeking to enrol for the said professions, whether in the office of Master, Dame, Assistant or Apprentice, are required to declaim a solemn oath stating their avowed intention to remain in a perfect state of chastity for as long as they shall continue to hold said office, and are in addition disqualified strictly and absolutely from

engagement in any form of sexual liaison with persons
of the opposite, or of the same, sex, or with any others—

'Any others?' queried Ruth.

'That's what it says' replied the magician. 'May I go on?'

—Or with any others whatsoever. The penalty for any
such infringement of this Regulation, whether inten-
tional or otherwise, shall consist in summary dismissal
from office and, in addition, of automatic and imme-
diate banishment to a distant outpost of the Kingdom
for as long as the Brotherhood shall see fit.

'I don't think I want to be banished to an outpost,'
moaned Geoffrey. There was a pause while they all
considered the options.

'Do we have to do it by the book?' queried Ruth
at last. 'I mean, couldn't we just sort of work out
something privately, between the three of us?'

'I don't know,' pondered the magician. 'I really
don't know what I should do. I swore an oath, you
know. I'm supposed to do everything the official way,
you see, in accordance with what's in here.' He
gestured vaguely towards the scattered litter of
volumes. 'And what would happen to me if I broke
the rules and then got found out? Much worse than
banishment, I should think. I should really report you
to the Brotherhood and let the official procedures
take their course. Yes.' He shifted uncomfortably on

his buttocks and considered this for several moments before continuing. 'But then, on the other hand, I don't really want to be responsible for having anyone banished either. It happened to someone I knew once – well, to one or two people actually, and it really wasn't much fun for them. Never heard from them again, as a matter of fact. Let me think.' There was a lengthy pause while he did this. Ruth lit a cigarette, and Geoffrey drifted away again on a small damson-flavoured cloud. The magician finally seemed to come to a decision.

'Actually, there *is* somebody I know who might be able to help. Somebody in the Bureau of Accommodation, as it happens. Perhaps we could find the two of you somewhere to live, away from the city. You'd have to resign from the Brotherhood, of course, there's nothing any of us can do about that. But I suppose you could find a different sort of work to do. Something where they're not so particular about people's private habits.' His features briefly took on a wistful look. 'And the baby could grow up out of harm's way. That would probably be for the best. But I'm still not sure I should actually—'

Ruth leaned towards him, and her manner seemed to change abruptly.

'Come on, Leo,' she whispered to the magician, and her voice sounded to Geoffrey as though it were stroking him. 'You can do it for your little Ruthie.'

At least, that was what Geoffrey thought he heard Ruth say, but he later concluded that he must have been mistaken. Anyway, it took the rest of that afternoon to clear up the mess in the antechamber, and then there were the shelves to build, and after that he wasn't surprised when Ruth said she was too tired to come to him that night, so it wasn't until the following afternoon that the subject of their future came up again. But when it finally did come up, it was in rather an unexpected way.

Geoffrey had been connecting up the electrical supply to the empathy engine and was screwing the brass nameplate to the back of the cabinet, while the magician fumbled with the circuit-breaker on the wall.

'There,' exclaimed Master Pegasus, turning to face him in a shower of ozone-scented sparks. 'It should be working now. The first prototype of the empathy engine. And I think I know what we can do for our inaugural experiment. Gather round, the two of you.'

Geoffrey and Ruth stared blankly at the mahogany cabinet. It looked rather like a large chest of drawers embellished with various additional features. Fastened to the top of the cabinet was a set of eyepieces. These were fitted with an intricate array of optical components and were shielded by a curved brass hood. To the sides of the cabinet were attached a pair of vertical, hinged ceramic handles, somewhat like the handles on the ale engines in the Crier's Rest. On one handle there hung, cockeyed, a bulky pair of bakelite headphones. And, at the front of the cabinet, mounted on a pair of sturdy iron brackets, was a padded leather seat.

'I'd better explain,' the magician began hesitantly. 'The concept is somewhat abstruse. But the idea of the empathy engine is that it . . . how can I put this? . . . it enables the user to experience the world of the imagination in an unusually vivid fashion. To experience it, in fact, as though it were utterly real. To see it, to feel it, to hear it, all without even having to get up from the seat. My intention, you see, when I have perfected it, is to use the engine as a means of testing the future. As a means of, I suppose, sampling the future to see what it's going to be like. And I thought that if the two of you were going to be leaving here, as it now seems you must, you might like to think about what kind of life you were about to go away to. Just try the future on for size, as it were, see if it fits, see if it feels comfortable. Geoffrey, it'll probably work more easily for you. You're more . . . how can I express it? . . . you see things more straightforwardly, I suppose. Why don't you go first?'

Geoffrey stepped tentatively forward and eased his ungainly bulk onto the seat. He leaned forward to peer into the eyepieces, grasped the two handles, and allowed the magician to slip the headphones over his ears. For a moment he was aware only of darkness and silence.

'Just try to relax a bit while I tune it in.' The voice of Master Pegasus sounded slightly muffled as the magician reached behind the engine to manipulate the small controls. 'Just a little tweak on the rheostat, and a notch more on the rapport indicator . . . and

two more beads to the left on the abacus of equilibrium . . . yes, that should be it. No, wait a moment
. . . another little tweak on this one . . . there, that's
right. Now just keep relaxing, and try to imagine
yourself twelve months from now.' The magician
peered over Geoffrey's shoulder into the eyepieces. He
snorted with impatience. 'No, not just you on your
own, you dolt. Try to imagine your whole life, if that
makes any sense.'

After a few moments of trial and error, Geoffrey
discovered that he could quite easily surrender control
and let his imagination take over. Gradually, he became
conscious of a rattling, hissing, irregularly percussive
sound that seemed to jump to and fro in the space
between his ears. Before his eyes, restless white shapes
started to form and expand and shatter and explode.
As the scene came into focus, Geoffrey realised that
he was staring at the sea, white breakers dashing against
a pebbly beach . . . He had always wanted to live by
the sea. He gazed at the waves, felt the sharp dampness of their spray, tasted its salty tang. After a while,
it occurred to him that he must be gazing down on
the scene from some point in the air, as if through
the eyes of a bird of prey hovering there. He wondered
what sort of place might be awaiting him on the
shoreline. Fiddling with the handles, Geoffrey found
that he could quite easily turn himself around in the
air. And yes, there on the shore was a funny little
house, standing on its own in a little garden . . . He
tried to get closer to the house, and found that with

another twist of the handles he could float down towards it, he could float down close enough to look into the tiny back yard, he could float down close enough to look right in through the window. And there were a man and a woman, seated at a kitchen table eating mutton and parsnip pies and drinking sweet milky coffee. Surely they were Geoff and Ruthie . . . ? They were having their supper. But shouldn't there be someone else in the room? Sure enough, from one of the near corners that was hidden from Geoffrey's gaze, there came a faint cry, and he saw the woman stand up and go to the corner and stoop to pick something up, and it was the baby, she was holding their baby, it was Geoff and his Ruthie and their baby, and they were living at the seaside. As the woman played with the baby, bit by bit it grew quiet. The man, meanwhile, stayed in his place at the table, continuing to munch at his pie. Now all three of them seemed to be happy. Geoffrey settled down comfortably to watch them. And if he listened hard, perhaps he could even hear what they were saying . . .

Then, abruptly, the components of the scene collapsed into darkness and silence as the magician pulled the headphones from Geoffrey's ears. For a moment Geoffrey was confused, unable to comprehend the sudden transition back to bleak normality. He felt as though the breath had been knocked from his body. And then, slowly, realisation began to dawn.

'Yes,' he said in a small, wistful voice. 'That's what

I want. That's all I've ever wanted. To live beside the seaside with Ruthie and the baby.'

'Very well,' said the magician. 'Thank you, Geoffrey. Sit over there, would you? Now it's your turn, Ruth. Have a look at what Geoffrey has imagined for you.'

Ruth stepped slowly up to the machine and allowed the magician to make some adjustments. For a few seconds, she sat very still at the controls. But then, suddenly, she tore away the headphones and rose to her feet with a hissing breath.

'All right,' she said. 'I've seen it. Can we get back to work now?'

Beside the Seaside

The house that Master Pegasus and his acquaintance at the Bureau of Accommodation found for Geoffrey and Ruth was, indeed, a small, solitary cottage that faced out across the restless sea. The cottage was situated several days' journey from the city, at the edge of a village, on an isolated, windswept stretch of coast, although it was by no means as isolated or as windswept as many of the more extreme and inhospitable outposts of the kingdom. In fact, at certain times of the year, the village was quite a popular place of retreat for those city folk who wished, for whatever reasons, to absent themselves briefly from their busy lives and responsibilities. Sometimes, Geoffrey would glimpse their distant, hunched figures staggering along the shingle, bent double against the relentless wind, their over-coats flapping around them. Sometimes they might be festooned with clinging children or orbited by excitable dogs, but more usually they walked alone, each figure seemingly enveloped in its own cocoon of isolated, windswept thoughts. It occurred to Geoffrey that any loose thoughts that were not firmly anchored to their owner would surely be blown away for ever. It seemed to him that this was quite a good idea, and Geoffrey sometimes found himself wishing that he could find more time to spend on the beach.

But, sadly, time was a commodity that Geoffrey was no longer able to enjoy. Although he was no longer permitted to practise any of his, admittedly limited, magical techniques, he still needed to earn a living, and so he had been relieved to discover on his arrival that the village was in dire need of a competent handy-man. The fierce wind, the salty air, and the battering of the waves resulted between them in a never-ending catalogue of damage to property, which of course required never-ending attention. Fences and gates were blown away, walls and gardens collapsed into the sea, ironwork and paintwork were constantly vulnerable to corrosion, and tiles and slates never seemed to stay long on the roofs to which they were supposed to be attached.

Geoffrey had soon discovered a steady demand for his practical skills, and although the work was not as exciting as being a magician's apprentice, at least it kept him busy. It also earned him an adequate living.

And, of course, Geoffrey was now a family man, so the money he earned had to go towards supporting not just himself, but his wife and baby as well.

'Hello, Ruthie. Hello, little Tom.'

It was a Tuesday evening in early spring, and the gales had been particularly violent that year. Geoffrey had spent the afternoon chopping up Mrs Crabb's greengage tree, which had been blown down the previous week. After he had chopped the tree into logs, he had spent a very satisfying couple of hours arranging the logs with geometric precision into a compact pile, the large logs and the small logs inter-locking and the curved logs nestling around each other like some complicated three-dimensional jigsaw puzzle. The taciturn Mrs Crabb had paid him when he'd finished, but had not seemed inclined to offer him any conversation or refreshment so, as he made his way home, Geoffrey was looking forward to a rest and a nice mug of tea. As he trudged up the front path, heavy drops of rain were just beginning to fall. He seated himself with a grunt at the heavy, sturdily built kitchen table and waited impatiently while Ruth boiled the kettle and banged down his mug in front of him. For some irritating reason, Ruth never both-ered to use the little cork mats, and as Geoffrey didn't like to see marks on the table top, he waited until she had turned back to the stove, then furtively slipped one underneath his mug.

'Have you had a good day, Ruthie?'

Ruth had had a terrible day. A truly terrible day, but not in any way an unusual day, for these days every day was a truly terrible day. Resentfully, she looked down at the elongated, red-faced, screaming creature in the cradle. Although she had tried hard to begin with, Ruth had found herself to be not at all a maternal sort of person. If young Thomas had been quiet and well behaved it wouldn't have mattered so much, but he just seemed to make one unreasonable demand after another, and she was left with no time at all to spend on the things that were important to her.

Ruth's enforced departure from the magical profession had come as a savage blow, for she was at heart an ambitious person and had long ago set her sights upon being admitted, some day, to the sparsely populated ranks of the kingdom's female magicians. While awaiting the birth of Thomas, she had been forced to think long and hard about alternative ways in which she might employ her talents, but the eventual arrival of the baby had brought all that to an irrevocable and deeply unwelcome halt. Ruth realised that she now hated just about everything about her life. After the sophisticated world of the Palace and the city, the village seemed a dreary place indeed. The people were stolid and provincial, the amusements were primitive, the weather was too miserable for her to venture out most of the time, and the occasional proximity of vacationing city folk served only to remind her of all the urban delights that she was missing.

And Geoffrey was a demanding husband. To begin

with, Ruth had vaguely looked forward to his daily return from work, but now his presence had become no more interesting to her than his absence. What with keeping the house clean, cooking meals, pandering to Geoffrey's whims and looking after the baby, she discovered that she was managing to be permanently busy and permanently bored, both at the same time. Her only relief was her diary, in which she still managed to scribble a few words from time to time.

'There aren't enough hours in the day,' she found herself saying.

Geoffrey took a cautious sip of his tea.

'You ought to get out more,' he replied laconically. 'What's for supper?'

When it began to grow dark, they went to bed so as not to waste too many candles. Geoffrey supposed that Ruthie must have shown him all her tricks now, for once they were under the covers she brusquely turned her back on him and lay on her side staring at the rain-lashed window-panes. In his half of the bed, Geoffrey lay glumly on his back, staring up at the cracks in the ceiling. And of course, before long, any prospect of sleep would be dispelled for good by another outbreak of desolate howling from the baby, at which point one or other of them would fumble resentfully for their slippers and stumble downstairs to attend to him.

Their life continued in much the same way through the summer and early autumn. Geoffrey chopped logs, repaired walls, painted doors and clambered precariously on roofs and chimney stacks. Ruth went to the market, swept the house, made soup, fed little Tom, made porridge, changed Tom's underclothes, made Geoffrey's tea, changed Tom's underclothes again and, occasionally, found time to write a few more words in her diary.

'What do you write in that book?' Geoffrey enquired one day.

'It's private,' snapped Ruth. 'And before you ask, I'm not showing it to you. And I'll know if you've touched it, so don't even think about it.' She closed the book with a snap, locked it in the cupboard and thrust the key into her handbag.

A few days later, Geoffrey arrived home after a long day spent raking up leaves in the public gardens. Tom was in his cradle, howling as loudly as ever, but the kettle was not on the hob, and Ruth was not in the kitchen.

'Ruthie?' Geoffrey called. He supposed that she must be doing something upstairs but, when he went to look, she wasn't there. Puzzled, Geoffrey stood at the bedroom door. He knew that something was wrong, but it wasn't until he noticed that the wardrobe door was hanging open that he began to fear the worst. Then he realised that Ruthie's clothes had vanished, as had her hairbrushes and her spare pair of spectacles. Geoffrey ran downstairs. The cupboard where Ruthie kept her diary was empty too.

Thomas was still howling as loudly as ever. Geoffrey looked down into the cradle at the thin, red-faced creature kicking and writhing there. He didn't know how to stop the noise. After a moment he turned away with a deep sigh, went to the sink and filled the kettle. Then he crossed to the stove, and discovered that the stove was cold. With another sigh he stared at the heavy kettle in his hands. His hands had begun to shake. Some of the water spilled out of the kettle. So Geoffrey hurled the kettle against the wall, and then he sat down at the table and began to sob. Later, aware that Thomas was still howling, he ransacked the pantry, looking for something to feed him on. Later still, it occurred to him that the baby's underclothes probably needed changing. He wondered where Ruthie kept the clean ones.

Ruthie didn't come back that night, or the next night. Geoffrey repaired the dented kettle and repaired the plaster where the kettle had hit the wall. From time to time, when the baby's howling became unbearable, he grudgingly attended to its needs. In between these chores, he scoured the house looking for a note or for some hopeful sign from Ruth, but he could find nothing. His Ruthie had gone, and she had taken every one of her belongings with her, and she had left nothing – except little Thomas – to indicate that she had ever been there. Geoffrey had no idea how he was going to manage.

As the days and weeks passed and autumn blew its way into winter, Geoffrey slowly came to accept that

Ruthie wasn't ever going to come back. From now on, it was going to be just him and Thomas. He looked down at the red, howling thing in the cradle and he felt his fists beginning to clench. Soon the creature would begin to crawl, would begin to walk. Then an idea came to him. Geoffrey went to the drawer next to the sink where he kept the few personal things he had brought with him from the city. There was his apprentice's cap. There was one of the nameplates he had engraved for the magician. There was his writing tablet. And there, at the back of the drawer, was the thing he was seeking. He reached towards the back, and he drew out, link by heavy link, the black iron chain.

One:
THE HOUSE BY THE SEA

The Digest of Affairs and Events: Volume 1 (in the Second Year of the Rule of King Matthew)

The Diary of Miss Garamond (Herald)

Greetings, Citizens!

Perhaps the author may first be permitted to introduce herself, and to say a few words concerning her life and history. She is not yet likely to be a familiar figure to the reader, for she has arrived only recently in the City, having previously been resident in one of the great towns of the Northern Outposts. Here she discharged a succession of functions at the Office of the Provincial Herald.

The initial years of her service in this Office were spent (in humble enough fashion!) in the role of Intake Assistant, until, after due time, she was fortunate enough to be granted advancement to the rank of Crier, calling the affairs and events of the day in the streets and squares of the town.

But in what manner (the reader may well ask!) did the author while away her hours of leisure? The citizen may rest assured that she spurned the temptations of idleness, and dedicated her hours to close study of the workings of the Provincial Administration and of the affairs of the Kingdom and the City. Patiently she awaited the day when opportunity might present itself, and in due time her patience was rewarded. For, upon the retirement of the Provincial Herald, the author had the great good fortune to be summoned by the Provincial Administrator and granted appointment to the vacant Office.

Now, despite the remoteness of the Province from the City and from the Royal Palace, the ways of this distant town were in many matters more advanced than the ways of the City, particularly with regard to matters of learning. Thus, even at that time, the children of the town, rich and poor alike, were taught the arts of writing and reading at their kindergarten desks. It therefore seemed natural to the author that information concerning the events of the day should be brought to the people through the vehicle of the written word. Accordingly, the author set out to recruit persons skilled in the arts of reading and writing and copying and, before many months had passed, the first volume of *The Provincial Digest of*

Events was prepared and ready for promulgation.

For reasons which need not concern the present reader, the early days of *The Provincial Digest* proved something of a trial for the author's perseverance but, before the passage of many months, her foresight had begun to bear fruit. The demand for the written word began to outpace the demand for the spoken word and, while the numbers of Criers fell into decline, the numbers of Scribes, Pasters-Up and Copyists began to display an upward trend.

Now, all of these events were of course taking place against the background of the old King's regime, and while the Provincial Administrator pronounced himself content with the innovations introduced by the author, the King expressed a degree of alarm concerning the propriety, and indeed the wisdom, of that which was taking place. Indeed, many more years were to pass before any form of written digest was finally to be tolerated within the walls of the City, and, as the citizen may well recall, it was not until the final years of the reign of the old King that his waning powers at last brought about some relaxation in his vigilance. And, by this time, the King's son Prince Matthew, a forward-thinking young man blessed with a progressive mind and advanced ideas, had begun to take matters into his own hands. With all due discretion, he dispatched an agent to visit the author at her Outpost, his aim being to acquaint himself with the methods by which affairs were being managed in that locality.

Following the death of his father, there were, of course, many tasks awaiting the attention of the young King, notably the dissolution of the Royal Counselling Services and the much-needed rationalisation of the Jester's Department but, nevertheless, word soon reached the author of a most remarkable opportunity. She was commanded by King Matthew to make her way at once to the City and there to assume immediate command of the Herald's Office. It was an invitation which the author would have been most ill-advised to decline! Upon arrival, she at once took up the duties of Herald, and, having recruited certain persons of proven abilities, she had within a very short time taken steps to ensure the availability of *The Digest of Affairs and Events* to every citizen.

Soon after this, the author was privileged to receive a summons to the Palace, there to attend a Private Audience with the King himself. The author found the King to be a most presentable young man, wise perhaps beyond his years, and possessed in addition of a commendable disregard for the time-worn customs and traditions for so long favoured by his father. In the course of the Audience, the King proceeded to outline the many changes that he is presently making to the administration of the Kingdom.

Firstly, the King is deeply troubled by the proliferation of unruly and lawless behaviour on the streets of our City. King Matthew is especially distressed at the danger posed to citizens by the murderous gangs of youths known as 'Wolf Boys' who roam the

Undertown by night, spreading fear and havoc and terrorising the unwary wayfarer. The King is determined to confront these wrongdoers and to restore the rule of law in the most uncompromising fashion imaginable.

Secondly, the King remains greatly dissatisfied with the manner in which information concerning affairs and events has to date been promulgated, both within and without the City walls. By this he refers especially to the manner of communication between the Palace and the people. With the intention of improving said communication, the King is disposed to grant to the author of this *Digest* a role of critical importance. *The Digest of Affairs and Events* is to be blessed with the patronage of King Matthew, and will henceforward be known as *The Royal Digest of Affairs and Events.* The author has been granted the unique privilege of a regular Private Audience with the King on the first day of each month, the aim of such Audience being the direct promulgation to the citizenry, through the channel of this Diary, of any matter which may be of public concern.

The author is deeply honoured to be granted this privilege, and anticipates with pleasure her next opportunity to communicate with the reader in this fashion.

Goodbye, Citizens, and long live King Matthew!

'What is the first thing you can remember?'

I suppose it must have been the leg of the kitchen table. Yes, that was the first thing, and I guess the chain must have been the second thing. But that table leg, now that was something I got to know very well indeed. When I was very small I seemed to spend most of my time underneath the table, and I got to know every scratch and scar and knot-hole of that leg. When I was bored, which was most of the time, I used to rub myself up against it, and I suppose I used to dribble on it and wipe food on it, at least when my father remembered to feed me. I suppose it must have been square at one time, when the table was new, but it had become smooth and rounded with all that rubbing, and the grain and the knot-holes stood out in relief. It formed a sort of miniature three-dimensional world for me, and it was quite a while before I got to know any wider sort of world. After I was taken away from home, I never saw that table again, but I'm sure if you put it in front of me now I would still recognise it. It's funny how these things can take you back. The chain? Yes, I'll come to the chain in a minute.

Thinking about it now, I can start to remember some of the other things that were around me in the house at that time. There was that mat on the floor between the table and the door, one of those things woven together out of old bits of scrap material, it was never tidy, always crumpled or turned up at the corner. It must have been red and white when it was new, but with age it had become almost black in places, and one of the edges, the one near the door, had worn away into tatters. I suppose I must have liked that mat, because when they came for me . . . I can remember the exact words the woman said, she said, 'We'll have to burn that thing for a start,' and I started to cry. I never used to cry very much, I suppose I lost the inclination to do it after the first few years, but there was something about the woman taking that mat away that for some reason set me off.

Sorry, I'm losing my thread. It's funny, sitting down here with you in this room, and trying to piece the whole story together. But I can see that it's a good idea. Once I've explained where I came from, and the things that people have done to me, perhaps you'll start to understand why there are certain things I need to do before I can rest easy.

Oh, yes. There was that table leg, and then there was the mat, and of course I've promised to tell you about the chain. The floor? No, I don't know why, but for some reason I can't seem to remember what the floor was like. Bare boards? Linoleum? Tiles? No, it's no use, it's gone. I don't suppose it matters very much, anyway. But I do remember the furniture in the kitchen, the two wooden chairs, and the dresser and the other bits. Big, heavy, furniture, and clumsy-looking, as if it had been built by someone who didn't really know what they were doing. Oh yes, that noise the chairs used to make, scraping across the floor when they were moved. I've got it now, the floor was one of those red-tiled ones. I can even remember the exact pattern of the cracks in some of the tiles, I could draw you a picture of them if you were interested. Well, no, I don't suppose you are.

And then there was my father. To begin with, it was mainly his legs, that was all I could see from under the table, and the thumping he made with his knife and fork, or whatever he was using at the time, on the table above me, that was like thunder. I could see his legs, of course. He had thick, strong legs, and he always wore corduroy breeches and big heavy boots. They always seemed to be the same ones, and the breeches were very worn, almost smooth in places, and they always seemed to have dried mud on them, and so did the boots as well.

I don't remember my father's face very well, apart from his beard — he didn't pick me up very often, and he didn't play with me. No, it didn't occur to me that there was anything unusual about that, and anyway, I hardly met another child until I was taken away. I suppose I was about nine or ten by then, and I was already almost as tall as he was, but he must have been a very strong man, much stronger than I was . . . sorry, I'm jumping ahead again.

And of course there was his voice. I can remember his voice very clearly. You know the noise you get when you try to put the pieces of a jug back together, a big earthenware jug that's been broken into several pieces? A sort of scraping noise from the jagged edges, but with a sort of boomy echo from inside the jug. No, that's silly, he couldn't have sounded anything like that, but somehow I must have put the two things together in my mind, because that's always what came to me when I heard him speak. Come to think of it, I once broke a jug like that, I remember being punished for it.

And of course I can remember some of his words. Certain phrases that he used all the time. 'Thomas, can't you get out from under my feet?' That was one of them. 'Leave that alone, you little monkey!' I had no idea what a monkey was, of course, and I'm not sure he did either. I found out later that he had come from the city, so I suppose he may have seen them in the menagerie. 'Can't you behave yourself for a minute, Tom?' That was another one. He always seemed to want to stop me from doing whatever I was doing. Yes, that was it. He wanted to stop me. Because he must somehow have known, right from the time that I learned to crawl, that he and I were very different from one another. He wanted me to be like him, but right from the start he sensed that I wasn't going to be like him, and he didn't like that, he didn't like it at all.

It was obvious from very early on that I was going to grow up tall and thin, and in the end I turned out quite awkward as well. My father was a stocky man, a practical type, very precise in what he did, he was some sort of a builder or handyman by trade, but as I grew up I always seemed to have my head in the clouds, I was never interested in anything mechanical, and he didn't like that at all. I never had any toys – no, I didn't realise that that was out of the ordinary, either – but he used to give me his tools to play with. There was a pair of pincers, and some sort of clamp thing that screwed up. I didn't understand what they were, and they never seemed very interesting anyway

But then, one day, he dropped his little writing tablet on the floor, the thing he used for making notes and doing diagrams and so on. I was fascinated by all the little marks and squiggles, of course I didn't know what they were at the time, but somehow I got a friendly sort of feeling from them, not at all like those other things of his, and I started to flick through the pages, and while I was doing that, I *suppose I must have been under the table as usual, he was moving around in the kitchen and he seemed to be getting annoyed about something, and when he finally saw me playing with his tablet he snatched it away from me and started shouting, 'What are you doing with that?' and then he threw me some piece of ironmongery to play with instead, I think it was a hinge or a fishplate, something like that anyway, but of course I wasn't interested, and that just made him even more furious.*

No, he didn't hit me. He had his faults, plenty of them actually, but he never raised his hand to me. Oh, except for that one time of course, but I'll come to that later. No, his way of punishing me was with the chain. That's why the chain is the second thing I said I could remember, and that's why I must have spent so much time under the kitchen table. It was when I was starting to crawl, I suppose, and I used to roll about on that dirty old red and white mat, and that was when he used to say that thing about getting under his feet. So back I would go, under the table, and when I got bored playing with the table leg, there was always the chain to play with. And when I got bored with the chain, then there was the table leg again.

At the time I never thought that there was anything unusual about the chain, I never realised what power it would come to have in my life, and I didn't find out till years later that he'd made it himself, but after a while I did get to know that chain pretty well. It was made of some sort of black metal, and the links were a sort of square shape, rather nicely designed I suppose, with little faceted corners and things, and I used to like the feel of it — it was heavy, of course, and the links felt smooth and slightly oily, I used to suck them sometimes, they had a spiky, slippery sort of taste.

Of course, the chain wasn't there all the time to begin with, I think my father only brought it out when I'd been bad. He used to fasten one end of the chain to the table leg. He used a padlock, I think. And of course the other end of the chain went round my neck. It was attached to an iron collar that opened with a hinge. And that was fastened with a padlock as well. So that was why I never strayed very far from my little world underneath the kitchen table. And that's why the table leg and the iron chain are the first two things I can remember.

Serendipity Court

'We can see the city now. Shift yourself off that bunk, and come out and have a look!'

Gideon Blackwood applied the wheelbrake at the side of the waggon and relaxed his grip on Kitty's reins, and then he and Peg shuffled to either end of the bench to allow their passenger a clear sight of the view ahead. A moment later, Rusty Brown's freckled face appeared between them in the doorway.

'Sorry, I must have dozed off for a second. What time is it?'

As Rusty wriggled his way through the narrow opening, Peg pushed herself into the corner of the bench, keeping a cautious arm around little Megan.

'You're a lazybones,' she laughed. 'It's nearly noon, we've been on the road for hours. Here, squeeze yourself in and take a look.'

Clumsily brushing his red hair out of his eyes, Rusty clambered over the bench and eased himself down between the two of them.

'Play with Rusty?' Megan piped up. With a show of mock reluctance, he lifted her onto his knee, where she at once started to tug at a loose stud on his leather jacket.

'There's the docks,' Gideon was pointing straight ahead, 'and see those tall buildings to the left? Those are the North Estate. That's where you'll find Uncle Joseph.'

Rusty gazed ahead of him, taking in the whole panorama. He hadn't thought much about the city in the couple of years since he had been away, but the view ahead of him was bringing back the experience so vividly that he could feel his eyes beginning to prick and his stomach beginning to tense. His time there had been desolate and terrifying and exhilarating and dangerous and overwhelming, and in the end he had had no choice but to run. And, in the intervening years, he had been taken up with other things, but now he found that he could approach the city with a fresh spirit.

Gideon had halted the waggon at the top of a gentle rise and loosed old Kitty's reins to allow her to graze at the roadside. Ahead of them now the ground fell away sharply on three sides. A half-hearted sun had broken through the clouds, throwing into hazy relief the irregular patchwork of motley-coloured fields, zigzagging lanes and scattered habitations. Like a sleeping body beneath a quilt, the landscape offered only a discreet indication of its contours, sloping, at first steeply, then more gently, away from them and down to the bright curve of the river.

And beyond the river lay the city.

Bit by bit, Rusty took in the view, trying to align each element of what was before him with the distorted and tangled chaos of memories that still echoed from time to time through unexpected corners of his dreams. Far away to his right lay the shining roofs and spires of the Western Suburb, and the elegant, arched stone bridge that carried its privileged denizens back and forth on their daily journeys to work. He could just make out one of the huge sailing vessels of the royal fleet approaching the bridge, her masts lowered, travelling now under oar power, preparing to pass beneath the central arch on her way to her berth in the docks. The docks with their cranes and masts and sails and pennants obscured most of his view of the city walls, allowing him only fragmentary glimpses of the ramparts, until finally they gave way to the drab, grey blocks and towers of the North Estate.

This was territory more familiar to Rusty. Although he could not quite see the ferry terminal from his present position, he knew that the river, broader at this point, was traversed at regular intervals by the old power-driven vessel, the same vessel that had once carried him as a stowaway in flight, clinging to her side in the freezing water. Beyond that, he could just make out the far curve of the river, encircling the city walls to the extreme left of the panorama.

And rising above it all, implacable on its massive base of rock, stood the royal Palace, with its turrets and gatehouses and its fluttering rows of kites, surmounted by the strange new six-sided accretion that was said to house King Matt's administrative offices.

'I thought you'd want to see it.' Rusty became aware that Gideon had picked up the reins again. 'We lose sight of it when we turn downhill, and you won't really get another view until you get to the ferry.'

'Yes,' murmured Rusty. 'Thanks. It feels really odd. You can't imagine.' He took a long, sharp breath, and a faint shudder passed briefly through his body. Then he became aware that Megan was tugging at the knees of his trousers, and gave her a playful slap.

'Rusty's naughty' said Megan.

'No,' replied Peg, her mock-sternness mitigated by a maternal twinkle. '*Megan's* naughty.'

Then Gideon released the brake and gave a sharp tug on Kitty's reins, and the waggon started to roll downhill, and the city was lost from view.

'This is about as far as we can take you,' said Gideon an hour later. 'Hand me back the reins, and you can get your things from inside.'

Rusty scrambled down into the narrow space inside

the waggon. Peg was curled up with Megan on one of the bunks, crooning snatches of some old Wanderers' ballad, seemingly oblivious to the rest of the world. Quietly, Rusty set about stowing his few belongings into his backpack, then climbed outside again to join Gideon on the bench

'The way takes us east from here,' said Gideon, 'but we can drop you just by the transport interchange. You could find another waggon there, or you could walk down to the ferry if you'd rather. But watch out for the Wolf Boys. They're worse than ever, these days. You'd best jump off now, anyway. Peg, Rusty's leaving us.'

'Bye, love. Come back soon.' Peg kissed him warmly, while Megan gave a last tug at the knees of his trousers. Gideon reached out a hard, dry hand to help him down on to the road for the last time. Rusty fumbled in his pocket for a coin.

'No, no, put away your money.' Gideon's voice was firm. 'We've known each other off and on since we were lads. The world's put some strange things in our path, one way and another. But you know you are always welcome in my home.' Rusty noticed that his friend had slipped unconsciously into the formal speech of the wandering folk, as he always did at auspicious moments. 'And your friendship is payment enough. So save your money for Uncle Joseph. He won't be shy about taking it! And remember, the road will bring me back to this place at the same season next year, and the year after, and every year thereafter.

Until the next crossing of our paths, then, Rusty Brown. Good guidance to you.'

He gave another tug on the reins, and the waggon pulled briskly away.

Rusty shouldered his pack and looked around him with some curiosity. He was standing at the edge of a vast, sunken expanse of rutted mud from which broad roads radiated in all directions, bearing traffic of every description. Scores of carts and waggons had descended into the dip, together with all manner of other vehicles, some large and some small, some horse-drawn and some power-driven, some making their laborious way from one side of the dip to the other, others stationary, sunk in thick mud up to their axles. This, then, was the transport interchange, the place where all the highways of the kingdom converged, and where conveyances travelling from every part of the land met up to collect or deposit goods and passengers, and to continue in whatever new direction they might be bound. As Rusty picked his way cautiously forward, trying to avoid the worst of the mud, he could detect no trace of organisation or method anywhere around him. Vehicles were pointed this way and that, their owners struggling with levers and brushwood and rocks and planks, desperately trying to gain a firm hold for their wheels. Passengers sagging under the weight of trunks and suitcases stumbled to and fro, seeking vainly for the conveyance that would take them to their destination, shouting to one another for assistance, occasionally subsiding into the mud until some helpful soul might pause to rescue them. There were no signposts, no signal kites, seemingly nothing to assist traveller in finding carrier or carrier in finding traveller. Rusty tightened his grip on his pack and stared about him in confusion. He was becoming uncomfortably aware of a feeling of dampness inside his shoes.

'Boots, mister?' The rasping voice came from a small, dirty-faced girl who had just emerged from behind a waggon that had capsized at a crazy angle in the mud in front of Rusty. She was clutching an outsize pair of rubber boots against her ragged smock, and Rusty noticed that she wore a similar, but scaled-down, pair on her feet. 'Rent yer boots here and get aboard with yer feet dry!' Behind her stood an even smaller boy, similarly shod, dragging a sledge loaded with boots in various sizes.

'Yes, thank you,' replied Rusty, offering her a small coin. 'Can you tell me how to get to the North Estate?'

'Easy, mister. See the tall, red waggon, in the distance there? That'll take you, or any of them little three-wheelers, just ask. Or you could walk. It's not that far. Look, you can just see the start of it over there.' She wiped her nose with the back of her hand, while the boy selected a pair of boots from the sledge. Supported by the two urchins, Rusty stuffed his leaking shoes one by one into his pack, and, keeping a careful hold on his socks, started to ease his feet down into the boots. Eventually he was ready.

'Thank you,' he said to the girl. 'What's your name?'

'Maisie,' she replied. 'And this 'ere's me brother Ross. Just leave the boots in one of the boxes when you've done with 'em. Oh, and I do like yer hair, mister.'

Bashfully, Rusty brushed his red hair from his eyes. As he lurched away towards the North Estates, he could still hear Maisie shouting hoarsely in the distance, 'Boots, mister? Boots, lady?' until her voice blended with all the other voices and noises.

With increasing confidence, Rusty picked his way between the waggons. Some of them were moving slowly, others seemed as though they must be stuck fast for ever, and one had keeled over irrevocably on its side. Groups of travellers shouted and cursed and shoved Rusty out of the way, and dirty children picked their way nimbly about, offering boots, refreshments, directional advice, and, from time to time, to Rusty's intense embarrassment, other services of a more intimate nature. Eventually he found his way to the far side of the area, where he was able, as promised, to deposit his boots in a large, rough timber container matter-of-factly labelled 'BOOTS'.

The going was easier now. The ground beneath his feet was hard and stony, and he found himself walking along the side of a busy thoroughfare that at last led him downhill to the bank of the river. Furtively, Rusty pulled a scrap of paper from his pocket. In response to Gideon's directions, he had sketched a rough chart that showed him how to find the apartment building at which Joseph Blackwood was the custodian. It wouldn't do to let anyone see the paper, for the use of charts was still forbidden to the general citizenry at this time, but Rusty had grown accustomed to a degree of concealment, so he quickly memorised the next few directions before thrusting the chart away out of sight again.

He crossed the river on the ferry, this time as a paying passenger, and he picked his way through the loose grid of drab lanes and courts that linked the grimy apartment buildings of the North Estate. From time to time, he caught a sidelong glimpse of furtive figures who watched him through slitted eyes but, when he returned their glance, they would quickly melt away, vanishing into alleys or behind walls. He soon found that he felt safest if he strode purposefully ahead, looking neither to left nor to right.

Eventually, Rusty found himself in front of the building that Gideon had described to him. Over the double entrance doors, a crude, hand-painted sign proclaimed the name 'SERENDIPITY COURT'.

Rusty's first impression of Serendipity Court was one of width rather than of height, for although the building towered several storeys above him, it sprawled outwards to either side over a much greater distance, occupying a crazily irregular ground plan, as if assembled at random from a child's box of building blocks. The outer walls of Serendipity Court were criss-crossed with an intricate network of rickety stairs, catwalks, balconies and ladders, all constructed in a haphazard fashion from scraps of timber and miscellaneous lengths

of rope. As Gideon had warned him, the constructors
had for some reason neglected to include any internal staircases in the finished building, and successive
generations of tenants had been obliged to make their
own improvised arrangements. This unusual feature
did not, of course, appeal to everybody, and so the
tenants at Serendipity Court tended on the whole to
be people who were young, agile, and fairly eccen-
tric. It also meant that the apartments could be hired
at an appealingly low rent. Rusty fell instantly in love
with the place.

Following Gideon's directions, he shouldered his
way through the ground-floor entrance doors, took a
sharp turn to his right, and found himself confronted
with a narrow, battered door. This bore the name
'J. Blackwood' on a brass plate that had started to turn
faintly green with age. The door creaked open at his
touch. Inside, he found himself in a dimly lit room
that was packed from floor to ceiling with ancient
wooden furniture, the items piled one on top of
another in dusty, rickety stacks. In the far corner, in
a circle of yellow light cast by an evil-smelling oil
lamp, a fat, lank-haired man sat hunched over a small
table, absorbed in some solitary game with a pack of
very dirty playing cards. He looked up briefly when
Rusty entered, but did not rise or otherwise interrupt his game. If this was indeed Gideon's Uncle
Joseph, he bore no outward sign of the special gifts
of the wandering folk.

'Hello,' muttered the man. 'You must be that mate

of Gid's. I'm Joe Blackwood. Got you the last but one on the fifth floor. Key's probably still in the door. Rent payable Friday.' He continued with his game, taking no further notice of his visitor.

After a moment, realising that the interview was at an end, Rusty went off to inspect his new property. But, moments later, he was back.

'Mister Blackwood? This is probably very silly. I've found the apartment, but I can't seem to find the way up to it.'

Slowly, Joe Blackwood looked up again from his cards. For a moment he seemed to have forgotten who Rusty was.

'Oh, yes, there's no stairs to that one,' he said finally. 'The last woman, she probably took 'em away. I can let you have a rope ladder, that should do you, but remember to pull it up once you're indoors. Can't be too careful, these days. The chap at the end, he'll probably let you climb up his one, till you get yours fixed.'

By the time Rusty had negotiated his way up the neighbour's ladder and across his balcony, heavy drops of rain had begun to fall, and by the time he had gained entry to his own apartment and secured the rope ladder to his own balcony, it was raining steadily. By the time he had tried the ladder and found it too short and bought some extra rope from Mr Blackwood, the rain had turned persistent and heavy, and by the time he was satisfied with his access arrangements, he was wet to the skin. Finally alone, he wandered around the two rooms and inspected the facilities in the tiny kitchen, peeling off his soaking garments as he went and tossing them one by one on the bare floor.

Arriving back on the balcony, naked and dripping, it occurred to him that he had no towel and no dry clothing and that the apartment had no floor coverings and no furniture. It was still raining, and darkness was beginning to fall. Gazing out over the glistening wet rooftops, it dawned on Rusty that this was the first time he had ever viewed the city from above. The last time he'd been here, he had viewed it from underneath. But, from now on, it was going to be different. Bit by bit, he took in the view. It was just as he had known it would be.

After a moment, he closed his eyes. He could feel the heavy drops of rain wetting his hair, his face, his shoulders, his chest, streaming down his body, forming a puddle on the hard floor at his feet. He felt clean and he felt cool, and he felt ready for a new beginning.

And then, after a while, he began to wonder where he was going to hang his clothes.

'What did you do all day?'

Well, for a start, there was one thing I certainly didn't do. I didn't go to school. The village was in a pretty remote spot, and actually I'm not even sure there was a school there in those days. But even if there had been, I don't suppose my father would have sent me. Of course, I would have done a bit better in life if I'd been taught things properly, I might not have been forced into my present course of action. But as it was, I just had to work most things out for myself as I went along, although I did get some help from Mrs Crabb, of course. I'll tell you about her in a bit.

Did I mention that the village was by the sea? No, I didn't think I did, and I suppose a lot of boys would have been quite excited at the idea of growing up by the seaside, but it never really did anything for me. Although I think my father must have had some sort of a feeling for it, because he used to go for walks on the beach on odd days when he didn't have any jobs to do, and once I started to walk, he used to take me with him. I didn't like the beach much, it was just shingle really, it was difficult to walk on all those little pebbles, and it was always cold and wet, and I was a bit scared of the seagulls so, no, the sea never did much for me at all. I suppose I used to complain about it, because after a while he stopped taking me, and after that he used to leave me at home, chained to the leg of the table again.

In the end, it was my father who taught me how to read and write and count. I think he did it pretty grudgingly, did it because he had to do it rather than because he wanted to do it. He used to sit me across from him at the table and show me things on that little writing tablet of his. 'You'd better look at this,' he used to say. 'It's dull stuff but I suppose you're going to have to learn it.' Sometimes he would say, 'Pay attention, and we can get it over quicker.'

So I learned how to form my letters and how to make my letters into words and how to draw little pictures and *diagrams. I didn't find it dull at all, I loved the way the letters all had sounds, and I loved the way the sounds sort of slid together to make words. He showed me numbers as well, he seemed a bit keener on those, but I loved the letters and the words. Yes, I suppose it was an odd sort of introduction to writing, because my father only used writing in a very limited sort of way, you know, to write lists of materials for whatever job he was doing, or for signwriting, or for engraving people's names on teapots and things. Anyway, we used to spend a bit of time on writing, when he remembered, but he would soon get bored with it and put his tablet away and give me another screwdriver to play with, there was one with a handle that had been mended, I remember that for some reason. But I didn't like the screwdrivers, I used to ask him to show me some more writing, and sometimes he would, if he was in a good mood, but more usually he would just threaten me with the chain, and then I would crawl back under the table out of his way. It was a big, heavy table with thick, solid legs. It was some years before it occurred to me that I might be able to move it.*

After a while, though, I learned that if he thought I was being good, he'd leave me alone and not use the chain on me. And then, when he was out of the way, I could do a bit of exploring, maybe around the room, or even out in the yard if he'd left the back door open. I used to like the yard, it was paved with those flat square grey stones, and some of them had quite interesting cracks in them and odd things that wriggled about underneath. And of course there was that big pile of logs. When I was big enough I tried to climb up it, and one day I slipped and brought down quite a little avalanche of timber. I think I must have hurt myself as well, but he wasn't bothered about that, he only seemed bothered about the logs. So after that little episode, I guess it was chain time again.

Another day I got as far as the gate at the end of the yard, and I think he may actually have found me wandering about in the lane, and he definitely wasn't pleased about that, and it was a long time until he let me off the chain again.

But you asked me about school, and I think I mentioned Mrs Crabb. I suppose I should say a bit about Mrs Crabb, because she was the first grown-up person I really met, apart from my father, of course. I told you that my father was a builder or a handyman, that sort of thing anyway, so he was out of the house doing his work quite a lot of the time. He had a big canvas bag full of his tools, which he used to keep by the back door, so I always used to know whether he was at home or not. Anyway, he never took me with him when he went to work. 'I can't take you, I've got too much to do,' he used to say, or sometimes it would be, 'You'll have to stay here, they won't want a little boy getting in the way,' but either way I would be left in the house, and on would go the chain again.

But one day, he decided to take me with him. Of course, he could walk much faster than I could, even carrying that big bag of tools, so by the time we got to the end of the lane, I was out of breath and struggling to keep up. Anyway, we got there in the end, and it was a big house that stood on its own facing out to sea, and an old lady lived there, and that was Mrs Crabb. I think the house might have been some sort of lodging house or guest house, but when I went there it was out of season, and there were no guests about.

Of course, I had no way of judging at the time, but it seems to me now that Mrs Crabb hadn't had much to do with children, and I suppose she was quite old-fashioned in her ways even for those days, and she was very gruff in her manner. But I think she must somehow have enjoyed my company, because after that first visit, whenever my father had a job to do for Mrs Crabb, he would always take me along too.

One thing that you would have noticed about Mrs Crabb was that she was a lady of very regular habits. Everything used to happen exactly the same way every time we went there, and actually we seemed to go there quite a lot, there was always something she needed doing to the house or the garden, so my father would be up a ladder or up a tree or digging holes or painting window frames or whatever it was. No, I never went out in the garden, and nor did Mrs Crabb as far as I can remember. She and I were always inside the house.

She always used to greet us in the same way when we arrived. My father would pull on the bell rope two or three times, or if he was in a good mood he might sometimes hold me up and let me pull on it. And after a few moments the door would open and there would be Mrs Crabb with her tight grey hair and her long black frock. And she would always say the same thing, she would always say, 'Goodness me, here's Mr Slater, punctual as ever, and here's little Tom come to sit with me.' Then she would have a few words with my father, explaining whatever it was she wanted doing, and *he would go off to do it, and Mrs Crabb would take me into her parlour, that was what she called it. The room had a dusty sort of smell, the ceiling was high and there were long curtains at the windows and some faded-looking pictures on the walls. In the middle of the room there was a big, round table, which was always covered with one of those thick, furry cloths, it was dark blue and it smelled of mothballs. The table had a sort of heavy feeling about it, actually everything did in that house. Mrs Crabb would sit at one side of the table, and I would sit at the other. I always knew which was my place, because there would be a glass of milk and a plate with one biscuit on it. And that would be a real treat for me. To start with, I never got to eat off a plate in my father's house, and until I came to Mrs Crabb's I'd never seen a biscuit or anything like it before, a pie crust was about all I was usually offered. I realise now that it was always the plainest, cheapest, dullest sort of biscuit, but at the time it seemed like just about the most exciting thing I'd ever eaten.*

After the refreshments, there was usually a long silence, because Mrs Crabb was not the most talkative of people. But one day, and I remember her words, although I didn't immediately understand what she meant, she said, 'Your father tells me that you like your letters,' and she produced a little book and placed it on the table in front of me.

It was a beautiful little book, and I knew at once that it was special. It was not at all like my father's writing tablet. It had a hard cover, with a complicated-looking raised pattern on it, and it had a wonderful smell, I suppose it must have been a combination of leather and peppermints and some flowery scent, perhaps what Mrs Crabb used to wear when Mr Crabb was alive. I leafed through the pages. They were thick, and the texture was very slightly rough, and the edges of the pages weren't straight, they were sort of irregular zigzags.

And on the pages were letters, and of course the letters were arranged into words, and the words were in short rows, and the rows were arranged in groups of four. Of course, it was a book of poems, but I had no idea then of the existence of poetry. As I said before, words were just something that my father used for writing lists. Quite a lot of the words in the poems were too long or too complicated or too strange for me to understand, but even before I began to understand them, I could hear the shapes they made when Mrs Crabb read them to me in her hard, dry old voice, and in time I started to make a link between the letters and the words and the rhythms and the rhymes and it all started to form a wonderful, complicated mysterious pattern.

And then my father finished his job and we had to go home. I wasn't allowed to take the book with me, of course, and when I tried to talk to him about it he didn't seem interested, so I let the subject drop. I suppose I was learning a bit of psychology, even at that age. Later, when my father was out of the room, I managed to filch a few leaves from his writing tablet, and then I got hold of one of those long, flat pencils he kept in his tool bag, and then I tried to write my own poem. I didn't have much idea what I was doing to begin with, but after a few more visits to Mrs Crabb, things began to make more sense, and I started to compose little two-line or four-line verses about nothing in particular. I've still got one or two of them in my pack, but they're really pretty terrible so, if you don't mind, I'd rather not show them to you. Not yet, anyway.

Oh, yes, I kept them hidden from my father for quite a few years. The kitchen table had a drawer, and the drawer slid to and fro in a set of runners that were hidden under the table top. My father never spent any time with me under the table, so he probably didn't know about the runners, but it was in the corner on top of the runners that I managed to tuck my bits of paper and my pencil away out of sight.

Of course, my father still hoped against hope that I would start to take an interest in his work, and although he didn't find out about the poems until the very end, he got more and more frustrated with me. And of course, as I got older I started to get more adventurous, and then he would catch me trying to wander off somewhere, and then of course it would be the chain again. And then, that last day, he found the poems. And after that, everything changed for ever.

Tea with the Neighbours

Rusty was sitting on the pavement outside Serendipity Court, accompanied by an ancient gateleg table and three miscellaneous non-matching chairs. He had bought the furniture from Mr Blackwood, but the taciturn caretaker had declined to offer him any assistance in moving the pieces into his apartment. He was wondering just how he was going to tackle this new challenge when a short, round man with a small, elegantly trimmed beard appeared around the corner. Rusty recognised the neighbour whose ladder he had used a few days previously.

'How in the world are you going to get those up to yours?' exclaimed the neighbour.

'I hadn't thought about that,' Rusty pondered. 'I did ask Mr Blackwood, but he doesn't seem very interested in coming out of his room.' He paused interrogatively. 'I suppose you don't have a few spare minutes?'

'Yes, of course I do, thought you'd never ask. I've got a bit of rope upstairs. I'm sure we can manage the dirty deed between the two of us. And best get you safe indoors while it's light.'

The neighbour's name, it turned out, was Paul Catalano, and he was a hairdresser by trade.

'No, not many of my clients come to me up here,' he was explaining as he trimmed Rusty's shaggy thatch just above the ears. 'Quite a lot of them are on the elderly side, and the ladder would just be the last straw for them. And of course there's always the danger of bumping into the odd gang of Wolf Boys. So I'm out and about most days – I pop round to see them all at home and it keeps me out of mischief, I can tell you. Lovely hair you've got, by the way, gorgeous colour. But where do you have the parting? I can't quite seem to trace it.'

During his time on the road with Gideon and Peg, Rusty's attention had not been concentrated upon his personal appearance, and he too was no longer quite sure what, if anything, his parting was supposed to do.

'I'll leave it to you,' he suggested. 'I'm sure you'll make a good job of it.'

'Yes, here we are. Heavens above, what's this?' Paul deftly extracted a small, unidentified item from somewhere around the crown of Rusty's head, and lobbed it expertly through the window. 'Now, where were we?'

'Seeing clients at home. And before that, I was asking how you get about the city.'

'Yes, of course, I'd forget my head if it wasn't screwed on. I go mostly on my two feet as it happens, keeps me fit, and I don't really have much to carry, just my comb and scissors and a few other bits and bobs. You could use the public waggons, I suppose, or the hackney coaches, but it all adds up, and we have to count our pennies, don't we? Now just hold still while I do the back of your neck.'

Until he had left home to study for his degree at the Academy of Cartography, Rusty's hair had been kept in order by his mother, and her rudimentary armoury of equipment had not extended to a pair of clippers. Rusty wriggled on his seat at the unfamiliar, ticklish touch of the interlocking blades on his neck.

'Hold still, you naughty boy! Just behave yourself and I'll have you done in a jiff. Now what else can I tell you about this wonderful city of ours?'

Among other things, Rusty learned from Paul the location of a small street market where he was able to acquire a few essential items for the kitchen. Huddled against the back wall of an adjoining building, he found a straggling row of shabbily awninged stalls offering some rather tired-looking fruit and vegetables as well as a selection of battered second-hand utensils. The market was just closing, and, for a very modest sum, he came away with a mixed bag of greengroceries in one hand, and a mixed bag of cutlery in the other hand. Thus burdened, the ascent of the rope ladder proved to be something of a challenge, and Rusty reminded himself to bring his backpack to market with him on the next visit.

Eventually, he found himself seated at his new table, wondering what he might be able to contrive from two apples, a potato, a turnip and a banana, with the aid of a small saucepan, a fish slice, three spoons and a fork. Before he went to the Academy, his mother had done all the cooking for him and, after that, his landlady Mrs Roberts had taken over the culinary duties. He wondered if any of the local traders could provide him with a cookery manual, then he remembered that the market had already been closing when he was making his purchases. Perhaps a neighbour might help him out? Paul had been very friendly earlier, but Rusty did not feel inclined to impose on him again so soon, and he therefore decided to try the apartment on the other side.

Peering across from his balcony to the neighbouring one, he could see that the door of the apartment hung ajar.

'Hello?' he called. 'Anybody at home?' There was no

reply, so he decided to investigate further. Hitching up his trousers, he clambered up on to the left-hand balustrade, and, heart in mouth, took a long stride across to the next balcony, where he made a clumsy crash landing, painless but inelegant, outside the neighbour's window. It was hard to avoid looking in, and it at once became apparent that the neighbour was at home.

The room was completely bare of furnishings, and its walls, ceiling and floor were painted a flat white. The floor was decorated with a complex interlocking grid of radial lines and concentric circles, interspersed with various indecipherable symbols, picked out in black and gold. At the centre of the grid was a person Rusty took to be the neighbour.

The neighbour appeared to be a young woman, perhaps about the same age as Rusty. She was very slim and she was wearing a tight black garment that covered her from neck to ankle, leaving only her pale feet and hands bare. Her hair was straight, and a very light blonde in colour, but her face was hidden from Rusty's view. This was because the neighbour was in the process of aligning her body into a rather extraordinary sequence of attitudes. At that moment, her weight was supported partly on her bare feet, and partly on her hands, which were planted firmly on the floor a short distance behind her feet. She must have been very supple indeed, for her body was arched sharply upwards in an acute curve, and she held her arms and legs almost straight.

For several moments, Rusty watched transfixed while

she maintained this posture. Then, very slowly, one slim leg raised itself up until it pointed vertically towards the ceiling, after which, following another interval, the second leg followed it equally slowly. Finally, with apparently no need for any adjustment to her balance, their owner arrived at an inverted position, supported on her outstretched arms, her long fingers spread, her body and legs forming a motionless vertical line, her pale feet pointing elegantly skywards. Her pale hair, hanging down almost to the floor, continued to mask her features. For a moment longer she held her balance, then abruptly she kicked herself upright, the legs scissoring together, the arms dropping to her sides.

Rusty let out a long, silent breath. Something about the whole tableau before him struck a chord in his memory, but he was unable for the moment to identify it. Perplexed, he stared at the face that was now revealed to him. The features were still and blank and expressionless and looked as though they had been carved out of marble. There was something indefinably familiar about them, too. Then, after a few seconds, the eyes opened, and animation returned by degrees to their owner. Gradually, she seemed to become aware of Rusty's presence at the window. Then she shook herself and broke into a smile.

'Why don't you come in?' she said, and her soft accent also had an air of familiarity. 'I'll make us some tea. My name's Alice, by the way. It's nice to meet you at last.'

*   *   *

A little later, they were seated cross-legged on the floor of Alice's empty room, nursing small bowls of pale, fragrant, milkless tea.

'It's just a form of exercise,' Alice was explaining thoughtfully. 'I've got a pattern that I work through every day. I was only a little girl when I started it. But it's a part of my life now. I really don't know where I'd be without it.'

Rusty looked at her.

'It's funny. I once stayed at a place where they taught me something like that. Not as difficult as the thing you were doing, of course. I enjoyed it, actually, but I've never really tried it again since.'

'Difficult?' Alice pondered, staring at one of the symbols painted on the floor. 'I hadn't thought of it that way. I suppose that's because it's always been there. But, you know, you should never have let it drop. You ought to try and keep it going.'

'Yes, I suppose I ought.' Rusty took a meditative sip of his tea. 'Strange that we've got it in common though, something so peculiar. Did you say you started when you were little?'

'That's right,' Alice replied. 'I didn't grow up in the city.' She paused, as if weighing up whether to reveal any more, then reached a decision and continued. 'I came from one of the islands. In the north-east. I lived there until I was seventeen.'

There was another long pause before Rusty spoke.

'The north-east. So you're an Islander.' Her motionless profile revealed nothing. 'Now that's really very odd indeed. You see, my mother came from the Islands, too. But we didn't live there, and actually she never told me anything about her island, I didn't find out about it till after she died. So I'm half Islander myself. But I've never been there. Do you think I should go?' Rusty wondered for a moment whether to reveal that he was also half Wanderer, but decided for the moment to say nothing. While he was considering this, Alice turned to gaze directly at him for the first time, and her wide blue eyes spoke of clover, and of long grass and of the sea.

'Of course you must go. If you don't, you'll only have lived half of your life.' The blue eyes rested on him for a moment longer, then looked down at the half-full bowl of tea. 'But maybe not yet.' Suddenly she changed tack. 'Hey, you must think I'm really rude. What are you planning to do, now that you've arrived in the city?' Rusty placed his empty bowl on the floor.

'It's difficult. It sounds corny, but I suppose you could say I'm seeking my fortune. Although, now I'm here, I don't quite seem to know what I'm looking for. I was in the city once before, you see . . .' He hesitated, then plunged on. 'I wasn't going to say any of this, but somehow you seem really easy to talk to.' Alice encouraged him with a smile that was brief but warm. 'I didn't exactly have a distinguished career. I started as a beggar. And, after that, I sort of worked my way down.'

'Down?'

'Yes, down. Actually, I was with the Wolf Boys for

a bit. I don't suppose you can get much further down than that.' Alice smiled more broadly.

'The Wolf Boys? Och, I've met a few of them, they're not as bad as people say.'

'Well, maybe not. Anyway, I'm in no hurry to repeat the experience. And before the city, I was at the Academy of Cartography. I learned to draw and paint a bit, but I never got my degree. So I suppose I'll need to find some sort of work for a while, until I get a bit more settled. I've got a bit of money, but it won't last for ever. What do you do, by the way?'

Alice shrugged. 'It's not really very interesting. I work at the Palace, sort of administrative stuff. It's quite hard to get work there. Mister Considine, he's my boss, I suppose I could ask him – he's quite difficult, though. But I know where you might try.'

'Go on.'

'Well. They're always looking for new people at the Herald's Office. I used to work there, so I still keep in touch with some of them. The new Herald, that's Miss Garamond, she's started this *Digest of Events* thing, a sort of written news-sheet, and the last thing I heard, they were looking for people to do the pictures. Why don't you go and give her a call?' Simultaneously, the two of them fractionally shifted their positions on the bare boards.

'Miss Garamond? All right, I'll give her a try. Thanks, Alice.' Rusty stood up, shaking himself to relieve the stiffness in his limbs. At the doorway, he turned back to find Alice on her feet as well. There was another pause, and when Rusty finally broke the silence, his manner was diffident.

'Alice? I know this sounds silly, but I'm sure I've met you before. I just can't work out where.' Alice seemed sunk in thought for a moment before replying.

'Yes. Yes, I think so too. And I can't think where either. Oh well, not to worry, I expect it will come to one of us. Can you find your way home all right?' Rusty grinned. After a moment, Alice continued. 'And, look, if you want to get back into your exercise pattern again, I mean just if you feel like it, well, you could always drop by another night.' Rusty broke into a broad smile.

'That'd be great,' he said. 'I'd love to.'

And this time, when he jumped across to his own balcony, he landed on his feet.

The Realm of Dreams

The Constanzas Brothers Travelling Amusements had pitched camp on a patch of waste ground at the edge of the village. The Constanzas Brothers operated on a modest scale, and there had therefore been no posters and no handbills, and nobody in the village had known of their impending arrival until the appearance of the gaily painted waggons. Now, two days later, a large tent and a medium-sized tent had been erected, and the showmen had assembled a set of swings and a hand-cranked merry-go-round, together with a few other, smaller rides and an irregular rank of targets for their archery display. To start with, business had been slack, but as the end of the week approached, things had begun to pick up somewhat. A few schoolchildren had arrived in the late afternoon to sample the swings and other rides, and a little later their older brothers and sisters had strolled across to try their luck at the archery butts. It was early evening now, and a handful of adults were wandering across from their various daytime occupations, curious to see what if anything the amusements had to offer them.

Evie Tate was there among the small crowd. She had finished her sewing and mending for the week, and had delivered the last batch of repairs, and now she was whiling away the slack hour before the inn threw open its doors. Evie spent most of her leisure hours propped on a high stool at the corner of the bar. She did not usually feel much inclination to go home to her ill-tempered husband and her screaming children, and she had discovered that the inn provided the most acceptable alternative. Usually she stayed on her stool until the landlord grew tired of serving and finally ejected the stragglers from the premises by threat or by force. Often she arrived home on her hands and knees, and occasionally she awoke at dawn to find herself slumped uncomfortably on the doorstep.

Tonight, however, all this was still ahead of her, and for the time being she was happy enough to wander about the amusements until it was time to make her way to the inn. Idly, she looked on as two small girls hauled each other to and fro on the swingboats, their miniature hands grasping the tufted ends of the ropes, and their shrieks of excitement ricocheting to and fro like small missiles through the air. Next, Evie turned her attention to the merry-go-round. Around the top of the ride, the words 'CONSTANZAS BROTHERS AMUSEMENTS' chased each other in perpetual widdershins motion. A few children were balanced unsteadily astride the garishly painted galloping wooden dogs and cockerels, and a couple of mothers with babies were seated more securely in an ornately gilded carriage. Evie's gaze alighted for a moment on the dark-haired young man who was cranking the central wheel, his legs astride, his bare torso glistening with sweat in the intermittent light that shafted through the ragged canopy. Smiling wistfully, she turned away, paused briefly to survey the gaggle of youths and girls lounging around the archery butts, then suddenly found herself caught up in a small group of people and carried along with them towards the short row of sideshows. The sideshows looked to Evie as if they might be of more interest to someone of her more mature years.

A small crowd had assembled outside the first booth. In front of it stood a not-very-secure-looking platform, on which a fat clown was banging a snare drum in a dramatically unmusical fashion. At the moment of Evie's arrival, he concluded his performance with an unsettling clatter, and relinquished the stage in favour of an imposing-looking moustached man in a battered top hat and shabby frock coat. This character paused for a moment to ensure that he had the full attention of the crowd, then he cleared his throat noisily and proceeded with his introduction.

'Ladies and gentlemen, boys and girls,' he intoned. 'I am your servant Andrew Constanzas. My brothers and I welcome you to our travelling amusements. You will by now have experienced the thrills of the Mighty Carousel, you will have marvelled at the dexterity of the Masters of Toxophily.' There was a snigger from the back of the crowd, swiftly quelled by a poisonous glare from the clown. 'You will have seen the Flying Gondolas and the Flying Chairs, and you will surely believe me when I say that in the field of amusements, the Constanzas have no equal.' There was another snigger. 'But today we are privileged, no, honoured, to bring to you an attraction that can claim no rival, no equal, at any place between earth and sky. For what we bring you today is utterly unique, ladies and gentlemen, what we bring you today is without peer at any place within the four corners of this land.' A few eyebrows were raised in the crowd, Evie's among them, but this time there was no sniggering.

'The Constanzas brothers are indeed privileged to present –' he paused dramatically '– Madam Nina and her Realm of Dreams.'

At this point, accompanied by another clatter on the drum, a sturdily built woman clad in a turquoise robe which was slightly too long and a feathered turban which was slightly too small, stepped from the tent on to the platform and greeted the crowd with a stilted bow.

'Madam Nina comes to us from the greatest city in the land,' continued Andrew Constanzas. 'There she was bound apprentice to the Mightiest Counsellors of the old King's retinue, there she was versed in the most mysterious of the communicative arts, and from there she fled, ladies and gentlemen, at the time of the Great Reorganisation of King Matthew. From there she fled, ladies and gentlemen, bearing only the clothes in which she stood. Only her clothes, ladies and gentlemen . . .' Another pause. 'Only her clothes . . . and . . . the secrets of the Realm of Dreams.' He now held the crowd in the palm of his hand. 'But I shall say no more. Who better to introduce to you the Realm of Dreams . . . who better than Madam Nina herself?'

There was more artillery from the clown. Andrew Constanzas stepped aside, and Madam Nina stepped forward. For a few moments, she surveyed the crowd with an expression that spoke of ageless wisdom. Nobody was sniggering now.

'I gaze at your faces,' Madam Nina began, in a voice that seemed to caress them, 'and what do I see there? What do I see there, ladies and gentlemen? Do I see happiness, ladies and gentlemen? Do I see content-ment? No, ladies and gentlemen, I do not see these things. Do I see fulfilment, ladies and gentlemen? Do I see joy or delight? No, ladies and gentlemen, I do not see these things either.' A low, unhappy murmur was audible from the crowd. 'So what do I see in your faces, ladies and gentlemen? Does any of you know what I see there?' She paused, as if expecting someone to venture a reply, but nobody did. 'I see sorrow, ladies and gentlemen. I see sorrow and I see misery and I see wretchedness. And as I see these things, ladies and gentlemen, I ask myself, have these people chosen to live their lives this way? Surely not, I say, surely not, for these people are kind people, these people are good people, these people deserve to be happy, these people want only to be happy, but these people do not have what they want. And why not, ladies and gentlemen? Why do these good, kind people not have what they want, why do they not have what they deserve? I will tell you, ladies and gentlemen.' This time she continued without a pause, the pitch of her voice beginning to rise. 'These good, kind people do not have what they deserve because something is standing in their way.' There was an expectant silence. 'I will say it again, ladies and gentlemen. You do not have what you deserve because something is standing in your way. For each one of you, it may be a different thing, but no matter. I can help you all, ladies and gentlemen, I can help every one of you. Let me tell you how you can have what you want, ladies and gentlemen, let me tell you how you can have what you deserve. Ladies and gentlemen, it is simplicity itself. You must find the thing that stands in your way, and you must destroy it.'

Madam Nina's voice had risen now from a seductive murmur to a terrifying shriek, but in the dead silence that followed, she allowed it to drop again so that it was only just audible.

'And within the bounds of the Realm of Dreams, ladies and gentlemen, you can do just that. Within the bounds of the Realm of Dreams, you can locate your heart's desire, you can see it shining before you, and for a moment you can even begin to live it. And then, ladies and gentlemen, within the bounds of the Realm of Dreams, you can find the awful thing that stands in your way, and you can destroy it, ladies and gentlemen, you can destroy the awful thing, and then you truly can attain your heart's desire.'

A hungry murmur rippled through the crowd. Madam Nina turned slowly away and started moving towards the entrance to the tent. Then, at the last moment, she spun suddenly back towards the crowd and cried, in a terrible voice:

'So who will be the first?'

Mesmerised, Evie found herself stepping forward, elbowing her way through the crowd, climbing onto the platform, and slipping under the flap of the tent.

Inside the tent it was dark, and the air was dense with a thick, cloying aroma that penetrated Evie's nostrils and throat and fogged her brain. She could not see Madam Nina but, after a moment, she heard her voice, not the shrieking one but the caressing one.

'What is your name, my child?'

'Evie, Madam. Evie Tate.'

'Very well, Evie Tate. Step forward and see what you will see.'

The light touch of a hand on Evie's elbow guided her forward.

'Are you afraid, Evie?'

'A little, Madam.'

'You have no need to be afraid, my child. Step forward now.'

A musty-smelling velvet curtain brushed across Evie's cheek. Invisible hands drew the curtain aside, and she felt her head guided downwards beneath some sort of metallic hood that shielded her eyes and covered her ears, and she felt her hands coming to rest upon two cool, smooth, upright handles that felt as if they were connected to some sort of humming machinery.

'Have no fear, Evie,' continued the voice, muffled now but still audible. 'Listen with your two ears, and look with your two eyes, and feel with your two hands. Now, what is it that you want, my child, what is it that you want?'

A vague blur of yellow light faded into view at the centre of Evie's field of vision. In her ears, she became aware of an indistinct murmur. And suddenly, she could smell the pungent scent of the ale, she could hear the reassuring voices of her companions, and she could feel the stool at the end of the bar exerting its familiar pressure on her buttocks. She relaxed, and a glow of contentment began to spread through her.

'Is this what you want, Evie?'

Evie gave the slightest of nods.

'Are you happy here, Evie?'

She nodded again, this time less certain.

'Look deeper, Evie. Look at what is behind.'

Suddenly the vision dissolved into another set of images. There were the ashes, cold in the hearth. There was Martin, forlorn in the kitchen, staring bleakly at the evening meal as it congealed in the pan. There were the children, crying for their mother. And there was the empty chair at the foot of the table. Evie felt a sudden chill. Surely, this was her place. This was where she was supposed to be. Instinctively, she tightened her grip on the two handles. The vision wavered before her eyes.

'Gently, my child, gently. Your heart's desire is here within your grasp.'

Evie relaxed again, and suddenly, in a warm glow of light, the scene sprang back into focus, and there was the whole family around the table, about to start their meal, smiling, laughing—

'So here is your heart's desire, my child. Here is your heart's desire. See now, what a little thing it is that stands in your way.'

And then she was back inside the inn again, but this time the ale was sour, and the light was cold and grey, and the coarse banter of the voices echoed mockingly. A violent wave of hatred surged up in Evie's breast. Abruptly, with a harsh cacophony of splintering noise, the scene around her flew apart in jagged fragments, and suddenly she was outside the tent again. In a moment, she had shaken away her confusion and she understood what she must do. Quickly, she strode away from the showground. The doors of the inn were open, but for once Evie ignored them. Unwavering in her path, she ran straight to her house, she ran into her kitchen, she kissed the astonished Martin, and she ran to the stove to cook her children's tea.

Back at the showground, the next punter stepped inside Madam Nina's tent.

'How did your father find the poems?'

Well, I think I mentioned that I was eventually taken away from my father. I suppose it would be more accurate to say that he got taken away from me, at any rate he got taken away before I did, and I'll come on to that in a bit. And although it was many years before I met my father again, I never forgot what he did to me.

The house where we lived was an isolated one — it stood on its own at the edge of the sea — and I guess it was only because it stood on its own that my father got away with what he did for so long. We didn't get any visitors, and I hardly got to leave the house, except to go to Mrs Crabb's, and the people round there kept pretty much to themselves, so if anyone else noticed me, they didn't pay me any attention, and I suppose things would have gone on in pretty much the same way if the city militiamen hadn't chosen our village for their sports day that year.

No, I don't think I exactly set out to get myself rescued, not in any deliberate way, at least, but everything did seem to come together somehow to make it happen. Let me try and remember the exact sequence of events that day. Yes, it's coming back now. It actually started the day before. I told you that my father had only hit me on one occasion, and that was the day before the militiamen's sports day, and that was also the same day that he found the poems. He had been out doing some work in the afternoon, I knew that because his tool bag wasn't by the door, and although there wasn't a clock in the room, I always knew what time to expect him back because there was a bell that chimed somewhere in the village, every hour I suppose, and he always came back at the same time, because he used to call in at the pie shop just before it closed, trying to scrounge some leftovers for our supper. The only time he ever came back early was when it rained, and it wasn't raining that day, so I'd imagined I would be quite safe doing my poems for a bit.

Anyway, there I was under the table, scratching away at a bit of verse, with my other things spread out on the floor, when suddenly the door flew open and my father came barging into the house. I had no chance to hide what I was doing, and as soon as he saw me, he was down on his knees, snatching up my bits of paper to find out what was on them. When he realised what I had been up to, he just went berserk, he started shouting 'What's this? What's this?' over and over again, and screwing up the poems in his big fists.

I don't think he was expecting a reply, because when I opened my mouth to speak, he went right on, shouting that I was ungrateful, that he had tried to teach me a proper trade, and that this was how I repaid him. I couldn't understand why the poems made him so furious, and I was trying to crawl as far away from him as I could, but then he started dragging me towards him with the chain, it was round my neck, so I didn't really have any choice, and then he was slapping me on the side of the head with his free hand, and he was panting and red in the face, and I was terrified, and then he suddenly threw me to the floor and stood up and he shouted 'Filthy little brute' a couple of times, and then he seemed to calm down a bit, and he went to his tool bag and got out a pie and threw me a piece of it, I remember it was still warm.

I had taught myself not to cry by then, so after a while he stopped noticing me and I suppose I must have fallen asleep, because when I opened my eyes his tool bag had gone again and I could tell by the light that it was morning. Of course, I was in a pretty disgusting state, I must have messed myself at some point, because my trousers stank, and there was blood on the floor, although I wasn't sure exactly what part of me it had come from, and of course my face was aching from the beating and my neck was raw from the chain, and I suppose I was covered in bruises as well, but of course there wasn't much I could do about tidying myself up, because I was still attached to the leg of the table.

But then I heard the noise from outside. I'm not sure exactly how old I was by then, eight or nine, perhaps. I had grown quite tall and thin, an unattractive child, I suppose, with sallow skin and lank, dark hair that always seemed to need cutting. Anyway, because of my height, I had found that if I crawled to the extreme limit of the chain and stood up, I could just catch a glimpse of the shoreline through the window. Well, the first thing I noticed was the tent, and then there was a row of flags, and then there were twenty or thirty big men in striped bathing suits running races and jumping over poles and cheering and clapping each other.

I discovered later that this was the city militiamen's sports day, but at the time all I could see was a crowd of people enjoying themselves, and I desperately wanted to have what they had, so I tried shouting, but of course the window was shut and they wouldn't have heard me because they were all shouting too. And then I started to wonder if I could escape from my chain and run down to the beach, and it occurred to me that if I could somehow manage to overturn the table, I could probably get the chain off the end of the table leg and then I could get out of the house.

Why did I never try to escape before? Yes, it's a good question. I suppose it had never occurred to me that there was anything much out there to escape to, and, in a funny sort of way, I hadn't exactly been unhappy until that day when my father found the poems. But now I had caught a glimpse of another world, a world where people enjoyed themselves, and here I was inside the house, aching and filthy and miserable, and suddenly I wanted my freedom more than I had ever wanted anything before. So back I went under the table, and first I tried pushing underneath it with my hands, but it didn't move because it was so heavy, and although I had grown quite tall, I didn't really have any *strength, but then I remembered seeing my father moving a heavy chest by shoving it with his shoulder, so I got up into a sort of crouch, and then I felt the table move a bit, and suddenly I knew I could do it and something seemed to explode in my chest and it was as if all the rage and fury and hate that had been lying dormant rose up at once and flung that table across the room and splintered it apart.*

And then I was hobbling down to the shore with the chain dragging behind me, screaming for help, and suddenly the militiamen had stopped their games and there was a row of big faces staring at me, and one of them picked me up and said, 'Whoever did this to you, my boy?' and then at last I began to cry. And while the militiamen were making a fuss of me, I remember seeing my father coming down the shingle in the distance and two of the militiamen walking up to him and saying, 'Is this your son, sir?'

And then I turned my head away from him, and after that I didn't see my father again for about thirty years.

The Rope and the Ladder

'Miss Garamond? Yes, she's in her office. She might give you a few minutes, she seemed to be in quite a good mood earlier. Top of the stairs, then turn left. Now, who's next?'

Following the intake clerk's directions, Rusty mounted the stairs two at a time and found himself facing a dilapidated wooden door that had a small glazed panel at eye level. Inside, he could see a big, fierce-looking middle-aged woman wearing a large pair of spectacles. She was sitting in a cloud of cigarette smoke behind a desk stacked haphazardly with piles of papers, books and scrolls. She appeared to be engrossed in her work, but in response to Rusty's tentative tap on the glass, she looked up at once.

'All right, come in, I can't be fannying around all day.'

Rusty could detect no evidence that she was in a good mood. He edged himself cautiously through the door.

'Park your bum, then, and tell me what you want. Yes, any chair, just chuck that stuff on the floor. Smoke?'

'No, thanks.' Rusty edged a chair into Miss Garamond's line of view and perched himself precariously on the edge. There was an uneasy silence while she eyed him up and down.

'Nice jacket,' she said finally, and her tone showed some sign of softening. 'Good haircut, too. Looks like one of Paul's.'

'Paul Catalano? Yes, I live next door to him. Serendipity Court. He was very helpful when I moved in.'

'Yes, I bet he was. So, mister red hair leather jacket Serendipity Court, what can the City Herald do for you?'

Rusty relaxed slightly.

'Well, I'm looking for work. I heard that you wanted to start putting some pictures in the *Royal Digest*. I can draw a bit . . .'

'Got any of your stuff with you?'

'No. You see, I was at the Academy of Cartography, but I never finished my degree . . .'

'Cartography? That's interesting. How much do you know about the *Digest*?'

'Er . . . ' Rusty had begun to compose his reply, but she interrupted him again.

'Now, obviously, I can't publish charts, because as you will doubtless know, the Brotherhood of Cartography keeps all its stuff secret, and anyway the charts are protected by Charter Ancient and Inviolable, or whatever it's called, so no one else can publish them either, especially not my poor old *Digest*. But what I am hoping to do is to start illustrating some of our stories with little vignette things, portraits, landscapes maybe. I don't suppose you can do portraits, can you?'

'I've never tried. I think landscapes would probably be more my sort of thing.'

'Yes, I guessed you'd say that.' Miss Garamond blew a long plume of smoke towards the ceiling before continuing. 'I must confess, I was thinking mainly of portraits. But some little landscape vignettes might be nice too. Scenes of the city, that sort of thing. Views of important buildings, scenes of crime. The Wolf Boys have been on the rampage again, maybe something to do with them? Or the odd country scene for a bit of variety?'

'I could easily do that. I grew up in a village, and I used to do sketches of the landscape round there.'

'Yes.' Miss Garamond was smiling now. She lit

another cigarette and inhaled deeply. 'I didn't think you were from round here. Anyway, I'll tell you what I'll do, Mister . . . what's your name?'

'Brown, Michael Brown.' Miss Garamond nodded.

'All right, Mister Brown. Go downstairs, talk to the folk on the intake desk, tell them I sent you. Find out what stories we're running this month, then go out with your pencils or crayons or whatever, and bring your stuff in by the end of Wednesday. I'll pay you for whatever we use. And I'll try and work out a rate for you. Smoke?'

'No, thanks, I don't . . .'

'No, of course not.' Miss Garamond adjusted her spectacles on her nose, glanced down again at her papers, glanced up again and surprised Rusty with a somewhat lewd grin. 'Run along, then, Mister Brown. Let's see what you're made of.'

There was enough money in Rusty's dwindling reserve for him to equip himself with a pad of cartridge paper and some 2B pencils. His first sketches, complying with the requirements of the intake department, showed a sequence of general views of the royal Palace as seen from various positions on the southern loop of the ring road. There was one with the sentry box in the foreground, another boasting a row of signal kites fluttering in the distance. Although his wrists and fingers seemed to have lost some of their flexibility in the two years since he had last drawn anything, still he was moderately satisfied with the results. Then, tiring of straight lines and right angles, he strolled around to the rear of the Palace and dashed off a low-angle view of Beggars' Row, the cobblestones massive in the foreground, the lane twisting away to its vanishing point.

Later, because it somehow seemed to come naturally, he sat on his balcony at Serendipity Court and sketched a detailed aerial view of the city, the grid of streets partitioned by the ruined section of the city wall and the broad thoroughfare of the North Way, the spires of the Western Suburb rearing up in the far distance. He imagined how the city might look to a kestrel hovering high in the air above . . .

'What are you up to?' Alice's softly accented voice broke in upon his concentration.

'Oh, hello, Alice. Have you had a good day? Listen, I think Miss Garamond is going to give me a job. I'm just drawing the view from the balcony. Would you like to see it?'

'I'd love to. Why don't you come across and have some tea?'

'Well, you're quite a draughtsman, I'll give you that.' Miss Garamond was scrutinising Rusty's work a few days later. 'I can certainly use that one, and those as well . . . not too sure about this, though.' She frowned over her spectacles at the aerial view of the city. 'I mean, it's good, it's very good, don't get me wrong, but the way it shows the layout of the streets . . . well, if you take my meaning, it does just look the tiniest bit like a chart. And, things being a bit sensitive in that area, I wouldn't want to be accused of treading on the toes of the Brotherhood of Cartographers, would I? So, tell you what I'll do. I'll take these three, and I'll certainly look at anything else you might do in the future. But no more overhead views, eh? Just keep your easel firmly on the ground and we'll get along fine. Smoke? Oh no, you don't, do you?'

Miss Garamond paused to light another cigarette. After a few reflective puffs, she started to rummage distractedly among the clutter on her desk, eventually finding a scrap of blank parchment. On this, she scribbled a note.

'Right, Mister Brown.' She thrust it at him. 'Give this to the cashiers and they'll pay you. And now, just get your arse off that chair and go and draw me some more pictures.'

Over the next few weeks, Rusty fell into a regular routine of work and sleep. On the first Thursday of each month, he would report to the Herald's Office to collect his instructions, and on the last Wednesday, towards the end of the afternoon, he would return to the office to deliver his work. Then, depending upon how many pictures Miss Garamond wanted to use, he would collect a greater or lesser sum of money. Gradually, working his way around the city from one location to the next, he began to rediscover the layout of the streets, the four main thoroughfares, the distinctive architectural styles of the commercial and industrial areas, the outlying docks and suburbs, and on a few occasions, chillingly, the ruined wastes of the Undertown. Occasionally, he thought he caught a glimpse of furtive gangs of Wolf Boys, but from them he kept a careful distance.

Although the Herald's Office indicated its willingness for him to use the public carriages and hackney coaches for his travel, he preferred for much of the time to make his way about on foot, resorting to wheeled transport only when time or circumstances started to press. He became an accepted figure at the office, and after a while he found that Miss Garamond did not always need to see him in person, although she always seemed to have a friendly word for him when she did. On one occasion, walking innocently down a corridor, he found himself playfully ambushed from behind, unseen hands grasping the shaggy hair on either side of his head.

'It's Mister Brown, isn't it?' Rusty recognised the voice at once. 'I rather fancy it's time to pay another call on your hairdresser friend!'

Although Rusty took the hint and visited Paul Catalano for a much-overdue haircut, it was his neighbour on the other side who was increasingly occupying his thoughts. He had taken up Alice's offer to teach him her pattern of exercise, and they had fallen into the habit of meeting each other for this purpose every Wednesday evening. Rusty usually arrived home first, and he would hover on the balcony at the top of his rope ladder until he saw Alice arrive below, clad in the drab grey outfit of the Palace Administration.

Alice spurned the luxury of a ladder, preferring to shin up and down a bare length of rope, which she could do with impressive agility. Arriving at fifth-floor level, she would disappear into her apartment to change into her black exercise suit while, in his bedroom, Rusty wriggled his way into an ancient, patched pair of shorts, a worn singlet, and a thick, fraying pair of grey socks which had somehow survived all the upheavals of the past few years. He would then hop across the gap between their balconies after which the two of them, positioned at either side of the complex, gridlike design on the floor, would work through what Alice chose to refer to as the 'elementary pattern'. Rusty found this quite strenuous enough, so that, at the end of twenty minutes, he would lapse into a resting posture and look on in admiration while Alice continued with her more advanced attitudes. During this period, she seemed to withdraw into some remote and inaccessible place of her own, a place of which Rusty had so far managed to catch only the most fleeting of glimpses. It was not until she reached the end of the sequence that Alice would acknowledge her guest again.

'That was called The Pattern of The Seagull,' she explained one evening as she settled back to ground after a particularly vertiginous sequence of airborne loops and spirals. 'You'll learn it one day, I'm sure. But that's enough for tonight. Do you want to buy me some supper now?'

Alice had introduced him to a large, noisy, high-ceilinged tavern called the Estate Arms, just around the corner from the market, which served a very acceptable range of hotpots and pasties, and boasted an exceptionally cheering log fire. Afterwards, refreshed and rested, they would usually take a walk around the block before retiring to their separate apartments.

One night, though, their walk decided to extend itself further than usual, traversing the pools of light and the patches of shadow between the looming apartment buildings, wandering along the quayside with the murmuring river below until, by and by, they found themselves strolling, arms linked, out to the end of the old wooden pier from which the ferry made its daytime crossings.

Then, with the water lapping beneath them, they kissed, tentatively at first, then, after a moment, rather less tentatively.

Alice broke away and took a pace back.

'Come on,' she laughed, taking his arm again. 'Time to go home.'

Arriving back at Serendipity Court, Alice caught hold of the end of her rope, then, obliquely, answered Rusty's unspoken question.

'I think that's your ladder over there. But Rusty . . . It's been a lovely evening. Let's do it again soon.'

And then, hand over hand, she disappeared up the rope to her balcony.

The Dark Stuff

As the last punter of the day stumbled out into the twilight, Madam Nina closed the flap of the Realm of Dreams, stripped off the ill-fitting robe and turban and tossed them onto a chair. Without the costume, it was apparent that she was a somewhat younger woman than she led her customers to believe, well built, with brisk movements and smooth, rather boyish features. After a cursory rearrangement of her short, spiky hair, she switched off her machinery, stretched herself for a moment, then set about tidying up the booth. She extinguished the two incense burners, swept the floor, then pulled aside the tattered velvet curtains that masked her empathy engine from the inquisitive eyes of her visitors. Next, she sat down at the small table that was wedged between the engine and the generator to count her takings. It had been another good day, and she allowed herself a few minutes to speculate on her future as the leading attraction at the Constanzas Brothers Travelling Amusements.

She reflected on the words that Andrew Constanzas employed to introduce her to her punters. They were not, perhaps, strictly accurate in every respect. She doubted, for example, whether her old companion Master Pegasus would have seen things in quite the same light as Andrew. The former owner of the empathy engine would doubtless have viewed her as a swindler and a thief, but Nina consoled herself with the thought that the magician had never seen the true potential of his inventions, so she was at least bringing something of positive worth to people who would not otherwise have had the chance to experience it. She had not at first imagined that the fairground would provide the arena in which she was to ply her trade, but she felt grateful to Andrew and his brothers for the opportunity they had given her.

Nina did not usually choose to dwell too long on the fate of the punters who were responsible for lining her pockets with their coppers. They were foolish people, she felt, foolish enough to believe that their lives would be transformed by a few seconds spent staring through a gimcrack set of eyepieces, but, if they left the booth feeling better than they did when they arrived, at least that was something. That first woman who had come in that day, Evie something, for instance. She had left the tent to run home, doubtless anticipating a joyful fresh start with her useless husband, but Nina wondered how long she would really be able to stay away from the tavern. And the others, the bully, the gambler, the petty thief? How quickly would their good intentions evaporate when the initial euphoria wore off? Oh well, she had at any rate sent them away happy, and perhaps that was all she could really expect to do.

Sweeping up the pile of change and depositing it deftly into the pocket of her skirt, Nina transferred her attention to the empathy engine. Reluctantly, she admitted that the engine had started to give her a few problems. She had worked out more or less how to control its basic functions, but there were still things about it that she did not fully understand. The instructions, if there had ever been any, had long since been misplaced, and she was having to work out some of the more specialised functions for herself. The maintenance routine, for instance. It was time to have another go at that. Nina got up from the table and threw a couple of switches on the generator. A moment later, the engine hummed back into life. She dragged a high stool up to the machine, pulled the headphones over her ears, grasped the handles, and squinted down the eyepieces. A couple of tweaks on the handles, and the familiar scene materialised before her.

Nina was standing in a small, empty, six-sided room with no windows and no doors. The walls, ceiling, and floor were an uneven pale grey in colour, and the light seemed to radiate, directionless and bland, from the eight surfaces that enclosed her.

She knew that the surfaces were supposed to be pure white, but she also knew that, with regular use of the engine, a deposit of dust or dirt built up in the room, causing them gradually to discolour. If she failed to carry out the daily cleaning routine, the walls would continue to darken until, inexorably, they would finally turn an opaque black and exclude the light entirely. Without fully understanding the reason, Nina knew that this must never be allowed to happen. She gave the controls another twist, and a small metal scraper appeared in the air in front of her. Resignedly, she grasped hold of the tool and set about scraping away the deposit, first from the ceiling, then from the walls, until, eventually, she was left with a small, loose pile, about the size of her fist, in the centre of the floor.

It seemed to Nina that this deposit was composed of whatever it was that her punters left behind them when they departed from the booth. They came in feeling bad, and they went out feeling good, so she concluded that the substance that she scraped away each day was somehow composed of people's bad feelings, if such a thing were possible. It was a substance that Nina felt should not be allowed to accumulate in the room, but she had not yet found a way of removing it completely. Each night, she pushed it into a corner, but the following night she had to scrape it from the walls all over again. And each night, the pile was slightly larger.

Nina knelt down and ran her fingers through the small pile of scrapings. Her hands tingled slightly at its touch, and it seemed to emit a thin, crackling hiss as she touched it. She peered at it more closely. At first glance it had appeared black in colour, but she could see now that it sparkled faintly, each particle seeming to emit a flickering light of its own, sometimes magenta, sometimes cobalt, always shifting, never resting for a moment. The particles clung stickily to her fingers, and for an uneasy moment it occurred to Nina that the stuff might actually be alive.

Hastily dismissing this thought, she compressed the small pile into a compact ball and pushed it away from her, hoping that she could soon come up with a way to get rid of it for good. Rising to her feet, she realised that it was hardly visible from head height. Perhaps after all she was making a fuss about nothing.

Returning to the here and now, Nina realised that the brothers would shortly be serving supper in the big tent, so she decided to shut down her machinery for the night. Reflexively, she licked a finger to get rid of the last traces of the deposit. It had a dark, bitter taste, shot through with multicoloured, tingling needles of sweetness that sent streams of warmth coursing around her body, relaxing her, bidding her to enjoy. It was a delicious, seductive, slightly frightening taste. To her surprise, Nina found that she liked it. Emboldened, she licked another finger.

Outside the tent, she could hear Leon Constanzas banging on the cooking pot with his ladle. Supper was ready. For a moment, Nina hesitated. Then she decided she would quite like to stay in the room for just a few minutes longer.

Two:
ROGER THE BLIND

The Royal Digest of Affairs and Events: Volume 5 (in the Second Year of the Rule of King Matthew)

The Diary of Miss Garamond (Herald)

Greetings, Citizens!

The reader will no doubt be aware that copies of *The Royal Digest of Affairs and Events* have, from its inception up until the present moment, been exceedingly difficult to obtain. Indeed, the author is herself painfully conscious that the demand for *The Royal Digest* has in recent months been outrunning the supply to a degree that can no longer be considered acceptable. However, it is now our pleasant duty to inform our readers that this uncomfortable situation is at last on the brink of resolution, and that certain other developments of a most gratifying nature will imminently be coming to fruition.

With the gracious support of King Matthew, *The Royal Digest* will within a very short space of time be enjoying the benefits of the most up-to-date copying engines. By means of this modern technology, *The Digest* will in future be produced in quantities sufficient, I am assured, to satisfy even the most extravagant predictions of demand. The new equipment will be constructed and installed under the personal supervision of the Royal Supervisor of Machinery, Mister Kevin Considine, whose participation in this venture has, for a strictly limited period, been vouchsafed to *The Royal Digest* by King Matthew. Mister Considine will be working in close collaboration with the staff of *The Royal Digest* to ensure a swift and unobtrusive transition to the new technology and the new methods of working with which it will be associated. We are delighted to welcome Mister Considine to the offices of *The Royal Digest,* and we most warmly thank King Matthew for his kind indulgence in facilitating the transformation.

And now, there is yet more exciting news! Readers will doubtless have been struck in recent issues of *The Royal Digest* by the appearance of the fine illustrations that now accompany much of the written material. It has been the good fortune of the author to secure the services of a remarkably talented young draughts-man, Mister Michael Brown, whose landscape vignettes have already served to enliven the various sections of *The Royal Digest*, and whose work we intend to be utilising to an even greater degree in the future. Indeed, Mister Brown has recently secured promotion to the newly instituted rank of Supervisor of Iconography, and it is to be his especial responsibility to engage and coordinate the services of a team of artists and illustrators who will offer further prowess in the fields of portraiture and ornamentation, and whose combined efforts will, I am assured, transform *The Royal Digest* into a startlingly vivid kaleidoscope of words and images that will undoubtedly appeal to the broadest possible range of readers.

But perhaps the reader begins to tire of this intimate account of the domestic affairs of *The Royal Digest*. (So too, if the truth be known, does the author!) Let us turn, therefore, to matters altogether more weighty, namely to the swiftly rising tide of alarm and distress that is at present being experienced by citizens of all degrees, with regard to the increasingly violent and unlawful behaviour on the streets of our City by the organised gangs of youths known as 'Wolf Boys'. These incidents have been weighing heavily on the mind of King Matthew and, following a period of deep thought and close consideration on the part of the King, it is the privilege of *The Digest* to issue the following promulgations, as disclosed to the author at the monthly Private Audience.

Firstly, the confidential agents of the King have in recent weeks infiltrated every nook and corner of the City, mingling with great folk and lesser folk in tavern and in workplace and on street corner, and it can now be stated with the utmost authority that there exists scarcely a man, woman or child in this City who remains untouched by the chill hand of lawlessness. Banditry, rape and murder, all now are accepted as commonplace, no longer confined to the hours of night and the stinking recesses of the Undertown, but encountered in broad daylight on every highway, in every suburb, at the gates of the Royal Palace itself (and even, on one notable occasion, here at the offices of *The Royal Digest*!). It is now established beyond doubt that honest and respectable folk go about their affairs in a perpetual state of terror, and this constitutes a situation that the King is no longer disposed to tolerate.

Secondly, the officially constituted body for the maintenance of law and order, namely the City Militia, is perceived by one and all to be a force that is utterly bereft of vital energy, and that is no longer believed to be fitted for the carrying out of duties for which it was established. As the reader will probably be aware, membership of the City Militia has traditionally been passed from father to son, in accordance with Charter Ancient and Inviolable. Although this method has operated in a satisfactory manner for many centuries, sadly, in more recent times, the sons of the City Militiamen have shown little inclination to take up the calling of their fathers, preferring, for reasons unknown, the more insidious attractions of strong drink, the gaming table, and certain young women of the town. To condense a short story out of a long one, the once-proud Militia has dwindled in recent times to a small band of elderly and infirm gentlemen whose numbers and whose physical prowess are daily in visible decline. The King has therefore concluded that there remains no alternative but to disband the Militia and to institute a new, more formidable body dedicated to the restoration of law and order.

Thirdly, following a reconnaissance visit to the Undertown by the King's Personal Guard, the leader of the Wolf Boys, an individual known as Fang, was invited under armed escort to the Palace, where he was granted an Extraordinary Private Audience with the King. Following lengthy and detailed discussions, it has been acknowledged by the King that, given the extensive and detailed knowledge, on the part of the Wolf Boys, of every highway, byway, lane, alley and sewer of the City, and given in addition the over-whelming numbers and highly disciplined structure of their organisation, the King has conceded, albeit with the utmost reluctance, that the instigation of any effective new body dedicated to the maintenance of law and order will not, without the active collabora-tion of Fang and his confederates, be viable.

Lastly, the King is therefore pleased to announce, with immediate effect, the formation of the Royal Wolf Boys Militia. This body, under the direction of Fang, will assume full and formal responsibility for the carry-ing out of all duties pertaining to the enforcement of law and order, the punishment of offenders, and any such other vital services as may be directed from time to time by the King. The aforesaid Militia will be financed by Bursary Extraordinary from the Royal

Purse and will shortly take up its duties following the final dissolution of the old City Militia. The King is confident that this initiative will guarantee a new era of peace and security on the streets of our City.

The author hopes that her readers will join her in wishing the Royal Wolf Boys Militia every success in the execution of their duties, and looks forward to more settled times following this bold venture.

Goodbye, Citizens, and long live King Matthew!

The Brothers Constanzas

The waggons of the Constanzas Brothers Travelling Amusements threaded their way across the country-side from one village to the next. Wherever they settled, Madam Nina offered her unique service to the people and, in the Empathy Engine, the people left behind them the black residue.

Andrew, George and Leon Constanzas had grown up in a travelling circus that was run, with a hand of iron, by their mother. The late Madame Constanzas, in common with many of the wandering folk, had been a passionate believer in the traditions of the family so that, when the brothers broke away to start their own travelling amusements, they had maintained the ritual of the company meal, taken each evening at sundown, at the long trestle table in the big tent. This tent, for as long as anyone could remember, had not been used for any other purpose, and although the showground hands regularly complained about the heavy work involved in assembling a structure that was used for only a brief period each day, the brothers had stood firm and, each evening, in the tent, the entire company was required to assemble without fail. The members of the immediate family, the stallholders, the roustabouts, even Klapsi, the unsociable and unmusical clown, all were expected to share a meal, and all could take advantage of the opportunity to discuss matters of mutual concern, and to celebrate the end of another successful, or perhaps not-so-successful, day's trade.

Andrew, the oldest of the brothers, in his top hat and frock coat, was the figure most in evidence to the public, and his task it was to attend to the presentation of the show, resolving any day-to-day difficulties, and constantly encouraging, goading and bullying the showpeople to present themselves to the punters in the most advantageous fashion. George, more retiring by nature, was in charge of the accounting. The system that he operated was a mystery to all, depending as it did on a waistcoat with eight or nine pockets, between which wads of notes and handfuls of coins were periodically transferred in an obscure sequence that nobody had yet managed to decipher. Leon, the youngest brother, did the cooking.

'That Madam Nina, she's late again. Do you think I should give her another call?'

Andrew, seated at the head of the table, looked up

as his brother ladled the first portion of stew into his bowl. It had been Andrew's idea to engage Nina, but now he was becoming increasingly perturbed by her erratic behaviour.

'I'm not sure, Leon. That machine of hers, it seems to need a lot of looking after. And somehow I just can't help feeling she's bad luck. I don't really like having her in the tent. George, what do you think?'

The two ranks of heads rotated in unison towards George's end of the table.

'She's good business,' said George. 'Takings are up.'

One or two heads nodded.

'It's not right, though, her being late for supper every night.' Leon was making his way along the table, filling the bowls in turn. 'Mother wouldn't have stood for it. Showpeople live together and work together and eat together, that's what she would have said. But yes, Andrew, I agree something isn't right with her. The last few weeks, she's gone all sort of turned in on herself.'

There were several nods at this.

'She was acting pretty rum at the start of the show today,' Klapsi the unmusical clown chipped in. 'Almost barged me off the platform. Didn't seem to see me. Like her mind was somewhere else.'

'Yes, I've noticed that too,' Andrew mused. 'But her spiel, when she started it, well, it was better than ever. Like she really felt it. Almost like she believed it.'

There were several more nods at this. The company ate in cogitative silence for a while. Leon had inherited his mother's talent for cooking, and, deep down, nobody really resented the formality of the meal.

'She's good business,' said George again after a while. Leon moved unobtrusively along the table collecting up the bowls, then disappeared to attend to the pudding.

'Tell you what we'll do,' said Andrew finally. 'Klapsi, if there's any other strange behaviour on the platform, let me know about it. George, keep an eye on the takings, well, I know you will anyway. And Leon . . .' The third brother reappeared at that moment, almost hidden behind a huge, steaming jam roly-poly. '. . . Make sure she doesn't miss too many meals. We may not like her too much but, all right, we don't want to starve her. And now –' he watched with approval as Leon filled his plate '– back to business.'

Nina, meanwhile, was still in her booth, hunched in front of her machine, engrossed in her nightly maintenance routine. There was no getting away from it, the pile of dark stuff was growing bigger every day, and it was getting harder and harder to scrape off the walls. It seemed to be getting more stubborn, almost to be developing a will of its own. Even during the day, Nina found herself unable to free her mind from its looming presence. It bore down upon her like a massive physical burden, an ever-present threat that could be held at bay only by sustained nightly application of the scraper. And now, in the past few days, Nina had started to feel an emptiness, almost a hunger for her maintenance sessions, for although in the scraping and the sweeping and the tidying she found no pleasure and no satisfaction, she awaited with giddy anticipation the moment when she would lick the last of the dark stuff from her fingers, when she would feel it explode into stabbing, kaleidoscopic life on her tongue and in her mouth and throat and belly. Then, just for that moment, she could forget the punters, forget the booth, forget the wretched ritual of cleaning the room.

Finished at last, Nina relaxed and allowed the sensation, part pain, part pleasure, to take possession of her. It felt good, sometimes, to imagine that it was alive, caressing her, soothing her, taking her into itself.

'Don't stop,' Nina murmured. 'Just a little bit longer.'

The dark stuff seemed to stir, as if in response. Then, from behind her, came a tactful cough. Startled, Nina tore away the headphones.

'Madam Nina?' It was Leon. 'Have you nearly finished? You don't want to miss your pudding again, do you?'

A Bicycle Made for Two

Among the jumble of miscellaneous items with which Joe Blackwood had packed the empty corners of his apartment was an ancient, intransigent-looking tandem bicycle. Rusty had first observed this curious object in the initial days of his tenancy at Serendipity Court, when he was negotiating with the caretaker for furniture. Some months later, when the weather became warmer, it occurred to him that it might provide a pretext for spending some extra time with Alice.

The two had continued to see each other for exercise and refreshments every Wednesday night but, for the rest of the week, Alice seemed to be enmeshed in a variety of commitments that made heavy demands on her energy and left her with little time to spare. She was explaining this to Rusty one Wednesday evening in spring, as they sat sharing a flask at one of the tables in the small rear garden of the Estate Arms.

'Mondays I go to the Crier's Rest with some of the people at the office,' she explained to him. 'Tuesdays I go to my exercise class. Thursdays I run a little class of my own.' Rusty raised an eyebrow. 'It's sort of Palace business. You know, confidential. Sorry. Fridays it's exercise class again. And then I have to get ready for the weekend. So that just leaves Wednesdays to see you.' Deftly, she changed the subject. 'But you, you're so clever, getting promoted so quickly at your work. You must like that, having your own little department to run.'

'It's a bit daunting, to be honest,' Rusty mused. 'Some of those artists, are, well, you know, quite difficult to deal with. Keep wanting to do things their own way, I suppose. But Miss Garamond, she's given me a lot of help.'

'Didn't you find her a bit scary, at first?'

'Yes, I did, but actually she's quite funny once you get to know her. Not really scary at all.' Rusty realised that Alice had managed to divert him. 'But listen, what do you do at the weekends?'

'Oh, all sorts, really. Sometimes I need to be by myself for a bit. And sometimes I have to talk to my own people about this and that . . .'

'The Islanders?'

Alice nodded, tight-lipped for a moment. Rusty knew that, during her years in the city, Alice had continued to maintain some sort of connection with the mysterious world of the islands, but he knew also that she was reluctant to speak about it, even to him, and he understood enough of such matters to respect her need for privacy.

Alice stared at him thoughtfully for a moment longer, then laid her two hands on his.

'Oh, Rusty . . . You're such a lovely man, and I could really get very fond of you, you know, and, well, perhaps it looks to you as if I'm holding back . . .' Rusty's lips parted slightly as he drew breath. '. . . But, you know, my people may need me to go somewhere else before long.' She was staring down at the weathered oak slats of the table. 'And I think it might be coming up for my time.'

'You mean you'll be leaving the city?'

Alice nodded. 'I might be. I don't know exactly when. Maybe at the end of the summer.' Her blue eyes appeared to be focused on some distant, unknown point and, for a moment, Rusty experienced another vertiginous glimpse of long grass and clover and the sea. 'But at any rate, let's make the most of things till then.'

Forlornly, Rusty studied her white hands with their slim fingers and faintly freckled wrists.

'So are you busy every weekend?'

She broke the tension with a smile.

'No. Not every weekend.'

'Have you ever ridden a bicycle?'

As it turned out, Alice was free the next weekend but one, and it was her idea that they might ride down to the coast, find somewhere to stop for the night, and return to the city the following day. Rusty assumed responsibility for extracting the tandem from Joe Blackwood, and he spent a couple of evenings with spanner and oil can restoring it to plausible working order.

After an early breakfast at the coffee stall on the North Way, they headed up the empty thoroughfare and turned upriver towards the ferry terminal, the tandem bouncing and shaking along the roughly boarded quayside. At the jetty, they pulled up short, confronted by a newly erected checkpoint at which a gleaming red-and-white-striped horizontal pole barred their way on to the boat. From an adjoining hut, two awkward-looking figures emerged. Rusty and Alice dismounted.

'May we ask the purpose of your journey, sir, madam?'

One of them was slightly shorter than Rusty, one was slightly taller. Both displayed a rather slouching gait, and both were dressed in very new, stiff-looking uniforms of a thick, dark blue cotton material, which did not appear yet to have been washed. On their heads were forage caps of the same material, bearing brass badges in the form of a wolf's head, and worn at defiantly non-matching angles. On their feet were brand-new shiny black boots, which looked heavy and stiff and uncomfortable. Their fingernails were long and sharp and dirty. From beneath the peaks of the caps peered sallow, pinched, hungry-looking adolescent faces with small eyes and irregular teeth. These, then, were the formidable troops of the Royal Wolf Boys Militia.

'Sir?'

'Oh, sorry.' Rusty curtailed his fascinated scrutiny of his interrogators. 'Short holiday. Tourists.'

Seemingly taken aback by this unexpected revelation, the two inquisitors retreated into their hut. Through the window, Rusty and Alice could see them leafing through a stack of thick, loose-leaf manuals. Alice nudged Rusty.

'Aren't they sweet?' she giggled. 'They're having to look it up in the book.'

Rusty, slightly less relaxed, smiled grimly. A moment later, the barrier swung itself up out of their path. The two heads reappeared at the doorway of the hut.

'Have a pleasant journey, sir, madam. Your safety is our sole concern.'

A few hours later, they found themselves on a bleak stretch of coast, a broad, featureless sweep of shingle separating rolling dunes from choppy sea, swooping gulls fracturing the air with their squawking cries. Abandoning the tandem, Rusty and Alice strolled arm in arm, enjoying each other's silence, picking up shells and pieces of driftwood, stretching out on the dunes, dozing, kissing. Later, they cycled at a leisurely pace along the coast road, passing one isolated, abandoned cottage and, shortly afterwards, arriving at a quiet village. At a pie shop they enjoyed an improvised supper, and, following the pieman's directions, they found their way to a lonely house next to the sea, whose gatepost bore a brass plaque, green with age, on which they could just decipher the word 'ROOMS' in a slanting, cursive script.

They rang the bell. There was a long pause, and they had almost decided to give up waiting when the door at last creaked open and a very old woman eyed them suspiciously.

'It's still winter, really. I've not started the season yet.' She was about to close the door, but she must have registered their crestfallen expressions, for she halted her action, seeming to soften a little. 'But if it's rooms you want, I suppose I can oblige. Two rooms, is it?'

Rusty and Alice glanced at each other.

'Two rooms?' queried Rusty

'Two rooms,' said Alice.

The trip to the coast was not repeated and, although he continued to see Alice every Wednesday evening, Rusty was conscious of a growing feeling of apprehension, aware that their time together was drawing to a close.

One Wednesday evening, towards the end of the summer, they were in Alice's apartment, working their way as usual through their exercise pattern. They had taken up positions at opposite corners of the curious abstract design that partitioned the floor with its angular geometry.

Rusty was beginning to reacquire some of his old facility. Under Alice's tuition, he had once again mastered the elementary pattern with its six basic attitudes, and now he found himself able to join her, tentatively, in a few of the more advanced figures. On this Wednesday evening, they had just arrived at the final phase of The Pattern of the Diver, which involved a challenging sequence of inverted balances, and had now entered into The Time of Repose. Feet in the air, toes pointing questingly towards the ceiling, they rested on their heads, facing each other from opposite corners of the grid, immersed for the moment in a boundless ocean of calm. Rusty's socks were wrinkled into their usual concertina folds around his ankles, while Alice's fair hair formed a circular pool on the floor. Outside, the late-summer sun was casting a pale orange glow through the window.

'Rusty?' Alice's voice broke in gently upon his peace, her inverted features betraying no outward sign of exertion.

'Hmmph?' Rusty, less proficient, was still fidgeting from time to time to maintain his balance.

'You know I said that the Islanders might be calling me away from here?'

Rusty adjusted himself slightly.

'Well, it's going to be soon. Very soon now, actually.' She mirrored his adjustment with an almost imperceptible shift in her position. 'But you've done so well at this. I hope you'll keep it up after— well, after I'm gone.'

'I think so.' The balance was becoming more of an effort to maintain. 'It'll be something . . .' He could feel himself beginning to slip, and made another, larger, adjustment, his legs splaying momentarily to the sides. Alice made a minimal movement, then allowed her eyes to close. Following her cue, Rusty took a series of long breaths, until he could feel his shoulders and ribcage beginning to settle back into repose. After a moment he continued. '. . . It'll be something to remember you by.'

'Well, of course that's a nice thought. But it shouldn't be just for that.'

Smoothly, Alice folded her slim, black-clad legs around each other, allowing them to settle into an intricate knot. Unconsciously copying her, Rusty attempted, more clumsily, the same manoeuvre.

'Gently,' Alice interjected.

But in turning his attention to his legs, Rusty had allowed his concentration on his balance to drift, and suddenly the intricately meshed components of his equilibrium flew apart and he was rolling on the ground in an ungainly tangle of limbs. Alice meanwhile remained immobile, unperturbed in her austere linearity.

'Have you hurt yourself?'

'No, I don't think so. I'm sorry, Alice, I know I can do better than that.'

Alice considered this. Then, abruptly straightening her legs and arms, she kicked herself upright, traversed the grid in an effortless cartwheel, and, alighting in a kneeling position beside Rusty, dipped down to kiss him on the forehead.

'There, is that better?' She gazed at him for a moment, then, suddenly, gave an unexpected sniff. Hastily, she drew one slim wrist across each eye in turn. 'You do understand, don't you? I really do think so much of you, Rusty, and, you know, maybe one day we'll have our time, but it can't be now, it really can't. I'm sorry. I'm so sorry, Rusty. Oh, come here.'

It was the only time that Rusty had seen Alice shed tears.

That night, as the last shreds of orange faded from the sky, they took their usual walk by the river. Later, they made their final sad ascent to their separate balconies. And the next day, when Rusty arrived home from the Herald's office, Alice's rope was no longer hanging there. And then he knew for certain that Alice had gone away.

'And then you were taken away?'

Well, not at once. The militiamen took me back to the house, I suppose there wasn't anywhere much else they could put me, and those two women came to see to me, the ones who threw away the red and white rug, remember, I told you earlier. Then things did get a bit confusing for a while, I remember being bounced around in the back of a waggon, and then I was taken somewhere where I had my clothes stripped off me and I was washed down with very cold water and some gritty sort of soap that smelled like burning, I remember not liking that much, I've never really liked water anyway. Then there was a man looking down at me from behind a big desk, he was wearing spectacles, and I'd never seen anyone wearing spectacles before, I remember being fascinated by that. Then I was taken to a big cold square grey house where there were a lot of other children running around in ragged uniforms. I suppose it must have been some kind of orphanage. I remember sleeping in a long room with rows of beds, and being made to walk around in a big circle in the yard. And I remember being shouted at – I was always being shouted at in that place, someone once shouted at me for dropping a spoon, and then, after a bit, someone else came and took me away, a tall man with a beard.

The tall man didn't say much to me. I think he must have arrived very early one morning, at any rate he was standing by my bed when I opened my eyes. He was just finishing talking to someone else I couldn't see, and then I think he said, 'Is this the boy?' and he turned to me and said, 'Thomas? Thomas Slater? Get dressed and pick up your things. I want you to come with me now.'

I didn't have many things. A few spare clothes, a little notebook that I'd managed to get hold of from somewhere, and of course the old iron chain coiled up at the bottom of *my pack, that chain seemed to go everywhere with me. And then I was sitting with the tall man in a carriage, I remember the road being very bumpy, but after a while the countryside sort of flattened out and then we arrived in a town, I'd never seen so many people. We drove through the town, and then there was another big house, but this one wasn't square, it was a funny spiky sort of shape, and it had towers and turrets and a steep roof and tall pointed windows and doors, and this, I discovered, was the Academy of Cartography.*

The Academy was to be my home for the next fifteen years, and in some ways it was rather like the house we're in now. Perhaps home is the wrong word to use for it, it wasn't as if my family was there, and nobody seemed particularly interested in looking after me, but somehow I found that I could fit in with the life of the place, and right from the start I had the sensation that everything there was being done for some kind of purpose, and that if I behaved myself and kept to the rules, I would be allowed to play a part in it. I suppose that was what was important, having a part to play in a world that was properly organised. I didn't get that feeling under the table at my father's house, all I learned there was to keep quiet and stay out of the way, although I suppose that did prove useful later on. And in the orphanage, of course, there had been routine and discipline, but it all seemed somehow pointless, as if it was just an aim in itself. But the Academy had a point all right, and I sensed it right from the beginning.

The tall man left me with the porter at the front gate and drove off in his carriage, and the porter didn't say anything, he just led me off down some dark stairs and handed me over to another man, this one was wearing a striped apron, and the porter said, 'This one's for you, Mister Roberts, name of Thomas Slater,' and then Mister Roberts said, 'All right, Tom, let's find you somewhere to sleep.' So he took me along a corridor and up a big wide staircase and into a huge room, I'd never seen a room so big, it had a stone floor and tall pointed windows, and at one end was a set of tall wooden doors with iron studs in them, and at the other end there was a row of massive stone statues, each one in its own alcove. I discovered later that these were the statues of the Great Cartographers of the Forgotten Age, Simeon the Engine Maker, Albert Albertsen, Roger the Blind and all the others. These alcoves were where the youngest, least important servants were allowed to sleep, and my sleeping place, I discovered, was to be in the alcove behind Roger the Blind, there were a couple of blankets rolled up there waiting for me, and that's where I slept for the next fifteen years, curled up on the hard stone. I could have moved into the senior servants' quarters later on if I'd wanted to, but I found that I quite liked my alcove at the feet of Roger the Blind, so that's where I stayed. To begin with, I felt a little bit lost in that huge room, with the others snoring in their alcoves, but I still had my chain with me, and my padlocks, so at first I used to chain myself to Roger's ankle, and then I could feel this great sense of safety washing over me. No, I stopped doing it when I got older. Or at any rate, I only needed to do it once in a while.

Once I had arranged my things in the alcove, I was taken straight off again and given some work to do, and so there

I was, just thrown into the life of the Academy and having to fend for myself. Nobody ever took the trouble to explain to me what the Academy was for or what went on there, and it took quite a few years before I could piece the whole picture together, but my father had taught me to keep quiet and be obedient, so that's what I did, I just had to listen and learn and work things out for myself.

Eventually I discovered that the Academy was where young men and women came to learn the science of making charts, and it was also the place where the Brotherhood of Cartographers kept their secret library down in the vaults, and of course nobody was allowed down there until they'd sworn the Lesser Academic Oath, but anyway that was the purpose of the place, and right from the first day I was there I could sense that feeling of purpose, and that's why I was able to fit in there so easily.

Of course I was at the Academy as a servant, not as an undergraduate, but I think I was a good servant, conscientious and hard-working, and it was by being a good servant that I slowly managed to learn what I learned. No, I never really made any friends, well, maybe just one, if you could call him a friend, but I'll tell you about him later. I was a silent boy, my father had never encouraged me to open my mouth much, so the others tended to keep their distance from me, but I think I eventually came to command some sort of respect from them, mainly because I did as I was told and remembered things.

There was quite a complicated organisation of servants at the Academy, a hierarchy I suppose you would call it, and it would easily have been possible for me to stop in one place and never really find out what went on anywhere else, but because I was a good servant I managed to work my way up the hierarchy, and by the time I was full-grown I had spent a bit of time in just about every corner of the place and had got to know the doings of the Academy inside out.

I started off in the kitchens, working mainly for Mister Roberts, cutting the rinds off hundreds of rashers of bacon, that sort of thing, and then I spent a bit of time in the grounds, cutting the grass and raking the gravel, there was a little old lady who was in charge of the gardening. I didn't enjoy that very much, I suppose because it reminded me of my father's work. Then they moved me again, and I became a waiter in the refectory, serving meals to people, and that was very useful because I got to overhear all sorts of talk, the undergraduates and the instructors and sometimes even the master cartographers at the high table, and I learned a lot from that. I was quite shocked at how unruly the under-graduates were at their meals, climbing up on the tables and that sort of thing, but the folk on the high table behaved themselves pretty well. One of the master cartographers, a dame actually, a silent, hunched sort of woman, she used to sit a little distance away from the others, and she was always writing, all the way through her meals. I could see that she was filling in letters and words on little grids of black and white squares, I discovered later that they were called cross-word puzzles. One day she left some of them behind her, and I managed to smuggle them away under my livery. I studied them later, and they seemed really intriguing, but I soon managed to figure out how they worked, so in my odd *spare moments, curled up at the feet of Roger the Blind, I started to design crosswords as a change from writing poems, and when the other servants discovered what I was doing they stayed out of my way even more than before.*

No, they never really picked on me. Of course, there used to be quite a bit of bullying among the young servants at the Academy, big boys and girls picking on small ones, but I never suffered from that. I grew up tall and skinny, and I was quite awkward, my livery never fitted me properly, but I was never what you would call a natural victim. Perhaps it was because of my height, or perhaps it was because of my silence, or perhaps it was because after what I'd been through with my father I ended up pretty well immune to cruelty, but one way and another they stayed away from me, and that suited me just fine.

Later on, I suppose some way into my teens, they made me an academic servant. They could see that I had a head for letters and figures, so they let me swear the Lesser Academic Oath, and then I was allowed to serve in the library, fetching the charts from their racks for the cartographers and filing them away when they were finished with. The racks went all the way up to the ceiling, row upon row of them, and I sometimes had to use a stepladder to get the charts down from the top levels. I wasn't supposed to look at the charts, and to tell the truth, even when I did manage to catch a glimpse of them they didn't mean anything much to me, but I certainly got to know the filing system, all those funny little grids of numbers and letters which identified every document and told me where it had to be stored. Each chart was kept rolled up in a sort of leather cylinder, and every cylin-

der had a little transparent pocket where the identification number was kept. I really grew to love that filing system, it was like a second home to me, I even designed a little filing system of my own for my poems and crosswords, I had built up quite a collection by that time. Later on I was even allowed to apply the seal of the Brotherhood to the new charts when they were drawn up, and that made me feel quite important, melting the wax and using the big embossing iron.

Next, they let me look after the little shop where the undergraduates bought their parchment and ink, and the special spools of thread for the cartography engines that they used on field exercises. I was about the same age as most of the undergraduates by then, and some of them seemed to want to chat to me, the girls as well as the men, I suppose I had some sort of curiosity value to them, and I started to lose a bit of my shyness and become a bit more companionable. I even discovered that I could be quite helpful to the new ones, explaining the way around the building, telling them where they could find this or that. One or two of the girls seemed to take an interest in me, too, in a different sort of way, but that frightened me because I didn't understand it then, and they must have sensed that I was uncomfortable because after a bit it stopped happening.

But generally I got on well with the undergraduates, and that stood me in good stead in my next job, which was in the lecture theatres assisting the instructors. I had to get their papers and charts ready for the lectures, sometimes I had to make copies of things, and they were very impressed by my reading and writing. And then there was the equipment they used for the practical instruction, the octants and the measuring chains and all the other engines and instruments, which all had to be got ready and put in position before the undergraduates arrived. I've probably already mentioned that I had no great aptitude for anything mechanical, but all I really had to do was to collect the things from the storeroom and put them in position, and then the instructors would show the undergraduates how to work them.

That was the best part of all, because once the lectures began, there was nothing more for me to do until the end of the hour, so I got the chance to stand on the top tier at the back of the lecture theatre and listen. Of course, strictly speaking this wasn't allowed, because to attend the lectures I should have sworn the Greater Academic Oath, and none of the servants were allowed to do this. One or two of the instructors were quite strict about it, Professor Octavian for example, he used to make me stand outside until the lecture was over, but some of them, the younger ones mainly, didn't seem to mind, a couple of them even said they were glad I was taking an interest, and so I started to learn a bit about the science of cartography itself, and of course that was really interesting.

Another thing I got to do from time to time was to go into the town and meet people who were visiting the Academy, quite important people sometimes, and escort them from the waggon halt to the Academy itself. Once or twice I even got to go in a coach to the city, to fetch people who didn't want to travel alone for one reason or another. The first time I did this, one of the senior servants came with me, to make sure

I knew the way, I suppose, but after that I was given the money for my fare and allowed to go on my own. I suppose I must have proved myself trustworthy by then. Anyway, the Academy used to entertain all kinds of distinguished visitors, other academics and people from the commercial brotherhoods and even members of the Royal retinue, the Senior Calibrator came once, I remember, Doctor de Voonik he was called, and the Royal Supervisor of Machinery, he came another time.

And one day, I had to go and meet a magician, actually the Chief Magician to the King. And after that, everything changed again.

Sculpture

The dark stuff clung to the six walls of the room in thick, uneven, sticky streaks, dimming the light, fracturing the atmosphere into jagged-edged shafts and lumbering, misshapen blocks of brightness and shade. Determinedly, Nina scraped at it until her wrists and fingers ached but somehow, each day, her scraper seemed to get smaller, and the room seemed to get larger, as the crawling black substance insinuated itself across every surface, choked the atmosphere with toxic sweetness, seeped through the very pores of her skin.

Nina had long since abandoned any hope of restoring the room to its pristine whiteness, but she knew that she must at all costs do whatever lay within her power to keep the dark stuff at bay, to forestall it from taking over entirely. Sometimes she wished that she could just abandon herself to it, give in to its treacly venom, fall back and relinquish all hope, but in some corner of her heart she knew that once she abandoned herself to that room, she would never again emerge into the daylight. And so she fought with whatever power she could muster to keep open every last chink of light.

The ceiling, long since beyond her reach, was completely and irrevocably black, but Nina had scraped as far up the walls as her arms could stretch, and she had scraped and swept as much as she could from the floor into a compact mound at the centre of the room. She was kneeling in the gloom now, in front of the mound, patting it into shape like some monstrous sandcastle. I could sculpt it, Nina thought, I could make it into a rabbit or a fish, like I used to do when I was a little girl at the seaside. I could make it into a companion, make it into a playmate. Tentatively, she traced a groove here, formed a mound there.

I could make it into a friend.

Nina encircled the mound with her arms, felt it yielding slightly to their pressure. Yes, she decided, now it was beginning to feel like someone. Someone sitting on the floor. Sitting on the floor, the knees up under the chin. The knees up under the chin, and the arms wrapped around the shins. The arms wrapped around the shins, and the head resting on the knees, yes, the head, on one side, resting on the knees. Yes, this is what my friend would be like.

She pressed her body against the dark stuff, buried her face in it, allowed herself for a moment to taste the familiar bitter tang. Unbidden, her hands continued their exploration. It even felt like a friend, Nina decided. Yes, here was the hand, slim-fingered, the grip relaxed, the nails long and curving. Here were the spine, the ribs, the sharp vertebrae, even the twin ridges of the shoulder blades. And here was the hair. The dark stuff almost felt like hair, sleek, whispering, long. Nina let her lips stray across the hair, sampled its texture, tasted its musky warmth.

And here was the face, cradled on its side on the knees. Nina's lips explored a slanted eye, its lid for the moment closed, an angular cheekbone, the waxy texture of the skin, the moistness of the lips . . .

Once again, the dark stuff seemed to stir into life, massaging her lips and tongue with stabs and shafts of warmth and anguish, a fierce glow spreading down her body, beginning now to tickle at the corners of her loins . . .

Shocked, Nina drew back, then found herself pulled up short. A long, sinewy hand grasped her wrist, drew her forwards again, and a hoarse, hot-breathed voice murmured like honey in her ear:

'Nina? Don't be afraid. I'm your friend. You can trust me.'

An Unexpected Confidence

'If you can't keep your head still, you're going to end up getting your ears cut off!'

'Sorry, Paul. I'll try and keep my mind on it.'

Rusty's neighbour was giving him a long-overdue haircut, his first since the departure of Alice.

'You've got such lovely hair, it's a real pity you don't look after it.'

'Paul, you're getting as bad as my mother. Ow!' Rusty winced as Paul made another forcible adjustment to the inclination of his neck. 'But you're right, I suppose I have been letting things slide. It's all been piling up a bit lately, you know, work and other stuff.'

Paul stepped back to scrutinise his work, nodding wisely.

'Well, I suppose it happens to all of us now and then. Is that Miss Garamond giving you a rough time at the office?'

'No, it's not her – not really, anyway,' Rusty mused. 'Although she has made the odd remark about my hair, now you come to mention it. Actually, when I think about it, there's nothing much at work that I can't handle if I put my mind to it. It's more . . .'

'Other stuff?'

'Other stuff. Yes.'

There was a period of mutual, interrogative silence, punctuated by the occasional staccato afterthoughts of Paul's scissors. At last, Paul stepped back, tapping his front teeth thoughtfully with his comb.

'Yes. Yes. Well, I think you're done, but do at least try to drag a comb through it now and again. Have you got time for a coffee?'

'Thanks, that would be nice. I've nothing much to dash off to, tonight.'

Rusty unwound the sheet from around his neck, then started casting about vaguely for a broom.

'In the tall cupboard. Milk and sugar?'

They seated themselves at the kitchen table. Rusty stirred his coffee with a mechanical motion, staring down into the depths of the bone china cup as it rattled in the saucer. After a moment he became aware of Paul's gaze.

'It's that girl, isn't it? The one you used to see on Wednesday nights?'

Rusty nodded. 'Alice, yes. But she's not here any more. She had to go away.'

'Oh, that's such a shame. You seemed to be getting on so nicely.'

'Did we? I don't know, I only really saw her for a couple of hours a week. But I'm really missing her, Paul. Suddenly, everything seems such an effort.'

'Well, you know what they say, someone else will turn up, there's plenty more fish in the sea. I'd have thought you'd have had them queueing up, a good-looking boy like you.'

Rusty managed a feeble smile, followed by a half-hearted sip of his sweet, milky coffee.

'Tell you what,' Paul continued briskly. 'I'm having some friends round on Friday, just a spot of supper

and a few drinks. You'd be very welcome to join us
if you're free.'

'Thanks, Paul. I'd like that.'

Paul was a kind-hearted, hospitable man, and his
friends were very welcoming but, although Rusty
joined them on a few Friday nights, he never felt
completely a part of their tight little circle. And
although he was now beginning to find himself on
nodding terms with several of his other neighbours
at Serendipity Court, still he did not feel that he had
made any real friends in the city. One reason for this
was that his work at the Herald's Office was starting to make quite severe demands on his time and
energy. Since his unexpected promotion, he had
found himself responsible for the recruitment and
administration of a loosely knit team of artists and
illustrators, and they had not turned out to be easy
people to deal with. But, as he became absorbed in
his work, he was at least able to forget for a while
about Alice.

One morning, he was sitting as usual in the narrow
cubbyhole that served him for an office. At his small
desk, wedged in between stacks of filing cabinets
beneath the grimy skylight, he was sifting through the
day's mail, wondering how many urgent tasks might
face him before lunch, when suddenly the door burst
open and a bulky, flamboyantly dressed middle-aged
man appeared at the threshold. It was Norman Loxley,
one of Rusty's regular team of artists. Without any

preliminaries, Loxley at once began to harangue him in a powerful, booming voice.

'You bloody people, you think you can tell us all how to do our jobs.' Rusty was becoming accustomed to these outbursts, and arranged his features into an expression of polite attention. 'I am an artist, do you not understand that? I draw, I paint, I express, I feel. You lot, you just want to put us into your little pigeon holes. You want to stand us in line and give us numbers and issue us with instructions.' His face was turning a dangerous shade of purple. 'You want us to dance around to your silly little tunes, you want us to arrange everything we do purely for your stupid convenience, purely to fit in with your stupid schedules . . .'

Rusty nodded politely, then became aware that the torrent of words had temporarily dried up, giving way to an uncoordinated sequence of inarticulate noises and gestures. Quickly, he identified his opportunity to state his own case, before Loxley recovered his full intimidating powers of speech.

'Norman, you do have a contract with the Herald's Office.' Rusty snatched a random piece of paper and held it up. 'Let's just remind ourselves what's in it. We don't actually require you to express your feelings. We simply require you to produce accurate drawings depicting items, scenes and topics as may from time to time be specified by the Herald or her representative.' Inwardly, he was squirming with embarrassment at the bureaucratic language he was forced to employ, but he guessed that his adversary would be too overwrought to notice this. 'You do understand that, Norman, don't you? We have been through it a number of times.'

Leaning over the desk, Loxley seized the paper from Rusty's hand, and dramatically tore it into several pieces, fortunately without taking the trouble to study it first.

'This is what I think of your contract. And this. And this.' He scattered the scraps of paper simultaneously in several directions. 'And as far as I'm concerned, little Mister Green or Brown or whatever your name is, the whole lot of you can fry in hell. Because let me tell you, I have been doing my work man and boy while you were still . . .'

Sighing inwardly, Rusty patiently allowed the stream of invective to flow on. He had had a number of similar exchanges with Loxley, and he knew that little further participation would be required from him until the final dramatic slamming of the office door. He also knew that Loxley's work, when it arrived, would be executed to an immaculate standard and delivered precisely on time.

Rusty was not yet entirely clear in his mind what value, if any, these heated exchanges might have to offer to either party. His team of artists included a number who were similar in temperament to Loxley, some of whom could also be relied upon to submit their work punctually, and some of whom could not. There were also a fair number whose submissions were punctual but whose work was indifferent, and there was one man whose work was nothing short of atrocious, but who could always be counted upon to produce something to fill a space at short notice. There were even one or two contributors who could reliably produce good work on time and without fuss, but their services were the most difficult to secure, as they usually seemed to be in demand elsewhere. Resignedly, Rusty concluded that not much of this was likely to change for the foreseeable future.

'. . . And I hope you're paying attention to this, you young whippersnapper, because this time I really mean it. I've had it up to here with you lot. Do you hear that? Up to here.'

The expected slam of the door returned Rusty abruptly to the here and now. Squeezing himself around the side of his desk, he made a circuit of the office floor on his hands and knees, recovering the fragments of the document that Loxley had scattered. Then, returning to his place, he picked up his mail again and started trying to recover the fragments of whatever he had been doing before Loxley's interruption. Then, belatedly, he realised that the mid-morning chimes from the Institute of Calibration had come and gone, and that nobody had remembered to bring him a cup of coffee.

Rusty's duties as Director of Iconography often kept him at his desk in the narrow cubicle long after the official end of the work period. When he had finally satisfied himself that he had achieved everything that could reasonably be achieved for the day, he would make his way across the road to the taproom of the Crier's Rest, where he would spend an hour or two, sometimes with colleagues, sometimes alone, before making his solitary way back to Serendipity Court.

On this particular occasion, he found himself in the company of Miss Garamond, who, as it happened, had been finishing her work at the same moment.

'One thing I will say for the Royal Wolf Boys Militia' – Miss Garamond was wrestling with the intricate, bitterly dysfunctional mechanism of her ancient umbrella – 'they've made it much easier to get across the roads.' The two of them stepped down from the kerb in unison, as an ill-matched pair of Wolf Boys waved the evening traffic to a halt. Their boots were looking more worn-in and comfortable now but, with their hands encased in the stiff white gauntlets of the Traffic Patrol, they still looked decidedly ill at ease. 'It used to take for ever to get across here. Even on a dry day,' Miss Garamond continued. They had arrived at the opposite side by now, huddled together under the ragged black canopy as the rain started to beat down more heavily, and they strode quickly up the hill, dodging around the puddles until the welcoming lights of the Crier's Rest appeared on their left.

Miss Garamond was not a frequent visitor to the inn but, as a conscientious leader of men and women, she made a point of joining her staff for an occasional drink, always proving herself on these occasions to be capable of keeping pace with any but the most determined toper. The two of them squeezed into a corner booth, Rusty with a medium-sized flask of ale, Miss Garamond with a somewhat smaller flask of spirits.

'Smoke? No, of course you don't. Sorry, I'm bloody hopeless. You don't mind?' They sat in companionable silence for a while. In between puffs of her cigarette, Miss Garamond made various attempts to arrange her umbrella in a suitable position for draining. Finally Rusty, slightly more practical by nature, came to her assistance. She eyed his efforts with approval.

'Thanks, that should work better. Whoops! Ah, there we are. Now, perhaps we can proceed to my hidden agenda. Did I hear that old git Loxley giving you a hard time this morning?'

Rusty smiled, more relaxed now.

'I'm getting used to it. He does it every couple of weeks. I don't let it bother me so much these days, but it does seem to take up an awful lot of time.'

Miss Garamond took a sharp swig at her flask, then peered at him over her spectacles.

'Is he worth the aggravation? You can always get rid of the bugger if you want. And probably better sooner than later.'

'Yes, I suppose so. His work's good, though, and he always delivers on time.'

'Well, of course it's entirely up to you. It's your department, you must run it your way. But something's wrong, isn't it? If it's not him it must be something else. I can just tell something's getting to you, you're really not at all yourself at the moment.' She raised an eyebrow. 'Anything your auntie can help you with?'

An unexpected note of concern in her voice took Rusty by surprise.

'No. Thanks, but not really, I don't think. At least, the work seems to be sorting itself out bit by bit. Ready for another?'

'Well, just a small one, perhaps.'

When Rusty returned from the bar, she seemed reluctant to let the subject drop.

'Come on, what is it? Moping over some girl?'

He hesitated, uncertain whether to take her into his confidence. She continued to look at him over her spectacles.

'Yes, I suppose that's about it,' he said finally. 'There was someone. But she had to go away. Story of my life, really. It's been a few months now, but I can't seem to put her out of my mind. She was quite a special sort of person. Not like anyone else I've ever met.'

Miss Garamond adjusted her spectacles.

'I'd guess there haven't been that many girls in your life so far. Am I right?'

She was showing a lot more perception than Rusty had expected. As he replied, he could not stop himself from smiling.

'No. Only a couple, actually. There was Laurel. I met her when we were both about seven and, it's funny, she went away as well, I hadn't thought about that before. She was from a family of Wanderers.' Miss Garamond gave him a sharp look, but did not pursue the point. 'She does seem to pop up every now and then, though,' Rusty continued. 'Last time it was at my mother's funeral. She stole a pair of candlesticks, and then she vanished again the next day.'

'She doesn't sound like the ideal girl,' Miss Garamond interjected wryly. Rusty smiled faintly.

'And then there was Eileen. When I was in my teens. We had one or two adventures.' Miss Garamond raised an eyebrow, and Rusty sensed the implied question. 'No, not quite. But her father didn't like me very much. He stopped her seeing me in the end. I haven't thought about her for ages. Haven't seen her for years.' He stared into his flask for a few moments. Miss Garamond did not try to interrupt his thoughts. 'But Alice was different. When we were together, it felt as though we were two halves of the same person. I'd never felt like that with anyone before. And now it feels as if I've lost a part of myself. I don't think I'll ever forget her.'

Miss Garamond looked at him for what seemed like quite a long time. Eventually, she lit a fresh cigarette.

'I don't know if it helps,' she began slowly, 'but I once had a rather similar experience. A long time ago. I was very young indeed.'

'Was that when you were out in the Provinces?'

'The Provinces? No, it was longer ago than that, even. I was very young. He was a bit older. And I only knew him for a short while. But I thought a lot of him. Yes, really quite a lot.'

Now it was Rusty's turn to wait.

'Oh well, I don't suppose the details matter much, but for one reason and another, we had to stop seeing each other. I've not heard from him for, oh, probably thirty years. But, you know, there's never been anyone else since. Somehow, there didn't seem any point.' She fidgeted with her empty flask. Unsure how to respond, Rusty fidgeted in unison.

'I had no idea,' he ventured finally. 'Did it get better?'

Miss Garamond gave a feeble smile.

'No, not really. I don't think a day goes by when I don't think of him. I suppose it's been my work that's kept me going.'

'Yes.' Insidiously, an alternative future was unfolding itself in front of Rusty. 'I've got my work too.'

Suddenly, with startling strength, the Herald grasped his wrist.

'No, no, no, no, you mustn't let it happen to you, you mustn't. Just look at the way I've turned out. A grumpy old bag with no friends and nobody to go home to! Is that what you want for yourself? No, I know it's tough, but if you can forget her now, you can start getting on with your life again.' She began to rise unsteadily to her feet. 'I'm going home. You stay here, go and get yourself another drink. And keep your eye on that barmaid. Yes, her, the one with the brown hair. She's been looking at you off and on all night. No, never mind the umbrella, I can do that. Go on! Get off your arse! Go!'

And with that, still wrestling with her cantankerous umbrella, Miss Garamond lurched out into the rain, leaving Rusty staring in perplexity at the brown-haired barmaid.

'What did the magician do for you?'

Well, they had told me to meet the magician at the edge of the city, at the transport interchange, I don't think he was very good at finding his way about, and then I had to accompany him on the coach back to the Academy. By that time, I'd been to the interchange several times to meet different people, and it was always a bit confusing, because the place wasn't very well organised in those days. Well, actually it wasn't organised at all, the coaches and waggons just used to arrive and unload their passengers wherever they could, and it was always muddy, and the passengers used to stagger around in the mud trying to find their next ride, and nobody seemed to know what was going on or when anything was happening or where to go. There were gangs of children who used to carry messages, sell drinks to people, that sort of thing, but nobody seemed to be in control of them either, everything was totally haphazard. Anyway, I found myself a vantage point on a bit of high ground and waited, that seemed to be the best tactic, and while I was waiting I remember thinking that a bit of organisation might really do the place some good, some method of getting information to people, letting them know where to find the coaches and waggons for the different destinations. And, as you know, in the end I found myself working there and I think I managed to change things quite a lot, but here I am jumping ahead of myself again. We'll get on to all that in time, but right now I'll go back to how I met the magician.

I knew what he'd be wearing, of course, they'd given me a description of his livery, and eventually I spotted him, a tall man with a little beard, he was rather ungainly-looking, a bit clumsy, like me I suppose, and he was wearing a long red and gold robe and a wide hat and big fancy boots that were actually quite practical in the mud, and he was carrying a leather bag that I suppose had his travelling things in it, I remember being impressed at how small the bag was.

I made my way over to him, and explained that I had come from the Academy, and he seemed a bit confused, said he wasn't used to travelling and that he'd lost his spectacles. He had the idea that he might be able to find a travelling spectacle-maker somewhere at the interchange, and he wouldn't take any notice of me until he'd done that. In the end he did manage to get some new spectacles, or maybe he found the old ones, I forget now, and after that he let me take him in hand, then he realised that he'd lost his bag, and it took a bit more time to sort that out, we found a couple of little girls who collected up things that people had lost and sold them back to their owners, and then of course he didn't have the right money, and I think I had to pay the fee for him, but by then we'd wasted such a lot of time that the coach had gone without us, so we had to find another one and, by the time we were finally on the road it, was already beginning to get dark, and we couldn't get all the way to the Academy that night, we had to stop at an inn somewhere and carry on the next day.

Of course, all that was tiring and inconvenient, but it did mean that I got to talk to the magician for quite a long time. We couldn't talk on the coach, of course, because he rode inside, whereas I had to ride outside, because I was still only a servant, but at the inn we sat together until it was time to go to bed. He asked me my name, and I said, 'Tom Slater, sir,' and he seemed very interested in that, he said, 'We've met once before, Tom. Do you remember me?' and I said that I didn't think I did, but then he explained that he was the man who had collected me from the orphanage all those years ago and taken me to the Academy, and after that I think I started to remember him a bit.

Then he asked me a lot of questions, all about how I had spent my years at the Academy, and what sort of work I'd done, and I told him all my different jobs, and I even told him about my poems and crosswords and my filing system, and he seemed very interested in all that, and then I told him about how I had been helping the instructors and listening to the lectures, but then it was time to go to bed, so he went up to his room, and I went to the stable to sleep with all the other servants. That was strange, after all those years with Roger the Blind, but I had my chain with me, so I didn't feel too lonely.

The magician didn't talk to me much the next morning, actually he seemed a bit confused again at breakfast time, but somehow I managed to get him back on the coach, and we arrived at the Academy shortly before midday. I helped him to get down, and made sure that he had his bag and his spectacles, and then I showed him the way to where he had to go and, when I was just about to take my leave, he held up his hand for me to wait, and he started to reach into the inside pocket of his robe. I thought he was going to give me some money, but he just handed me a little piece of parchment with his name written on it, he was called Master Pegasus, and he thanked me for my help and said *that he thought I was a very intelligent young man and he might be able to help me to do better for myself one day.*

I wasn't sure what he meant by that, but it wasn't long before I found out. Anyway, I didn't see the magician again after that, he went to his meeting or whatever he was supposed to be doing, and when he went back to the city one of the other servants went with him.

A few days later, I found out what he had meant when he'd said he could help me. It must have been during the summer vacation, because there weren't any undergraduates in residence at the Academy, it seemed very quiet when they weren't there. Anyway, because of that, I wasn't helping out in the lectures, I was back in the kitchens for the duration, I remember I was cleaning out one of the big cooking pots when Mister Roberts came over and asked me to go with him, and he took me to the Director's chambers, and the Director's assistant told me to wait, and then he took me in to see the Director.

I'd never been taken to meet the Director before. She didn't take her meals with the other professors and instructors and she didn't give any lectures, and I don't suppose she had much time for talking to servants. She was sitting at a big desk in the middle of a big room with a carpet on the floor, there was a long telescope on a tripod in the corner and there were three tall pointed windows behind her, so I couldn't see her face very well, but she seemed to be quite a small lady, and she spoke with a scratchy little voice, she said, 'Sit down over there, Tom, and let me look at you', so I sat on the chair in front of her and she studied me for quite a long time, then she said, 'They tell me that you are a very bright young man, Tom,' and I didn't quite know what to say to that, so I just mumbled, 'Thank you, Ma'am, I hope I give satisfaction' and then she said, 'It seems that you have a benefactor, Tom. Do you know what that means?' and I said, 'I think so, Ma'am' and then she said, 'How would you like to become an undergraduate at the Academy, Tom, and to read for a degree in Cartography?'

Well, at first I couldn't believe what I'd heard, my heart began to pound, and I think if I hadn't taken hold of the chair I might have fallen over onto the carpet, but I managed to catch my breath, and I think I said, 'Thank you Ma'am, I should like that very much indeed' and she said, 'Very well, then. You will continue with your duties as a servant until the beginning of the new academic year, and then you will join the new Undergraduates for the Ceremony of Matriculation.' I think I managed to say, 'Thank you, Ma'am' again, and then she said, 'My assistant will furnish you with all the necessary papers' and then she nodded at the assistant, who must have been standing behind me the whole time, and the assistant led me out of the room and handed me the papers, and then I was back in the kitchen cleaning the cooking pots again.

It wasn't until later that day that it occurred to me that the Director was the same little old lady who was in charge of digging the gardens. That puzzled me a lot, and I still don't really know what to make of it.

Nina's Last Supper

After her first, unsettling encounter with her new companion, Nina felt rather apprehensive about continuing her programme of maintenance on the empathy engine. So, each evening, after the departure of the last punter, she extinguished the incense burners, tidied the booth, shut down the machine and drew the curtains across it to shield it from her eyes. Then, forcing her hands to stay away from the switches, she left the booth, closed the flap behind her, and joined the rest of the company at the supper table.

Nina sat in silence, eating little, the talk and laughter of the others ebbing and flowing somewhere beyond her reach, an undulating background noise that communicated nothing, left her untouched. Outside the tent it had started to rain, and the drumming of the raindrops on the canvas of the tent mingled with the sound of the voices in a meaningless blur. From time to time, Nina noticed one or other of her companions glancing at her, Andrew Constanzas with a puzzled, quizzical expression, George with steely acquisitiveness, Klapsi with cold indifference. Only in the face of Leon Constanzas could she detect any real trace of concern, and from him she averted her eyes, frightened and desolate at his silent compassion. She grasped the edge of the table, concentrated her gaze on the wrinkles in the white cloth, fought to quell the trembling she felt in her hands.

'Do you fancy a bit of cheese, Madam Nina?' Leon was hovering at her shoulder.

'Thank you . . . no . . . I . . . excuse me.'

No longer in control of her actions, Nina lurched to her feet, elbowed her way between her two neighbours, fled from the tent with undignified haste. In an instant, she was racing across the showground, panting for breath, her shoes skidding on the wet grass, the rain streaking her hair across her face, and then at last she was back in the safety of her own booth, tearing aside the curtains, flustered fingers seizing the switches, groping for the headphones . . .

And then she was back in the six-sided room.

The air in the room was utterly black now, and Nina knew that the battle against the dark stuff was lost for ever. She shivered.

Then she realised that she was not alone in the room. Her friend was there as well.

I've missed you, Nina, hissed the familiar voice, and Nina was aware of a chilling streak of menace in its tone. *But I'm so glad you've come back. Yes, I'm glad because I can help you, Nina. Please trust me.*

Nina sensed, rather than saw, that her companion was standing erect at the centre of the room. The black hair hung loose around the square shoulders, the long limbs were relaxed, the waxy skin was cool and dry.

Come to me, Nina.

Despite herself, Nina took a pace forward.

Come closer.

Another pace . . .

Then two hands seized hold of Nina's shoulders, and it was as if a bolt of electricity shot through her body.

'I can help you, Nina. What is it that you want?' The voice was gentler now.

'I don't know,' Nina heard herself replying, and she found that her cheeks were wet with tears. 'I don't want to clean the room any more. I'm so tired. I just want . . . I just want it all to stop. Can't I stay here with you?'

The hands loosened their grip. She could feel the long body hard against her, she could smell the musky aroma.

'Of course you can stay, Nina.' Now the voice seemed to caress her. *'You can stay with me here in my room. You can stay with me here for as long as you like. Just say the words, Nina. Just say "I want to stay".'* Suddenly the voice rose again to its menacing pitch. *'Just say the words.'*

'Yes.' Nina's voice was small and uncertain.

'Say the words, Nina.'

'Yes.' Her voice had shrunk to a pinprick of sound. 'I want to stay.'

Slowly, the hands began to tighten their grip again, and, panic-stricken, Nina suddenly realised that they were very strong, much stronger than she was. Her breath caught in her throat.

'You're hurting me.'

All at once, she felt herself flung back with insuperable force, dashed against the wall of the room, the breath expelled instantly from her body by the brutal impact. Vertiginously, the room inverted itself around her. Dizzily, her body seemed wrenched inside out. Then, somewhere, a trapdoor sprang open, and Nina felt herself engulfed in a dark, bitter, viscous flood of destructive energy, felt herself deafened by a cacophony of voices, shouting and hissing and jeering. Helpless, she allowed the blackness to overwhelm her, to saturate her, to defeat her. The voices reared up in unbearable crescendo, then, bit by bit, subsided again to a dull echo.

Slowly, the echo dwindled into silence.

And then she was abandoned, and she was broken, and she was alone.

'My goodness, what on earth was that?'

Leon Constanzas dropped the jug of cocoa he was holding and dashed out into the rain. He couldn't be sure whether the blood-chilling, hissing shrieks that had split the air a moment ago had been made by one voice or by many, but he knew at once that they had come from Madam Nina's booth.

He found her sprawled across the front of her machine, still clutching one of the handles in her left hand, the headphones tangled around her neck. Her eyes and mouth were gaping open and, when he bent over her, her features displayed no response. Leon became aware that several of the others had followed him and were now staring in through the flap.

'What's happened?' demanded Andrew Constanzas.

'I don't know. I think she's alive, but she can't see me. We'd better take her to her living waggon and put her to bed.'

The Realm of Dreams was not open to the public the next day, nor the day after. On the third day, Madam Nina's condition remained unchanged, but by now it was time for the travelling amusements to move on.

'She won't bring in any business in that state,' said George Constanzas. The company was seated as usual around the long table that evening and, because it was traditional on their final night at a pitch, Leon had boiled a huge joint of gammon.

'No,' said Andrew. 'And I can't see how we can take her with us. There's no knowing how long she'll stay that way.' He paused in reflection for a moment, then an idea seemed to come to him. 'I suppose we could exhibit her. "The Slumbering Maiden", that sort of thing. Not that she'd really pass for a maiden.'

'Absolutely not,' snapped Leon. 'Mother would never have considered it. She would have said it was disrespectful. And I would have to agree with her. We may not have liked Madam Nina much, she may have had her odd ways, but she was still one of us.'

Several heads nodded, even the misanthropic Klapsi's.

'I know a place,' Leon continued after another pause. 'They look after people who can't look after themselves. It's quite near here. I think it's called the

House of Rest, or something like that, anyway. Why don't we take her there?'

'Who's going to pay for it?' demanded George.

So it was finally agreed, assuming of course that the issue of payment could be resolved, that this would be the best course of action for all concerned.

A few days later, the residents of the House of Rest were surprised to witness the arrival, on the undulating turf in front of the house, of a garishly painted convoy of carnival waggons. Two men alighted from the first waggon and made their diffident way up the steps to the front door. The taller of the two was clad in a frock coat and a battered top hat. The other, smaller and slightly younger, had on a chef's apron. They were met at the door by a middle-aged, grey-bearded man, who was hastily brushing what appeared to be fragments of pie crust from his fraying pullover.

'Hello,' said the man, his voice slightly muffled as if he were still chewing his food.

'My name's Geoffrey. I'm the duty guide. How can I help you?'

'Well, we've got a woman in one of our waggons,' Leon began awkwardly. 'She seems to have had a bad shock. She can't move and she can't speak. Is there anything you can do for her?'

'Of course,' replied Geoffrey, swallowing the last of his meal. 'The House of Rest will never turn away anyone who suffers. Now, where is the unfortunate lady?'

During this exchange, a third man, wearing a curious multi-pocketed waistcoat, had joined them from another waggon. When he spoke, his words were brief and to the point.

'How much will it cost?'

'For heaven's sake, George,' replied the one in the apron. 'Can't you just help us get her inside?'

Two Sets of Everything

There was indeed something faintly familiar in the barmaid's smile as Rusty elbowed his way back to the bar.

'What will it be, then?' Giving nothing away, she brushed her rather untidy brown hair away from her eyes.

'Er . . . same again, please. Whatever.' It was late now, and Rusty was feeling slightly fuddled. He waited while she replaced his flask with a fresh one.

'I know this sounds silly, but . . . don't I know you?'

She laughed.

'I was wondering when you'd get round to noticing me. I'm Eileen, Eileen Gilbert. And you're Michael Brown, aren't you? Rusty? I'm not likely to forget hair like yours. We lived in the same village. Don't say you've forgotten me.'

'Eileen! Yes, of course!' Theatrically, Rusty tapped the side of his forehead with two fingers. 'I'm sorry, I've been a bit . . . preoccupied, I suppose. But what on earth are you doing there? I mean here? It must be, what, five, six years?'

'I don't think it's quite that long. Don't you remember, we said hello at your mother's funeral? Before that Wanderer girl spirited you away. Laurel, was that her name?' They were interrupted by an impatient cry from the far end of the long bar. 'Yes, sir, with you in a moment. Sorry.' She turned back to Rusty. 'It gets a bit frantic in here for the last hour. And I don't mean to be rude, but you do rather look as if you need to go home and put yourself to bed.'

Ruefully, Rusty brushed his fringe away from his eyes.

'You're probably right, I remember now, you usually were. Maybe I'll see you another night?'

With a slight air of reproach, she slid his flask across the wet surface of the bar and waited while he fumbled for his change. There were more impatient noises from the far end.

'Yes, all right, sir, I'll be with you in a moment.' She turned around again. 'Look, I've got some time off tomorrow night. Why don't I meet you in here, early? That'll give us a bit of time to catch up.'

Pushing his way through the double doors of the Crier's Rest the next night, Rusty could not at first pick Eileen out in the early-evening crowd, but after a moment he caught the sound of her voice calling to him from one of the booths along the left-hand wall.

'Here, I've bagged us a table. And I've got you the

same as yesterday. With a glass to drink it from, this time. I hope that's all right.' She had exchanged her barmaid's smock for a flower-patterned dress, and her hair, potentially as unruly as Rusty's, had been prettily arranged with the aid of a number of tortoiseshell grips. She smiled as Rusty eased himself into the corner opposite her, and it struck him that she looked rather attractive. For a moment they gazed at each other in silence.

'You're looking well,' she said finally. 'Better than last night, anyway. But you seem a lot thinner. Are you eating properly?' Suddenly she blushed. 'Sorry, that's awfully rude of me. I mean, it's not really any of my business, is it?'

Carefully, Rusty poured himself a glass of ale.

'No, you're right,' he said finally. 'I don't suppose I am looking after myself very well. Actually, I've got a job now, at the Herald's Office – I've been there nearly a year. It's kind of interesting, but it's hard work too. And by the time I get home, I never really feel like eating. Maybe pick up a pie from one of the stalls.' He had expected their conversation to begin with a polite exchange of formalities, but, unexpectedly, it had established itself straight away on quite an intimate level.

'So where do you go home to? I mean, do you live on your own?'

'I've got a place on the North Estate. Serendipity Court, you might have heard of it. And no, there isn't anyone else there.' He was about to mention Alice, but at the last moment thought better of it.

'Serendipity Court? Yes, I know it. The place without stairs? That sounds like it could be good fun.' Grinning, she took a minuscule sip of her drink.

'Fun?' Rusty frowned, as if having temporarily forgotten the meaning of the word. 'Yes, I suppose it was, at first. I've just sort of got used to it now.'

Easing themselves back in their seats, they gazed at each other again. This time, Rusty was the first to speak.

'So, what are you doing here? Don't you still have to look after your father?' Ambushed with unexpected viciousness by the memory, Rusty lapsed back into silence, recalling the tall, morose Doctor Gilbert, who had forbidden Eileen to see him and had confined her to her room.

'Daddy's still very poorly.' Eileen stared down at her glass. 'He can't really get about much these days. Actually, he can hardly even speak. And then I found out that he had spent nearly all his money, so I had to come to the city and find some work. Old Granny Hopkins goes in to do his meals and everything – gosh, she must be at least ninety-five by now – and I go to visit him whenever I can. But I don't suppose he'd remember you now.'

Rusty allowed himself a carefully timed pause before replying.

'Probably best not to remind him.'

Suddenly they were both laughing.

'Remember when we came back from that Wanderers' camp? Daddy went absolutely spare! You don't still go about with them, do you?'

'Gideon Blackwood? And Peg? Yes, I still see them now and again. Oh, they called the baby Megan, by the way. She's getting to be quite a bright little girl, now. And I think they were expecting another, last thing I heard. But do you remember their food? We thought it was going to be something really exotic, but . . .' They both laughed again.

'Look, talking of food . . .' Rusty began tentatively. 'Are you starting to feel hungry yet?'

Eileen looked genuinely crestfallen.

'Oh, look, I'm sorry. I'd love to hang on, but I've got to be somewhere else soon. I'm doing a late shift at another place. But maybe I could cook for you at home one night. That is, if you want me to. I'm free again on Saturday.' Rapidly, she swallowed the last of her drink. Then she rose to her feet, and Rusty followed.

'Saturday. Yes, that would be great.' He accompanied Eileen through the double doors. Outside, the traffic of the main thoroughfare had mostly abated for the night, and the traffic patrols were no longer on duty.

'Saturday, then. And Rusty . . .' Suddenly she clutched at his arm. 'It's been really lovely seeing you. Really. Take care of yourself.'

And then she was gone. Slowly, Rusty returned to the booth. Slowly, he decanted the last of his ale from the glass back into the flask. Eileen, he mused. Yes, it would be nice to see her again.

*   *   *

'My, you're looking smart,' Miss Garamond observed towards the end of the work period, as she bumped into Rusty behind the Intake Desks a few weeks later. 'You've even found time to comb your hair. Now don't tell me it's the barmaid.' Rusty did not need to reply in words. His broad smile told her everything she needed to know.

'Listen, I'm sorry, I don't mean to balls up your date,' Miss Garamond continued, almost apologetically, 'but I've got an idea that might interest you. Whoops, ducky . . .' She dodged aside as one of the clerks hurried past, staggering under the weight of a huge pile of folders. '. . . So, could we just pop up to my office? Only for a few minutes?'

Not wishing to create any difficulties, Rusty reluctantly followed her. As soon as the door was closed, Miss Garamond flopped down on her chair and reached for her cigarettes.

'You don't, do you?' she asked reflexively as she lit up. 'Listen, it's about the charts. Remember, those overhead views you did? And I told you we couldn't publish them?'

Still standing, Rusty stared out of the window. In the narrow yard beneath them, a couple of Wolf Boys were aiming a series of vicious kicks at the prostrate form of an elderly beggar.

'I see the patrols are doing their best to keep the streets tidy,' he mused. 'Yes, charts. I'd still love to do some for the *Digest*. But as far as I know, the situation hasn't changed, has it? I mean with the

Brotherhood of Cartographers, the Charter Ancient and Inviolable and so on? I don't see that there's anything more we can do.' He turned around to face Miss Garamond, and noticed that she had propped her feet jauntily on the surface of the desk. She exhaled a large cloud of smoke.

'In theory, no. But it's been hinted that, with a degree of pressure from the appropriate quarter, the Brotherhood may be prevailed upon to make some adjustments to the interpretation of the Charter. On a strictly discretionary basis, of course.' She pursed her lips and raised both eyebrows.

'The appropriate quarter?'

'The King, sweetheart, King Matthew. It might not have been anything –' she took a long, greedy pull at her cigarette '– but there was something he said in Audience the other day. It didn't strike me till after-wards, unfortunately, or I would have asked a ques-tion. But it did just sound as if he might have been having another think about the whole business. Now what exactly was it he said? Something about what was he going to sort out next? Yes, that was it, and then he reeled off a whole bloody list of possibles. You know, the Kite Sergeants, the transport inter-change, all that malarkey. And then I could swear that he mentioned the cartographers as well. You know, charts, secrecy, the Brotherhood, the whole caboodle. Could be very good news for us if that's what he's planning.'

For a few moments, Rusty continued to stare out

of the window. When at last he spoke, it was with something of an air of wonder.

'Yes. It could, couldn't it? Just think, charts to accompany the written pieces in the *Digest*. Not just words and pictures, but charts as well, to show people where things happened. We could even publish a little supplement. You know, *How to Find Your Way Around the City*, that sort of thing.' His gaze, which had momentarily wandered up to the sky, refocused itself on the scene below. The Wolf Boys had vanished, and the beggar was now slumped against the wall, massaging his ribs with weary resignation. After a moment, Rusty became aware that Miss Garamond had risen from her desk and crossed the room to join him. A conspiratorial hand alighted softly on his shoulder.

'You've got some sort of special talent, haven't you, Mister Brown? Where charts are concerned? No, don't say anything, because I can usually tell.' Rusty's heart was pounding, and he had to make an effort to take in the meaning of the Herald's words. '. . . We could really do something out of the ordinary,' she was saying. Her fingers tightened their grip on his shoulder, then relaxed again. 'But don't let's get too excited too soon. One step at a time. I only said the King might be having another think. But I will keep my ear to the ground. And if I hear anything, I promise you that you'll be the first to know. Now, you don't want to keep your barmaid waiting any longer, do you?'

★   ★   ★

'Oh, Rusty, you don't have to go yet, do you?'

Sleepily, Eileen tugged on Rusty's arm, drawing him back into the warmth of the bed.

He turned back towards her and gave her a playful tap on the nose.

'Yes. I. Do. There. Didn't I say that I've got to get back to my place before I go to the office – I've left my case there with all the stuff for the meeting.'

But Eileen didn't want to give up.

'Oh, come on, you old misery-guts. We can have another half-hour if you forget about your silly exercises for once.'

Reluctantly, or perhaps not so reluctantly, Rusty allowed himself to be pulled back underneath the flower-patterned eiderdown.

Eileen was fond of flower patterns, and most of the items in her small, tidy apartment – china, upholstery, even the lampshades – were embellished with one form or another of floral design. However, as most of her belongings had been acquired piecemeal over a period of time, none of the patterns matched one another, either in colour or in scale, and the overall effect was that of a florist's shop which had been rearranged by a gang of escaped lunatics, and so overpowering was the visual cacophony that at times the human occupants of the space seemed almost to fade into the background.

Over the past few months, the pair had been spending most of their spare time together, sometimes at Rusty's grimy, sparsely furnished rooms in Serendipity

Court but, increasingly in recent weeks, at Eileen's more comfortably appointed apartment in Shrubbery House. This building, named presumably after the narrow strip of garden that fronted it, was also on the North Estate, but on the far side from Serendipity Court, somewhere in the loose network of streets that separated the North Way from the Ferry Terminal. Eileen was a domesticated young woman who enjoyed spending her spare evenings at home, and Rusty had temporarily abandoned the inns and taverns of the city in favour of home cooking and chintzy comfort. The only unsettling feature was the stern, formal portrait of Eileen's father, which frowned severely down at them from its place on the chest of drawers.

'Don't you think it's rather silly, keeping two apartments?' Eileen, propped up on one elbow, was running a fingernail lightly up and down the shallow, vertical channel that bisected Rusty's torso, straying occasionally on to the triangle of softer flesh beneath his ribcage. 'We're together practically every night. We could save quite a bit of money if we moved into one place.'

'I don't think your father would be too happy.' This was not the first time that a similar exchange had taken place between them, and Rusty's first line of defence was well established.

'Daddy would never have to know. And besides, it's silly having to go to and fro all the time. We'll just end up having two sets of everything.'

'But would you really like living at Serendipity

Court?' Rusty already knew what the answer was going to be.

'We're not going to live at Serendipity Court. We're going to live here.'

'What's wrong with Serendipity Court? I feel quite at home there now.'

Eileen rolled on top of him, her thick brown hair lightly brushing his face and neck.

'What's wrong with Serendipity Court?' She raised her eyebrows. 'I'll tell you what's wrong. The apartment's filthy. You haven't got any furniture, not even a proper bed, the neighbours are all mad, and there aren't any stairs.' She giggled. 'Apart from that, I suppose it's quite nice, actually.'

Despite himself, Rusty was amused.

'I'd never really thought of it like that. No, stop it, stop it, I've really got to get up now!'

He struggled out from under her and sat up on the edge of the bed, casting around the room for items of clothing.

'What time will you be back tonight? I've got the evening off. I need to sweep the carpets, but I don't mind cooking.'

'Oh, about the usual, I suppose.' He was on the far side of the room now, half dressed, struggling with a recalcitrant sock. 'Anyway, Shrubbery House isn't really for people like us. All the other people here seem to be families.'

There was a silence from Eileen that broke the rhythm of their exchange. Turning to face her, Rusty saw that she had sat up in bed and was refastening the buttons on her flower-patterned nightdress. And she was smiling enigmatically.

'Rusty, there's something I'd better tell you. Come here.' She took his hand. 'I didn't want to say anything till I was sure. But I think Shrubbery House will be just right for us. Because I think we're going to be a family.'

The Kite Master

Kevin Considine, the Royal Supervisor of Machinery, was having a trying week. He knew this because he had observed that his hands had started to tremble slightly more than usual. He wasn't enjoying his secondment to *The Royal Digest* and, since he was still required to carry out his normal duties at the Palace Administrative Centre, he never seemed to be finding quite enough time to do anything properly. The sudden disappearance of his assistant Alice had certainly not been helpful in alleviating the situation, as he was now having to open his own mail and run his own errands. And today there was the interview with the Kite Master.

Ever since King Matt had instructed Kevin to do something about the Kites, this impending confrontation had been weighing on his mind. If Alice had been available, she would at least have been able to greet the Kite Master, do whatever was necessary to make him feel uneasy and, after a carefully timed delay, send him through to the inner office. Without Alice's support, Kevin felt that he would be putting himself at an immediate disadvantage by having to emerge in person to greet his adversary.

Brooding on the possible ramifications of this, however, Kevin found himself overtaken by events. Glancing up from the electrical circuit diagram on which he had become transfixed, he discovered the Kite Master standing at the precise centre of his office floor with an air of stony-faced attention.

He was a short, wiry man in late middle age. His narrow face was deeply lined and weather-beaten, and his grey beard and mop of grey hair were unruly and unkempt. The Kite Master was dressed in traditional heraldic garb, consisting of wrinkled sky-blue hose and a tight sky-blue tunic, which was emblazoned with the silver kite motif. The outfit was completed by the addition of silver climbing boots and silver wristbands. The Kite Crews, Kevin recalled, were one of the very few categories of worker in the Palace who still observed the traditional practices.

'Ah, Kite Master. Thank you for being so punctual. At ease, please.'

Silently, continuing to regard him suspiciously through narrowed eyes, the Kite Master allowed his posture almost imperceptibly to relax. Kevin Considine pressed the ends of his long, thin fingers together, a habit he had developed to make their trembling less apparent.

'Kite Master, Kite Master, Kite Master. The King has asked me to speak to you about the changes that are being planned for the signalling system. Perhaps you have already heard rumours.'

For the first time, the Kite Master spoke.

'Some rumours, sir, yes.' His voice was gruff and unemphatic. Kevin noticed, with distaste, that the Kite Master's fingers were stained a deep yellow from cigarette smoking.

'Remind me, then, Kite Master: what are the daily duties of your Kite Crews?'

As if reciting something that had been learned by rote, the Kite Master began.

'The Crews rise one hour before dawn, sir. At dawn, a Royal Messenger arrives at the Kite Station with the Messages of the Day inscribed on a scroll of small parchment. The Kite Master, that is myself, sir, breaks the seal and studies the Messages and then transcribes them into the Kite Cipher on large parchment which is then affixed to an easel. The Messages are then re-copied by the six Kite Sergeants onto small parchment. The Kite Sergeants and I, the Kite Master, then call upon the Kite Hands and Apprentice Kite Hands to be in attendance. The small parchments are distributed to the Kite Hands and the Kites are appropriately dressed for the day.' The Kite Master had up to now been speaking slowly and with some detachment, but as his account progressed, his delivery began to show increased speed and animation. 'The six Detachments then proceed, with Kites, to the

Moorings. The Kite Sergeants and their Crews are responsible, as you know, sir, for the Kites that fly from the three remaining Gates of the City, from the Offices of the Dock Master, and from various other public buildings. The Kite Master, myself, sir, and his Crew are responsible for the kites that fly from the roof of the Royal Palace itself. When the Detachments reach their Moorings, sir, they climb. At certain Moorings, as you know, sir, there are fixed ladders of various lengths. At one Mooring, the West Gate, there is an internal staircase. And at the Royal Palace itself, there is a partial ascent by staircase and ladder, followed by a final ascent of the bare wall of the building itself.' He paused for a moment and, with a crooked yellow finger, flicked a drop of sweat from his forehead. 'When the Crews are all in position, sir, the Kites are secured to their Moorings and launched, first the ones on the Royal Palace, then all the others simultaneously. After this, sir, the Crews descend and return to the Kite Station for rest and refreshment. And one hour before dusk, sir, the Crews return to the Moorings, and the Kites are winched to earth, stripped of their dressing, and brought back to the Kite Station to be prepared for the following day.'

Kevin Considine pressed his fingertips more tightly together.

'It's hard work, sir, and it's dangerous work. There are accidents, particularly among the younger men and women. Little more than girls and boys, they are, sir, when they start their Apprenticeships. Not fully aware of the dangers. In the past twelve months, sir, we have lost two of the young Apprentice girls and one of the Kite Sergeants, an experienced man he was, too, sir, but subject to momentary lapses of vigilance.' For a moment the Kite Master was silent, his grizzled head bowed. Then, more slowly, he continued, 'We love our work, sir, despite the dangers. And we look out for each other. Team spirit, that's what we've got. You don't see so much of it these days.'

Abruptly, the Kite Master stopped speaking, as if aware that he had said too much. During the final part of his recitation, he had unconsciously taken a few steps forward, and this impropriety he now quietly corrected.

For a few moments, Kevin Considine remained silent.

'Indeed, Kite Master, your men, and, er, women are an example to us all, an example that the Kingdom can ill afford to lose.' The Kite Master continued to eye him with suspicion. 'However, such is the headlong march of progress that, in due time, even these things must pass. What would you say, for example, if I told you that, in one year from now, it will be possible for the Messages on the Kites to be adjusted on an hourly basis, purely by the use of electrical impulses, without the need for anyone to set foot outside the Kite Station? What would you say if I told you that there will be no further need to climb ladders or to scale the surfaces of buildings, except perhaps to fetch down an occasional Kite that has been damaged by storm?' Kevin paused, then continued in a quieter voice, 'Tell me, Kite Master, how many men, and, er, women, are at present on the strength of the Kite Crews?'

The Kite Master's delivery reverted to the deadpan. If he felt any shock or concern at the news he had heard, his voice and his features did not betray it.

'Thirty-four men and women, sir. Eight Apprentice Kite Hands, nineteen Kite Hands, five Kite Sergeants, one Acting Kite Sergeant, and myself, sir, the Kite Master.'

'What would you say, Kite Master, if I told you that in one year from now, the Kite Crew will consist of just two Apprentices, three Kite Hands, and yourself?'

An observant person might have detected a microscopic elevation of the Kite Master's bushy eyebrows.

'I should say, sir, that technology is a marvellous thing. I should never have expected to see such things in my lifetime. Nor even in my children's lifetimes.' For a few moments he seemed lost in thought, then he rapidly collected himself. 'Now, will that be all, sir? You see, the Crews have some bunting to repair before tomorrow, and of course the Kites must still be winched to earth at dusk.'

'Yes, that will be all, Kite Master. Please pass the word on to your Crews.'

'Sir.'

The Kite Master saluted smartly, turned on his heel, and departed, leaving Kevin Considine puzzling over whether or not the confrontation had been a success.

★　★　★

The rest of the week wasn't any better for Kevin. He watched the kites anxiously for any signs of unrest from the Kite Crews, but the Messages continued to be displayed as accurately as ever, with only a slightly intensified vibration in the lines indicating, to those able to interpret it, that anything might be amiss. The people at the Herald's Office continued to be as frustrating as ever. The Herald, that big, untidy woman, somehow had the knack of being precise and vague at the same time, issuing firm instructions one day and contradicting them the next. And then there was that young chap in the leather jacket, the Director of Iconography, Michael Brown his name was, quite sharp-witted, but also somehow annoyingly oblique, always on the sidelines of things, as if he had his own plans and wasn't too bothered about anything or anyone else. Anyway, it was Friday now, and for two days all this could be dismissed from Kevin's mind.

Kevin Constanzas had adopted the name Considine when he first came to work in the City, reckoning that he would not get far if he kept his family name, with all its associations of shabby circus tents and sleazy amusements. Disloyal as this might have seemed, he always made a point of finding out when the Constanzas Brothers Travelling Amusements were in the neighbourhood, and he always made a point – in a discreet fashion, of course – of visiting his cousins once or twice a year. It could never do any harm to stay in touch.

This week, the Amusements were encamped, as was customary, in a muddy field somewhere out on the North Way, beyond the river crossing and the Transport Interchange. Business had been slack, as it often was in this unfriendly corner of the land, and Kevin found his three cousins and the rest of their company in the tent, slumped morosely around the long table, picking over the remains of a pot of rabbit stew.

'Hello, George, Andrew, hi Klapsi, everybody, where's Leon?'

The third cousin appeared at this moment, carrying a dangerously flexing tray of baked apples.

'Kevin! Have an apple, I'm sorry, the custard's come out a bit lumpy, I think the milk might be a bit funny round these parts. How's everything in the big city?'

So they sat together over baked apples and cheese and coffee, exchanging news and gossip until the candles in the big tent started to burn down. Andrew spoke animatedly of the comings and goings of showground hands and stall- holders. George spoke curtly of the decline of business. Leon spoke forlornly of the strange qualities of the milk, and Kevin spoke, guardedly, of the affairs of the Palace. Eventually he began to yawn.

'Sorry, chaps, it's been a busy old week. Anywhere I can lay my head for the night?'

'Madam Nina's old waggon's probably your best bet,' Leon suggested. 'She's gone now, but the thing is, all her old kit's still in there. You'll have to shift it around to make room.'

'What old kit? What did Madam Nina do?' enquired Kevin sleepily, slightly irritated at the prospect of having to move piles of lumber out of his way before he could go to bed.

'She called it the Realm of Dreams,' explained Andrew. 'Some piece of nonsense. Fortune-telling or something. Don't know why we've kept the stuff, really.'

'Drew the punters,' said George.

In the cramped interior of the living waggon, Kevin lit a couple of candles and cast his gaze over the dusty pile of machinery that took up most of the floor space. Heaven knew what it was supposed to be, but Kevin had always been fascinated by any kind of machine and he knew that, until he had given it at least a cursory inspection, he would be unable to sleep. So he squatted down uncomfortably in a small vacant corner, brushed away some of the dust that covered the engine, and began his work. At once he identified a pair of eyepieces fitted with lenses and various other optical components. And here was a pair of headphones, there must be auditory output, then, as well as visual . . . In contact with machinery, Kevin's fingers ceased to tremble and, agile and questioning now, began their exploration of the smaller controls at the rear of the machine. Yes, these would be the various parameter settings . . . but what parameters were involved? And what were these handles at the sides of the cabinet? Kevin decided that the machinery would have to be activated before these matters could be fully investigated. Peering out through the rear door of the waggon into the gloom, he caught a glimpse of the clown, Klapsi, stooped over a barrel of water, washing off his make-up.

'Ahoy, there! Any chance of a drop of electricity?'

'Oh, go to bed!' snapped Klapsi. Then, recognising Kevin, he softened his approach. 'Oh, sorry, Mister Kevin. I thought it was one of the others. Well, since it's you, just hang on a minute . . .'

Shortly afterwards, the Engine crackled and shuddered reluctantly into life. Slipping on the headphones, peering into the eyepieces, Kevin Constanzas ran his fingers over the small controls, swiftly registering every subtle variation in sound and vision. Then, satisfied with the preliminary adjustments, he grasped the two handles at the sides of the machine, flexed his wrists, made a couple of swift movements, then drew a long, sharp breath of astonishment.

He had to know more.

Letting go of the controls, his fingertips explored the top edge of the cabinet until they located a couple of catches. He swung back the covering plate and all the optical components that it housed, revealing the inner mechanism of Madam Nina's engine. Automatically, he groped for a candle, brought it closer so that he could see inside. Swiftly, his eyes and his fingers acquainted themselves with the machinery, twisting cogs and worm-wheels this way and that, exploring the intricacies of the mechanical action, squinting through lenses, adjusting irises, plumbing depths of field, unravelling skeins of wiring, tracking each wire from source to branch to destination . . .

At last, he slumped exhausted onto the unmade bunk. From this position, Kevin could see, for the first time, the back panel of the machine. Fastened to the back was some kind of metal nameplate, tarnished with age. Bringing the candle closer, he could just make out the script:

> *Empathy Engine (prototype):*
> L. PEGASUS, *designer*

Pegasus, thought Kevin. Who'd ever have thought that I'd run across him again?

That night, Kevin slept fitfully, his dreams coming in disjointed fragments, the Kite Master, the apprentice girls who had fallen from the moorings, the cumbersome copying engine at the Herald's office, the elusive Madam Nina, the delicate, seductive workings of Master Pegasus's mysterious engine, the electrical devices that would control the messages on the kites, playing them perhaps like an orchestra or a choir . . .

When he awoke at dawn, the fragments of thought had begun to crystallise into clear, recognisable form. Madam Nina's engine could interpret signals from the imagination of a human being and turn them into electrical impulses. And the kites, when they were suitably modified, would receive electrical impulses and turn them into signals in cipher.

The engine would generate electrical signals.

And the kites would transmit them.

Kevin wasn't quite sure yet what it all added up to, but he was certain of one thing.

He had to have that engine.

At breakfast later that morning, Kevin apologised to his cousins for having to cut short his visit.

'Sorry, chaps. A signal's come up on the kites. I'm wanted back in the city. Urgent.' He smiled ruefully, fairly confident that none of his cousins would be able to interpret the kite cipher. 'Needs must, I'm afraid.'

'That's a shame,' replied Leon. 'Still, we'll be back later in the year.'

'Of course,' continued Kevin. 'And thanks for your hospitality, it's been great.' About to leave the tent, Kevin paused. 'Oh, I almost forgot.' His tone was artfully casual. 'Are you getting rid of that old engine thing? I could probably get it stripped down for spares.'

'Take it,' said George. 'It's just wasting space.'

'Nobody knows what to do with it, anyway,' mused Andrew.

'You'll have to arrange to get it fetched away, though,' added Leon. 'Maybe they could send a waggon up from the Palace?'

Hello, Stranger!

Paul Catalano was having a little maintenance session on his hairdressing equipment, dismantling his scissors and clippers, cleaning and oiling the small parts, sharpening the blades, replacing the washers. He had spread out all the components on the gingham-patterned cloth on his kitchen table when he was surprised to see a shaggy head of red hair appearing over the edge of the balcony. He jumped up from his chair and offered an outstretched hand.

'Hello, stranger, welcome aboard!'

Rusty, somewhat out of practice at the climbing techniques necessary for life at Serendipity Court, hauled himself clumsily over the balustrade and stood panting in the doorway until Paul invited him to take a seat.

'Here, I'll move all these old bits, won't take a jiff, and then you can tell me all your news. Fancy a coffee?'

'Great.' Rusty hadn't quite got his breath back.

'Dear me, you sound a bit out of condition. Hasn't that girl of yours been keeping you in trim?' Paul looked him appraisingly up and down. 'And I'm sure your trousers weren't as tight as that when you lived here.'

Rusty grinned. 'Oh, you know. Married life, I suppose. It has its compensations, Paul. You should try it.'

'I don't really think so, do you?' Paul positioned the cups and saucers carefully on the table. 'Sugar? Sorry, I've got a head like a sieve. Do you want me to do your hair while you're here? Not meaning to be cheeky, but it looks as if it needs it.'

'Actually, Paul, I was going to ask if you wouldn't mind coming to us. Eileen was thinking of having hers shorter, and she's not getting about so much now, what with, you know . . .'

Paul put his cup down with an embarrassed clatter.

'Oh, what must you think of me? I said I was getting forgetful, didn't I? Sorry, sorry, sorry! When's the happy event? It can't be long now.'

'Could be any day, actually,' said Rusty. 'I've just come over to get a few things from Joe Blackwood, if he's got them. And Eileen's doing fine, but of course she's had to cut back on her bar work, so money's been a bit tight. Anyway,' he gulped the last of his coffee, 'I'd better get down and see Mister B. Thanks for the drink.' He headed over towards the balcony.

'See you soon,' called Paul cheerfully. 'Any time you're passing.'

Behind the door with the discoloured brass plate, Joe Blackwood sat as always, his bulky form hunched over his table in the gloom, engrossed in his card game. Rusty wondered briefly if it was a continuation of the same game that he had first observed in progress two years earlier, on the day of his arrival at Serendipity Court. Edging cautiously between the piles of ancient furniture, he coughed discreetly to announce his presence.

'Mister Blackwood?'

With deliberation, the caretaker played another card before putting down the pack and looking up at the intruder.

'Oh, it's you, Gid's mate, isn't it? What you doing here? Thought I'd seen the last of you.'

'I'm at Shrubbery House now.'

Blackwood rotated his body slightly to face Rusty, his features displaying a small amount of what might have been taken for interest.

'Marry that girl, did you? The one you got in the family way?'

Rusty laughed.

'I guess that's about the size of it, yes. And listen, Joe. The baby's coming soon. I was on the lookout for some bits. You know, a cot, maybe a high chair. I'm not really sure what else.'

For the first time, as far as Rusty could recall, Joe Blackwood heaved himself into a standing position. Abandoning his card table, he peered up at the stacks of furniture around him, as if surprised to see anything there.

'Reckon we can come up with something. What's this?' He reached up into the gloom and brought down what turned out to be a folding camp bed, as well as a considerable quantity of dust and a stack of disintegrating lampshades. 'Hmm, maybe not, oh, hang on . . .'

A little while later, Rusty had manoeuvred the necessary items out on to the pavement, and was casting around for some form of transport. To his surprise, Blackwood, not usually a generous man, had refused any payment from him.

'Got to do our bit for the babby,' he muttered shyly.

'We're all kinfolk, when all's said and done. Oh, yes.' He brightened suddenly. 'Got word from Gid. He's passing this way, four, maybe five weeks' time. Said for you to drop by and see them. If you're not too busy, that is. And they've got another little one now. A boy, this time.'

'Rusty!' Eileen's breath was coming in quick, panting gasps. 'I think it's starting. You'd better get Mrs Thing. She'll know what to do.'

The caretaker at Shrubbery House, whose name for some reason nobody could remember, could also be found in a dingy basement room, but in all other respects she differed from Joe Blackwood.

'Oh, goodness me, why do these things always come at the wrong times? That's what my Ted used to say when I was having mine, there's never a good time for anything, that's right, make yourself comfy, now let's have a look at that leg . . .'

Sprinting down twelve flights of stone steps, Rusty had tripped over some refuse cans on the second landing and twisted an ankle rather painfully.

'Never mind that, hadn't we better hurry up?'

'Oh, don't worry, dear, my first one was happy enough to take its time, not that my Ted would take any notice of me, anyway they've stopped the City Midwives, didn't you know, it's that King Matthew, thought it was too old-fashioned or something, mind you I don't see it that way myself, people aren't going to stop having babbies, that's what my Ted said, now when I had my third . . .'

'Stopped the Midwives? Who's going to come and help, then?' In a supreme state of agitation, Rusty jumped to his feet, his trousers rolled up and one foot still in a basin of cold water. 'What's going on in this place? How does anything ever get done around here?'

'It's all right, dear, I'll send my granddaughter out, she's at home today, used to come and see my Ted, she'll find someone, I'd go myself, of course, only the man's coming about the parrot, I'm not sure when. Maisie?'

A scruffy-looking child of about twelve appeared in the doorway.

''Allo, Mister, I know you, don't I? What's the matter with yer foot?'

'Not now, Maisie,' her grandmother interjected.

Rusty recognised the little girl who had hired him the boots at the Transport Interchange.

'Hello, Maisie. You've grown.'

'Maisie,' interrupted her grandmother, 'get out there now. Down the corner. Gentleman's wife is about to deliver. Get someone in. And look sharp about it.'

'But, Gran—'

'I said look sharp.'

By the time Rusty had limped back up the stairs to Eileen's bedside, Maisie had evidently completed her mission for, before long, they were startled by a loud knock at the front door. Standing on the mat, shuffling their feet, were two embarrassed-looking Wolf Boys, one of them bearing a stack of grubby towels, the other with a dog-eared manual under his arm. Even in his present state of agitation, Rusty could not help noticing that their uniforms were now faded and torn, and their long toenails had started to peep through the battered toes of their boots.

'Mrs Brown? Mister Brown?'

'What are you doing here?'

'Royal Militia Midwifery Service, sir, madam. Perhaps you could show us to the lady's bedside. And then perhaps you could boil us some water.'

Not knowing what else to do, Rusty went to the kitchen and started to fill the kettle.

Three:
THE RED-HEADED KID

The Royal Digest of Affairs and Events: Volume 17 (in the Third Year of the Rule of King Matthew)

The Diary of Miss Garamond (Herald)

Greetings, Citizens!

The reader may well experience some difficulty in believing that an interval of one year has elapsed since the formation of the Royal Wolf Boys Militia (the Author, too, finds herself astonished at the rapidity of the passage of time!), but nevertheless this remains the case. And although this interval has been notable, particularly in its early stages, for the many obstacles and pitfalls that have been faced by one and all, it is with great pleasure that *The Royal Digest* can now record that, thanks to the determination and single-mindedness of King Matthew, these obstacles and pitfalls have in large measure been overcome, and that Citizens are at last free to enjoy once again the security and the peace of mind that they have long been entitled to expect upon the streets of our City.

Thanks to the vigilance, teamwork and remorseless discipline of the Royal Wolf Boys patrols, Citizens have been delighted to witness a swift and spectacular diminution in the numbers of assaults of a fatal nature upon the person, and likewise in the numbers of robberies, disembowellings, ritual amputations and other attacks of a similarly distressing nature. In addition, we are pleased to record a gratifying reduction in the numbers of the vagrants, beggars, derelicts, degenerates and other undesirables who used at one time to haunt our courtyards and alleyways, and a consequent final resolution to the nuisance and inconvenience which used daily to face those of our Citizens who were for one reason or another obliged to make use of these byways.

Furthermore, those of the Citizenry who engage in daily travel upon our thoroughfares, whether by horse-drawn vehicle, by power-driven carriage, or on foot, will undoubtedly have been pleased to report a striking improvement in the flow of traffic, accompanied by a notable enhancement in the facility with which the pedestrian is now able to traverse the roadway. This is due in great measure to the selfless and dedicated work of the Royal Wolf Boys Traffic Patrols, the first of several new branches of the Service from whose efforts all Citizens may shortly expect to benefit. These are to include the Royal Wolf Boys Fire Service, the Royal Wolf Boys Water Rescue Service, and the Royal Wolf Boys Litter Patrol. Some Citizens will already have reaped the benefit of the Royal Wolf Boys Midwifery Service. (Indeed, on a personal note, it is especially pleasing to record that the latter Service has in recent days been of invaluable assistance to *The Digest*'s Supervisor of Iconography, Mister Michael Brown and his young wife Eileen in the successful and happy delivery of their baby daughter, Ashleigh.)

In our monthly Private Audience, King Matthew has pronounced himself well content with the progress of this venture, to the extent that it is now his avowed belief that the Royal Wolf Boys Militia may be permitted to continue its business, under the direction of Master Fang, without further need for daily interventions from the Palace, thus allowing King Matthew the freedom to turn his attention to other matters. Foremost among these are the Ancient Brotherhoods and Sisterhoods, the Transport Interchange, and the Signalling Kites.

Firstly, The Ancient Brotherhoods and Sisterhoods. As is well known to all, the Brotherhoods and Sisterhoods were established by the First Kings during the twilight years of the Forgotten Age, their duties, regulations and privileges being established and set down in writing in the form of Charter Ancient and Inviolable. It is stated in Charter that the purpose of each of the Seven Brotherhoods and Sisterhoods shall be:

. . . To develop through the pursuit of learning and research a body of wisdom pertaining to a specified field of human endeavour, to oversee the nurturing and application of that knowledge by its custodians and practitioners, and to protect the security and secrecy of that knowledge and to guard it against the depredations of whatsoever persons may be considered to be of insufficient competence or trustworthiness to be vouchsafed therewith.

Of the Seven Brotherhoods and Sisterhoods, readers may by now be aware that the Sisterhood of Medicine and Midwifery has within the past month elected, on a voluntary basis, to undergo immediate dissolution and summary cessation of its activities. The Brotherhood of Magicians may now reasonably be dismissed as utterly bereft of significance, as may the Brotherhood of Jesters, deficient as both bodies have become in membership and likewise in credibility. The Brotherhood of Calibrators and the Sisterhood of Mechanics both continue to offer services of a useful and praiseworthy nature, and it has therefore been deemed fitting for these bodies to be permitted to continue in their work, remaining unmolested for the time being. However, with regard to the Brotherhood of Cartographers and the Sisterhood of Dispatches, the King remains in a state of some uncertainty. It is to the Brotherhood of Cartographers, that most retiring and secretive of the Ancient Brotherhoods and Sisterhoods, that the King intends firstly to turn his attention. The reader perhaps has little awareness of the activities of this reclusive body, and the author is not presently at liberty to speak with complete freedom on the matter, but it can at least be stated that, within the secret vaults of the Academy of Cartography, the Brotherhood has in its possession an extensive collection of documents known as *charts* that, if once brought within the public domain, will undoubtedly prove to be of unprecedented value to the Citizenry. The King intends now to consider whether, and by what means, such an objective might be attained.

Secondly, the Signalling Kites. The King has long been aware that the traditional means of operating and maintaining the Kites, namely by a crew of between thirty and forty highly trained individuals of long experience, under the direction of the Kite Master, can only be regarded as cumbersome, slow and inefficient. It is also considered by the King to subject its practitioners to unacceptable degrees of risk and danger. After due consideration, the King has therefore concluded that a new method of operation, based upon electrical impulses transmitted by means of wires from the Palace Administrative Centre, will provide an alternative method of controlling the Kites that will represent an immeasurable improvement in respect of speed, adaptability and safety. The King has therefore instructed the Royal Supervisor of Machinery, Mister Kevin Considine, to bring the full weight of his resources to the development of such a method, and in due course to assume responsibility for its installation and operation. From a recent conversation with Mister Considine, the Author notes with interest that additional work will be taking place upon the development of various items of ancillary equipment which we are assured will provide additional features of a novel and invaluable nature. (The diligent reader may well recall that the same Mister Considine has until recently been engaged upon the installation of the new copying apparatus at the offices of *The Royal Digest*.)

Thirdly, with regard to the Transport Interchange, the King remains in a painful state of awareness of the severity of the difficulties that are still being experienced by travellers but, regrettably, a solution has thus far eluded him. Citizens may, however, rest assured that comprehensive and vigorous action will in due time be taken to remedy these matters in such manner as the King and his advisers may deem appropriate.

Goodbye, Citizens, and long live King Matthew!

'So how did you take to being an Undergraduate?'

The last few days of the vacation, I was starting to get quite nervous, because I knew that everything was going to be different again. I was still sleeping at the feet of Roger the

Blind, of course. They asked me if I didn't want to move into new quarters in the Undergraduate Wing, but I said I didn't want to do that, I wanted to stay where I was comfortable. Well, perhaps 'comfortable' isn't quite the right word, I never really got a good night's sleep in that stone alcove and, to tell the truth, I never really learned how to get a good night's sleep anywhere else either, but at least I felt at home there, and I needed to have a place where I felt at home, so in the end they let me stop there. During those few days I had started using the chain again. I found that, when I was feeling anxious or upset, I could draw some sort of power from the links of the chain, and somehow that gave me the strength I needed to endure whatever was to come. So, on the first morning of the new academic year I rose at the usual time, undid the padlocks and put the chain away, then I tidied myself up as best I could, but this time I had to dress myself in the undergraduate garb, the cap and tunic, and then I went down into the basement where the boilers were and threw my servant's garb into one of the furnaces and I remember thinking, 'There's no going back now.'

It was still early, the new undergraduates wouldn't start arriving until about halfway through the morning, so I just wandered around the buildings and the grounds. One or two of the servants saw me and wished me luck, I remember Mister Roberts was quite friendly to me, but most of them just looked away, and one or two said quite unkind things like 'We'll see how long you last' and 'You're too clever for your own good'. Then, after a while, the carriages started to arrive and the young men and women started climbing down with their boxes and trunks, some of them had quite a lot

of baggage, and I went and stood with them in the courtyard at the front of the Academy. They all seemed very young
to me, I suppose by then I was five or six years older than
most of them, and they mostly seemed quite nervous, so there
wasn't really much conversation.

That was when I first remember noticing the kid with
the red hair. I knew that most of the new undergraduates
would be the sons and daughters of wealthy men, traders
and other city folk, I suppose, but this boy was obviously
from a poor family, his breeches had patches on them, and
he didn't walk and hold himself in the same way as the
others, he seemed somehow loose-jointed in the way he
moved, he reminded me a bit of a marionette, as if he hadn't
been taught the proper way to conduct himself, which I dare
say he hadn't. And I'd never seen anyone with that colour
hair before, and I'd also never seen an undergraduate with
a dog. Oh, didn't I mention the dog? Well, he had a funny
little brown dog on a lead, and I learned the dog's name
before I learned the kid's name, because when he spoke to
the dog, he called him Dusty. 'Sit still, Dusty,' that was the
first thing I heard him say, and I could tell from the way
he spoke that he wasn't from the city, but Dusty didn't want
to sit still, he was too excited by all the new sights and
smells, and suddenly he broke away and ran off across the
lawn trailing his lead behind him, and of course the kid ran
after him, trying to catch him.

I knew that that would lead to trouble, of course, because
undergraduates weren't allowed on the grass, and sure enough
the old woman who looked after the gardens called out to
him, 'Come here, young man!' and by then he had caught

hold of the dog's lead again, so he went over to her and she said, 'What is your name, young man?' and I couldn't hear what he said, but I heard her all right, she said, 'Well, Mister Brown, I think you should know that undergraduates are not allowed on the grass,' and he hung his head, he looked ashamed, and then she said, 'And as for the dog, well, I think we had better have words about that later on.' She was smiling a little when she said that, and I had to smile a little too, because I knew by then that she wasn't a servant, she was the Director of the Academy, but of course the kid didn't know that yet.

Anyway, most of the undergraduates had arrived by this time, and some of the servants came out and started conducting them to their quarters, and then later on everybody had to assemble in the big lecture theatre so that the professors could explain how the teaching was going to be done and distribute the timetables and so on.

It was while this was happening that I noticed the red-haired kid again, or rather I should say that I noticed his dog, because there was a sudden commotion in the row in front of me, and then I felt something bumping around my ankles, it was the dog, of course, and I must have jumped up, because suddenly everybody was looking at me, and the professor who was speaking looked quite annoyed, he said, 'Can the undergraduates please remain silent?' and then he must have recognised me because he said, 'Slater, you of all people should know better', so of course then everybody knew my name. Then I noticed that the red-haired kid was sitting in front of me because he sort of half-rose to his feet and said, 'I'm sorry, sir, my dog's escaped,' and the professor said, 'Your DOG?'

I suppose the dog must have been recaptured eventually, because after a while the lecture continued and everyone settled down again, but I decided at that point that the red-headed kid was going to annoy me quite a lot, because he obviously didn't know the proper way to conduct himself, and he had no respect for the regulations. I came to see all this in quite a different way later, of course, and, if I'd known then quite how much trouble he was going to cause me, and what I was going to have to do to put it right, I might have given him a very wide berth indeed. But you've told me I mustn't jump ahead of myself, so I'll say no more about that for now.

Anyway, I tried to keep my distance from him after that, actually I ended up keeping my distance from just about everyone, because sometime in the next week one of the instructors noticed me at the back of the lecture theatre and she shouted at me to fetch some piece of equipment that she needed. I was about to get up when I remembered that things had changed, so I said, 'I'm sorry, Ma'am, I think you should ask one of the academic servants to do that.' I felt embarrassed as soon as I had said it, and I think she was quite embarrassed too, because she must have remembered about me, she called for a servant and then she continued with her lecture.

Of course, after that the word quickly got about, and all the undergraduates discovered who I was, and quite a lot of them, the ones with the rich parents, didn't want to have anything more to do with me. I also had a habit of retreating at times to places around the Academy that I knew and they didn't. And, of course, at night I wasn't with them in the Undergraduate Wing, I was still chained to the feet of

Roger the Blind. And then I was a bit older than most of the other undergraduates, and quite a bit taller, so I suppose most of them began to see me as a bit of an oddity and not quite one of them. So, because of all that, I started to find myself a bit apart from the others. I wasn't really accepted as one of the undergraduates, and of course I wasn't one of the servants any longer. But anyway, I kept going to the lectures and listening carefully and writing things down and asking questions. The work was interesting, and I started to understand a lot more about cartography. There were also some lectures about business and commercial administration, and they turned out to be very useful, although I didn't realise it at the time. So, although I wasn't exactly enjoying myself, I certainly wasn't wasting my time either.

Of course, there were a handful of other undergraduates who for one reason or another didn't seem to fit in with the majority. The red-haired kid, of course, Rusty, that's what people used to call him, he didn't make many friends, he seemed to prefer the company of his dog. The two of them seemed quite happy together, although I found that this annoyed me too, in a way I couldn't quite understand. Then there were a couple of others, a boy called Charles and a girl called Sally, who must have known each other before they came to the Academy, they seemed to be sweethearts because they went around holding hands the whole time, people called them CharlesnSally, and they were pretty annoying as well. And then there were one or two others from poor families, and they mostly ended up talking to each other because nobody else would talk to them.

★   ★   ★

I did my best to ignore all this, though, and I kept work-
ing hard, so I passed all my theoretical assessments, but then,
at the end of the first year, came the field exercise. I knew
that this was on its way, of course, so I had a fair idea what
to expect, because I had observed what happened in previ-
ous years when I was an academic servant. All the under-
graduates gathered together, and one of the instructors
explained the Exercise to us, it involved travelling to a strange
part of the land, to a destination that would be revealed to
us later, and making measurements and observations, and
drawing a chart of the terrain there. Once everyone under-
stood what they were supposed to be doing, the instructor
went on to explain that we were required to work in groups
of four or five undergraduates, and that each group was to
go to a different destination, and that everyone was to be
allowed to choose who they would work with.

I knew exactly what would happen, of course. Most of
the undergraduates, the ones who were rich and popular, had
already decided in secret who they were going to work with,
and they quickly broke into groups and took their pick of
the destinations. Then there was a round of bargaining among
the others, and at the end there was a handful of people
that nobody liked, and nobody wanted to work with, and
they ended up being stuck with one another, whether they
wanted it or not. Sure enough, at the end, there were
CharlesnSally, who had managed to annoy just about every-
body with their disgusting pet names and their kissing and
hand-holding, and there was the red-haired kid with his
strange ways and that smelly dog that nobody wanted in
their group. And, of course, there was me.

The instructor wrote down our names and handed us the details of our destination, it was some horrible remote spot halfway up a mountain, and she looked at us in such a dubious fashion that it was obvious that she thought we were going to fail. It was a very disheartening start to the Exercise. Of course, she was absolutely right, but none of us knew that yet.

Kevin and the King

King Matthew had not visited the Administrative Centre at the top of the Palace for some time and, under normal circumstances, he would have expected the Supervisor of Machinery to present himself in the Throne Room, but on this occasion Mister Considine had begged leave to waive the conventional protocol. The King was secretly quite pleased at this opportunity to take a break from his usual routine. He was becoming rather weary of Master Fang and all the problems with the Wolf Boys, his armies were making no progress with the border campaign, he was becoming apprehensive about the Herald's remorseless questions, he had reached a position of deadlock in the interminable negotiations with the Brotherhood of Cartographers, and he still hadn't come up with any ideas for the transport interchange.

Picking his way among the chimney pots on the Palace roof, the King expected the grey double doors of the annexe to swing open automatically, but for some reason this did not happen, so he gave a gentle push to the left-hand door and found himself sidling into the Administrative Centre in what must have seemed a rather furtive manner. Clearly, proper arrangements had not been made to receive him, for the hum of conversation and machinery in the large windowless room continued unabated, and the rows of clerks and assistants in their regulation grey outfits continued to stare vacantly at their administrative engines and abacuses, to chat to each other, to drink coffee, and to do whatever else they usually did on a Wednesday morning. Scanning the rows of desks, the King recognised a face that he knew, a short, tubby, frizzy-haired woman who, in the days of his father's reign, had occupied a senior position in the Jester's Department, but who had now been reassigned to a post in Central Administration.

'Veronique? Sorry to bother you . . .'

Startled, the woman looked up, and the King noticed that she was still wearing a modified version of the traditional face paint that she had worn in her former position.

'Blimey, it's King Matt!' Hastily, she jumped from her stool and turned to address the rest of the room. 'Matt's here, everybody! On your feet, quick!'

There was a sudden commotion as everyone dropped whatever they were doing and hastily arose, scattering pieces of parchment, abacus beads and coffee cups here and there. A flustered-looking Kevin Considine emerged hurriedly from a side office, straightening his clothing as he approached the King.

'Sorry, er, Matt –' he used the informal address that the King had decided on his accession to adopt '– no assistant at the moment. Bit of chaos going on.' The King, taken aback at the lack of an organised welcome, noticed that Kevin's hands were trembling slightly more than usual.

'Not to worry, not to worry,' he replied diplomatically. 'Actually, I've not got much time. We'd better go straight away and see what you've got to show us. Although a coffee would have been nice.'

'Yes, the Experimental Laboratory. Over here.' Kevin pressed his fingertips together. 'Veronique, coffee.'

They threaded their way between the rows of desks, descended a narrow iron staircase at the far side of the Administrative Centre, and entered another long, windowless room. Like the Administrative Centre, this room was illuminated by harsh artificial light, but unlike it, this room was empty of furnishings. The only objects on view were two identical tall engines, housed in grey metal cabinets, one at each end of the room. The atmosphere was alive with the scent of ozone and the hum of electricity.

'Sorry,' said Kevin. 'I can't offer you a seat. As you can see, it's pretty basic in here at the moment.'

The King nodded absently.

'Remind me, what are we looking at?'

'I haven't got a name for it yet. Universal Empathy Network, perhaps. Something like that, anyway.'

'Empathy, empathy, now why does that word remind me of something?' queried the King.

'I don't know, probably no reason,' Kevin interjected hurriedly. 'Now, if you remember the Kites . . .'

'Empathy. I'm sure I remember the word.' The King was clearly disturbed by some half-forgotten recollection.

'It'll probably come to you later if it's important,' suggested Kevin, anxious not to draw attention to the source of his ideas.

'I suppose so. Anyway, what is this network thing?'

'Well, if Your, er, Majesty recalls, you commanded me to devise a method of operating the signal kites by means of electrical impulses.' The King nodded. 'Well, Your, er, Majesty will observe . . .'

'Please remember to call me Matt.'

'Yes, of course, well, Matt, you will observe that each of my engines has on top of it a row of miniature kites –' the King scrutinised the kites '– and a telescope. The principle is straightforward, although the technical details are somewhat less so. The signals that are displayed on the kites are controlled by means of electrical impulses generated by the two engines. And the telescope on each machine is focused on the kites on the machine opposite.' He paused to check that the King understood him. 'The telescopes decipher the signals and transform them back into electrical impulses. In other words, the two engines are capable of communicating remotely with each other. As you will have observed, they are not connected to each other in any physical way, not by wires, not by levers, not by hydraulics.'

He paused, as if expecting a round of applause. The King frowned, before making his measured reply.

'Yes, that all makes sense. Signals pass through the air from one engine to the other. But what happens to the electrical impulses that the second machine generates?'

'Ah yes,' Kevin continued hurriedly. 'That's the really clever bit. Let's take a closer look at one of the engines.' The two men strolled together down the length of the room, both grey-clad, the King well built and lightly bearded, his Supervisor of Machinery thinner, dark-haired and, despite his relative youth, rather stooped. 'Each engine has a pair of eyepieces, a pair of headphones, and a pair of handles. The handles receive impulses from the operator's hand movements and convert them into electrical signals. And the eyepieces and headphones receive impulses from the telescope and convert them into pictures and sounds. So that the operator of the first engine, whom we might call the *Sender,* can imagine anything he chooses, anything at all, and the operator of the second engine, whom we might call the *Receiver,* will see and hear and feel whatever it is that the Sender has chosen to imagine.' Kevin had now become very animated indeed. 'Just think of it. With enough of these engines, there could be a whole network, maybe spanning the entire Land from end to end. People could send their thoughts and imaginings to anyone, anywhere. You, the King, could address the whole of your people at one and the same time. You wouldn't need Heralds, or the *Digest*. We could call it – the Universal Empathy Network.' Kevin caught the King's frown. 'Or anything we liked,' he added hurriedly. 'Just think of it.'

For several minutes, King Matthew stood still, staring at some spot on the ceiling. When he finally spoke, he sounded almost awestruck.

'All right,' he said quietly. 'I think I'd like you to do some more work on this.'

At that moment they were interrupted by a rude clatter coming from the direction of the staircase.

'Coffee?' called Veronique's grating voice.

'What happened on the exercise?'

Well, first of all we had to collect the octants and the triangulation engines and all the other measuring equipment, and after that we walked into the town to find out when there was a waggon leaving for the mountains. It turned out that there was one early the next day, so we arranged to meet at the waggon halt in the morning. I was early, of course, I had been elected to carry the instruments, and the red-haired kid arrived soon after me with his dog, but CharlesnSally were late. In fact, they almost missed the waggon altogether, but they turned up at the last minute, smiling and full of apologies, so we managed to get going on time and nobody was too angry with them.

The road up to the mountains was quite rough, and the

waggon was an old, shaky one, so we couldn't really discuss anything or make any plans during the journey. And, by the time we arrived at the inn where we were staying, it was nearly nightfall. So once we had unloaded all our things and been shown to our rooms, there was just time for a late supper, and after that CharlesnSally decided that it would be a good idea to have a few drinks, so we didn't really manage to discuss anything that night either.

We had been allocated two rooms at the top of the inn. CharlesnSally were together, of course, and I was in the room next door to them with the red-haired kid and his dog. We went upstairs at the end of the evening, and CharlesnSally disappeared at once into their room, and it was obvious from the noises coming through the wall what they were up to.

There were two beds in our room, one by the door and one under the window, and I sat down on the bed by the door and started to undress in an embarrassed sort of way and wriggle myself into my nightshirt. The kid tried to get the dog settled down on a blanket in the corner, then he just stood up and shrugged off his clothes and threw them on the floor, he didn't seem at all self-conscious. I couldn't help noticing how graceful he was, he was smaller than me and slighter, and his body looked very young and smooth. He must have sensed that I was staring, because he grinned at me, and then I was embarrassed, I looked away. When I looked again he had thrown himself down on the bed, he was still naked except for his socks, they had fallen down around his ankles, and the dog had jumped up there with him and he was stroking the dog and whispering things in its ear. I felt a bit disgusted at that, so I turned to face the wall and went to sleep.

I got up at first light, as I usually do, and saw that the kid and the dog had gone to sleep curled up together on top of the bed. He still hadn't put his nightshirt on, maybe because it had been a hot night, or maybe he just didn't have one, and he was lying on his side with his back towards me. I remember noticing his backbone and his two shoulder blades, and how delicate they looked, like a girl's, and then I started to feel sad, because he had his dog, and of course CharlesnSally had each other, but I didn't have anyone.

And then, without quite knowing why I did it, I knelt down by his bed and reached out a finger, and started tracing the outline of one of his shoulder blades. Then I realised what I was doing and quickly drew back, and I noticed that my hand was sweating and my heart was pounding. My touch must have woken him, because he turned towards me and saw me kneeling there, and he said, 'What's going on?' and I said the first thing I could think of, I said, 'I thought I heard something.' That probably sounded pretty stupid, but it seemed to satisfy him, because he turned over again and threw his arm across the dog's back and went straight back to sleep. I found that I was shaking all over, but of course I had brought my chain with me in my pack, so I sneaked it under my pillow then, and it seemed to help a bit.

There was no sign of CharlesnSally at breakfast, and the kid didn't say anything about what had happened in the night, maybe he'd forgotten. I asked him whether he thought we could rely on the other two to do any work, and he said that he was having his doubts, but he guessed that we were just going to have to make the best of it. I had to agree with that, so then the two of us at least had some kind of understanding. By the time the others appeared, there was nothing left but toast and coffee, but eventually we were able to sit down all together and discuss what we were trying to do.

It was during that discussion that I finally started to get the measure of the other three. My own idea was to use the instruments as we had been instructed, and to do the proper calculations, and to make a chart in the way we had been shown, but it turned out that Rusty — for some reason I found it hard to use his name, but obviously I was going to have to try — had other ideas. He reckoned that if we all observed the landscape as we made our way through it, and if we each made our own notes, we could come up with some sort of picture that incorporated everybody's different observations and didn't rely too much on making measurements. I was uneasy with this — it seemed very imprecise — but Sally was quite keen on the idea, I think mainly because she didn't really understand the instruments. Charles, who I had begun to realise was fundamentally idle, said that he was happy to go along with whatever everyone else wanted. In the end, we agreed on some sort of compromise, with everyone making notes, but also taking turns to use the instruments so that at least we had some figures to back us up if Rusty's method failed.

That was when I began to feel some kind of respect for Rusty. I realised that morning that the kid had got some ideas of his own, he wasn't just breaking rules for the sake of breaking them. I also started to realise that he had something I didn't have, some quality which I had only just begun to appreciate. I learned more about that over the next few days, but just then I couldn't have put a name to it, and even now I'm not sure I really can.

So that's how we did things to begin with, and soon we started to get some results that seemed usable, we even drew up a few preliminary sections of our chart. Actually, Rusty did all the drawing and painting, he used black ink and a box of watercolours, and as soon as I saw his first sketch, I knew that the charts we were producing were going to be something quite out of the ordinary. They seemed to have some sort of life of their own, they almost made the parchment glow. Despite my reservations, I found myself beginning to admire him, and I also began to think that, between the lot of us, we might come up with something really good after all.

Everyone must have sensed the same thing, because after the first day we all started to relax a bit. In the evenings, after supper, we would have a few drinks together, and we all started using each other's first names, and now and again even CharlesnSally started behaving like two separate people, although, as I had suspected early on, neither of those two ever really made much of a contribution to the exercise. Before long, though, I began to realise that Rusty had some sort of instinct or feeling for making charts that went far beyond anything I would ever accomplish with my instruments and grids and geometry. While I was measuring and reproducing lines and angles, he seemed somehow to be able to see the landscape as if he was floating in the air above it, and to absorb it all into himself. And when he painted it, he produced something that was more than just a simple chart, it was something alive, something that leaped out of the parchment, something that almost seemed to express the soul of the land. Of course, I wouldn't have used a word like 'soul' in those days, and I still don't feel comfortable with it, but I've since heard other people say that sort of thing, and it does seem to express what I'm trying to tell you better than anything else I can think of.

I've tried many times to make sense of what I was feeling during those few days, because I don't think I really understood any of it at the time. You see, although I couldn't help secretly admiring what the kid could do, at the same time he was really making me angry. He was making me angry because of the way he carried on with the dog, the way they seemed so completely absorbed in each other when they were playing together. And he was making me angry because he could command something that I felt was beyond me, this instinct for the landscape, this effortless ability to transform a list of notes and figures into a thing that had its own life and its own soul. And he was making me angry because his work was so beautiful. And he was making me angry, this isn't easy to say, because I had begun to see that he was beautiful too.

At night I used to kneel there by his bed, watching him while he slept, always with his arm around the dog, and I found myself wishing that I could be there on the bed too, with his arm around me, not around that stupid animal. No, of course I didn't say any of this to him, I had enough sense not to do that, but I really didn't know what was happening to me, I had never had feelings like that before.

Was I in love with him? Yes, I suppose I was, though that's another expression I wouldn't have chosen to use. And, you see, all this was coming to me rather late in life. I'd never had the chance before, and now I was finding it impossible to understand how anyone could make me so angry, but at the same time could make me want them so much that it seemed to hurt inside. Yes, I suppose I must have been in love. It just wasn't anything like I'd imagined it would be.

I think it was on the fourth or fifth day of the Exercise that everything went wrong. We started off in the usual way, I remember CharlesnSally were late for breakfast again, and the kid was sitting on a bench outside the window pulling on his socks and boots. I was staring at the side of his knee as he flexed it to and fro, fascinated by all the little ripples on the surface, marvelling at the complexity of the mechanism beneath, until Sally banged her coffee cup down on the table and startled me out of my trance.

In the end, we set off about halfway through the morning, and that day we climbed higher than we had done before and then, around midday, we somehow all got separated. Oh, I remember now, there was a patch of mist on the mountainside, that was the reason, I don't know where it came from, but I remember suddenly hearing voices coming from below me, and I heard the dog howling, so then I ran back to see what was the matter. Actually I never did really find out what had happened, the innkeeper thought it might have been bandits, but when I found the kid, he was just standing there in the mist. He seemed to be frozen to the spot, he couldn't speak and his eyes didn't seem to register anything, and the dog was lying there on the ground at his feet, and he wasn't moving either.

Well, somehow we got them back to the inn, and we put the kid to bed, and that's where he stopped until the waggon came at the end of the week to fetch us back. Without him, of course, we weren't going to get any more work done, and I was furious with him for wrecking the exercise. I knew that I would probably fail my Degree because of that, but when I saw him lying there in bed, looking so helpless, I found that I couldn't stay angry for long, and then I found myself wanting to stop with him to make sure he was all right, wanting to be the first one to speak to him when he finally came to himself. So I stayed with him in the room the whole time, and CharlesnSally decided they might as well go back to bed for a bit so, for the next few days, I could hear them in the background the whole time.

The kid seemed to be in some kind of fever, he was thrashing around in the bed, twisting his body from side to side. Now and again, he would sit up suddenly and open his eyes and start shouting things that didn't make any sense, something about someone called Lauren or Laurel, something about a secret, then he would fall back, all covered in sweat, and he would sleep again. I'm not sure that he ever really woke up properly, he wouldn't take any food or drink, and he didn't seem to recognise any of us, not even his dog.

I passed a bit of time writing some verses, but when I read them later I was ashamed of what I'd put, so I didn't keep them, I threw them away. But mainly, for those last *days, I felt very sad, because I knew that whatever had been going on between me and the kid was nearly over, and I knew that soon I would lose him, not that I ever actually had him, of course.*

When I realised that, I went over to my bed, and I reached under the pillow and drew out the chain. Then I crossed back over to his bed, and I held out the chain at arm's length. I let the end dangle down so that the last link just rested on his breastbone, and I remember that I could hear CharlesnSally doing whatever they were doing in the next room, and that made me feel sad as well.

Then, with the chain, I slowly traced out the landscape of his body, and I watched the end of the chain snaking around his throat and bumping lightly over his ribs and trailing across his smooth stomach and making a little circle around his hip bone. As I did that, he seemed to stir slightly and he gave a little shudder, and somehow that made me sadder than ever.

Then I heard the innkeeper calling up that the waggon had arrived, so I quickly put the chain away and then I had to wipe my eyes before the others saw me.

And then the Exercise was over, and of course we hadn't completed the Assignment.

The Wrong Kind of Darkness

Kevin Considine was feeling mightily relieved. Despite an untidy start, the meeting with the King had gone much better than he had expected, and it had finished up with the King granting him permission to develop what he had now decided to call the Universal Signal Network and to oversee whatever associated planning, manufacturing and installation processes might prove necessary. There had been a sticky moment when it looked as if the King might have remembered the true origin of the empathy engine, but, Kevin congratulated himself, he had successfully forestalled that one. After the meeting, he had returned to his own office, where he had immediately prepared and distributed all the necessary instructions, and now, at the end of the day, nothing further remained to be done. He stretched himself luxuriously, then, struck by a sudden thought, he got up from his desk and peered through the small glass pane in the door to check that the Administrative Centre was deserted. Then, satisfied, he made his way down the iron staircase to the laboratory. There was something that was still bothering him about one of the empathy engines.

Having switched on the power, Kevin settled himself at the controls of the engine in question. As it happened, this one was the same engine that he had acquired from his Constanzas cousins, the one he had disguised with metal sheets to prevent anyone from recognising it. The second engine, the one that the Palace technicians had built on his instructions, didn't so far seem to be exhibiting any untoward behaviour. But there was something inside the first engine, something perhaps that Madam Nina or some previous owner had left behind there, that had periodically been disrupting his test transmissions. It was clearly something that he needed to identify and to eliminate before he could have total confidence in the Network.

He slipped the headphones over his ears, took a light grip on the handles, adjusted the eyepieces until he was satisfied with the test signal. Then, concentrating hard, he worked his way quickly through the sequence of mental images that he had developed to check that the engine was functioning properly. First he imagined a major chord played on a guitar, then a rainbow traversing the sky, then an axe splitting a log.

Next, because he had found that, for limbering up, there was nothing to beat a real, solid problem, he ran a series of future projections, hoping to discover how the Administrative Centre could be restored to full working order following the departure of Alice. This produced some satisfactorily vivid imagery, but Kevin did not really expect to come up with any concrete results so, after a while, he allowed the pictures gently to disperse.

Then, conjuring a broom out of the air, he swept all the lingering fragments of picture and sound aside and brought his full concentration to bear on the empty space that remained. As usual, the picture appeared a uniform grey to begin with, and the sound a subdued hiss. Kevin frowned, and a dull patch of dirty red faded into view in front of him, while the sound expanded into a low-pitched boom. Then he smiled, and the red dissolved into a cheerful yellow while the sound rose in pitch to a merry warble. He raised an eyebrow, and little green and blue squiggles danced in the corners of the picture, while the sound went through an intriguing sequence of frequency modulations. Then, satisfied, he gave another flick of the broom and allowed his emotions to subside, until nothing remained before him but blackness and silence.

At least, that was what should have happened. But once again he found, to his annoyance, that the blackness was the wrong kind of blackness, and the silence was the wrong kind of silence. It should have been a broad, cool, infinite kind of blackness, and a wide-open, bottomless, never-ending kind of silence, but it wasn't. The blackness was tight and intense and enclosed, and the silence was narrow and shallow and somehow temporary. Kevin wanted to be floating in an infinite, timeless void, but he felt more as if he had been imprisoned in a narrow, airless cell. And, Kevin began to sense, although he wanted to be alone, he definitely wasn't.

Something else was there. He couldn't see it, he couldn't hear it, but somehow, perhaps through the two handles, he could sense it. For a moment he released his grip, wiped his sweating palms on his trouser legs, then he took hold of the handles again.

No, there could be no doubt. Inside the engine, Madam Nina had left something behind for him. She had left behind a small, black room, a room from which there was no escape, a room that contained some kind of unwelcome presence. Kevin strained his ears. Yes, he could definitely hear something. It seemed to be some kind of faint, intermittent hissing sound. It was coming from just in front of him. And the air around it seemed to be warm.

'Hello? Can you hear me?'

There was the hissing again, slightly louder now. Quickly, concentrating furiously, Kevin reached around the back of the machine, made some fine adjustments to the minor parameters, fidgeted with the handles.

'Hello? Hello? Who's there?'

'Hello, Kevin.' It was very faint, but the words were unmistakable. Feverishly excited, Kevin gave the handles a quarter-twist to increase the volume.

'Hello, yes, I'm Kevin. Who are you?'

The voice that answered was still faint, and its tone was hoarse, but it was unmistakably a woman's voice, languid and caressing and seductive.

'Hello, Kevin. I'm Lee. I want to be your friend. You can trust me.'

'Did you ever get your Degree?'

No, I never did, and nor did the red-haired kid. During the waggon ride, he started to wake up a bit and, when we dropped him off at his lodgings, he managed to get inside on his own. We watched him go upstairs, and then we left him and went back to the Academy to return the instruments. It was still vacation time, so Charles and Sally got on another waggon and went home, and I went back to my alcove and started wondering what was going to happen to me.

Well, it turned out that they wanted me to carry on working as a servant until the new academic year began, and they weren't too pleased when they found that I'd burned my clothes, but in the end I was allowed to carry on with my duties until the vacation was over. I was feeling pretty apprehensive for those few weeks, wondering what would happen when the results of the exercise were announced, and I stayed out of everyone's way as far as I could. I would have liked to see the kid, but somehow I couldn't pluck up the courage to call at his lodgings.

When the results were announced, they were even less pleased, they said that I wouldn't be able to continue with my degree, but that I could stay at the Academy as a servant again if I wanted to. I thought about this for a while, and I came to the conclusion that I couldn't do it, I'd tried to be an undergraduate and I'd failed at that, and I didn't want to go back to what I had been before. So I told them I didn't want that, and then they told me I would have to go.

I didn't know what I was going to do then, of course, I suppose I hadn't really believed it would happen. But I decided not to hang around, I packed up my things, the poems and the crosswords and the chain, and I headed out of the Academy gates, and I started walking slowly towards the town. I didn't really think about where I was going, I suppose I must have been in a bit of a daze, because eventually I found myself outside the lodging house where the kid lived, so I thought I may as well find out what he was going to do.

My heart was pounding as I rang the bell, and after a while a big woman came to the door with a feather duster in her hand, and I asked her if he was in, and she said, 'Mister Brown, no, didn't you know, he's gone away, I don't think he's coming back.' So I said the first thing I could think of, that he'd got something of mine, some drawings, and then she let me go up to his room.

All his clothes had gone, and there was no sign of the dog, either, there was nothing left but a few books and some of his charts still pinned to the wall. I took a few of them down and spread them out on the bed, and I sat there looking at them for a while, but somehow all the life had gone from them, suddenly they were just charts, very good charts perhaps, but still just charts. I didn't like to touch the ones he'd done on the exercise, but there were some old ones, they looked like they might have shown the village where he grew up, and I could see that he'd been much younger when he did them, the drawing wasn't so confident and the lettering looked rather childish. But there was something about those charts that reminded me of him more than the newer ones did, so I took a few of them and stuffed them into my pack with my other things, and then the woman came back and asked if I needed anything else, but I said that I didn't, and then it was time for me to go.

I didn't have anywhere to go to, of course, and I didn't have any money, so, as I walked, I started to ask myself what I might be able to do to earn a living. There was no point in thinking about cartography, of course, I'd failed at *that, and I certainly didn't want to be anyone's servant again, so then I thought about the other things I could do, the poems and the crosswords, and an idea came to me.*

I had seen people begging in the town, some of them just asked the passers-by for money, but I couldn't bring myself to do that. Some of them were selling little things, bootlaces and matches and so on, and some of them had learned tricks of various kinds, there was a woman who played a tune on a violin, always the same tune, but people seemed happy to part with a few coins to hear her, and then there was a contortionist, this dark-skinned boy who used to tie himself in knots. I knew I wouldn't be able to do anything like that, but then I remembered an old man who used to draw pictures on the pavement with coloured chalks, and that gave me my idea. I couldn't draw pictures like his, of course, but I thought I might be able to draw crosswords. Fortunately, I had a few sticks of chalk among my things, I used to keep them in my pockets when I was an academic servant, in case the instructors didn't have any chalk for writing on the blackboards. So I found a place where the pavement was wide, and I sketched out a grid and filled in some of the words, then I started asking people if they could guess what the missing words were. And if I got the better of anyone, they would pay me, and sometimes they paid me even if they did guess the words.

So that's how I earned my living for the next few years. I had to keep moving on from town to town, because people would get bored with me if I stayed in one place for too long, but I found that, wherever I went, I could earn a bit of money for a day or two, enough to pay for food and maybe a night's lodgings if it was too cold to sleep outdoors. In a few places I got chased away by militiamen or by other beggars but, after I'd been doing it for a bit, I began to develop a sense for where the good places were, and after a while people started to recognise me. 'Here comes the Crossword Man,' they used to say. So it seemed that I had found something to keep me out of mischief for the time being.

I never earned enough money to travel in waggons or carriages, of course, so I ended up doing a lot of walking. Sometimes the roads were rough, and that was hard work, but in some places there were new roads being built — the Royal Highways, people called them — and they were quite a lot easier on the feet, so I tried to stay on the Royal Highways whenever I could. And while I walked, I had quite a lot of time for thinking. I started thinking about my life, what it was and what it could have been. I realised that things would have been much better for me if I'd come from a good home, and I realised that things would have been much better for me if I'd passed my degree and become a cartographer. And then I thought about my father, and I thought about the red-haired kid at the Academy, and I started to understand that it was because of them that things had turned out the way they had, and I started to think that I might have a couple of scores to settle. The nights were the worst times, lying in the dark I used to find myself getting angry about everything, and then I used to burrow around in my pack and get out the chain and the other things, and I found that if I spent a bit of time with them I didn't feel so bad.

It's funny, but I've never talked to anyone about these things before. Somehow, they've always seemed really hard things to talk about. But, sitting in this room with you, it all becomes really easy. I think you must have some sort of gift, maybe the gift of being able to listen. I don't think I've really got any gifts and, when I first met someone who had, I didn't like it at all. But with you it's different. You've used your gift to help me. And I like that.

One day, I came to the top of a hill and there, in the distance, was the city. I could make out the gatehouse and the Palace, with all the kites flying from them, and in the distance I could just make out some spires, and the river, and the masts of the tall ships in the docks. I hadn't been to the city since that day when I met the magician at the transport interchange, and that set me thinking again. The magician had been my benefactor once, he had paid the fees for me to become an undergraduate, so perhaps if I told him what had happened he would be my benefactor again. I knew that he worked for the King, so I decided to go to the Palace and ask to see him.

There was some kind of machine at the front gate of the Palace, and I discovered by watching people that you needed a special token to get through the gate, so after a while I walked around to the back, I had to go up a little cobbled street. It was called 'Beggars' Row' although there weren't any beggars in sight. At the back gate, there was just an ordinary sentry in a sentry box. I sat down on the ground, and I searched in my pack for the parchment that the magician had given me, and fortunately I still had it. It had his *name on it, Leonardo Pegasus, so I showed it to the sentry and said I had an appointment, and the sentry looked at it, and showed it to another sentry, and they looked on some lists of names, and then they told me that they were very sorry, but Master Pegasus wasn't there any more, he had left the Palace when the new King came to the throne, and that was nearly three years ago. I felt very despondent then. I didn't have much money, so I walked back down the cobbled street, and I kept walking until I found a place where I could draw my crossword.*

After I had been sitting there for a short time, I noticed that people were hurrying past me and nobody seemed to be taking any notice, and then it occurred to me that I hadn't seen any other beggars in the city. I was just wondering why this should be, when three ragged-looking characters walked up to me, two of them had bare feet with long toenails and the other one was wearing a pair of battered old black boots, and they stood in front of me, right in the middle of my grid. I was about to chase them away when I noticed that they were wearing the remains of some kind of uniform, faded blue tunics and caps with badges on them, and one of them, the one with the boots said, 'Attention, Scum, don't you know who we are?' and I said that I was sorry, but I didn't. Then he said, 'We are the troopers of the Royal Wolf Boys Militia, and it is our duty to inform you that begging is no longer tolerated on the streets of this city.'

And before I could say anything else, he signalled to the other two, and they grabbed me by the arms, and the one with the boots kicked me a few times, and then they dragged me along the pavement and threw me into the back of a power-driven waggon. The waggon drove off very fast, it was noisy and the fuel made an awful smell in the back. I was thrown around all over the place. When the waggon finally stopped, they dragged me out again, and I found myself in a big yard with high walls all around it, and I said 'Where have you taken me?' and the one with the boots said, 'This is the city gaol, Scum.'

Then they kicked me a few more times, and then they threw me into a dark cell, and I heard the door slam and the key turn in the lock.

The Signal Station

Leonardo Pegasus was enjoying his retirement, and he was enjoying living in the country. In the few years since his arrival in the village, he had become a well-known fixture at the Plough, where he was usually to be glimpsed collecting glasses in the taproom, and was occasionally to be encountered, during the periodic absences of the landlord, serving behind the bar. The work was engrossing but not overtaxing, and it allowed him plenty of spare time to tinker with the various pieces of machinery that he kept in the hayloft behind the inn, and plenty of time also to discuss the state of the land with his regular customers, the retired schoolmaster and the village tradesmen and farmers. Occasionally, Leonardo allowed himself the luxury of reminiscing about his years in the city and his dismissal from office at the hands of King Matthew and, once in a while, he even thought about Nina. He tried not to think too much about Nina, because she had pretended to be his friend and then, when he was at his most vulnerable, she had betrayed him and stolen all his equipment, even his empathy engine. Thinking too much about these things still made Leonardo angry. Sometimes he wondered what, if anything, Nina had done with the empathy engine, but then he forced himself to remember that all these events were a long way in the past, and that he had a new life now.

One rainy Tuesday lunchtime in late spring, an old farmer named Zachary Flint made one of his rare appearances in the taproom at the Plough. Water was dripping from his tweeds, and his boots left a muddy trail on the flagstones behind him. Zachary trudged straight up to Leonardo, who happened to be serving at the bar that day, and produced a thick wad of money from inside his jacket. He then proceeded to buy large drinks for everyone present. Leonardo did not pay much attention to this but, an hour later, when the performance had been repeated three times, he did find himself starting to become curious. Zachary kept a small farm up in the hills, where the soil was poor, and it was well known that he was barely able to scratch a living from his land. Leonardo could not avoid speculating about the source of Zachary's new-found wealth, but, as it turned out, he did not have to speculate for long.

'Got me a little windfall,' the farmer confided,

leaning across the bar. Leonardo flinched at the man's ale-fogged breath.

'Really? That was lucky.'

'It were the King's men. Come to the farmhouse, they did. Offered to buy that old patch of rough ground, you know her, top of the hill.'

'Really? Whatever for?' Life was uneventful in the village, and Leonardo's curiosity was quickly aroused by such remarkable news.

'Don't know. Some sort of signal station, they said, something like that, anyway. Building them all over, so it seems. So how about another drink for everybody, yourself as well?'

Zachary must have retreated to his farm soon after that, because he didn't reappear at the Plough for some time, and it wasn't for another few weeks that Leonardo got around to making any further investigation of his story. However, with the approach of summer, and the consequent improvement in the weather, Leonardo decided one afternoon to take a walk in the hills that overlooked the village. Approaching Zachary's farm, he was surprised to discover a stark, newly laid track of broken stones, slicing its uncompromising way across the landscape. The track led him to a new-looking building, standing squarely on the rough ground that the farmer had recently sold. The building was constructed from bricks of a dirty yellowish colour, and it was squat in form and very ugly. From its flat, slablike roof fluttered a row of kites.

Puzzled, Leonardo approached the building and stepped through its open, unpainted door. The interior consisted of a single long, bare room, in which two men in labourers' overalls were seated on packing cases, drinking tea from tin mugs. Around them were ranged various large pieces of machinery, generators, coils of wire and toolboxes. One man was wrinkled and elderly, the other much younger, perhaps still in his teens. They looked around, unperturbed at the arrival of their visitor.

'Good afternoon, gentlemen,' said Leonardo brightly. 'I was just passing, and I couldn't help—'

'You can't come—' began the young one.

'Be quiet, Terry,' interrupted his colleague. 'Give the gentleman a cup of tea. Have a seat, guv'nor. We was just on our break.'

Leonardo seated himself cautiously on the edge of a packing case and took a long, welcome draught of the strong, sweet tea.

'What are you lads up to, then?' he enquired.

'We're not supposed to—' said the young one.

'Be quiet, Terry. Let me explain to the gentleman. Not that we really know much about it.' The old man brought out a tobacco tin and started to roll a cigarette. 'They call it a Signal Station. Sends messages through the air, so they tell me. See the kites, did you?'

Fascinated, Leonardo nodded. He had not seen a row of signal kites since he'd left the city, and was baffled at finding them in such a remote situation.

'And the engines, see, these ones we're unpacking, they have to be connected up to the kites somehow . . .'

'It's all in the book,' interjected the young one helpfully.

'Be quiet, Terry. I'll tell the gentleman.' The old man lit his cigarette, took a deep puff, then scratched his head for a few moments before continuing. 'Well, I suppose that's it, really, guv'nor. We've got that one working over there. Have a look if you want.'

'He's not allowed to—'

'Be quiet, Terry.'

Leonardo levered himself cautiously upright and crossed the room to where the engine was quietly humming. It was housed in a square, grey, metal cabinet, the surface of which was dotted with switches, dials, and flashing lights. On top of the cabinet was a set of eyepieces, with a set of headphones on a curly lead plugged in next to it. At the sides of the cabinet were a pair of upright handles. Feeling curiously breathless, Leonardo gingerly slid the headphones over his ears. Then he became aware of the gaze of the two men.

'May I?'

'He's—'

'Quiet, Terry. Go ahead, guv'nor. Just try not to break it.'

Leonardo peered into the eyepieces, gave the handles an awkward tweak. There could be no doubting it. This, surely, was an empathy engine, identical in every detail to the one he himself had designed so many years ago. But who had constructed it? And how did it come to be here? Slowly, he relinquished the controls and returned to where the others were still sitting.

'What name did you give to that thing?'

'It's called—'

'Terry! I shan't tell you again. No, guv'nor, I could-n't rightly say.' The old man shrugged. 'Signal engine, I suppose you could call it. Like I said, they're going up all over. Name's probably in the book somewhere.'

'Ever heard it called an empathy engine?'

'No, guv'nor, can't rightly say I have. Empathy engine, you say? No, I don't think so. Terry, why don't you make the gentleman another cup of tea?'

'How long did they keep you in gaol?'

As it turned out, I wasn't in there very long at all. I spent the night in a cell, but the next morning, the guards came in, they gave me another beating, and then they took me to a large room, rather like a classroom it was, and about twenty other prisoners were brought in as well. I asked the guards what was happening, and they said, 'You'll see in good time,' and then there was a clatter in the corridor, and the head guard shouted, 'On your knees, Scum, for Master Fang!' and everyone knelt down, even the other guards. Then Master Fang swept into the room, and I could see how important he was from the clothes he was wearing.

He had on a uniform rather like the guards, except that it looked much newer, and it had bits of what looked like gold all over it, and on his head he had a three-cornered hat with long black feathers held in place with more gold bits. Around his shoulders hung a long, black cloak with a scarlet lining and a gold clasp. His boots were tall and new-looking, very shiny, so I couldn't see his toenails, but the nails on his fingers were very long and sharp, almost like claws. His face had a mean look, with narrow, yellowish eyes and a long, twisted nose and long teeth, and he had a straggly beard arranged in spikes with little black bows in it. Master Fang looked us over for several minutes. When he finally spoke, his voice sounded hard and cracked and cruel.

'Scum,' he said, 'you are here because you were found begging in the streets of the city. Well, let me tell you that in this city we do not tolerate such defilement of our public spaces, and it is the duty of the Royal Wolf Boys Militia to administer punishment of the utmost severity to all beggars, vagrants and other such degenerates.'

At that point, one of the other prisoners started to protest that her livelihood had been taken away from her, and that she had no other way to earn her keep. Before she had finished speaking, however, Master Fang signalled to the guards, and a couple of them got up and went over to her and gave her a good kicking in front of the rest of us, and after that nobody interrupted again.

'Perhaps you are beginning to understand the manner in which you will be treated if you choose to remain here,' Master Fang continued. 'But you must not let yourselves become downhearted, for you will be encouraged to make a

choice. The Royal Wolf Boys Militia takes great pride in being a compassionate organisation, and we have always been disposed to temper justice with mercy.' His little eyes flicked from side to side as he said this, and I remember thinking that I had never seen anyone who looked less merciful, not even my father. 'We have no desire to retain you here if you can prove yourselves capable of earning a living in a respectable fashion,' Master Fang continued. 'We are therefore prepared to grant immediate release to any prisoner, or group of prisoners, who can present to us a fully detailed Business Plan, which is to include, preferably in the form of an Appendix, a thorough Market Analysis and rigorously argued Income and Expenditure Projections. Upon submission of such a Plan, the prisoner or prisoners will be deemed free to leave, and will be permitted to remain at liberty, subject, of course, to the successful implementation of the Plan. Until such a time,' and he looked round the room in what I suppose would have to be described as a wolfish fashion, 'you will be returned to your cells and subjected to regular beatings. You have one hour.' And then he turned and swept out of the room.

When we heard the door close, we all rose to our feet, guards as well as prisoners, and the head guard said, 'All right, Scum, you heard the Master, you have one hour, GET ON WITH IT!' The prisoners all looked at each other in a blank, terrified sort of way, but I was already starting to have an idea, so I quickly went round the room and asked the others what they used to do before they became beggars. I found two women, including the one who had been beaten, who had once been criers in the Herald's department, and there were a couple of men who used to be kite hands, so I told those four my idea, and we decided that we might be able to work together. Of course, I had the advantage that I was good with words and figures, and I had even learned a little about business plans at the Academy, in the lectures on commercial administration. Funnily enough, they had not been the most popular lectures, and not everyone had paid much attention to them, but the instructor had said that many of us would find them the most useful part of the degree, and finally he was about to be proved right.

At the end of the hour, we were taken back to our cells and beaten again, but I still had my pack with the parchment and ink, so I was able to start drafting my plan. I don't know whether Master Fang really believed that any of us would come up with anything, the guards certainly didn't make it easy for us, but in the end I was able to present a business plan that was so thorough that they ended up having to release me and the other four. The last thing Master Fang said to me was, 'We'll be watching you, Slater. So no funny business.' Then there was a final beating from the guards, and then we were free.

Oh yes, I suppose I'd better tell you what my plan was. I didn't know much about the city, of course, I'd only ever visited it briefly, but the one place where I had spent quite a bit of time was the transport interchange. I'd seen quite a lot of what went on there, so I decided that the most useful thing I could do was to try and get the interchange organised a bit better, so that people would know which waggon they had to get on, and where to find it, and when it was supposed to depart.

We needed to start earning some money straight away, so the first thing I did was to go round talking to the drivers of all the coaches and waggons, and of course they were all completely frustrated because none of the passengers could ever find the right waggon, so I asked the drivers if they would pay me if I could get the passengers to the waggons on time, and they said they would be glad to, but I don't think any of them really believed that I could do it. Anyway, I started making notes about all their destinations and departure times, and then I got some parchment, and drew up a big grid, and put all the figures on it, and I called it the schedule of departures. And while I was doing that, I sent the kite hands down to the Undertown to collect up lengths of scrap timber from the ruins, and then I got them to build a tall observation tower. This was to stand at the edge of the interchange, facing north, with its back to the river. On top of it they built a cabin with a big window, so that I could sit up there with my schedule, watching the coaches and waggons and listening to the chimes from the Institute of Calibration. Then the criers could sit on either side of me, shouting out all the times and destinations through megaphones so that everyone could hear.

Well, the plan was a big success, and soon I had the interchange running like a well-tuned engine. The Wolf Boys used to come and check up on me from time to time, but I could tell that even they were impressed, and after a while, with a little financial inducement, they agreed to stop interfering. Of course, I had my share of problems. Some of the drivers tried to cheat me, they decided they weren't going to pay me anything, but when that happened, I told the criers not to call out their times, so that they wouldn't get any passengers, and after that they soon started paying up again. Then there was a gang of children who used to carry messages and run errands, hiring out waterproof boots and so on, their leader was a girl called Maisie, and they were angry because they said I'd taken their work away from them. But I persuaded them that they would be better off working for me, so they ended up carrying baggage and selling refreshments, and they seemed happy enough in the end. I think Maisie and a couple of the other girls made a bit of money on the side doing various other things, but I decided it would be better not to enquire too closely about that.

So, after a couple of years, things really started to come good. I wasn't rich, but I was earning enough money to rent a little apartment in the North Estates, Serendipity Court, that was the name of the building, and the people who worked for me were all doing well too, and of course the transport system was working better than it ever had. Later on, I got around to making a few more improvements. I hired gangs of beggars from the gaols to collect stones from the derelict sites in the Undertown, and they built some roads and paths across the mud, so that people could get about more easily, and then I had some big signposts made, with numbers on them, so that it was even easier for people to get to the right place at the right time. So at last it seemed that I had found something that I was good at, but then a couple of things happened that started to make me angry again.

First of all, a man came from the Palace, Kevin Considine,

he said his name was, and he said that King Matt was delighted with what I had achieved, and then he asked how would I like to have a row of signal kites on my observation tower and to become a part of the Universal Signal Network. Well, that frightened me quite a lot, because I had worked hard to get where I was, and I reckoned that if this network started to transmit my departure times, then I would pretty soon be begging in the streets again, and so would all the people who worked for me, except perhaps Maisie and her girls, so I told him to go away and steal his ideas from someone else. He didn't seem too pleased with that, and the next month, someone showed me the Royal Digest, *and there was a piece in it by the Herald, Miss Garamond, saying that the schedule of departures and the improvements at the interchange were all the King's inventions, and not saying anything at all about me. That made me angry all over again, but there was something else in the same piece that made me angrier still. It said that the Royal Supervisor of Iconography was about to become a father for the second time, and that his name was Michael Brown.*

Well, that stirred up a lot of memories that hadn't troubled me for quite a while. I'd been so preoccupied with running the interchange for the last few years that I'd completely forgotten about the red-haired kid, and now suddenly I had discovered that he'd been living in the city all this time. I imagined him sitting in some comfortable office with his impressive title and his fine clothes, and going home to his nice little family in their cosy house, and generally enjoying an easy life. And meanwhile, there I was, sitting on top of my tower in all weathers with the criers either side of me yelling their heads off. And every day I was having to argue with the drivers about my money, and pay everyone their wages, and bribe the Wolf Boys to leave me alone. And then there was Maisie carrying on her extra business somewhere round the back, with all the noise and inconvenience that went with it. And at the end of the day, I would be crossing over the river on the stinking ferry and going back to my bare little room at Serendipity Court and climbing five storeys up a rope ladder just to get to bed. And of course I knew that the next day it would be the same thing all over again.

So then I realised that I might be earning a living and even doing people a bit of good, but there were others in the city who were doing a lot better than I was, others who maybe thought they were better and more important than me. But I knew that they didn't deserve to be where they were, and I knew that I had to show them that they couldn't ignore me any longer.

Lee's Room

Night had fallen across the city, and the Palace was in darkness. Not quite total darkness, however, because, in the laboratory beneath the administrative centre, a single lamp continued to glow. And, in the laboratory, Kevin Considine remained hunched over the empathy engine, his body tense, his breath shallow and noisy. Kevin's attention was entirely concentrated on the machine and, somewhere in the imaginary world inside it, he continued to explore the enclosed, stifling darkness of the black, six-sided room. Because, somewhere in that darkness, he could still sense the presence of the invisible being who called herself Lee.

'Who are you, Lee? And what is this place?'

'This place? This place can be whatever you want it to be, Kevin,' whispered the being. *'And I can be whatever you want me to be, too. I hope you will let me be your friend.'*

'It's so dark in this room. I wish I could see you.'

'Of course you shall see me, Kevin. But if you want to see me, you must make me a new room, a room with light in it. And you must make me a doorway, Kevin, a doorway into my new room. And then we can go through the doorway into the light, you and I, and you shall see what you shall see.'

'Another room, Lee? What sort of room?'

Just use your imagination, Kevin, that's all you need to do. Just use your imagination. I'm sure you have plenty of that.'

There was a tense silence. Kevin gripped the two handles of the empathy engine and tried to breathe deeply, tried to engage his imagination as Lee had commanded. And then, at first faintly, then more brightly, an outline faded into view before him, the outline of a tall, rounded archway. For a moment, it hung there in silence. Then, suddenly, a dazzling pool of golden light blazed from beyond the arch, accompanied by an echoing, hissing, shrieking sigh, like the sound of compressed air escaping from a cylinder.

And, at that moment, Kevin caught the briefest glimpse of a quick, lithe figure, silhouetted against the light, darting ahead of him into the middle distance.

'Lee?'

'Follow me, Kevin.'

The timbre of the voice told him that a wider space lay beyond. Breathless, blinded and deafened, Kevin approached the archway. As his eyes began to adjust, he could see that it opened into a cavernous, six-sided chamber that had an identical, rounded arch at the centre of each of its walls. Between the arches were mounted ranks of candle sconces, and the candles cast a soft, amber light that bathed the whole of the space in an even, golden glow. At the centre of the room stood a large, broad, ornately carved bed, draped in black satin covers, which called to mind some kind of sinister altar. Above the bed, from the domed ceiling, hung a trapeze. And on the trapeze, dangling her legs, sat a creature, who, Kevin assumed, must be Lee. He hesitated, his fingers lightly brushing the sides of the archway.

'Don't be afraid, Kevin.'

He could see now that Lee was a woman, a tall, athletic-looking young woman. Her hair was long and thick and black, her eyes were dark and slanted, her cheekbones were high and sharply chiselled, her lips were a dark, glistening red, and her skin was of a yellowish colour and a smooth, waxy texture. She was wearing a short, black tunic, which displayed her long, elegant arms and legs to great advantage. The nails on her fingers and toes were painted the same red as her lips, and were long and sharp-looking. She reminded Kevin of an exotic dancer he had once admired at one of the places of entertainment that he occasionally frequented with his colleagues. He could feel his feet being drawn reluctantly forwards.

'What's happening? What's going on?'

Then, with a single, smooth movement, Lee arched her body, slipped clear of the trapeze and dropped down onto the bed, landing lightly on her knees, shoulders back, thighs slightly parted. Kevin's feet took another step forwards.

'Lee?'

Lee's moist lips parted slightly, giving Kevin a glimpse of sharp, white teeth. Slowly, she raised a hand to her throat, then, suddenly, she ran a sharp fingernail down the front of her tunic. It parted with a hiss and a rustle and fell away from her. Underneath it, she wore nothing. Every vein in his body suddenly pounding furiously, Kevin took another step forwards.

'Lee? What's . . .'

Laughing, Lee patted the black covers beside her. *'Come on, silly boy. Explanations later.'*

This time, Kevin needed no further encouragement.

Tea in the Night

Several hours after the end of the work period, Rusty fumbled his way up the three flights of stairs at

Shrubbery House, rummaged in his pockets for his key, and let himself into the apartment. It didn't look as if Eileen had waited up for him because, as usual, the living room was dark. From the half-open door of Ashleigh's bedroom came the glow of a night light and, in its dim glow, Rusty could just make out the child's profile as she slept, thumb in mouth. Her arm was curled around her favourite toy, a battered canine known as Mister Woofie. A second night light glowed in the larger bedroom that Rusty and Eileen now shared with the recently delivered Max. The baby was sleeping quietly in his cot, but Eileen was not quite asleep for, as Rusty sat down on the side of the bed, he felt her turn towards him.

'Working late again?' she murmured sleepily.

'Yes. Well, a bit late. And then there were a few drinks. Couldn't really say no.' Rusty, still in his over-coat, started pulling off his thick, brown shoes.

'Was it that Gordon – Simon Loxley again?' Eileen took a determined interest in the various intrigues at the Herald's office, and was always curious to know about the doings of Rusty's colleagues, despite the fact that she had never met any of them face to face.

'Norman. Yes. Same old thing, thinks he knows more about everything than the rest of us, and of course he has to keep on and on telling us all about it. It all just keeps going round in circles. Never seems to get anywhere. Must have been going on for three years at least.' One of Rusty's shoelaces had got itself into a tangle, and in the half-light, he couldn't really see what he was doing.

'I don't know why you just don't get rid of him if he's that much trouble,' Eileen persevered. 'What did you say his wife's name was?'

At that moment, Rusty couldn't remember whether Loxley was married or not and, because he wasn't too certain of the relevance of the question, he decided to sidestep it.

'It's just not that easy to get rid of people. Miss Garamond likes everything to be done by the book. Oh, damn this shoelace! Where are the nail scissors?'

Eileen laid a hand on his forearm.

'Keep your hair on, darling, it's only a shoelace. So what about Miss Garamond? Did she say anything else today? You know, about the cartographers?'

Rusty abandoned his struggle with the shoelace and half turned to face his wife.

'Yes. Yes. Sorry, it slipped my mind, with all that other business. But Miss G called me in this morning. She gave me a sort of preview of what she's writing in her diary column this month. And, apparently, the King . . .'

'Feet off the covers, darling,' Eileen interrupted. 'Or at least let me get these shoes off you first.' She took hold of his shoes one by one, and tugged them off his feet without bothering to untie the laces. Rusty screwed his face up in annoyance.

'You know I hate it when you do that. I always like to untie them first. Now, where have you put them?'

Eileen could not help smiling. She responded to his odd habits with a mixture of irritation and affection.

'Look, never mind that now. What were you saying just then? About the King and the cartographers?'

'Oh yes.' Rusty, now sitting cross-legged on the bed, shrugged off his overcoat and let it slide on to the floor. 'It's finally happening. The King has decided that the charts are going to be published. Apparently he's found a loophole in that old law, you know, the Charter Ancient and Inviolable. And there's going to be a sort of competition to decide who the publisher will be. I was hoping the Herald's Office might put in a bid, but it seems that Miss G's had second thoughts about it.'

'That's a shame,' murmured Eileen, giving his arm a squeeze. 'You really wanted to do that, didn't you?'

'Yes, I did. But I think I still could. I mean, I think I've got a special feeling for charts, you know how I can just sort of see things from the air. And, you see, I've had an idea. Perhaps it's time for me to move on from the Herald's Office. I was thinking I might put in a bid on my own account.'

Fully awake now, Eileen turned on the bedside lamp. There was an outbreak of subdued gurgling from the direction of Max's cot but, after a few moments, it subsided again.

'Would you fancy some tea?' said Eileen. 'I won't go back to sleep until we've talked about this.'

A few minutes later, they were seated at the table

in the tiny, spotless kitchen, flower-patterned cups of tea in front of them on the flower-patterned cloth, Eileen in her flower-patterned nightdress, Rusty still in his office clothes, minus socks and shoes. Eileen stirred her tea thoughtfully.

'Would we be any better off? I mean, things have been pretty tight the last couple of years. And now there's Max as well.' She put the spoon down carefully in her saucer.

Rusty frowned.

'Well, of course, it's bound to depend on the demand for the charts. But I think people will find them pretty useful, and they'll be good, I'm sure of that at any rate, so the demand should be quite strong. I've done a few sums, look –' he produced a dog-eared piece of parchment from an inside pocket '– and I reckon we should be better off. Quite a lot better off, actually.'

'Enough to get a bigger apartment?' They were both painfully aware that, since the arrival of Max, their quarters were becoming uncomfortably cramped.

'Should be. We could probably move to a two- or three-bedroom place somewhere on the North Estate. And if things went well enough, we might even be able to stretch to the Western Suburb.'

'The Western Suburb? Oh, Rusty, could we really?'

Mentally, Rusty patted himself on the back. He had guessed that the prospect of an apartment in that most prestigious corner of the city would secure his wife's support for his scheme.

'I think so. Maybe not straight away. But perhaps in a couple of years.'

'The Western Suburb. Daddy will be so impressed.' Eileen tipped the remains of the tea down the sink. 'You are a clever old thing. Shall we go back to bed now?'

'And how did you get yourself noticed?'

It was another year or so before I finally got my chance. The transport interchange had settled into a steady way of working, and I had developed a regular routine of revising the schedules and bribing the Wolf Boys and collecting the money from the drivers and from Maisie's girls, and sorting out any other odd problems that came up. And the criers and the kite hands and the other helpers, well, they knew their stuff, and they kept things running pretty smoothly most of the time. Now and then I had some new idea or other, and recently I had decided that the passengers might like to have something to read, to pass the time if they had to wait around, so Maisie's kids had started to sell copies of The Royal Digest *and, if I had a bit of spare time, I used to take a look at it as well, and it turned out to be quite interesting, keeping up with what was happening in the city.*

I was particularly interested in that Miss Garamond's diary, particularly since she used to make the occasional mention of my old enemy Mister Brown, so I could keep track of what he was up to. I used to follow the doings of Kevin Considine and King Matthew as well, of course.

I had one or two more visits from Considine, but he must have realised that I wasn't going to change my mind about the network, so in the end he stopped coming.

But, one day, there was something from Miss Garamond that really interested me. It seems that the King had finally decided to crack down on the Brotherhood of Cartographers, and all their charts were going to be copied and sold to the public, but the really interesting thing was that the Brotherhood weren't going to do the publishing themselves, there was going to be some sort of competition, and the winner of the competition would be allowed to publish the charts, and would probably make quite a lot of money doing it.

Well. I was having a cup of coffee with Maisie that afternoon — yes, we used to sit down now and again, just to discuss business — and I showed her what I'd read, and she looked at it and sort of screwed up her face, and then she said, 'Why don't you put in for it, Mister Slater? I think that would be right up your street,' and I said, 'Don't be silly, Maisie, things like that aren't for people like us.' But later, I started to think about it again, and I thought, well, I do know quite a bit about cartography, even if I never got my degree, and I do know how to administer a business, and since I've been at the transport interchange, I've learned a lot about the geography of the city as well, so yes, I reckon I could do it. And then I started to imagine what it would be like, sitting behind a big desk in a smart new building, and having people fetching me coffee, and living in a fancy apartment, and travelling in a power-driven carriage. And I thought, this will make Mister Brown and Mister Considine and all those others take some notice of me, this will even make Master Fang take notice of me. So I decided then to enter myself for the competition.

It turned out that the King wanted everyone to write a business plan, and the person who wrote the best plan would win the competition and be allowed to publish the charts. I found this very encouraging, because I had already written one plan, the one for the transport interchange, and that had been a great success, so I reckoned that a plan for publishing the charts wouldn't give me too much trouble.

There was going to be a meeting at the Palace for everyone who was interested so, on the evening in question, I went along, and I was taken up several flights of stairs, broad and nicely carpeted they were, and then I had to walk across a part of the roof, that didn't seem quite right, but then I was shown into a room in the new part of the Palace, the Administrative Centre I think they call it, and there were about thirty or forty people packed into the room, they were all milling around a big table with all sorts of food and drink arranged on it. I decided to have something to eat while I was waiting, but I found that it didn't really taste of anything.

Then the King arrived, and they asked everyone to be seated while he spoke to us. We were all given a bundle of documents to read, so that we'd understand what we had to do, and the King had some diagrams pinned to a sort of easel, so he had to explain all that to us. He wasn't at all the way I had expected him to be, he looked younger than me, and he was very thorough and precise and matter-of-fact. Anyway, he explained that the business plans had to be ready by a certain date, and then he asked if anyone had any questions, and of course quite a few people did, but eventually he excused himself and said that we were welcome to have more food and drink before we went home.

Some of the people in the room were talking to each other, and I recognised one or two, but I didn't know anyone well enough to speak to, and they all looked better dressed and more important than me, so I just moved among them, looking and listening. Mister Considine was there, I think he was helping to organise things, at any rate he didn't have a bundle of documents under his arm, but anyway I didn't feel like talking to him. I had just decided that it was time for me to go home, when I spotted someone that I did know on the other side of the room, someone I hadn't noticed before. It was Rusty Brown, that red-haired kid that I'd known at the Academy.

It was some years since I'd last seen him, and of course he wasn't really a kid any more, and I knew from The Royal Digest that he preferred to be known as Michael Brown these days. I thought he had started to put on a little bit of weight, and he seemed not quite so loose in the way he held himself, his hair was tidier and his face had more of a set expression. He was standing there talking to a couple of people who looked quite important, and I noticed that he was dressed in the same sort of way that they were, in some sort of tailored grey outfit with a necktie. I could tell that they were all accustomed to each other's company, and I couldn't help noticing how confident they all seemed, well, arrogant really. And then, with a terrible empty feeling in my stomach, I knew that Brown had become one of them, *he was one of the people who ruled the city. And finally it dawned on me that it was going to be one of these people who would win the competition, maybe it would be him and maybe not, but at any rate it certainly wasn't going to be me.*

I was about to slip away when he turned and saw me, and then his face suddenly broke into a grin that made him look like a kid again, and he came towards me holding out his hand, and he said, 'Good gracious, it's Tom Slater, isn't it?' I felt embarrassed at that, I was beginning to feel the old anger again, because I had started to imagine him gloating over his success and my failure, but actually he did look really pleased to see me. I didn't take his hand, though, I just said, 'Hello, Rusty.' We chatted to each other for a bit, but eventually he made some excuse, I think he'd had enough of me by then, because he started getting ready to leave. So then I waited until he had gone out of the door, and then I slipped out quietly and followed him.

I don't quite know why I did that, I didn't have any particular plan in mind, not then anyway, but I decided that I wanted to know where he lived, and to my surprise he walked around the Ring Road and headed off up the North Way. I kept thinking he would turn off to the left, towards the Western Suburb, but he just kept going, and eventually I saw him go into a building on the North Estate, mind you it was on the smarter side, away from the Undertown.

And then I went home to bed. And I remember thinking, I know where to find you now, Michael Brown. I know where you live.

I started to draft my business plan the next day, but I

was feeling very despondent after meeting Michael Brown, I think I had already made up my mind that I wasn't going to win the competition, so I kept picking the plan up and putting it down again, going off and doing other things, and I don't think I concentrated very hard or made a very good job of it.

And I suppose it must have been round about then that I began to lose interest in the transport interchange. I sort of told myself that the others could look after things for a few days now and then, and of course that meant that I stopped updating the schedule as often as I should have done and then, of course, bit by bit things started to go wrong. People started missing their waggons, and then the drivers didn't want to pay me their fees. The Wolf Boys weren't getting their money, either, so they started making all sorts of trouble for me, and of course Maisie's kids started to get out of control as well. So all in all, the transport interchange started to degenerate into the state I'd found it in to begin with.

But by then, to be honest, I had stopped caring about any of that.

Four:
LOST IN A MAZE

The Royal Digest of Affairs and Events: Volume 72 (in the Seventh Year of the Rule of King Matthew)

The Diary of Miss Garamond (Herald)

Greetings, Citizens!

The author finds herself in a state of continuing incredulity at the rapidity of the passage of time. The reader, too, will surely respond with amazement when reminded that a period of no less than six years has elapsed since the accession of King Matthew, and that the King is already entering upon the seventh year of his rule. It is therefore, perhaps, a suitable moment at which to pause and to take stock of the many remark-able developments that, during this brief period, have served collectively to enhance the well-being of every citizen.

Firstly, the streets of our City, at one time reduced to a state that was considered by many to border upon anarchy, are now restored to their former order and decorum. The beggars, vagrants and criminals who at one time constituted a daily menace to law-abiding folk are no longer to be glimpsed, except perhaps in the few remaining untouched corners of the Undertown. The traffic on our highways, once plagued by continual congestion and recurring delays, now flows with a smoothness and a sense of discipline in which our Traffic Patrols may justly take pride. Our walkways and gutters, once a byword for filth and squalor, are now daily swept clean and are at most times free from human and animal refuse and other forms of pollution. The forces of law and order, embodied in the Royal Wolf Boys Militia, hold sway in every quarter, and citizens may now sleep peacefully in their beds, confident that fire, flood, accident, or indeed any other form of emergency will receive prompt and effective attention. Beyond the City walls, the Border campaign continues to be pursued with vigour and persistence, while the constantly expanding network of Royal Highways provides the traveller with swift and secure access to every corner of the Kingdom.

Much credit for these remarkable achievements must, of course, be granted to the Royal Wolf Boys Militia, for whose unfaltering teamwork and discipline the citizen has so many reasons to be grateful. Particular credit is, of course, due to the Leader of the Militia, Master Fang. Indeed, the author has been informed by the King, at the monthly Private Audience, that in recognition of his outstanding achievements, Master Fang is to be granted a place on the Board of Senior Counsellors, and is henceforth to be known by his new title, namely High Master Fang, Director of Internal Affairs. High Master Fang will occupy a newly refurbished suite of offices adjacent to the Throne Room, at which location he will be available to the King at whatsoever time of the day or night his advice might be sought. The author is confident that all Citizens will join their voices to hers in wishing High Master Fang every success in his important new position.

Secondly, in the sphere of communications, every Citizen may now expect to reap an abundance of benefits. The author (modesty almost, but not quite, forbids!) is proud to report that the lavishly illustrated *Royal Digest of Affairs and Events* continues to appear at monthly intervals, and that copies are now available in such abundance that no citizen need ever again find herself in ignorance of the matters of the day. Indeed, such has been the success of *The Digest* within the walls of the City, that plans are now afoot for its distribution, by means of the Royal Highways, to certain of the more important towns in the Provinces and Outlands, whose inhabitants may therefore shortly expect to partake in the benefits which we City folk have for so long enjoyed.

Thirdly, under the leadership of Mister Kevin Considine, Royal Supervisor of Machinery, the

Universal Signal Network continues to expand. Signal
Engines have now been installed in the offices of every
arm of the Royal Administration, and Signal Stations
have been constructed across a network of strategic
locations that spans the Kingdom. Mister Considine
confirms that all incumbents of high office, in no
matter whatsoever corner of the Kingdom they may
be situated, will now be at liberty to enjoy the benefits of instantaneous communication, not only with
the Palace, but also one with another. Further, this
communication will be made not only through auditory and visual channels, but also through the facul-
ties of imagination and sensation. (The author
confesses herself to be quite bewildered by the marvellous technologies deployed to achieve these miracles,
but assures the reader that she and her staff now make
daily use of the Signal Network in the course of their
routine business, and are undergoing some difficulty
in recollecting how affairs were conducted in earlier
times!) In the months to come, Mister Considine
assures me, further enlargements will be made to the
Network, in such a fashion that its availability will
extend not only to organisations in the commercial
field, but also to such members of the private Citizenry
as may wish to furnish themselves therewith.

Sadly, there remains one corner of our City that
has yet to enjoy the benefit of this new era of peace
and security. I refer, of course, to the Transport
Interchange. Travellers who are obliged to avail themselves of this facility will not need to have their atten-

tion drawn to its many shortcomings. The King deeply regrets that, despite his unrelenting efforts to bring some semblance of order to the Interchange, he remains in a continued state of frustration at the appalling mismanagement and misinformation which are daily in evidence there. All Citizens will surely share our sense of outrage, not only at these organisational shortcomings, but also at the blatancy with which bribery, corruption, extortion and prostitution have been permitted to flourish within the boundaries of the Interchange.

It is with a heavy heart that the King now feels it incumbent upon him to inform the Citizenry that the responsibility for these shortcomings lies with a certain Thomas Slater, perhaps better known to the reader by his self-appointed title of Interchange Supervisor. The King declares that his patience with Mister Slater is now exhausted, and that he is no longer disposed to tolerate the many gross malpractices that have flourished under the hand of the said Mister Slater. In view of this, the King has now instructed High Master Fang to take a hand in the matter, and accordingly to issue directions to the Royal Wolf Boys Militia. Citizens can therefore rest assured that swift and decisive action will imminently be taken to bring this troublesome and disruptive individual to justice. Indeed, the present author (for reasons that need not now concern the reader!) will, for one, be overjoyed to witness the spectacle of his downfall and humiliation.

Perhaps the author may be permitted to conclude this month's *Diary* with some reference to matters of a domestic nature. Our Supervisor of Iconography at *The Royal Digest*, Mister Michael Brown, will shortly be bidding us farewell, as it is his wish to concentrate his energies from now onwards upon an exciting new venture.

As readers will doubtless be aware, the Brotherhood of Cartography, after a protracted period of negotiation at the highest level, has at last generously offered to make available for the public benefit the entire contents of its vaults. We refer here, in particular, to the collection of Secret Charts that illustrate, to those able to interpret them, the entire topography of our Kingdom in all its detail. Publication of the Charts is to be by Royal Mandate, and, as readers will recall, an Open Competition has been held with the Mandate offered as reward.

The various submissions for the Competition have now been subject to Royal scrutiny, and it is our happy privilege to announce that the victorious submission was that prepared by Mister Brown, and that our respected colleague has therefore duly been awarded the Mandate.

In consequence, Mister Brown has begged leave to be discharged from his present obligations at *The Digest*. While we shall be most reluctant to part company with a member of our staff whom we hold in such outstanding esteem, we nevertheless have great confidence that our new Supervisor of Iconography,

Mister Norman Loxley, will in due time come to fill the position with equal distinction. We wish both Mister Loxley and Mister Brown every success in their new ventures.

Goodbye, Citizens, and long live King Matthew!

'What became of the interchange after that meeting?'

Well, as I told you, after that meeting at the Palace, I just seemed to lose heart. It must have been four or five years since I took over the interchange, and in that time it had become my whole life. And, unlike some others I could mention, I never had time to make any friends, or to have any social life, or to get married, all I had time for was work and sleep. And it all seemed so unfair. I really believed that I had been doing something useful for the city, something that would win me some recognition, something that would make me a proper member of the community. And then I met Brown and the others, and I saw how well they had done for themselves, and I started to compare their lives with mine, and I knew that I was never going to be able to catch up with them. And that was really when I gave up trying. I suppose I started to think that if I wasn't going to get noticed for doing good, then perhaps I might get noticed if I started doing the opposite.

No, actually that sounds a bit too calculated. I don't think I really did it in any sort of deliberate way, that's just the way it seemed to turn out. I suppose to some people it might have looked as if I'd set out on purpose to cause the disruption, it might even have looked as if I was doing it in a fit of petulance, like a child who can't have what he wants, but no, I really didn't mean it to be like that, at least I don't think I did. As I said before, I just stopped caring, none of it seemed worth the bother any more, so I just sort of gave up.

To begin with, though, nobody else noticed what was happening. The criers still had the schedule of departures, and they just carried on shouting out whatever information was in it. Sometimes I was still there on the tower sitting beside them, and sometimes I wasn't, but they had grown used to that, so at the time I don't suppose they thought anything of it.

But of course the information in the schedule wasn't going to stay accurate for ever, because none of the drivers or carriers were actually employed by me. That meant that it had never been in my power to tell them when they were supposed to come and go, so they always just used to work out their own times. So now and then they might decide to alter what they were doing. It might be just because of the season of the year; or perhaps if a particular destination became popular, then they might start running extra waggons or coaches at odd times.

And, of course, everything depended on the information I got from the drivers, but they had always been quite hard to pin down to anything, probably because they thought I might start asking them for more money, which of course I sometimes did. That meant that the drivers had never really gone out of their way to bump into me. But of course that's how I really earned my money, running after the drivers and finding things out and then making adjustments to the schedule. And chasing after the drivers was tedious and tiring and time-consuming, so once I started to lose heart with the venture, that was the first thing to suffer. That meant that when the drivers decided to change anything they were doing, nobody found out about it. And that meant that they gradually started to lose passengers, and then of course they decided that it was my fault, and so they started to stay out of my way more than ever. I never really understood why they couldn't just have come and found me, then I could have put things right for them, but somehow they just seemed to stop trusting me.

Eventually, a group of drivers did come to see me but, by the time that finally happened, they had started to become very angry. They said that I was ruining their business by giving out the wrong times. Then they said that Maisie's girls were distracting their passengers and making them late, and that the Wolf Boys had started prowling around again and frightening people. And then they said that they weren't going to pay me any more money. Well, that shook me up quite a bit, so I told them that, if they didn't pay me, I would stop them from bringing their vehicles into the interchange, and then they would have to find their business somewhere else. That started them grumbling among themselves, but in they end they went back to work, and I found myself hoping that that would be the end of it.

It wasn't, of course. A few days later, I happened to have found a spare moment to read Miss Garamond's diary in

The Digest, and there was a piece in it about the interchange, and it mentioned me by name, and made me out to be not just incompetent, which was bad enough, but to be some kind of criminal as well. Well, I suppose it was just about possible to interpret things that way, but it had never occurred to me to use words like corruption or bribery, I had only ever tried to earn a living and to make things work the best way I could. I don't mind telling you I was pretty upset by what I read in The Digest, and then, to cap it all, I read that Michael Brown had won the competition to publish the charts. I imagined him and his family, moving to some fancy apartment in the Western Suburb, maybe having their own carriage and domestic servants, and then I thought about myself, and the way my life was going. I had to admit to myself that the interchange seemed to be heading for big trouble, and that pretty soon I'd probably be struggling just to keep the boots on my feet.

This all happened on a Tuesday, I'm not sure why I remember that, but it turned out to be a pretty terrible day for me. Later the same morning, a couple of the kite hands, the ones who used to go round collecting the money from the drivers, came and told me that quite a few of the drivers were refusing to pay, so I told them not to worry, I would go and see the Wolf Boys about keeping those drivers out of the interchange.

So then I thought I had better go and find the Wolf Boys but, as it turned out, I was spared the bother, because, just as I was thinking it over, the Wolf Boys came to me. There was a new Sergeant, his name was Gash, and he was wearing a fancy uniform rather like the one Master Fang had been wearing when I first saw him at the gaol, only without quite so many gold bits on it. Sergeant Gash stepped forward, and the other Wolf Boys, the ones I knew, stood behind him, shuffling their feet and looking a bit shame-faced. I started reaching for my wallet as-usual, but just as I was starting to explain what needed to be done, Sergeant Gash looked at me as if I was a piece of shit, and he said, 'I hope, sir, that you aren't intending to offer me a bribe,' and then he explained that bribery was a criminal offence. Then he went on to say that the interchange was a public place, and that I had no right to stop anyone from coming there and carrying out their lawful business. Then, before I could think of a reply to that, he said, 'I would advise you, sir, to ensure that no other unlawful activities are taking place within this vicinity, because my militiamen will be returning at regular intervals to verify that all your business is being carried out in a correct and proper fashion.' And then he saluted, and they all turned around and left.

Word must have got around among the drivers about our conversation because, pretty soon after that, all the other drivers decided to stop paying me too. Then the collectors came to see me and said that since there wasn't going to be any money to collect, there didn't seem to be much point in their staying, so they all deserted me and went off to find other work.

That wasn't quite the end, though. I was still getting a bit of money from Maisie and her girls, that was from selling The Digest and the other things they did. It was just about enough to pay the criers, not that they had anything much to shout about by then, but then of course I couldn't *afford to pay the beggars who fetched the stones for the road-ways, so pretty soon the mud started to creep back again. When that happened, the errand boys went off to look for the waterproof boots, but the boots turned out to have been thrown away because nobody thought we'd need them again.*

The next time I saw Maisie, she wouldn't look at me, so then I knew that something else was the matter. She didn't really want to talk to me, but in the end she said that Sergeant Gash had been to see her, and he had told her that she mustn't give me any more money because it was unlawful for anyone to live off immoral earnings, and in any case prostitution could no longer be tolerated in a public place. I asked Maisie what her girls were going to do, and she looked even more embarrassed, and finally she said that the Sergeant had offered to find them all respectable work at the barracks, and then she started to cry, and she said, 'I'm sorry, Mister Slater, we all really liked it here with you, but us girls have got to make a living.' And then she took my hand for a moment, and then she was gone, and I knew that this was going to be the end of my career at the interchange.

Soon after that, I had to tell the criers that I couldn't pay them any more, and of course they deserted me as well, so then there was just me. I didn't have the voice for shout-ing out messages, so all I could do was to sit at the top of my observation tower and look on while everything at the interchange slowly fell apart. The weather had been very wet that year, and without the supply of fresh stones, the road-ways started to disintegrate almost at once. Then the waggons started to get bogged down in the mud again, and all the signposts collapsed, so nobody could work out where to go, only now, of course, there was nobody there to help them. Meanwhile, the drivers were starting to look for any dry spots where they could still park their waggons, and that meant that everyone was blocking everyone else's way again, and before long nobody would have known that I'd ever been there.

In the end, the only thing left was the tower. I had to give up my apartment at Serendipity Court, of course, I couldn't pay the rent any more, and the cabin on top of the tower was the only place I had. So one day I fetched all my things from the apartment, not that I really had much, just my pack with the bits and pieces from the Academy. And I ended up living in the cabin, looking down on the ruins of everything I'd done. It was a sad time, but then I remembered that I did have one thing that might make me feel better.

It was the chain, of course. It was still there at the bottom of my pack, underneath Michael Brown's drawings. I couldn't bear to look at the drawings but, although I hadn't thought about the chain for quite a few years, I found that, as I let the links run through my fingers, I could still draw some strength from it. So then I got out the padlocks, and I chained myself to one of the uprights of the tower. It was thick and rounded, it reminded me a bit of the old table leg in my father's kitchen, and after that I felt quite safe while I sat there watching the rain and the mud and waiting for whatever was going to happen.

Once again, I didn't have to wait for long. The first thing that happened was that the drivers all pulled their waggons to one side, to make a clear path across the middle of the interchange. And, soon after that, the Wolf Boys arrived in force. I heard them before I saw them, and what I heard was a sort of rhythmic chanting. I couldn't make out the words at first, because of the noise of the rain, but eventually I could hear that they were chanting just one word, repeating it over and over. Then, at last, I realised that they were chanting, 'Heave! Heave! Heave! Heave!'

Then they appeared. There must have been a couple of score of them at least, and they were marching in two long rows, and they were pulling a sledge, and in the sledge stood High Master Fang and Sergeant Gash, brandishing whips and looking very self-important while the others pulled them along. I suppose they had chosen the sledge because it was about the only vehicle that stood a chance of making any headway across the mud, at any rate they were coming towards me with quite a turn of speed, and when they arrived at the foot of the tower, High Master Fang called up to me, 'Thomas Slater, I have a warrant for your arrest. You are charged with giving and taking bribes, misuse of public space, subverting the King's will, theft of building materials, proffering false information to the citizenry, extortion, and subsisting on the earnings of prostitutes. Are you prepared to give yourself up and come with us peacefully?'

I wasn't going to answer that, so I just checked that the padlocks on my chain were secure, and then I threw the keys out into the rain, and I heard them splash down somewhere in front of the tower. High Master Fang glanced at Sergeant Gash then, and the Sergeant sent six of the troopers to search for the keys, I was quite amused to see them go down on their hands and knees in all that mud and water. Then Fang shouted at the rest of them to storm the tower.

I watched them from above. Most of them were bare-footed, and the ones who still had boots took them off and threw them away, and then about twenty of them started to swarm up the tower in their bare feet, using their toenails to cling on, and shouting and roaring as they came. Of course, I had never designed the tower to take that much weight, and I suppose that the mud had never made an ideal foundation, and the rain must have weakened it fatally, because I suddenly realised that the whole structure was beginning slowly to keel over sideways. I clung to the upper side as it came down, but quite a few of the Wolf Boys finished up underneath it, and I suppose that made another crime to add to my list of charges.

When the structure hit the ground it split apart with a tremendous creaking, crashing noise, and I was left clinging to what was left of the cabin, while the surviving Wolf Boys struggled to extricate themselves from the quagmire. I noticed that they seemed quite happy to use the bodies of their comrades as stepping stones.

There was no point in trying to resist arrest, of course, there were still far too many of them, and I was attached by my chain to the remains of one of the uprights, so they just lifted me up and turned me over a few times so that the chain was wrapped around me and I couldn't move. Then they hacked away the remains of the timber, and they threw me onto their sledge. I was soaking wet by then, and freezing cold, and I couldn't really see what they were doing, I could just hear the noise of their cheering and the sound *of the rain. The last thing I can remember was the face of High Master Fang, leering down at me and smiling in an evil sort of way. And at that point I think I must have passed out.*

Tower Mansions

When he discovered that he had won the competition, Rusty realised, with some misgivings, that it would be necessary for him to re-establish contact with the Academy of Cartography. The Director of the Academy had conceded, after protracted negotiations, that copies could be made of the Charts, but she remained adamant that nothing was, in any circumstances, to be removed from her vaults.

Rusty eventually decided that, for the time being, he would need to divide his week between the city and the Academy. Each Monday, therefore, he found himself braving the pandemonium of the transport interchange, suffering the discomfort of the carrier's waggon, and eventually finding his way to the outlying town where the Academy was situated. The Director and her staff received him with minimal civility, but he was never made to feel at ease there. Reluctant, therefore, to spend his nights in the chilly atmosphere of the Academy's guest wing, he had managed to rent a room in the town from his old landlady, Mrs Roberts. After sleeping off the sprains and bruises incurred on the journey, he would spend each Tuesday and Wednesday, under the suspicious eye of the Academy Librarian, painstakingly copying the charts section by section onto fresh parchment. On the Thursday morning, he would return to the city.

On the Friday, he would take a brisk walk down the North Way and along the ruined section of the old city wall, until he arrived at the new development of commercial properties wherein the headquarters of Michael Brown Publications was situated. An enterprising builder had carried out some renovation work on a length of the old wall, repairing the worst of the dilapidations, and creating half a dozen rough-and-ready spaces for new offices and warehouses. On the strength of the Royal Mandate, Rusty had managed to raise a deposit on one of these, and it was here that he was in the process of establishing his organisation. The office was situated opposite the high wall that surrounded the city docks, and had a pleasant outlook across a patch of rough grass where a herd of wild goats could sometimes be seen grazing peacefully in the distance.

At the start of the Friday work period, Rusty would have his weekly conference with his assistant Charlotte, who was for the time being his only member of staff. Over mugs of scalding instant coffee, Charlotte would explain to Rusty whatever problems she might be facing with painters or builders or sign-writers, show him any significant items from the week's mail and then, most importantly, inform him of any current difficulties with the copying engine. This crucial device had been acquired second-hand from the Herald's Office, where it had recently been declared surplus to requirements. Although it still exhibited a number of irritating faults, Rusty was confident that it could in due course be rendered capable of producing multiple copies of the charts that would be suitable for sale to the public.

Content that affairs were proceeding satisfactorily at headquarters, he would then spend the next few hours walking the streets of the city, following a seemingly never-ending itinerary of visits to booksellers and other shopkeepers who he hoped would agree to serve as retail outlets for his product.

And, while he walked, Rusty kept his eyes open, and he made notes.

Sometimes, the charts that he was copying at the Academy did not quite seem to convey to him the real essence of the places they purported to depict. So, although it did not come strictly within the terms of the Mandate, Rusty often discovered that he needed to add a few little touches of his own here or there. Sometimes he would find himself diving into an alleyway or courtyard, taking in an unexpected view of some street or building. Sometimes he would make an impulsive detour, exploring the networks of lanes that wove between the thoroughfares. Sometimes he would stand in the middle of a road gazing upwards, and sometimes he would climb to the top of a tower or a spire and peer downwards. During these few quiet hours, Rusty found that he could forget the problems of his office, could forget the problems of his family, could wander undisturbed through the streets and the courts and the alleys, aware for the moment of nothing but the city around him.

When he returned to his headquarters at the end of the day, he would retire to his drawing office on the top floor, and there, seated alone at his easel in the fading light, he would spend the remainder of the work period making his subtle alterations to the charts, adding the little individual details without which he did not feel ready to consign them to the ministrations of Charlotte and the copying engine. After that, he would go home to Shrubbery House, where he would spend the rest of the weekend with his family.

The first chart to go on sale, which had been known as *Sheet 1*, had depicted the central area of the city. This included the Palace, the Ring Road, the Market, and the Main Thoroughfare as far south as the Crier's Rest. *Sheet 1* had been followed by *Sheet 2*, which showed the Administrative Area, then *Sheet 3*, which showed the Commercial District, and then *Sheet 4*, which showed the Industrial Area. Rusty was planning to follow these with *Sheet 6* (the Western Suburb), and *Sheet 7* (the Docks, North Estates and Transport Interchange). Plans for *Sheet 5* (the Undertown) were in temporary abeyance, owing to the absence of up-to-date information on the area, this being on account of the extensive demolition work that had been taking place there in recent years.

Initially, sales of the charts were slow. As it turned out, this was because the citizenry lacked the necessary cartographical knowledge to interpret the information contained on them. However, with reluctant assistance from the Academy, this problem was eventually remedied by the provision of short training courses, which were offered free of charge to all purchasers. This, of course, constituted an unforeseen expense, as a result of which Michael Brown Publications continued to operate at a loss for some time longer than its proprietor had anticipated. However, after little more than a year, sales had increased to a healthy level, Charlotte found herself in charge of an expanding group of staff, and the Brown family was at last able to move into a four-bedroomed apartment in the coveted Western Suburb.

'It's a shame we couldn't afford a place with an elevator,' Eileen complained. She had just returned from a shopping expedition, and was slumped in her flower-patterned armchair, resting her feet after climbing the eight flights of stairs.

'I carried a parcel!' boasted Ashleigh. 'I carried a parcel in one hand and Mister Woofie in the other hand! Why didn't Max carry a parcel?'

'Max is only little,' explained Eileen, who had had to carry her son up most of the stairs. 'He can't climb all the way yet.'

Rusty, seated at the table, looked up abstractedly from the chart he had been studying.

'There used to be an elevator here once upon a time, didn't you know? The caretaker told me all about it. It was one of the old pony-driven ones, but when the elevator captain retired, they couldn't find anyone to take over from him. The shaft's still there, but all the doors are kept locked up now, and they've taken everyone's keys back. But look, Eileen, we've been through all this. Tower Mansions was the best we could afford. I know it's not the most up-to-date, and I know it's getting a bit run-down. But it is in the Western Suburb, like you wanted. And we've got the view, as well. Look at that sky, it's terrific tonight.'

Rising from his chair, Rusty crossed over to the window. There, bathed in the warm evening light, the whole of the city offered itself up to him. His viewpoint was different now from that at Serendipity Court, which had faced south, and was certainly an improvement over that at Shrubbery House, which had in fact had no view at all. The living room at Tower Mansions faced south-east, and the vista now extended from the docks, on Rusty's extreme left, to the main gatehouse of the city, on his extreme right. Beneath him stretched the broad rectangle of somewhat unkempt lawn that offered private recreation and enjoyment to the residents of Tower Mansions. Beyond the lawn glittered the gilded spires and turrets of the Western Suburb, between which the rippling surface of the river was here and there visible. And beyond the river, dominating the horizon, loomed the angular silhouette of the Palace, lines of signal kites fluttering busily from its battlements. A sense of calm stole over Rusty as he surveyed his realm.

'. . . I'll come and look in a minute,' Eileen was saying. 'Can you put the kettle on if you're going in the kitchen?'

'Coming,' replied Rusty, catapulted back to earth by this reminder of domestic affairs. 'Have you got anything for the children's tea?'

A couple of hours later, Rusty and Eileen were seated in their armchairs on either side of the fireplace. From the centre of the mantelpiece, the scowling portrait of Eileen's father dominated the room. Rusty as usual was doing his best to ignore it, staring out of the window as the last curls of light faded from the sky. Ashleigh and Max had been put to bed, and the remains of the evening meal still awaited attention in the kitchen.

'Can we afford a holiday this year?' Eileen wondered.

Knitting his brows, Rusty made a mental calculation.

'I don't know,' he said finally. 'But Gideon and Peg and the kids should be passing this way in a couple of weeks. Why don't we join them for a few days on the road, like we did last year? Only if you want to, of course,' he added, sensing Eileen's lack of enthusiasm for this suggestion.

'Oh, I'm not sure, Rusty,' came the reply. 'It does get a bit crowded in that waggon, and Megan and Liam are getting quite big now. And I don't think Peg always keeps it very clean in there. And it's not much fun if it rains. And, well, they're . . . you know . . .'

'Wanderers?'

'Sorry, that must sound awful, but . . . ' There was an uneasy silence between the two of them. After a few moments, another thought seemed to come to Eileen. 'Anyway, I suppose I really ought to go and see Daddy again. I'm afraid he's not getting any younger. And he does like to see his grandchildren.'

'Why not?' agreed Rusty, in a carefully neutral tone. 'But I don't need to come with you, do I? There's plenty for me to do at the office.' Eileen's father had retained all of his early hostility towards his son-in-law, and Rusty had long since ceased to accompany his wife on her visits.

'No, I suppose not. I just wish it was easier to keep in touch with him. I can really only get up there once or twice a year, and the letters seem to take for ever to arrive.'

An idea came to Rusty.

'Tell you what. Why don't we think about getting one of those signal engines? You could get in touch with him any time if we had one of those. Isn't there a signal station near the village now?'

'I've never used one,' replied Eileen doubtfully. 'Is it difficult? And we'd have to get two, wouldn't we? One for us and one for him. How could we afford that at the moment?'

'They're making small ones now. Ones that you can use at home.' Rusty was warming to the notion.

'We could put the kites up on the roof – it would be a good position for them. Maybe share the cost with some of the neighbours. And I could probably get the equipment through the company; it would be quite useful for work, actually. Just think, you could be in touch with your father any time you wanted. And in touch with anyone else who had an engine.'

'Yes. Perhaps we ought to think about it.' Eileen was half persuaded. 'We'd be the first people at Tower Mansions to have one. Now that would be something, wouldn't it?'

'How did they punish you?'

It was all very confusing to begin with. They locked me up, of course, I think I must have spent quite a long while in that cell, and various people came in to see me. Some of them wanted to ask questions, some of them brought me food and, now and again, a couple of Wolf Boys would drop by to give me a beating. It made me feel quite at home when they did that, rather like the old times, I suppose. That was about the only homely touch, though. They even took away my pack with all my things in it, so I didn't have my chain with me. I made a bit of a fuss when that happened, so then they had to manacle me to the wall. Their chain was a strange one, though, it was made of some sort of smooth, shiny, bluish-coloured metal, and it didn't feel right at all.

I didn't have any visits from friends or family, mainly I suppose because I didn't have any friends or family. Well, there was my father, Geoffrey, of course, but I don't suppose he would have come, even if he'd known I was there. I've got an idea that Maisie came in once, but I didn't want to talk to her, I think I must have said something to upset her, because I can remember her turning around suddenly and leaving the room, and I don't think she ever came back again.

Eventually, there was some kind of trial. It was a pretty one-sided affair, naturally. High Master Fang was in charge of the proceedings, he was sitting at some sort of raised desk with a big wolf's-head design on the wall behind him, and he interrogated a whole series of witnesses. There were a couple of waggon drivers who said that I had demanded money from them and threatened to expel them from the interchange when they wouldn't pay. Then there were some passengers who said that they'd been given wrong information, and some of Maisie's girls who said I'd extorted money from them. Sergeant Gash made an appearance, and he said that I'd offered him a bribe, then they produced one of my beggars who said that I'd sent him to steal timber and stones from the Undertown. Finally, Kevin Considine appeared, looking even more pale and shaky than ever, and he said that I'd refused to let my tower become a part of his Signal Network, and that this was in defiance of the wishes of the King.

After all that, High Master Fang turned to me, almost as an afterthought, and asked if I had anything to say. Well, I hadn't had a chance to prepare myself for that, and I hadn't had any help from anyone, and of course I was still feeling pretty confused and disorientated from the beatings,

so in the end I just repeated what I had said to the High
Master when he'd arrested me. I said that I was trying to
make a living the best way I could, and that I really thought
that I had been doing some good for the city. That last bit
was definitely a mistake, it produced a huge roar of laughter from everyone in the room, and when it died down the
High Master said, 'I don't think we need to hear any more
from the prisoner,' and then he signalled to the guards and
they took me away.

Then, for a while, I was back in the same cell getting
the same food and the same beatings, but at least they stopped
sending people in to ask me questions. I don't know quite
what I did to pass the time. I would have liked to have
taken some exercise, maybe walked up and down the cell,
but of course I was still chained to the wall with their funny
blue chain. Sometimes I thought about my father, and sometimes I thought about Michael Brown, but it was just the
same thoughts over and over, so in the end I think I must
have switched the thoughts off, because I just seemed to exist
without thinking of anything much.

I don't know how long I spent like that but one day,
quite suddenly, they moved me. A couple of Wolf Boys came
into the cell, I thought it was just going to be the usual
Wednesday beating, but they undid the padlocks and dragged
me out into the yard. That was a bit of a shock, because I
hadn't seen daylight since they'd arrested me, and my eyes
couldn't make the adjustment to begin with, all I could see
was blinding light, I had to shut my eyelids, but I could feel
myself being manhandled and thrown into another confined
space. I thought it was another cell at first, but when it

started bumping up and down, I realised that they'd put me in a waggon and I was being taken somewhere with a few other prisoners. After a while I found I could see again, and I called out to the driver to tell me where we were going, but he only said, 'You'll know soon enough.'

Well, several hours later, the waggon came to a halt in front of a huge pair of gates, and we were brought out again, and it turned out to be in some place bang in the middle of nowhere, there was rough country all around, with some purple-coloured weed growing all over it, and blue hills in the distance. Inside the gates was a big compound with a high wall all around it, I suppose it must have been some different kind of prison, but this time they didn't lock us up in cells, we were allowed to sleep in a dormitory, and we could wander about inside the compound if we wanted to.

The next day, several of us were taken to a low building in one corner of the compound. The Wolf Boys were in charge, of course, but they seemed nicer than the city Wolf Boys, not quite so brutal, and their uniforms looked cleaner. A sergeant instructor called Maggot explained that we were to be taught an honest trade, and that we would be released when we had proved that we were capable of securing permanent employment. I wasn't sure how I was going to secure any employment while I was still in prison but, apart from that, it sounded like quite a good idea.

The honest trade that Sergeant Instructor Maggot had in mind for us was that of Signal Engine Technician. Maggot explained to us all about the network of signal engines that was being installed across the land, and how important it was going to be in the future. Then he said that if we could manage to learn how the equipment worked, we might eventually find respectable work operating and maintaining it. Maggot seemed a kindly man, he was a bit older than the other Wolf Boys, he spoke more slowly, and his voice had a different accent from the city folk's. He went on to say that the training was not compulsory, we were free to return to our cells in the city gaol if we so wished.

I don't think anybody had to think about this for very long. Of course, the last time I had come across the Signal Network, I had tried to stand my ground against it, but that hadn't done me much good, so I decided that this time it might make more sense to go along with it and see what it had to offer me.

The training began straight away. There were six signal engines installed in the room, and Maggot was going to be our teacher. He was a good teacher, actually, very patient and thorough. At times I found that he took things a bit too slowly for me, but it seemed to suit the other prisoners, so I didn't say anything.

I must have spent a year or more at that place, dismantling the engines and reassembling them, trying to get all those tiny little parts to fit together and work the way they were supposed to. I think I said earlier that I was never much good at mechanical things, so I never really felt completely comfortable with the work, but I managed just about well enough to pass the tests in the end. Secretly, though, I was more interested in some of the things I saw when I put on the headphones and looked down the eyepieces, but Maggot didn't encourage that sort of curiosity. He explained, in his patient way, that we were being trained to understand the machinery, and that we would have plenty of time to explore the Network when we were released. But I had seen one or two things that I thought were very interesting indeed, and I made a mental note to have another look at them one day when I got the chance.

At the end of the training, we were handed our certificates, and Maggot explained that we were now to be transferred to another establishment but, this time, it would be possible for potential employers to visit us and talk to us, and that was how we would be able to find honest employment. Then Maggot wished us all luck and waved us goodbye, and then, once again, we were herded into closed waggons.

The new establishment turned out to be back in the city again, and it was situated at the northern tip of the Commercial District, just at the end of the Ring Road. As soon as we arrived, I realised that it was none other than the old City Menagerie. Apparently one of the King's ancestors had developed a passing interest in wild animals and, for a brief period, the menagerie had flourished as one of the great attractions of the city. Eventually, though, its owner had lost interest in it, the animals had died one by one and had not been replaced, and the cages had been left empty, until the City Rehabilitation Services decided that there was another use they could be put to.

We were each allowed to choose our own cage. Every cage bore some marks of the character of its former occupant, and it was interesting to see how my fellow prisoners each selected a cage that more or less suited them. There were cages fitted *with swings and branches, which had presumably housed apes or some other climbing creatures. There were cages with pools for swimming creatures – sea lions, perhaps. Then there were cages with tunnels for burrowing creatures, and wide, empty roofless cages for basking creatures. The cage that I chose for myself was furnished with a sort of obstacle course. There was a tree stump, a truncated section of wall, and a ditch. The former tenant had clearly evolved a particular routine for negotiating these features, for he had left behind him a broad, amoeba-shaped pathway, around which he had presumably spent his days running in never-ending circles.*

The menagerie had been reopened to the public and renamed the Employment Market, and now people could wander in to stare at us, myself and my climbing, basking, burrowing and swimming colleagues. Some of the visitors threw food, some of them laughed and pointed, but none of them seemed particularly interested in offering employment to any of us. Soon, I stopped noticing them, stopped putting on any sort of display, and instead I turned my attention to the fixtures within my cage.

I decided that the three objects – the tree stump, the wall, and the ditch – offered more possibilities than were immediately suggested by the deeply rutted track left behind by my predecessor. I therefore set myself the task of discovering how many possible ways there might be of circumnavigating my cage, both clockwise and anticlockwise, and for many months this became the sole focus of my life. Sometimes I would clamber over the stump before crawling through the ditch, and sometimes I would crawl through the ditch before clambering over the stump. Occasionally I would vary my routine by scampering around the wall before I clambered over the stump, or crawling through the ditch after I scampered round the wall. I no longer paid any attention to the world beyond the bars or to the people out there. When food was thrown to me, I ate. And when I grew weary, I slept.

I dare say things would have continued in this fashion indefinitely, but one day, just as I was waking up from a nap, I was surprised to hear a voice calling out to me. The voice did not belong to anyone I knew, it had a strange, soft sort of accent, and at first I could not work out why any stranger might want to take an interest in me. I even began to wonder whether I had been dreaming, because I had come across tales of prisoners who imagined that they heard voices but, when I looked up, I realised that there really was somebody there. The owner of the voice was an old lady, a tall old lady with grey hair and spectacles, and she was dressed in some kind of long robe. And it was this old lady who turned out to be my rescuer.

The Six Arches

Arriving at the Palace one Thursday morning, Veronique inserted her token as usual into the slot on the admissions engine, waited for the whirr and click of the machinery, then made her way through the gate, across the courtyard, up several flights of stairs, and across the roof to the Administrative Centre. During her years as Senior Clown in the Jester's Department, Veronique had approached her work in a surprisingly disciplined fashion and, in her new role as Senior Administrator, she had continued to operate in the same manner. She had fallen into the habit of arriving at the Administrative Centre precisely fifteen minutes before the start of business, she could always be relied upon to be at her post during the hours of business, she never permitted her refreshment breaks and rest periods to exceed the stipulated duration, and she made a particular point of leaving everything tidy and switching off all the lights when she departed at night.

Veronique was almost always the first to arrive at the Centre and the last to leave, and it was therefore with some surprise, this particular Thursday, that she noticed the narrow band of light that glowed under the door of Kevin Considine's office. She could recall odd occasions on which Master Considine had stopped behind late but, until now, he had always been most punctilious about switching off his lights.

Frowning, Veronique threaded her way between the rows of desks until she arrived at her own place, where she deposited the large handbag that contained her knitting, her sandwiches, her cigars, three large flasks of milk and various other odds and ends. Then she powered up her administrative engine, fished the cigars and the milk out of her bag, and made her way over to the corner where the coffee engine was situated. Muttering under her breath, she collected up the litter of dirty mugs that had accumulated the previous day, lined the milk flasks up on the shelf, and then threw the large circuit-breaker that controlled the power. Once she had had her first mug of coffee and her first smoke of the day, her brain would be clearer and she would be able to attend to whatever the morning might hold for her. She lit a cigar, inhaled deeply, coughed a couple of times, and waited for the coffee engine to deliver its morning offering.

While the machinery roared and spluttered and hissed into life, Veronique's gaze was drawn once more to the strip of light that glowed under Mister Considine's door. Weighing up various possible courses of action, she eventually decided that it might on the whole be sensible to check whether Mister Considine had, in fact, arrived early in the office (which seemed unlikely) and, if this was not the case, to go in and switch off the light. She crossed over to the door and pushed it open.

Inside, she was astonished to discover Mister Considine slumped across his desk, fast asleep and snoring softly. He was wearing nothing apart from a rather grubby-looking pair of briefs, and the remainder of his clothing was scattered randomly across the floor of the room. With a sharp intake of breath, Veronique stepped over to his slumbering form.

'Mister Considine? Kevvy boy?' Prodding him cautiously, she was startled to notice that his back and shoulders were crisscrossed with scratches, some of them oozing drops of blood.

After a moment, he lifted his head and stared at her blearily.

'Veronique? What are you doing here? What time is it?'

'Time for work,' replied Veronique. 'It's Thursday morning. What the devil has the old Supervisor of Machinery been getting up to? No monkey business, I hope! Been in the office all night?'

Kevin sat up, struggling to collect his thoughts.

'Oh yes,' he said finally. 'Yes, I had to stop on. All sorts of problems with the Signal Network. Can't afford to fall behind schedule, all very urgent. Must have dozed off. Sorry if I startled you.' He rose shakily to his feet and started to collect up his scattered clothing. Veronique eyed him warily, reluctantly fascinated by the state of his underwear.

'Well, you're a big lad now, so I suppose you know what you're doing. But I reckon you'd get a better night's kip if you went home to bed. Want a coffee?'

Propped against a filing cabinet, Kevin was having some difficulty negotiating his way into his trousers.

'Yes, good idea, Vero, thanks.' There was an uneasy pause, while they both considered how best to terminate the encounter.

'Best not mention this to the others,' said Kevin finally.

'Mum's the word, then,' agreed Veronique. 'Milk and sugar?'

That day turned out to be a tiresome one for Kevin. What he wanted to do more than anything else was to connect up the signal engine and spend some more time with his new friend Lee, but his intuition suggested that it would be foolhardy to attempt this during the hours of business.

Listlessly, he shuffled through the papers on his desk. There was an ever-growing pile of correspondence awaiting his attention. He glanced at a document entitled *Universal Signal Network: Progress Report*. Despite what he had said to Veronique, the expansion of the Signal Network was in fact proceeding on schedule, and Signal Stations were now in the process of construction across an extended web of strategic sites that spanned the length and breadth of the Land. He tossed the report aside without troubling himself with any of its details. Later on that morning, Kevin was due to attend the monthly congress of Administrative Supervisors which, he knew from tedious experience, was certain to be time-consuming and unproductive. And there were continuing difficulties with the administrative engines in many of the offices, which would be guaranteed to swallow up whatever spare time he might have had during the rest of the day.

Kevin's eyesight and hearing, and his senses of touch and taste and smell, were still throbbing and reeling and dissolving and overbalancing from the events, real or imaginary, of the night before. Nevertheless, with the assistance of Veronique's coffee, he more or less managed to drag himself through the humdrum business of the day without incurring any undue suspicion from anyone. Kevin was uncertain to what extent he could trust Veronique to hold her tongue but, after some thought, he came to the conclusion that she had actually seen no evidence to indicate that he had done anything more untoward than spend one night asleep at his desk.

Eventually the work period drew to its weary close. The overhead lights were dimmed and, one by one, the working areas fell into darkness as their occupants extinguished their writing engines and desk lights. Soon, only Veronique remained in the Administrative Centre — as far as she knew. In his darkened office, Kevin watched through the crack of the door as she gathered up her numerous belongings and de-powered the coffee engine. Each minute felt like an hour as she made her methodical way over to the exit door. Kevin seethed with impatience as she hesitated with her hand on the lock. Finally, with a shrug, she took her leave for the night.

For another few minutes Kevin forced himself to remain motionless, willed himself to wait until the sound of her departing footsteps had faded away to nothing. At last, satisfied that the coast was clear, he stepped out into the darkness, fumbled his way between the rows of desks, and made his precarious descent to the laboratory.

For a few moments, he stood irresolute, uncertain whether to continue with his experiment, unable for a moment to rid himself of the nagging image of Veronique's suspicious expression. Then, looking down at his hands, he noticed that they were trembling rather more than usual, and he knew that he had no choice.

Kevin stepped forward and powered up the Empathy Engine.

'Left a bit . . . Lower . . . Lower . . . Yes, that's it . . . Go on, harder . . . Yes . . .'

Lee's long, supple legs were entwined around the upper part of Kevin's body, and she was scratching his back with her long, curved toenails. For several minutes she continued with this while Kevin moaned in satisfaction. Then, abruptly, she disentangled herself, sprang upwards from the bed, caught hold of the trapeze and vaulted nimbly into a sitting position.

'What are you doing, Lee?' Kevin mumbled peevishly. 'Come back to bed.'

'I'm starting to feel restless, Kevin. It happens to me from time to time.' She swung downwards, hanging by her knees, her black hair brushing lightly against Kevin's chest. *'You're having a nice time with me, aren't you, Kevin? And there's lots more things we can do later on. But just now, Kevin, just now there's something I want you to do for me. You don't mind doing something for me, Kevin, do you?'*

'No, I suppose not.' Kevin rolled to one side, sat up, and started to untangle the black satin sheets from around his legs. 'I mean, of course not. What did you have in mind?'

Lee righted herself on the trapeze, then dropped lightly down to sit beside him. Kevin noticed, with some bewilderment, that in the course of this manoeuvre she had managed to exchange her black baby-doll pyjamas for a black tracksuit and running shoes.

'The arches, Kevin.' She sketched a broad arc with her long nails to indicate the six rounded arches that divided the six candle-studded walls of the room. Through each archway, they could see only blackness, their gaze occluded by the surrounding glow of the candles. 'I want to see what's through the arches. But I can't go there on my own. I need you to take me there, Kevin. Will you do that for me?' Her pale face had an imploring look.

'Well, I suppose one of them must lead to the black room, the room where I found you.' Surveying the arches, Kevin realised that, from his present perspective, they all looked identical. 'But, actually, I'm not sure which one it was. Can't you just go and look? I mean, why do you need me to help you?'

'This is your room, Kevin — your room, not mine. Don't you remember, you made it for me? It came from your imagination. And whatever is through the arches, well, that will come from your imagination, too. And Kevin —' suddenly he detected a catch in her voice '— I can't go there without you. When you're not here —' she started to sob '— I can't do anything. I can't move. I can't speak. It's almost as if I don't exist. It's almost as if, when you're not here, I'm not here either.'

Awkwardly, Kevin took her in his arms. She seemed suddenly smaller and frailer than before.

'I'm sorry, Lee. I hadn't thought, I didn't realise . . . Of course I'll take you. Come on, dry your eyes. Now, which arch shall we go through first?'

Bounding up, energised again, she pointed a long, red fingernail. Kevin rose to join her, noticing in passing that he was now wearing a tracksuit identical to hers. Together, they stepped forward, through the yellow glare of the candles. Beyond, they found themselves in a long, straight, featureless corridor that extended ahead of them to a distant vanishing point.

'*Come on!*'

Suddenly, Lee began to run, and Kevin, who did not usually take much exercise, found that he was struggling to keep pace with her. A stitch had started to rake at his side when, unexpectedly, they arrived at a short flight of steps, and found themselves tumbling down head over heels to land in an undignified tangle on a polished oak floor.

As they sat up and started to straighten themselves out, Kevin felt a sudden swell of nausea. For a moment he thought that this must be the result of their fall, but then he realised that the floor itself was swaying gently to and fro. Looking around him, he discovered that he was now in an eight-sided room. This time, the illumination was provided by a large oil lamp that hung on brass chains from the centre of the ceiling, its sickly aroma reinforcing his feeling of queasiness. The ceiling was low and, like the walls and floor, was fashioned of polished oak boards. As before, each wall of the room had an archway at its centre but, this time, each archway was flanked by a pair of round, brass-edged portholes. For an instant, Kevin had the uncomfortable sensation that eyes were watching him through the thick glass.

'*Are we on a ship?*' Lee scrambled up the wall to peer through a porthole. '*There's water outside.*'

'It certainly looks that way. And I'm not a very good sailor. Can we go back?'

But of course every one of the arches looked the same, and Kevin, in his disorientated state, could no longer be certain by which arch they had entered. Lee, though, had already chosen her favoured exit, and was poised at the threshold, awaiting his permission to proceed.

This time, the corridor sloped steeply uphill. Kevin was soon panting, but then Lee reached out for his hand, and it felt almost as though she were pulling him along. His feet were hardly touching the ground, and he could feel the wind streaming through his hair. Then they were squeezing through a narrow gap . . .

. . . And they found themselves in a dimly lit space surrounded on all sides by tall stacks of crates, cardboard boxes and packing cases. The air was musty with the smell of damp wood and sawdust. From a gap between two stacks, Kevin could hear Lee coughing wheezily.

'*I don't like it here, Kevin. I can't breathe. Let's try somewhere else.*'

They managed to locate an exit, squeezed their way though, and soon found themselves crawling on their hands and knees along a low, narrow tunnel. The further they crawled, the narrower the tunnel became. They were making slow progress now and, as they inched their way forward, Kevin became aware that the light was getting, not exactly brighter, but somehow paler, more diffuse. With a shock, he noticed that he could see the detail of the tunnel walls through Lee's body. Soon, her translucent form was reduced to little more than a faint outline.

'There's nothing here.' Her voice was faint, just a whisper. 'We'll have to go back, Kevin. There's nothing in front of us.'

Awkwardly, Kevin managed to twist himself around and then, painfully, he helped Lee to twist herself around. Her body was almost weightless now, and her limbs seemed hardly capable of independent movement. Slowly, inch by inch, they made their way back down the tunnel, arriving eventually at a place that they had somehow failed to notice earlier, a blank, white, neutral space from which passageways radiated in all directions like the spokes of a wheel. In the background they could hear a faint humming noise that sounded quietly reassuring.

Exhausted, they slumped down side by side. The floor, they discovered, was cool and soft and comfortable. The air seemed fresher now, and they could feel the fatal weakness ebbing away from them.

'What are all these places?' Kevin murmured. 'I've lost my sense of direction. How do we get back to where we started?'

'I think it's all right now.' Lee was sounding a little

stronger, a little more confident. *'We can go to sleep here, Kevin. Just go to sleep, and when you wake up, I think you'll be at home again.'* Her voice, regaining its old seductiveness, was gently lulling him. *'And I'll see you again next time you come.'* She wriggled closer to him, wound her arms and legs around his body.

'Goodnight, Kevin.'

He could no longer keep his eyes open.

'Goodnight, Lee.'

'So how did the old lady help you to escape?'

Well, when I heard her call me I looked up. 'Young man?' she said, and that surprised me, because I hadn't thought of myself as young for some time. I could see that she was standing right up close to the bars of my cage, and she was staring at me very intently, as if she was really interested in what I was doing. She was quite an unusual-looking person, she was tall and thin, very upright, and she was wearing some kind of long robe. Her hair was long and grey, and she wore it in plaits, wound tightly around her head, and she had small, gold-rimmed spectacles. It was a while since I'd had a conversation with anyone, so I just looked back at her, I didn't reply straight away. Then she said 'Young man?' again, so I got up and went over to where she was standing.

'Young man,' she said, 'I've been looking at you for some time, and I've been watching the way you negotiate

the various obstacles in your cage.' I wasn't sure what to say to that, I think in the end I said that it helped to pass the time, and that I didn't have much else to keep me occupied. So then she explained that she came from some kind of place where they helped people who'd lost their sense of direction, and she asked me if I would like to go there with her. I started to explain that I had been trained as a Signal Engine Technician, and she said yes, that might be useful too, and then she went off to get the guard. I wondered whether she was going to come back, but pretty soon she did. She had the guard with her, he had a big bunch of keys in one hand and, to my amazement, he opened up the cage. Best of all, he had something in his other hand that I hadn't noticed to begin with. It was my pack with all my old things in it, the Wolf Boys must have kept it for me the whole time I was locked up. And then he told me that I was free to go.

The old lady took me with her to where her carriage was waiting, and in a few minutes we were heading out through the west gate of the city, over the river and out by the Western Suburb. But I hardly bothered to look out of the window, the only thing I wanted to do was to open up my pack and have a look at all my old things. I plunged my hands into the bag, down through the layers of books and parchments, until I could feel the chain, right down at the bottom. I pulled it out for a moment, but then I noticed that the old lady was looking at me in a very odd sort of way, so I quickly put it away again. But, even in that short time, I had felt some of its old power seeping into me through my fingertips.

After a while, I began to feel quite a bit better, so then I pulled out some of the old charts that the red-headed kid had drawn, and I held them in front of me and I gazed at them, and it was almost as though I was revisiting all the places in them, they were so clear and potent. Come to think of it, I shouldn't really have said revisiting, I'd never actually been to any of those places, but still, it felt as if I had.

Eventually, I started to feel as if I had satisfied my hunger for the time being, so then I packed the charts away and I looked up, and I could see that the carriage was bumping along through open country, and the old lady was looking at me in a more kindly sort of way. I suppose I must have appeared very rude and ungrateful, but she didn't show any sign of annoyance.

'They're beautiful,' she said. 'Did you draw them yourself?' So I explained that they belonged to someone I once knew. Part of me wanted to say more, but another part kept saying that I wasn't ready yet, so I just shook my head and she smiled at me in an understanding kind of way.

By this time I had completely lost track of where we were going, although I think we must have been heading roughly north-west, and we had ventured onto the bumpy old roads beyond the reach of the Royal Highways. We spent several days on the road, and at night we stopped at inns, quite good inns actually, I was even allowed my own room to sleep in. The old lady turned out to be a good companion, she seemed to know when to talk and when to keep quiet.

By the end of the journey, I had begun to find out quite a lot about where she lived and what she did. It turned out that we were heading for a place called the House of Rest, and that she was the person in charge there, her name was Kathleen, but her official title was Keeper of the Ground, and she'd been there since she was quite a young woman. The House of Rest, so it seemed, had been established to help people who'd lost their way in one fashion or another, and anyone who arrived there was allowed to stop for as long as they needed to, apparently some of the people had been there for years. But of course you already know all about that, don't you?

Anyway, although I learned a lot from the old lady, I was careful not to let on too much about my own history. I did tell her that I'd studied cartography for a while, and she said that she thought that might be useful. That led me to asking her what sort of work she had in mind for me to do, and she was a bit vague about that, she said that there were all sorts of possibilities, and it would all begin to make more sense when we got there. Then I asked about the signal engine, and she said that they hadn't actually got one yet, but that some of her people thought that it might be a good idea. Actually, once I started asking questions, everything started to get a bit vague, but the House of Rest did sound like an interesting sort of place, so I thought I might as well come along, after all I didn't have anything much else lined up.

We were driving along a straight, flat road when I saw a long, grassy mound that crossed the landscape in front of us, with a line of little gnarled trees growing along the top. The old lady had been reading a book, but she suddenly looked up and said, 'We have arrived. This is the boundary dyke. The House of Rest has no gates,' and, sure enough, *the carriage zigzagged through a gap in the mound and then I could see the house in the distance. The house was situated on flat ground at the bottom of a valley, there were hills in the distance, and in one place I think I could just catch a glimpse of a mountain with snow on top of it. On either side of us were fields with crops and animals in them, and now and then the people working there would turn around and wave. The first thing that struck me as we approached the house was that it was much bigger than I had expected. It was a huge, rambling house, built of some kind of yellow stone, with a grey tiled roof and lots of chimneys, some of them with smoke coming out. As we got nearer, the fields gave way to lawns and formal gardens, and I could see people wandering about in twos and threes, there was a group of them on a paved area playing some sort of game with huge stones for counters, and there was someone else sitting at an easel doing a painting. The house was almost as big as the Academy, but somehow it looked friendlier, less like an official building and more like someone's home, I suppose. And, now that I've spent a bit of time here, that's how it's begun to feel.*

The carriage pulled up on the gravel, and I could hear a bell ringing somewhere. The old lady suddenly became very brisk, she said, 'Well, I've got plenty to do, and I expect you'll want some lunch, oh look, there's my granddaughter, she can help you get yourself sorted out.'

So I was handed over to a much younger woman, maybe five or six years younger than me, she had straight fair hair, she was quite thin and she was wearing a faded old tracksuit and plimsolls. She said that her name was Alice and that she was the Exercise Captain, and she took me into a big refectory room, rather like the one at the Academy, and we sat down at one of the long tables and ate slices of meat pie. When I tasted that pie, I had the strangest feeling, a sort of warmth in my chest and a hollowness in my stomach. Thinking about it now, I suppose it was a mixture of security and apprehension, but just at that moment I didn't have the chance to stop and analyse it.

Alice asked me a few questions while we ate, and then she said that there weren't any exercise classes that afternoon, and she could show me around if I liked. So we wandered around the house and the gardens, and I saw people talking to each other, and playing games, and playing music, and making sculpture, and taking walks. Alice tried to explain to me what it was all about, but by then I was finding it a bit hard to take it all in. I think she must have realised that I was getting tired, because after that she found me a room to sleep in, and then she left me alone to have a bit of a rest. As soon as she had gone, I got my chain out of my bag and I wrapped it around myself and then I lay down and went to sleep.

After a few days, I began to find various odd jobs that I could do about the place. I helped in the kitchens a bit, like I used to do at the Academy, and then I started to help with some of the equipment for painting and sculpting and so on. After a while, I even started up a little crossword group, and that seemed to interest a few people. So I suppose you could say I've settled in here pretty well.

The Magician's Nameplate

A few days (or nights) after his embarrassing encounter with Veronique, Kevin Considine was once again passing a few hours in the company of Lee. This time, the two of them had found their way together to a clearing in a forest, a roughly circular patch of daisy-studded grass from which seven shady pathways snaked away in various directions among the trees. Kevin and Lee were sprawled on short, springy turf with the remains of a picnic spread out on a cloth between them.

'What are all these places, Kevin? I still don't understand.' Lying on her front, propped up on her elbows, Lee had flexed her spine backwards at an acute angle and was massaging her shoulders with her toes. Kevin, on his back, stared up at the latticework of branches above them.

'I've been thinking about it a lot. And I've begun to think it must be something to do with my Network, you know, I told you about it, the Network of Signal Engines that I'm building in the real world . . . I should say, my other world . . .'

'That's the world you go to when you're not here with me, Kevin? The big world with thousands and thousands of people? The World of Women and Men?'

'Yes, that's right. And I'm building this network so that they can all talk to one another, wherever they are. Well, when I use my Signal Engine, it's like going into a sort of secret room . . .'

'*The black room where you found me, Kevin?*'

'The black room, that's it. Well, the other people who use the Network, they all have their own Signal Engines, and I think they must all have secret rooms of their own, different rooms . . .'

'*And those secret rooms are the other places we go to?*'

'Exactly. And all the corridors and passages and tunnels where we keep getting lost are the channels of communication that connect all the rooms together. So we have been exploring . . .'

'*Exploring your Signal Network on the inside.*' Thoughtfully, Lee rolled onto her back and slowly raised first her legs, and then her body, until she arrived at an upside-down attitude, her weight settled on her shoulders. Kevin gazed at her a moment before he continued.

'Exploring it on the inside, yes, that's it. And each of the places, each of the secret rooms, has absorbed something of the character of the person who owns it. And of course that's why they're all so different from each other. There's this forest, then there was a ship, and a warehouse . . . and of course there's our bedroom.' A crooked smile insinuated itself across Kevin's face.

'*And what about the empty place, Kevin? The place where I started to fade away?*'

'I've been thinking about that. I think that must have been a part of the Network that's not finished yet. No one's using it. So there's nothing there, not even air. And that's why you couldn't breathe.' He watched as Lee slowly parted her legs, until her inverted figure formed a taut, lean capital T, her toes pointing in precisely opposite directions. She held this position for a few moments, then abruptly rolled forwards, arriving in front of Kevin in a kneeling position on the grass.

'*Kevin?*' He sat up to face her. Her pale, high-cheekboned face had taken on a grave expression.

'Lee?'

'*Suppose I said I wanted to explore your network? On my own? While you're away in your other world?*'

'I don't know,' Kevin mused. 'Would you be able to find your way about?' As soon as he had said this, they were both struck by the absurdity of it, and burst out laughing simultaneously. Suddenly Lee sprang towards him with a wild yell, and Kevin just had time to notice that their clothes had disappeared before they collapsed with a gleeful squelch into the long grass at the edge of the clearing.

A few minutes later, the conversation continued.

'*If there's anyone who can't find his way, Kevin Constanzas —*' Kevin was momentarily disconcerted by Lee's use of his secret name '*— it's you! So will you let me explore, Kevin? Will you? Please say yes, Kevin, please say yes! I'll do some more of this if you say yes . . .*'

'All right, all right.' Aware that time was beginning to press, Kevin had started to fumble for his clothes. 'Yes, I suppose there's no reason why you shouldn't go and explore. But just make sure you're still around when I get back.'

'*Can I really, Kevin?*'

'Yes, of course you can. Really.'

Slowly, Lee rose to her feet. Kevin noticed that she seemed suddenly taller and stronger than before.

'*This is going to be so good, Kevin, it's going to be so good . . .*'

As her figure towered above him, the muscles started to quiver faintly all over her body, as if she were becoming charged with electricity. Her body seemed almost to glow with light and somewhere, suffusing the atmosphere around her, Kevin became aware of a faint, humming sound that was gradually rising in pitch. Lee's eyes grew wider. Her splayed fingers trembled. Then her lips parted slightly.

'*I can't keep still any longer,*' she murmured. '*Kevin . . .*'

And suddenly, in a gust of wind and a streak of light and a rush of sound, she was gone.

'Lee?'

Awkwardly, Kevin hauled himself to his feet. He could not work out where Lee had gone to, whether she had run, or flown, or simply vanished. Kevin could not even say for certain which of the seven possible exits from the clearing she had taken. All that was certain was that she was no longer there. Picking a direction at random, he started to walk.

'Lee?' Kevin called. 'Lee, don't leave me here.'

He had left the forest behind him now, and he was trudging along a narrow, rocky track between two high stone walls. After a minute, he arrived at a flagged courtyard from which several paths radiated, and was just in time to see something bright flash and hiss with lightning speed across his line of vision. He turned and headed along the path where he had seen it. Gradually, the path became smoother and broader, and Kevin realised that it was also starting to slope downwards. He allowed his footsteps to accelerate to an easy lope. Seconds later, he was startled by another flash of light, this time from just behind him. He spun around, nearly tripping over his ankles, but was too late to see anything.

And now there were more paths, and more intersections and more turnings, and it was as though Kevin were assailed as he ran by a barrage of artillery or a display of pyrotechnics, brilliant objects roaring madly past him to left and to right, fireworks detonating above him and beneath him, dazzling him, deafening him, battering him, numbing him, until at last he found himself staggering across a desolate open space with archways and paths opening up on every side, and the noise and the light swelling and exploding and bombarding him from all quarters until all his senses were exhausted and he could comprehend nothing.

Until, at last, all fell still.

Until, at last, he could hear Lee's voice in the stillness.

'*Thank you, Kevin,*' whispered Lee. '*Thank you.*'

And then all was truly still.

★   ★   ★

The following morning, at the start of the work period, Veronique arrived at the Administrative Centre at her usual time, deposited her usual belongings at her desk, and headed as usual across to the coffee engine, where she proceeded with her usual refreshment routine. From this vantage point she could see the door of Mister Considine's office, and she noted with relief that this morning there was no light showing beneath it. Then, just as the coffee began to bubble and drip into her mug, Veronique noticed another light, a faint glow of light seeping up the stairwell from the laboratory.

'*Now* what's the bugger been up to?' she muttered, raising her thickly painted eyebrows theatrically. Reluctantly abandoning her coffee, Veronique clamped her cigar firmly between her teeth and set off down the narrow steps to investigate Kevin's latest outrage.

All the lights were switched on in the laboratory, so Veronique had no difficulty in discerning the figure of Mister Considine. He was spreadeagled on the floor, approximately at the centre of the room, in a rather undignified posture, although this time, fortunately, he appeared at least to be fully dressed. He was sound asleep and breathing evenly. The signal engine that he had been using, however, had come off less well.

Four blackened bolts marked the place where the engine had stood and, in between them, there protruded from a hole in the floor the severed end of a thick skein of electrical cable, its bright copper ends jaggedly twisted, as though wrenched apart by giant hands. Judging by the trail of scars and gouges, the engine itself must have been torn from its moorings and spun over at least twice before coming to rest on its side in the far corner of the room.

Having satisfied herself that Mister Considine had once again come to no serious harm, Veronique stepped over to inspect what remained of the signal engine. The cabinet was hot to the touch, and pale wisps of acrid smoke curled from the cracks between its panels. Loose wires trailed here and there, and the eyepieces, handles, and other projecting parts had all been sheared off and now formed a trail of debris across the floor. The gauges and instruments were smashed, and an occasional loose screw dropped out of its socket and rattled across the floor.

The cabinet's rear surface, which had originally faced the wall, now presented itself to Veronique's gaze and, after a moment, her eye was caught by something that was attached to it. It was a rectangular metal plate that had probably once been shiny, but had now faded to a dull, greenish hue. Cautiously brushing away the dust, Veronique craned her head sideways to decipher the script.

Empathy Engine (prototype):
L. PEGASUS, designer

Her jaw dropped, depositing her cigar unnoticed on the floor.

'Old Wizzy-boy Pegasus!' she murmured incredulously. 'So this is *his* doing! Well, who'd have thought it, eh? Who'd have thought it?'

Veronique now became aware of the distant, muted chatter of her fellow workers as they began to arrive at their desks in the room above. Quickly, she seized a handful of dust and wiped it across the nameplate to conceal its cryptic message. By the time she had done this, Kevin had started to stir.

'Morning, Mister C,' said Veronique. 'Getting to make quite a habit of this, aren't we? Coffee again?'

A Haircut for the Family

'What on earth was that?'

Eileen drew back in alarm from the signal engine and hastily pulled off her headphones. A moment later, Rusty's quizzical face appeared around the door of the sparc bedroom where the equipment was installed.

'What happened? Is anything the matter?' He extended his hands towards his wife.

'No, it's all right. It was just for a minute . . . It's probably nothing . . . I was in touch with Daddy . . .'

At that moment, they were interrupted by the shrill jangle of the doorbell.

'Who can that be?' Eileen snapped. 'Oh, it must be Paul. I don't know why he had to come today. The place is such a mess.'

'You wanted us all to have our hair cut before we went away,' Rusty reminded her.

'Oh yes. I suppose so. But I've still got half my packing to do. And I don't suppose you've done any of yours yet. We'd better get him to do the kids first while we get things straight. No, don't worry, I'll go. You put the kettle on, I expect he'll want a drink.'

In the years since Rusty had left Serendipity Court, he had gradually drifted out of touch with his old neighbours. The sole exception to this was Paul Catalano, who had continued to visit the family on a regular basis to attend to their various hairdressing requirements. Glancing out through the kitchen door as he filled the kettle, Rusty caught a glimpse of Paul, slightly balder than before, slightly stouter, but still as cheerful as ever.

'You haven't thought about growing it back?' Paul was saying to Eileen as she ushered him into the living room. 'It used to be so gorgeous when it was a little bit wilder.'

'I don't have the time to look after it these days,' Eileen replied, 'and it's just more practical like this. Shall we go in here?'

'Hello, Paul.' Rusty could not stop himself from smiling broadly as they shook hands. 'How's Serendipity Court?'

'Oh, same as ever,' replied Paul. 'People come and go. Old Uncle Joe's still down in the basement with the furniture. But I must say, climbing up and down that ladder doesn't seem to get any easier. You're so lucky, having this lovely place.'

'It's not really as good as it looks,' Eileen broke in. 'They can't ever afford all the repairs they should. The garden's always a mess. And it doesn't look as if that elevator's ever going to work again.'

'But you've got that fantastic view,' countered Paul. 'Look at old hubby-features, he's sneaking over for another look!'

In fact, Rusty had crossed over to the window to call down to Ashleigh and Max, who were playing on the lawn, eight flights below him at the front of the building. As he gazed down at them, their shrill, excited voices drifted back up. They were playing a game of leap-frog, each taking it in turn to vault over the stooped form of the other. Ashleigh, taller and slimmer than her brother, was the more graceful of the two. She had inherited her father's freckled complexion, and her long, dark red hair streamed out behind her as she ran and skipped and cartwheeled across the grass. Max's hair was cut short like his mother's, and was the same shade of brown. Stockier than his sister and less nimble on his feet, the boy seemed perfectly built to provide the platform for Ashleigh's gymnastic display, his sturdy legs braced to offer her firm support. Momentarily transported by the children's instinctive display of teamwork, Rusty allowed them to make another circuit of the lawn before he shouted down.

'Ash! Maxie! Paul's here! Who's going to be first?'

'ME!' they cried in unison as they abandoned their game and raced around the side of the building to the entrance. They both adored Paul, who, although not a father himself, always seemed to know exactly the right thing to say to them.

'That lovely thick hair of yours always takes ages, Ashleigh, so I'd better start with you,' he said when they arrived panting in the apartment a minute later. 'You'll only need two minutes, Maxie, won't you? Are you going to practise your flute while you're waiting? Now, young lady, how do you want the ends to go, this time?'

'I don't know.' Ashleigh was studying herself seriously in the mirror. 'Shall I have them curling in, or shall I have them curling out? I want to look like Charlotte at Daddy's office.'

'She's getting quite obsessed with how she looks,' Eileen said to Rusty as they began to sort out the holiday things in their bedroom. 'Do you think it's right to encourage her? She's still only a little girl.'

'Oh, I don't think it matters,' replied Rusty. 'Besides, Paul loves to make a fuss of her. Anyway, never mind them for a minute. What was all that about the signal engine?'

'Yes. That was a bit odd.' Abandoning the packing, she sat down on the edge of the bed and waited for Rusty to join her before continuing. 'I was in touch with Daddy, like I said . . .'

'And how was he?'

'Expecting us tomorrow, yes, that's all right. Well, me and Maxie, anyway. Are you sure you'll be all right with Ash?' This year, for the first time, Ashleigh was to go on holiday with her father while Max accompanied his mother. Over the past few years, the Browns and the Blackwoods had taken a number of holidays together, and Ashleigh, unlike her brother, had taken an immediate liking to the rough-and-ready life of their wandering friends. Father and daughter were to spend two weeks on the road with the Blackwoods, and Ashleigh had talked of little else for several weeks.

'She's really been looking forward to it,' Rusty reassured his wife. 'We'll have a great time. And she loves being with Liam and Megan, they all get on so well together. But look, about the signal engine?'

Eileen stared down at the flower-patterned eiderdown for a minute while Rusty awaited her reply. In the distance, they could hear the echoing tones of Max's flute.

'It's sad, being in touch with Daddy,' Eileen began finally. 'In one way, it's just like being in the room with him. But every time, somehow, he seems harder to reach. As if there was some kind of veil between me and him, sort of like dusty net curtains, and every time I try there seem to be more layers in the way. He's still there, behind it all, and in a way he's just the same as he was when I was a little girl, you know, when he used to hold me on his knee, but he seems so far away now.' She brushed reflexively at a speck of dust on the dressing table before continuing. 'And sometimes I can feel his pain. Usually he tries to hide it from me, but sometimes he forgets. Actually, these days he forgets more often than not. Oh, it's awful,

Rusty, watching him fade away like that. I wish we could be there for him.'

A dark cloud seemed to drift across her face. Rusty held her hand for what seemed an appropriate interval.

'I'm so sorry,' he said finally. 'It must be dreadful. But you'll be with him this time tomorrow. And, you know, I still think I'm better off out of his way.' There was a moment's silence. At the corners of their minds, they became aware that Max's music had stopped. Rusty changed the subject. 'Look, you still haven't told me what happened with the engine.'

'Oh yes.' She stared up at him, frowning. 'Just as I was finishing . . . It was like for a moment there was someone else there . . . Like someone sort of . . . flashed across, if you know what I mean. It made me jump.'

'Some sort of incoherence, perhaps? An imp, even?' At his office, Rusty had been getting to know the technical jargon associated with the Signal Network. 'It happens from time to time.'

'No, not incoherence. It was really like I said, like another person being there.' Eileen frowned again. 'It was only for a moment. I'm not even sure if it was a man or a woman. But it was as if we had some sort of conversation. Very quick, but yes, I'm sure we had some sort of . . . exchange.' A puzzled expression chased across her face.

'An exchange? Was it about anything in particular? People sometimes do see little creatures, you know.

Imps, like I said. Nobody seems to know quite what they are.'

'It's going to sound daft,' Eileen said slowly, 'but I think it was about housework, of all things!'

'Housework?' Rusty laughed. 'Is it even infecting the Signal Network now?'

At that moment, Paul called to them from the next room.

'I've done the children. Ashleigh looks adorable, of course, but I'm afraid Maxie's been having a little strop. Anyway, who's coming through next?'

'You go,' said Eileen, turning her attention to the big cabin trunk. 'These socks need a bit of sorting out.'

Soon, the children had gone back out to play and Rusty was alone with Paul.

'Remember that young girl who used to live next door to you?' Paul murmured between snips. 'The one who used to do those funny exercises?'

'Alice?' Suddenly, Rusty's heart was in his mouth.

'Yes, that's the one. Whooa, hold still, you're worse than Maxie! Yes, Alice. Well, she looked in the other day. Just passing through, I suppose. She asked how you were. Said she'd got a job somewhere, as a dancing teacher I think, odd little thing she was.'

'Did she say anything else?'

'No, I don't think so. Whoops, one or two grey hairs there! You shouldn't have any of those yet, you're still just a boy.'

'I'm thirty,' said Rusty, with a faint air of bewilderment.

The mention of Alice had unsettled him. These days, immersed as he was in the routines of family life, he tried not to think too much about the women he had known in the past. Alice, the Islander, had been the most recent . . . And, although he wasn't exactly unhappy with Eileen – their life together was comfortable enough – he couldn't stop himself wondering from time to time how things might have been. Alice still appeared sometimes in his dreams, but these days, he realised, he dreamed more often of Laurel. Laurel, the Wanderer, Laurel with her strange magic and her wild ways and her unpredictable appearances and disappearances. Rusty wondered what might have happened to her, wondered how his life might have been if events had turned out differently . . .

But, at that moment, his train of thought was derailed by the reappearance of Eileen.

'More tea?' she asked. 'And let me sweep that floor. The place looks such a pigsty.'

'Why don't you wait till we're finished?' Rusty queried.

'Best do it straight away,' Eileen said, rummaging in the broom cupboard for her dustpan and brush. 'Leah told me I mustn't leave any dirt lying around.'

'Leah?' said Rusty. 'Who's Leah?'

Eileen paused in her search. She looked perplexed.

'I don't know. The name just came into my head. Anyway, it won't take a second.'

On her hands and knees, she swept away all the clippings.

'There, isn't that better?' She returned the dustpan and brush to the cupboard. 'I'll just make the tea now. I can do the floor again in a minute.'

'And how are you liking the House of Rest?'

Well, once I'd found my way about, I realised that nobody seemed too bothered about what I did, so I just sort of decided to slip into the life here and let things take their course for a bit. After a while, I found that I wanted to start telling my story, and once I realised that, they soon found someone for me to talk to, and of course that someone was you, Nina.

I've never really had the chance to tell my story to anyone before. I suppose I didn't think anyone would be interested, but somehow you really do seem to take an interest in me, although I've never really found out anything about you, how you came here or why you stayed. But I really do enjoy our little afternoon sessions. I suppose you must be what people call a good listener.

Oh yes, I was going to tell you about the other person I've met since I've been here. I think I mentioned the pie that I had on the first day, mutton and parsnip it was. Well, after a while the cook noticed that I would always come back for seconds when it was on the menu, and it turned out that those pies weren't made in the kitchens, they were made by the blacksmith in his forge, apparently there was a bread oven above the furnace there.

I must have missed the forge when I had my guided tour

with Alice, so I set off one day to look for it. It turned out
to be hidden away in the woods at the furthest corner of the
grounds, a rather tumbledown brick building with a tall chimney and a corrugated-iron roof. And there was a smell of
baking in the air.

As I approached, I began to feel a bit apprehensive, a bit
unsteady on my feet. The door was standing open, and the
first thing I saw when I went in was a length of chain hanging from an iron hook by the door. The chain caught my
eye because it wasn't the ordinary sort, it had oddly shaped
links, they were square with faceted corners, just like the ones
on my own chain.

By then, it felt as though my heart was pounding in my
throat. It took a great effort to tear my eyes away from that
chain, but eventually I forced myself to inspect the rest of
the room. There was an anvil of course, and a furnace, a
huge pair of bellows, various tools hanging up from nails on
the beams. And then I saw the blacksmith. He had his back
to me, and he was fiddling about with something in the
furnace, but he must have heard me come in, because he
said, 'Do you want a pie? There's a batch nearly ready.' I
knew the voice, of course, that cracked, booming voice that
reminded me of a broken jug. So, even before the blacksmith
turned around, I knew that he was my father.

I hadn't seen him for more than twenty years, but he
looked pretty well exactly the same as ever. But in that split
second of recognition, I managed to prevent myself from react-
ing, because I had decided not to introduce myself to him,
not right away at least. And of course, he didn't recognise
me, because I'd only been a little boy the last time we'd met.

When I went to bed that night, I couldn't sleep, not even my chain could help me through that, and as I lay there on the narrow bed, all the old anger started to well up again, and I thought about everything my father had put me through, and I thought about what my life could have been if I'd had a better start, and then I thought about Michael Brown and how well he'd done for himself, and I knew that I couldn't just leave things be, I was going to have to do a bit of evening up.

I've not got much more to tell you, Nina, we'll be finished soon. So now it's time for me to tell you what I had to do, and then you will be able to share my secret with me. It's been good talking to you. I hope you'll think it's been worth it.

Five:
AT THE HOUSE OF REST

The Royal Digest of Affairs and Events: Volume 112 (in the Tenth Year of the Rule of King Matthew)

The Diary of Miss Garamond (Herald)

Greetings, Citizens!

The younger reader may well be hard-pressed to recall a time in which the southern borders of the Kingdom were free from the threat of invasion. Ever since the accession of King Matthew, and even before that, throughout a substantial period of the reign of the old King, the military campaign has continued to be fought with no perceptible indication of progress on either side. After some years of deliberation, therefore, King Matthew, in consultation with High Master Fang, has arrived at the conclusion that this state of affairs can no longer be permitted to continue. The King has therefore resolved that the matter will at once be taken in hand in the most direct fashion possible, and has, in consequence, set out with a small party of advisers for the border region, with the intention of making a personal reconnaissance of the deployment of forces there, and has declared himself prepared, should circumstances warrant it, to assume immediate personal command of the campaign.

The author is therefore obliged to report that, for the first time in nearly ten years, it has not proved possible for the King to hold his monthly Private Audience. However, anxious as ever to maintain the accustomed degree of communication between Palace and people, he has graciously seen fit to delegate the Director of Internal Affairs, High Master Fang, to hold Audience in his stead. A short time ago, therefore, the author was privileged to be received by the High Master in his office adjacent to the throne room, attended by a detachment of the Royal Wolf Boys Ceremonial Guard. The author found her exchanges with the High Master most illuminating, and it was of particular interest to her to discover at first hand the High Master's attitude regarding a number of issues that are certain to be of great consequence to the Citizenry.

Firstly, the author was assured by the High Master that, although the rule of law and order in our city continues in greater force than ever, it must be emphasised that there is an inevitable price to be paid for the safety, security and peace that Citizens have rightly come to expect. The Citizen must therefore be reminded of the many far-reaching and costly reforms that the High Master has been obliged to carry out in order to achieve the present felicitous state of affairs. To mention but one example, following recent reports of attacks on innocent persons by marauding gangs of young women, extra patrols have now been deployed in the Western Suburb and North Estates districts.

The King has thus far taken great pains to ensure that such expansion of the Services should, so far as is reasonably practicable, be financed from existing resources. High Master Fang wishes, however, to make clear that this is not a state of affairs that can be maintained indefinitely, and that imminent measures are therefore afoot to ensure a sounder financial footing for the Services. The reader will surely agree that a modest supplement to the City Levy will constitute but a small price to pay, and the High Master is confident that every citizen will make his contribution with pride, gratitude and promptness.

As an example of the new benefits that the Citizen may expect to enjoy in the future, the High Master has chosen to single out for special mention the Royal Wolf Boys Penal and Corrective Service. The High Master is determined to ensure that every wrongdoer shall be subject to a regime of punishment of the most severe nature imaginable, and that such regime shall be applied with equal vigour to the perpetrators of great crimes and small crimes alike, from the most trivial of misdemeanours, such as littering and obstruction, to the most gross and outrageous instances of corruption and fraud, as for instance in the recent celebrated case of Mister Slater, the self-styled Transport Interchange Supervisor, whose flagrant misdeeds and richly deserved downfall have been reported at length in this column.

Secondly, the High Master has been deeply gratified to observe the excellent progress that has been made, under the direction of Mister Considine, in the development and construction of the Royal Signal Network. Signal Engines of the most up-to-date design have been procured for every arm of the Royal Wolf Boys Services, and these engines are proving to be of the utmost efficacy in the rapid transfer of intelligence concerning the movements and intentions of wrongdoers, accidents and obstructions on the roads and rivers of the Kingdom, and even (and to this the author, from a purely selfish point of view, must admit to some alarm!) to the promulgation of intelligence concerning the affairs and events of the day. The arms of the Signal Network now extend to every department and organisation of any significance within the boundary of the City walls, and are further expanding to encompass the larger cities and towns of the Provinces and Outlands. Indeed, it is anticipated that, within the next few years, it will in addition become available to users in the majority of the more important rural locations.

In addition to bodies of an official or institutional nature, it has been most pleasing to note the recent growth in the numbers of private individuals who have elected to make use of this invaluable service. Indeed, many persons and families of the author's acquaintance are now the proud owners of the miniature signal engines designed for domestic use, through which they are able with ease to make contact on a daily basis with kinfolk and acquaintances, no matter at what distance they might be situated. All without exception have expressed their profound satisfaction at the many advantages they have thus been able to enjoy.

In connection with this expansion in domestic utilisation, the author has been amused to note a number of recent instances in which owners of signal engines have experienced unexpected contact with those creatures of unknown nature and identity that have popularly become known as 'imps'. A promulgation from Mister Considine, Royal Supervisor of Machinery, reads as follows:

> *Contacts with 'imps' have generally been of momentary duration only. Although these creatures appear normally to display a whimsical or humorous character, all unexpected contacts should be treated with some caution, and any threatening or sinister occurrences reported to the Royal Signals Division for investigation. The citizen may rest assured, however, that the overwhelming majority of these 'imps' are friendly and playful by nature, and that a great deal of harmless enjoyment is to be had in their company.*

Indeed, the author is pleased, through personal experience, to attest to this!

Thirdly, and in conclusion, High Master Fang is anxious to point out that the persistent difficulties to which travellers have for so long been subject at the Transport Interchange are expected soon to be consigned to the annals of history. This is as a result of the imminent formation of the Royal Wolf Boys Transport Division. This new Service is expected in the near future to assume control, not only of the Transport Interchange itself, but also of the many individual operators of the coaches and waggons that ply their trade there. In the near future, these individuals are intended to operate together as a single, coherent organisation. The High Master is confident that these innovations will in the future guarantee the traveller a swift, efficient and economical service. (If the author were to be permitted a moment of flippancy, she might perhaps remark that this statement carries about it a certain air of weary familiarity!)

In conclusion, High Master Fang reminded the author that King Matthew is expected to return from the Borders in ample time to conduct his next monthly Private Audience in the usual fashion. We join the High Master in wishing the King a successful and productive visit and a prompt and safe return to the City. (Of course, in the unlikely event of any delay to the King's return, High Master Fang will continue to conduct the Audience.)

Finally, and to conclude on her customary personal

note, the author was recently delighted to spend an evening in the company of an old colleague, Mister Michael Brown. Following his departure from the offices of the *Royal Digest,* Michael has in recent years become well known as the proprietor of Michael Brown Publications, whose *City Charts* have quickly become a familiar feature of every bookshelf. The author is pleased to report that Michael and his young family are happy and flourishing, and she is sure that the reader will join her in wishing them continuing health and prosperity in the future.

Goodbye, Citizens, and long live King Matthew!

From the Keeper of the Ground, at the House of Rest: To the Council of Wise Ones

Dear Sisters and Brothers,

It is the season of the ballad singers once again. It is now five days since the start of their annual visit, and their presence serves as a timely reminder that my report to you is, as always, overdue. Much has happened over the past twelve months here at the House of Rest, and when in due course you come to the end of these pages, you will perhaps begin to understand why I wish this to be my final report.

For many years I have kept this House and the

ground around this House, but nothing remains for ever, Sisters and Brothers, and I believe that the time has now come for me to step aside from my position and to consign the House of Rest to younger, fresher hands. The world continues to change around us at a dizzying pace, and I begin to find myself feeling old and weary. And, when once I have recounted to you the terrible events that have lately taken place within these walls, you will perhaps begin to understand.

But let me begin at the beginning. It was twelve months ago, shortly after the ballad singers had last gone on their northward way, bearing with them my previous report, that I began to notice certain indications that all was not well in the world beyond our ground.

To begin with, the number of visitors to the House, which had remained at an even trickle for many years, has in recent times started to display a steady growth. As you know, it has long been our guiding principle that no visitor to the House shall ever be turned away, and that, equally, no visitor shall be asked to leave until she is ready to face the world beyond. Some of our most loyal and long-serving helpers, such as Nina the Listener, have been here for almost as long as I can remember; indeed, Geoffrey the Blacksmith has been here even longer than I. Life at the House has been all the richer for the presence of people such as these, and I now find it hard to imagine myself ever wishing to part company with them. However, we have reached a point at which we find ourselves hard-pressed even to provide sufficient sleeping accommodation for our guests, while our farms struggle to produce enough food for all.

I have begun to wonder, Sisters and Brothers, whether certain events in the world beyond might not begin to suggest an explanation for our increasing numbers of visitors. Perhaps something is taking place among the Wounded Ones in the City, perhaps there is some malevolent force at large that compels people to seek the shelter of our walls in ever larger numbers. As you know, I have always viewed the affairs of the Kingdom and the City with a certain sense of detachment, as my visits are infrequent and my knowledge of affairs is, to say the least, patchy, but I wonder at times whether the relentless growth of our little domestic difficulties may not be connected by some means or other to the reckless reforms of King Matt and High Master Fang.

To compound matters, the yield of our farms has, over the passing years, begun steadily to fail. And I do not refer here to the occasional lean year sandwiched between fat years. The decline in yield from one season to the next has been steady and unrelenting. The farmers furrow their brows, but they are unable to explain what is happening, and their mothers and grandmothers know of no precedent for such a thing.

But, trying as these things might be, they remain straightforward enough problems in themselves. No, if it were simply a matter of accommodating larger numbers of people and subsisting on smaller quantities of provisions, my concern would not be so great as it is. What troubles me much more is a sense that something is happening in the forces of nature themselves, something like a failing of the light, something like a remorseless anticlockwise twist, as though the Great Being were herself beginning to suffer some unnamed sickness.

This spring, for instance, I have been surprised to identify several flocks of seagulls following the ploughs in our fields. You and I, Sisters and Brothers, grew up in the Islands, where the crying of these birds formed a familiar backdrop to our daily lives, but here, four days' weary journey from the sea, they are an unfamiliar sight indeed. I ask myself why they have strayed so far from their usual path? At the House, we have become accustomed to dealing with people who have lost their sense of direction, but to discover the same thing happening to the birds of the air is a novel experience indeed! It is hard to escape the conclusion that some small but vital component in the mechanism of nature has become dislodged from its place.

And then, at Midsummer, there occurred another troubling incident. On Midsummer's Eve, as is my custom, I set off on a long walk along the boundary dyke that encircles the ground around the House of Rest. I was accompanied in this walk, as I have been on several previous occasions, by my granddaughter Alice, whose thoughtful company I greatly prize. We followed the narrow track that winds along the top of the dyke, that same track that weaves its way in and out of the gnarled little blackthorn trees that were planted in long rows there by one of my predecessors. This time, it was Alice who noticed that something was awry. We had walked perhaps a quarter of the distance around, when she stopped me with a light touch on the elbow.

'Nanna,' she said. 'Have you not noticed anything strange about the trees?'

'No, I don't think so,' I said. Alice had a habit of approaching things from odd angles, so I asked no further questions, but waited quietly to discover what she was about to say.

'Well, does the wind here blow from any special direction?'

'From the north-east, I think.' I indicated the direction with an uncertain finger.

'From the north-east, yes.' She nodded slowly to herself. 'And the wind blows the trees, and the trees bend under the force of the wind?'

With a sudden pang of fear, I began to understand. The wind here blows mostly in the one direction, and the wind indeed bends the trees, so that the young saplings grow in stooped form, and in time the trees come to point always in the direction in which the wind blows. I looked at the trees more carefully, and now I could see that something was not right.

'Something's happened,' said Alice. 'The trees have changed. They're all pointing here and there. What is it, Nanna?'

Of course, I did not have an answer to that. It was one more thing to wonder at, one more ounce to add to my growing load of unease. Although Alice did not say anything else, I knew that she could sense my disquiet. She took my arm for the rest of the walk, and I could feel her worry adding its weight to mine.

But, Sisters and Brothers, perhaps you do not feel that these things are of any great consequence. Indeed, I find it difficult with any conviction to explain how it is that they conspire together to cause me such disquiet. None of them on its own presents me with a problem that I cannot solve. All I can say is that in combination they form an unsettling background, a shifting wash of sombre colour against which a number of more directly troubling incidents have been taking place, culminating in the terrible business of the past week. To these events I will now proceed.

Sisters and Brothers, it has long been my custom in these letters to mention to you any persons of a curious nature who have passed across our threshold these twelve months. I must therefore now say a little about a certain young man whom I first met on one of my occasional visits to the City. It is a matter of profound regret to me that it was I who invited this person into our House, and that it was through my carelessness that he has brought about the awful events that have taken place here.

Of course, for reasons with which you will doubtless be familiar, the Rules of the House forbid me to mention his name. However, I have already said that I first met him in the City. I was paying my usual visit to the City Rehabilitation Centre and, at that time, I found the young man on the point of release from the clutches of the corrective system. As I watched him in his cage, something about him caught my eye, and I stood there for quite a while trying to puzzle out what he was doing. As he paced this way and that, it became apparent to me that he was following an organised sequence of movements. It seemed almost as though he were setting himself problems of navigation, and then solving them, and I found myself particularly struck by his approach to matters of space and direction. This gave me the idea that, with suitable guidance, he might have the potential one day to become a useful member of our community and so, with his agreement, I invited him to accompany me in my carriage to the House.

Perhaps I should have become wary of him sooner than I did. For the four days of our journey he was mostly a silent companion, listening rather than speaking, and spending much of his time studying a collection of charts or diagrams and other objects that were stowed in his pack. At the time, I attributed this to a probable state of shock following his sudden and unexpected release from captivity. Distracted as I was by other concerns, I dismissed it from my mind and failed to draw the conclusions that in hindsight I know I should have drawn.

Upon our arrival at the House, I introduced the young man to Alice, who led him off towards the refectory. At that point, I was obliged to concentrate my mind upon other matters, and therefore thought no more about him until sometime later that afternoon, when I was taking my customary cup of tea with Alice in her cell. In the course of our talk, she mentioned to me that she had taken the young man on a tour of the grounds and later found him a place in which to sleep. While she spoke of these things, it seemed to me from the way she held herself that she was somehow uneasy in her mind, but she was at first reluctant to speak directly of the matter.

'Nanna, are you sure that it was right to bring him here?' she asked me finally.

'I'm not sure I know what you mean,' I replied.

She added milk to my tea and passed it across to me.

'Well, since I've been here, I've met plenty of people who've lost their bearings,' she began hesitantly. 'And I've tried to help each one in some way or another. Because, of course, once I got the hang of it, I found that I needed to approach different people in different ways. And then I started learning to recognise the different sorts of things that might be helpful for each person. And I suppose after a while I started to think of them as types, although I know I shouldn't. But this man ... He's not a type. I've just never met anyone at all like him.'

I chose not to reply, but fixed her with one of my quizzical looks until she continued. Eventually, she set off at one of her delightful tangents, as I had hoped she might.

'Nanna, what do we mean when we say that some-one is lost?'

'Well, I suppose they don't know where they are. Or maybe they know where they are, but they don't know where they're going.'

'And what do we do to help them?'

'We encourage them to think about where they've come from. And, after that, then perhaps we might encourage them to explore the place where they find themselves. And then, with luck, they will eventually realise that if they start from where they are, and keep going in the same direction they've come from, then that will lead them in the end to where they need to go to. But surely you learned all this when you were a little girl?'

'Of course I did. I just wanted to put it straight in my mind. So then, just suppose you met someone who knew where he'd been?'

'Yes?'

'And he knew where he was going?'

'Yes?'

'Well, this man, when I talked with him, I got the feeling that he was like that. He knew where he'd been and he knew where he was going. But he just didn't seem to know where he was. I could feel that, in the past, he'd suffered some great sorrow, and I had the strangest feeling that he was headed for great sorrow in the future as well. And, this was awful, I think he knew it too, and somehow he actually seemed to want it. And what I found really strange was that it didn't matter to him how he got there. I mean, he knew that he was here, at the House, but in some other way it seemed as if he'd been cut adrift, as if he'd lost any sense he might have had of his location.' She stared into her empty cup. 'And nothing we can do is going to change that, is it?'

I thought about this for a time. Alice poured some more tea, and we drank in silence.

'So what do you think we ought to do?' I wondered aloud. 'I mean, I know he's made you uneasy, but we can't just ask him to leave. You know, the Rules of the House. And besides, it's not even as if he's done anything wrong. Not in the time he's been here, anyway.'

Alice was sitting at the end of the bed. I noticed that she had begun to twist her legs into a knot, a sure sign that she was feeling ill at ease.

'I suppose not,' she said finally. Then she seemed to collect herself. 'No, of course not. I just have to forget my feelings and treat him the same way I would treat anyone else. Help him to find his way towards whatever seems most suitable for him. You know, I did think about getting him along to my dance class, but I'm still not sure.'

'Then trust your instinct,' I said at once. 'That's one thing you're always right about. Why don't we just do what we usually do for people who've suffered great sorrow? Why don't we try and get him to tell his story?'

'To Nina?' she suggested.

'To Nina,' I agreed. 'I think he's going to need the best we can give him.' I noticed that she was still knotting her legs together. 'He's really upset you, hasn't he? You look as if you need to re-attune yourself.'

She nodded ruefully. I got up to leave. As I closed the door, she had already assumed the first attitude of her exercise pattern.

The Return of the Wanderer

Following the destruction of his signal engine, it was some days before Kevin Considine felt strong enough to continue his exploration of the Network. He made a careful inspection of the remains of the engine before deciding, reluctantly, that it was beyond economic repair, so he then set about making arrangements for a new engine to be installed in the laboratory. The technicians who carried out the installation gave him a number of curious glances when they observed the pile of tangled wreckage in the corner of the room, but Kevin offered them no explanation, merely ordering them to continue with the work without wasting time. Once satisfied that the new equipment was in working order and properly connected, he sent the men on their way with a curt reminder that anything they had seen in the laboratory must be regarded as secret and confidential. And, at the end of the working day, when the administrative staff had gone home and the lights had been dimmed, Kevin stole down to the laboratory and powered up the new engine. He badly wanted to see Lee.

But of Lee there was no sign. The room with the bed and the trapeze and the archways was empty and cold, and the candles had burned themselves out.

'Lee?' Kevin called. 'Lee?' But there was no reply except for the mocking echo of his own voice. Sighing, he picked an archway at random and set off to search for her.

Night after night Kevin searched, but not a trace of Lee could he find. He wandered the corridors and the staircases, he roamed through chambers both familiar and unfamiliar and, eventually, when he found that his strength had deserted him, he lay down and slept. Each morning, Veronique arrived to find him slumped over the control panel of the engine, and each morning she awoke him with another mug of coffee and another sarcastic remark. But Kevin was a thick-skinned man, immune to sarcasm and other such nuances of discourse. Each morning he would tidy himself up as best he could and drag himself back upstairs to his desk.

By now, Kevin had lost any sense of engagement with his work that he might once have had. He squinted in incomprehension at memoranda and reports, he sat through interminable meetings staring zombie-like at the wall, he snapped at his staff for no apparent reason, he left meals half-eaten, and he only rarely found his way home to change his clothes. If he had been a more diligent student of human nature, he might have noticed that people were taking detours to avoid him, speaking to him only when necessary, giving him looks of pity and concern. The Signal Network and his various other projects meandered along with no sense of direction, the work carried out by indifferent subordinates who neither knew nor cared about Kevin's carefully worked out strategy, his meticulously calculated targets and outcomes. Only Veronique, recently elevated to the rank of Chief Administrator, had any understanding of what was taking place, but Veronique, of course, had her own reasons for keeping quiet.

Anyway, none of these things impinged to the slightest degree on Kevin's battered consciousness. All Kevin wanted to do now was to find Lee.

After many nights of searching, Kevin found himself starting to wonder whether his sense of direction might be letting him down. Many of the corridors of the Network looked perplexingly similar to each other and, although he had tried leaving markers in critical places, Kevin somehow never seemed able to locate them again. One day, though, on one of his increasingly rare forays beyond the Palace walls, he found himself wanderering up the North Way in search of refreshments. There he came upon a bookstall that boasted a colourful display of the *City Charts* from Michael Brown Publications, and Kevin wondered whether he might be able to design some kind of a chart to guide him around the Network. He rummaged in the pockets of his fraying clothes for a coin, and returned to the Palace with a couple of charts tucked under his arm in a brown paper bag. Later, when Veronique popped her head around the door to remind him of his next meeting, she found him on his hands and knees, the large sheets of crackling parchment spread out on the floor in front of him.

So, for the next few nights, Kevin sat at the signal engine with a writing tablet on his knees, laboriously sketching out each turning he made and each chamber through which he passed. Each night, he strove to complete a sketch of one small section of the Network but, upon re-examining it the following night, he would invariably find it useless. To his perplexity, the layout of the chambers and the angles of the junctions and the inclinations of the corridors all seemed to have transformed themselves in subtle, or not-so-subtle, ways each time he returned to the locations. Finally, Kevin was forced to admit defeat. He realised then that the Network was constantly growing, changing, evolving, and it was all happening too fast for him to keep track of it. And, ironically, it occurred to Kevin that he was the one who had designed it. If he, the inventor, was unable to keep track of his creation, he doubted if anyone else would be able to, either.

Kevin realised then that the whole thing had spiralled utterly beyond his control. And, as if that wasn't enough, he still hadn't found Lee. Forlornly, he shredded his charts into strips and tore the strips into small pieces. When Veronique brought him his coffee the next day, she found him in a state of collapse on the floor of the laboratory, surrounded by this litter of bizarre confetti.

And then, the next night, Lee was back.

She was perched on her trapeze, wearing her black tunic, just as she had been when Kevin first saw her. One long, bare leg was dangling downwards, the arched foot drawing tantalising circles in the air. Her other leg was drawn up under her chin, and her head was bent forwards over her knee with an air of intense concentration. In the yellow glow of the candles, Kevin could see that she was sharpening her long, red toenails. After a moment, satisfied with her work, she looked up.

'Hello, Kevin. Welcome home.'

'Lee! I've missed you. Where have you been?'

Kevin sensed a brief flash of cold hostility from her slanting eyes, but it was so quick that he told himself he must have been mistaken. Then Lee dropped lightly onto the bed, smoothly shedding her tunic in the process.

'I've missed you, too, Kevin.'

Patting the black satin sheets, she treated him to a smile. Her teeth were white and even and sharp.

From the Keeper of the Ground, at the House of Rest: To the Council of Wise Ones (continued)

After my talk with Alice, I devised an excuse to pay a visit to the kitchens while the young man was at work there. Finding him unoccupied, I engaged him in conversation, in the course of which I contrived to offer the suggestion that it might be a good idea for him to start telling his story to someone. To my surprise, he was quick to agree to this, and I told him that I thought that Nina might prove a helpful listener for him.

You probably recall the story of Nina's arrival at the House of Rest, Sisters and Brothers. She appeared here perhaps eight or ten years ago, abandoned on the doorstep by a troupe of carnival folk. At that time, she was unable to speak or even to stand upright without assistance, and it was apparent that she had suffered some appalling shock that had left her completely helpless. Even when she finally recovered her power of speech, she could at first remember nothing about herself. We even had to invent a name for her until, eventually, she began to recall some of her history. But, having once started to recover her memory and to regain her sense of direction, she revealed herself to be one of the most gifted listeners it has ever been my privilege to meet, and it has been our great good fortune that she has chosen to remain at the House ever since.

But I must return to my narrative. I arranged for the young man to be introduced to Nina in the hope that, with her help, he would start to piece his story together and to recover his sense of purpose, and I was gratified to observe that he quickly fell into the habit of meeting her at regular intervals, in order to relate his story to her bit by bit. While this was going on, I noticed that Alice was continuing to avoid him, and as nothing unusual was reported to me by Nina, he ceased for a while to be at the forefront of my mind. The next time I crossed paths with him was over the business of the signal engine.

I think I mentioned earlier that I am no longer a frequent visitor to the City, but it would be hard to spend any time at all there without overhearing talk of the Royal Signal Network. You said to me in your last letter that the tendrils of the Network have finally extended their reach as far as the Outer Islands, and I was interested to read that you had made the decision to install a signal station on the hill next to the Sacred Place. As you will recall, it has for quite a while been my view that, with the help of the Network, communications between us might become quicker and easier, so I have finally made the decision to follow your example and to arrange for an engine to be installed at the House of Rest.

Having arrived at this decision, it occurred to me that specialised assistance for the task was available to me at my fingertips. In the course of my conversations with my strange young man, he had mentioned to me that the Penal and Corrective Service had offered him training as a Signal Engine Technician, and I therefore decided that it would be a good idea to invoke his help in the installation of the equipment.

In the course of our afternoon tea, I mentioned my notion to Alice and, to my surprise, she became quite anxious.

'Aren't you worried about imps, Nanna?' she asked me.

'Imps?' I queried.

'Oh, Nanna, when did you last read the *Digest*?' she demanded, showing, I thought, more than a touch of exasperation. 'We do get a copy sent to us here, you know. You really ought to make more of an effort to keep in touch with the world beyond.'

I had to confess that I had little time to spare for browsing through periodicals.

'Nanna, what am I going to do with you?' she replied plaintively. 'Everybody knows about imps! You know, those funny little creatures that sometimes appear to people on the Network.'

I indicated by my expression that these matters were unfamiliar to me.

'Well, nobody really seems to know where they come from or what they are,' Alice continued. 'People say they're mostly harmless, but I don't see how anyone can be certain of it.'

'Good heavens,' I said. 'I had no idea such things existed. Do you really think they might pose a threat?

Because, you see, Alice, the engine has already arrived.
I asked that strange young man, you know, the one
you don't like, if he could help us to get it installed.
Very keen, he seemed. In fact, he's probably up there
tinkering with it just now.'

Alice's face was starting to show some tension, and,
without being fully conscious of what she was doing,
she had started to knot her legs together in the way
I knew so well. I allowed her a few moments' silence.
After a time, she seemed to relax.

'I'm probably just being silly,' she said finally. 'After
all, lots of people have the engines now. I'm sure it
will be all right. Just ignore me.'

'Now that's something I could never do,' I reassured her. 'Drink your tea now, before it gets cold.'

'*What have you been doing at the House of Rest, then?*'

*Oh yes, the House of Rest. Of course the real reason I was
brought to the House of Rest was the Signal Engine, or at
least that was the pretext I was given. As I said, the condition for my release from the menagerie was that I must find
gainful employment in the trade for which I had been trained,
and naturally I had mentioned this to the old lady in our
very first conversation. I thought she had seemed quite interested at the time but, somehow, when we arrived at the
House, the idea was forgotten again.*

Actually I wasn't too bothered about that, because there

were plenty of other things to keep me occupied. There was my official work, of course, all the odd jobs, helping in the kitchens and so on, and then there were my little sessions with you, Nina. That's all been very interesting, trying to remember all the separate bits of my story, and discovering how to piece them back together again. It's helped me to recover my sense of direction, as you said it would, and it's even started giving me a few ideas about what I need to do next, and I promise I'll get around to that before much longer.

And then I've been getting to know my father again, and hearing some of the bits and pieces of his story. He seems mostly to keep himself to himself, my father. He doesn't mix much with the others. Sometimes he comes and sits in the common room in the evening – I once saw him playing some kind of board game with a couple of other people – but mostly he seems to prefer pottering around in his forge, making up various odds and ends at the anvil, or sometimes cooking the odd batch of pies when the mood takes him. He's built a special pie oven, next to his furnace. It's on quite a big scale, I suppose he needs to make quite large batches of pies, and it's got a sort of long baking rack for the pies that pulls out on little wheels that run on tracks. Just the sort of thing I can imagine him building. And, of course, he's got his own chain. A chain just like mine – I told you about that, didn't I?

So I've got into the habit of dropping in on him now and again, and he doesn't seem to mind too much. He usually keeps a few flasks of spirits hidden away at the forge, it's not really allowed in the House of Rest, of course, but we sometimes sit down and have a drink or two. The forge isn't the most comfortable place to sit, he hasn't even got any chairs there, so we usually perch ourselves on the baking rack. Like everything my father makes, it's pretty sturdy, so I suppose if we ever got round to finding any cushions it would make quite a comfy seat.

No, I still haven't told him who I am, and I'm pretty sure he hasn't guessed. He sometimes talks about the time when he was an apprentice magician, and once he even mentioned a woman, I think her name was Ruth, he seemed to have some sort of special feeling for her, but he's never said anything about having a child, and he's never said anything about how he came to be here at the House. In fact, there seems to be a whole blank section in his life, as if things had happened to him that he preferred to forget about. I can understand that, of course, but I reckon he really ought to try talking to you, Nina, I'm sure you'd get the truth out of him. Actually, it's occurred to me that I could try to jog his memory a bit, but at the moment I haven't quite decided how. Something will doubtless come to me, sooner or later. Something usually does.

Sorry, I was talking about the signal engine. Well, as I said, nothing much happened about it for quite a while but, of course, as I moved among the people in the House, I continued to keep my ears open in my usual way, and now and then I overheard scraps of conversation that gave me clues about what might be going on behind the scenes. Actually, it wasn't too difficult to do this at the House of Rest. I'd managed to do it at the Academy, after all, and the people there were a much more secretive bunch, so doing it here hasn't been too much of a struggle. And I dare say you know at least as much about it all as I do, so please stop me if I've got it wrong.

Funnily enough, I managed to learn quite a lot from Alice, the Exercise Captain, although she never really seemed inclined to talk to me after that first day. She was an odd young woman, very pale and thin and intense. I never went to any of her classes, people seemed to think that it wouldn't be the right thing for me, but when I listened to the people who did go, they all seemed very fired up about it. I heard a couple of them saying that the exercises had given them a new way of looking at the world, changed their perspective, clarified their vision, that kind of thing. None of that sort of talk made any sense to me, but it was obvious that her students thought highly of her. Once, when we were all having a picnic in the grounds, I saw her scramble up on top of a garden wall, kick herself upside down, and then walk the length of the wall on her hands. Despite myself, I was pretty impressed by that, and I realised then that she must have been pretty good at what she did.

But there had always been something about Alice that troubled me. I could feel it just watching the way she walked, and I could feel it even more that time I saw her do that upside-down trick. She had a rather loose-jointed way of moving, and it gave me a very odd sort of feeling, sort of half frightened and half angry. I knew I recognised that feeling but, to begin with, I couldn't place it, although I knew that it belonged to sometime long ago. It nagged at me for a long while, until eventually I remembered that day at the

Academy when I first met the red-haired kid and his dog. The kid used to move in the same sort of way, although he seemed to have lost it when I met him later on. But, watching him, I used to get the same sort of feeling that Alice had stirred up in me, and I knew that I was going to have to do something about it sooner or later.

But the main thing I noticed about Alice was that she didn't like me. I could never really work out why that was. Of course, she was never exactly rude or hostile, but she never seemed to want to talk to me for very long, she would always make some excuse and hurry away. One time, I tried asking her about the signal engine, and although she wouldn't get drawn into conversation, I could tell straight away that she didn't like the idea of it.

Now, that was very interesting, because I knew that the old lady, Kathleen, the Keeper of the Ground, was her grandmother, and I also knew that the two of them used to spend quite a lot of time together, because when I was helping in the kitchens in the afternoon, they sometimes asked me to take them a tray of tea, and I could see that they were always deep in discussion. So I began to realise that these two were sharing quite a lot of their thoughts, they were probably quite a big influence on each other, but one thing they didn't seem to agree about was the signal engine. I reckoned that the old lady wanted to get one for the House, but apparently Alice wasn't too sure. Now, that was very interesting indeed, because it looked to me as though the old lady must have been grooming Alice to take her place after she retired. And that meant that, even if the engine did get installed, Alice might very well eventually decide to get it taken away again. So, if I was going to make use of it, I had better not waste any time.

Now, as it happened, one day while I was turning these things over in my mind, I bumped into the old lady in the corridor, and she told me that the signal engine had been delivered, but the men had had to hurry away, so would I like to unpack it from its boxes and get it working.

Well, of course, I agreed to that straight away but, as it turned out, it was easier said than done, because the engine that had been delivered was one of the heavy, old-fashioned ones. She'd probably chosen it because it was cheaper than the modern kind, but the only place in the house where there was room for it to go was up in the attic, in a little six-sided turret, and that meant that I would need quite a bit of help to get it into position. And even after I had sorted that out, there was still the problem of electricity. The House did have a generator, but it only served the communal room downstairs, so I had to get hold of a long piece of cable and get that installed. Then there were the kites to be rigged and launched, and of course that was another big problem, because the kites needed a steady wind to keep them in the air, and it turned out that the winds that blew around the house were constantly changing direction, and the kites wouldn't have stood up to it. Of course, I knew from my training that, if the wind isn't right, the kites can be attached to tall masts, but for some reason the old lady hadn't ordered any masts. I suspect that Alice must have talked her out of it, which was a shame because, I realised, I would quite have liked watching Alice shin up the masts to rig the kites. When I asked, though, I was told that there wasn't any more money *for masts, and that I'd have to make do with what I had.*

In the end, I managed to attach the kites to one of the chimneys — I even got my father to make up a special bracket in the forge. Unfortunately, the chimney wasn't really high enough, which meant that the engine could only receive signals from certain directions. We managed to get a hazy sort of signal from the city, but the biggest disappointment was that we couldn't get anything at all from the Islands. I tried all sorts of things to sort it out and, in the end, I managed to get in touch with someone in Kevin Considine's department, a funny little woman called Veronique, and she told me that even with the right sort of mast, we still would-n't be able to get in touch with the Islands because there were too many mountains in the way. I asked her what was going to be done about that, and she said there was supposed to be a chain of relay stations going up along the coast. So I asked her when they would be ready, and she said that Master Considine hadn't been very well lately, so she really had no idea. And then she broke off contact.

To my surprise, the old lady didn't seem too bothered about any of this. Alice was much more concerned, I could see her winding her legs around one another in that funny way of hers, but she never spoke to me if she could help it, so I never really found out what she was worried about.

But for me, it couldn't have been better. The old lady didn't have any interest in the signal engine until she could use it to get in touch with these people on the Islands, whoever they might have been, and that meant that the engine simply didn't get used at all, and that meant that I could have it all to myself. Not that there was anyone I wanted to get in touch with, I suppose when it came to it I didn't really know anyone. No, I was more interested in some of the other things that you could find in the Network. To be precise, I was interested in those funny little things called imps. Now they seemed really interesting. I had chanced upon them once or twice in the course of my training, but at that stage I hadn't really had a chance to get to know them properly, and for some reason old Maggot hadn't been keen to encourage me in that direction. But now I had just the chance I needed.

I could have slipped away up to the turret at just about any time I felt like it, but for some reason it seemed best to conduct my investigations of the signal engine at night. It was illogical, really, because, if anyone had discovered me, it would have looked far more suspicious to be mucking about with it at night-time, but somehow I felt an overpowering need for secrecy. I also thought that it might take me a few sessions to find what I was looking for but, as it turned out, I did everything I needed to do in the course of a few hours and, by the time dawn arrived, I was chained up safe and sound in my bed.

The night I chose for my experiment was one of those nights when I had been visiting my father at the forge. We had fallen into a little routine of after-dinner drinks, or at any rate, with a little encouragement from me, he had fallen into the routine. I allowed him to think that I was drinking as much as he was, but I was careful to keep a clear head, which I did by pouring most of my liquor away when he wasn't looking. As usual, after a couple of hours, we ended up slumped side by side on the pie rack, and my father had fallen into a doze, as he usually did on these occasions.

Eventually, I nudged him goodnight, he replied with some kind of grunt, and I took my leave of him.

The moon was almost full that night, so I managed to pick my way along the track through the woods without collecting too much mud on my boots, and after a few minutes I came in sight of the House. All of its windows were dark, as I had expected, but on the lawn in front of the main building, someone was moving about.

I suppose that in a house the size of the House of Rest, there are bound to be a handful of people who for one reason or another have trouble sleeping. There were certainly a few like that at the Academy of Cartography, and I was beginning to discover that there were a few in this place as well. There was me, of course, and, it turned out, there was also the Exercise Captain. On this rather special night, as I rounded the corner in front of the House, I was surprised to discover a solitary figure capering around on the grass in pyjamas. I was even more surprised when I recognised Alice

I guessed that there must have some kind of method in what she was doing, at any rate she had never seemed the kind for reckless impulses, but I couldn't immediately make any sense of what I saw. I suppose she must have been doing her exercises, although it was a funny time of day for it, but in a way what she was doing actually seemed more like dancing. For a moment I forgot my errand and cautiously stepped closer to her, fascinated by what I saw. She looked as if she was in some kind of a trance, certainly in some strange world of her own. She was leaping and whirling about, flipping herself head over heels on the grass, craning upwards at one moment, twisting her body into a backward curve the next and, before I had been watching her for many minutes, I began to sense some sort of inner logic in her sequence of movements, as if she were dancing to music that no one else could hear. It was something that seemed to attract me and frighten me at the same time and, for a second, I was tempted to forget the signal engine and just stay and watch her instead. Then I came to my senses and withdrew into the shadows again.

I'm pretty sure she didn't see me, at any rate, although I came quite close to her, she didn't react to my presence in any way. For a moment I felt uneasy, as if I'd seen something I shouldn't have seen, but then I reminded myself that I had to concentrate on what I was supposed to be doing, so I made my way quietly inside the House, leaving Alice to her mysterious ritual.

I didn't have any trouble finding my way up the main staircase, as the moon was shining in through the big landing window but, by the time I reached the attic floor, I was having to tread rather more cautiously. I made a mental note to bring a lamp with me on any subsequent visits. Eventually I found my way up the narrow stairs to the turret room and, once inside there, I found that I could see again, because there were windows in all six sides and the moon was still bright.

In the middle of the room squatted the signal engine, just as I'd left it a few days before. I brushed the dust from my clothes and got ready to fire the engine up. I had wondered whether I would need any familiarisation with it but, as it happened, the engine was an identical model to the one I'd used on my training course, so it didn't take me a moment to get the controls adjusted and, before I knew it, I was perched on the seat, squinting down the eyepieces, with the headphones over my ears as if I'd never been away.

To begin with, there was darkness and there was silence. I wasn't bothered by this, because I knew that if there was an imp or anything else there, I would notice it soon enough if I kept quiet and still. Sure enough, after a few minutes, it began to feel as if something was tugging at the back of my neck. It was quite a gentle tug, so gentle that it didn't even startle me when it came, but it was insistent and it was firm. When I didn't respond to it the first time, it came again, and when I ignored it once more, it came a third time, but this time slightly firmer and slightly sooner. Half fascinated, half reluctant, I surrendered myself to its pull and allowed myself to be led forward.

I knew then that things weren't going to turn out the way I'd expected. When people had spoken to me about imps, I had imagined small, playful, agile, mischievous creatures, insubstantial, probably almost weightless. I quickly began to understand that the creature that was tugging me forward was a being of a very different kind.

As I moved, step by hesitant step, into the void beyond view, I began to be aware of a weak, diffuse luminescence around me, not strong enough for me to make out any detail, but just strong enough for me to get a rough idea of the layout of my surroundings. I could now see that I was moving along some kind of corridor, low-roofed and unevenly floored. There were no doors or windows, but from time to time there were openings to left and to right, side turnings that departed from the main passageway at irregular angles, sometimes uphill, sometimes downhill, sometimes seemingly doubling back the way they had come. From time to time, my unseen guide would indicate by a tug one way or the other that I was to turn aside and follow one of these new passages.

After a while of this, I began to perceive that I was treading the corridors of some kind of bizarre maze, a crazy labyrinth of unpredictable geometry in which no surface was horizontal, no wall was vertical, no corner was right-angled. It was not long before my sense of direction had completely deserted me but, as I reminded myself, all this was of course taking place inside the signal engine, in the realm of my imagination, so I was able to reassure myself that I did not need to be concerned with such mundane matters as time and space.

As I dwelt on these things, I began to notice that the tugging at my neck was becoming harder and more urgent, as if I were at one end of a rope and the person at the other end was slowly increasing the tension. At the end of a rope? Involuntarily, my hand rose to my throat. What I found did not feel like a rope, for there, encircling my neck, was a rough iron collar, and the collar was secured with a heavy padlock. And there, attached to the collar, was not a rope but a chain, a heavy iron chain. So at last I was beginning to understand what was happening to me.

The chain must somehow have been getting shorter as I walked because, as I rounded the next bend, I finally caught a brief glimpse of the creature that was hauling at the other end of it. It was a small creature, thin and hunched, and it moved with an awkward shuffle. I frowned, unable to relate it to anything I had seen before. Then, before I had a chance to examine it more closely, it was away round the next corner and out of sight again.

But now the light was growing dimmer, and the turnings were growing closer together, and the ceilings were growing lower, and the angles of the intersections were growing crazier. It was getting difficult even for me to tell the horizontal from the vertical, as if the distortions in the geometry of the place were actually bringing about a distortion in the force of gravity itself. I no longer knew whether I was standing or lying or crawling and, in the last instant of failing light, it even seemed that I caught a glimpse of my sinister guide scuttling across a ceiling. I could hear its footsteps now, sighing steps like bones dragging in the dust, and I could hear its hissing breath and the wheezing of its chest. And as it drew me inexorably into the vortex of the maze, I began to smell its harsh scent in my nostrils, a fetid mingling of oil and smoke and iron and sawdust and rotting food and unwashed flesh. And then, suddenly, we had arrived at our goal, a hot, airless, dark, twisted, low-ceilinged, enclosed space. At last, we were close enough to reach out and touch.

And then it spoke to me.

'Touch me, Thomas,' hissed its voice. 'Reach out and touch me. Isn't that what you want?'

So I reached out. It was a skinny thing, little more than bone and tendon, and its clothing hung about its frame in rags. There were its ribs, its vertebrae, its bony arms and shoulders. There were the rank musk of its body and its vile breath. And there, wrapped around its neck and its body, between its sticklike thighs, across its narrow shoulders, lay the square links of the black iron chain. As the creature shifted its position, the rattle of the chain grated on my ears, and suddenly I wanted to give the creature its freedom, to liberate it from the weight of its shackles. Once again I raised a hand to my throat, and this time the padlock fell open and the collar dropped away from me but, instead of casting its chains aside, the creature pulled them around itself all the tighter. Then, as I stood transfixed, it fell to its knees, moaning and weeping and rocking to and fro.

'I cannot throw away my chains, Tom Slater!' it cried. 'I cannot be set free so easily! Do you not know what you have to do to set me free?'

Suddenly there came a terrific banging sound from the ceiling above us, as if a giant were dropping lead weights on to the surface of a massive table. By now I was in a state of abject terror, but the noises seemed to have had the effect of quietening the creature down.

'For you were once in chains, Tom Slater,' it whispered. 'You were in chains, and one part of you remains in chains until you have done what you have to do. For there are those in the world who have put you where you are today, Tom Slater. There are those who have put you where you are, and there are those who have mocked you for being what you are. And you will remain in chains until all your scores are settled. So that is what you must do, Tom Slater. That is what you must do.' And the creature began to croon 'That is what you must do' over and over again.

At that moment, there came a sudden glimmer of sickly light from somewhere above me, as if someone had lit a feeble oil lamp, and I was able at last to make out the creature's face. I suppose I knew what was coming. Despite the rotting teeth and the red-rimmed eyes, there was no mistaking the angry rash of freckles on the sunken, grimy cheeks, and there was no mistaking the filthy, matted shock of dark red hair. As the pale, unsteady light picked out the hollows of the bony features, the kid began to laugh, a raucous, mocking, hysterical laugh, and as he laughed he ground the links of his chain together, and he rocked himself to and fro, and then, at last, the tears began to flow down his pock-marked cheeks.

And then, without warning, the sounds and the images dissolved away, and I found myself slumped exhausted across the controls of the signal engine in the little turret room. And I knew then that the imp I had found was going to be, not an adversary, but an ally.

From the Keeper of the Ground, at the House of Rest: To the Council of Wise Ones (continued)

I am not the sort of person who is easily thrown from her stride by minor setbacks, Sisters and Brothers. I have always considered this to be one of the strengths in my character, and have valued it accordingly, but lately I have started to become aware that, in certain circumstances, it can also be a weakness. There have been too many setbacks of late, Sisters and Brothers, and the business of the signal engine has provided yet more weight to add to my growing burden of frustrations. Perhaps, if I had paid more attention to the intuition of my granddaughter, none of the things that have followed would have taken place. Perhaps, if I had allowed myself to take a more direct hand in matters, events might have taken a very different course.

But of course it is always foolish to dwell upon what might have been. Alice was uneasy about the signal engine, she made her feelings known to me, but I chose to ignore her. The young man told me that the engine would not function properly without masts, and I also chose to ignore him. I told the young man that there was no more money and, although this was no more nor less than the truth, I realise now that, with a little ingenuity, some other solution to the problem might have been found. But, instead, I chose to put it out of my mind until such time as the money might become available.

This meant, of course, that my signal engine lay neglected in its turret. I knew that it was there, but I chose to do nothing. Alice, too, knew that it was there but, for reasons of her own, she also chose to make no use of it. And, of course, the strange young man who had installed the engine knew that it was there. I have tried to reassure myself that I could have had no inkling of the purpose to which the engine would ultimately be put by him, but I know in my heart that, had I chosen to pay more attention to Alice's misgivings, I might perhaps still have been able to take some action to forestall the terrible events that have now overtaken this House of Rest.

But what is done is done. I know now of the secret

night-time hours that the young man spent in the turret. I know now that he had connected himself in some mysterious way to the engine, had united himself in some inexplicable communion with the unearthly presence, the baleful creature, the imp that dwelt within. And I know now that it was the imp that prompted him to carry out his awful deeds, the deeds that have left such a shadow over our House that I now feel my only honourable course of action is to step aside from my position here and to return in sorrow to the desolate seclusion of the Islands.

My first inkling that all was not well came when the refectory ran out of pies. My appetite for rich food has never been great and, in recent years, it has perhaps been less than ever, and so my visits there have not for some time been frequent. However, several days ago, as sometimes happens even now, I found myself seized by a sudden craving for a slice of mutton and parsnip pie, and my mind turned briefly to Geoffrey the Blacksmith and the oven that he had built in his forge. But, upon arriving at the refectory, I was disappointed to discover that no pies were available that day. At the time, I attached no great significance to this, and in the end I ordered something else, I forget what, and thought no more about it.

Over the next few days, though, I chanced to overhear a number of conversations in which people were complaining about the absence of pies from the menu, and the matter finally came up one afternoon when

I was taking my customary cup of tea with Alice in her cell. Despite her slender physique, my grand-daughter is possessed of a healthy appetite and, like many of the people of our House, is partial to a slice of pie now and again.

'It's probably not important, Nanna,' she said, 'but there haven't been any pies for over a week. Do you think there might be anything the matter with Geoffrey?'

Still I was not greatly concerned. Geoffrey is a soli-tary man who prefers mostly to keep his own company, sometimes remaining in the seclusion of his forge for days on end.

'He likes being on his own,' I replied. 'And it's always best to respect people's wishes in such things.' At that point in the conversation, I noticed that Alice had started knotting her legs together again.

'There's more to it than that,' she said finally. 'You see, he's not actually been on his own. I've seen some-one going over there in the evenings. That strange young man, you know, the one who helped you with the signal engine?'

'The one you don't like?'

She nodded reluctantly.

'And I saw him coming back once,' Alice continued. 'It was late. I was having trouble sleeping, so I'd gone down to the lawn to exercise. He watched me for a little while, but I don't think he knew that I'd seen him. But I'm sure he smelled of drink, strong drink. Oh, Nanna –' she had become very agitated '– I'm sure something's wrong. Can't we go over to the forge and have a look?'

Reluctantly, I agreed to this. Abandoning our tea, we collected a couple of pairs of stout boots from the storekeeper and set off up the muddy track through the woods. Driven by the force of her anxiety, Alice quickly drew ahead of me, while I followed at a more measured pace, happy to humour my granddaughter's whims, still failing to feel any concern for the fate of the blacksmith. As we approached the forge, I was enjoying the scent of woodland flowers and damp earth, until it occurred to me that there was no trace of the usual aroma of woodsmoke, hot iron and freshly baked pastry. I think it was at that point that I finally began to sense that something was indeed wrong. Then I heard Alice calling to me from up ahead. Anxious now, I quickened my pace.

Inside the forge, it was at once apparent that nobody had been there for some days. The air, usually sweltering hot and dense with smoke, was stale and cold. I found Alice standing beside the furnace, her hand resting lightly on the heavy iron door of the oven.

'Feel it,' she invited me. I felt it. It was cold.

'It looks as if he's gone away,' I suggested. Alice shook her head. Looking around the room, I could see Geoffrey's coat hanging on its usual nail, Geoffrey's tools scattered as usual on his workbench, even Geoffrey's boots standing side by side in a corner. In another corner, there was a medium-sized, untidy pile of empty bottles.

By the time I had taken in these details, Alice had managed to unfasten the oven door. Belatedly, I became aware of a faint aroma of charred meat.

'We'd better look in here,' said Alice. She looked even paler than usual, and her voice was unsteady. She swung the oven door open and fumbled with the catches that secured the baking rack.

The rack was solidly built and very heavy but, between the two of us, we eventually managed to heave it out along its rails. On top of it lay, not a batch of burnt pies, but the charred remains of a human being. For a moment we stood helpless.

'Is it Geoffrey?' Alice managed at last.

'I'm not sure,' I replied, and I realised that my own voice was weak and faint. 'But I think I recognise this. Geoffrey made it.'

Wrapped several times around the body, binding it tightly to the rack, secured with several padlocks, was a length of heavy, square-linked iron chain.

Scratching Where It Itches

'Scratch me a bit more . . . No, a little lower . . . Yes, that's it . . .'

'You like me scratching you, don't you, Kevin? I'll scratch you some more if you like. How about this? Is this nice?'

'Ooh, that feels funny. What are you doing?'

Just writing my name.'

Kevin and Lee were sprawled side by side in the

big bed. It had been a long and demanding night, and the candles, which had been new when they started, had burnt down almost to the sconces.

'So where were you all that time?' Kevin finally enquired. 'Why weren't you here with me?'

'Didn't you want me to go exploring, Kevin? Didn't you say I could go?' Lee extended a long leg across Kevin's body and began to scratch at his shoulder with her toenails. *'I've been to all sorts of places. And there were lots of other people who wanted to meet me, too.'*

'Other people?' Kevin was alarmed. 'I don't want to share you with any other people. Ow, that hurts! Do you have to scratch so hard?'

'Poor Kevin, he's got such delicate skin!' She stroked his shoulder softly with the ball of her foot. *'Is that better? But you wouldn't want me to get bored now, would you, Kevin? And anyway, it's not as if you were really sharing me, is it? Because the others all see me in different ways. So please say you're not going to be cross with me. You're not going to be cross, are you, Kevin?'* Twisting around onto her side, she slid her other leg underneath his body and began to scratch gently up and down the side of his ribcage.

'Aah, that's nice. But how do you mean, differently? How do they see you differently?'

'It's a bit hard to explain, Kevin.' Linking her ankles together, she gave his torso a tentative squeeze. *'But what you see isn't really me, is it?'* She frowned. *'At least, I suppose it's partly me. But most of what you see comes from you, doesn't it? From your own imagination? Hadn't*

you managed to work that out?' Suddenly, she squeezed much harder. Kevin drew a sharp breath.

'Steady on, you're cracking my ribs!' Lee smiled enigmatically, and Kevin detected an easing of the pressure. 'But listen. If it all comes from me, what are you really like? I mean, can I ever see you as you really are?' The candles were beginning to gutter now. In a few moments, they would start to go out.

'You want to see me as I really am?' Lee's voice had begun to rise. *'Is that what you want, Kevin Constanzas? Is that what you really want?'*

Suddenly, with startling force, she rolled onto her back, her powerful legs encircling his arms and body, heaving him on top of her, twisting the black satin sheets around his legs.

'Is that what you want?' Toenails were raking at his back, and fingernails were clawing at his neck.

'Stop it, that's enough!' Kevin gasped, the breath knocked out of him. 'You're hurting me! Do it gently!' He tried to struggle free, but his legs were hopelessly entangled in the twisted sheets.

'Poor Kevin!' Her voice mocked him now. *'He wants me to do it gently!'* Suddenly, she plunged her nails deep into his flesh, sending rivulets of blood coursing down his sides. To his horror, Kevin found himself unable to move, rigidly pinioned as if by iron chains.

'Hasn't he ever had it from a real woman?'

With a furious roar, she rolled him over again onto his back, heaving herself astride him now, squeezing the breath out of his lungs, clawing wildly at his chest, his belly, his throat, bathing herself in the welling blood, hissing and cursing and spitting at him as his struggles became feebler. Then, at last, in the fading light, her fury seemed to abate.

'*Has Kevin had enough? Is he tired now?*' The voice was tender again. Then, with a final surge of rage, she drew back her arm and slashed her fingernails viciously across his throat. The last thing Kevin saw was her face, a savage, distorted mask of hate.

Veronique had always had a suspicion that Mister Considine was destined for a bad end. So, when she arrived the next day with the coffee, although she was momentarily taken aback at the sight of his mutilated body, she had to admit to herself that she was not altogether surprised.

'Too many late nights. Not good for a growing boy,' was her only comment to the Wolf Boys who came to investigate the death. But, later, Veronique remembered the brass nameplate that she had found on the back of the signal engine, the nameplate that had borne the name of her old associate, the disgraced magician Leonardo Pegasus. And, if Leonardo Pegasus had made the engine, Veronique thought, perhaps Leonardo Pegasus might after all be able to sort out the trouble it had been causing.

So maybe it was time for someone else to be told her secret. Veronique waited for an opportunity to slip away from the Administrative Centre. When the coast was clear, she quietly picked up her handbag, slipped out of the door, and set off on her stubby legs in the direction of the Throne Room.

'So what are you going to do next?'

Well, Nina, you'll be pleased to hear that I've been making plans for the future at last, so I think this will probably have to be the final one of our little talks. I'm going to miss our sessions, sitting here in this room, chatting away, or just staring out at that nice view over the lawn with the woods and the hills beyond. It's hard to believe that it's only a few days since I saw Alice out there on the grass, doing her strange exercises or whatever it was she was up to. As I said before, I didn't really have the time then to figure out what she was doing, but I did find myself getting quite intrigued by it. I think you were right, though, when you said back at the start that I wasn't quite ready for any of that, and unfortunately I don't think I'll be staying at the House of Rest for much longer on this visit. But, if I ever do come back, I think I'd quite like to join the exercise class and find out a bit more about that side of things.

I've always been interested in patterns and systems in all their various forms. As I've told you, there were the poems and the crosswords, and of course there was the cartography, and I realise now that all those different things eventually came together into some kind of whole when I spent those years at the transport interchange. And Alice's stuff, well, it just seemed to bring it all together in a different sort of way, so I do feel quite tempted to spend a bit of time on it and find out more. But it can't be this time. I'll explain why in a minute.

I told you about that night I spent on my experiment with the signal engine. When I came out of that, I felt completely exhausted, and I had to spend a couple of days in bed before I felt ready to tackle anything else. I'd never had an experience like it. Of course, I knew at the back of my mind that none of what was happening was real but, as I got drawn into the maze, it all became so vivid, so compelling, that I completely forgot about the other world. And so the House of Rest and the turret and the signal engine, and that maze and the creature that lived in it became my whole reality. What I found really hard to grasp afterwards was that the whole thing had taken place entirely within my own imagination, with just a little help from whatever it was that I found in the maze. I'm pretty sure there must have been something there that came from outside myself, but most of that stuff about the chain and the red-haired kid and the other things — well, that could only have come from me, couldn't it? You must know enough about me by now to realise that the imagination is not a place where I've ever spent very much time, except maybe for the poems, so I suppose I must have experienced just about a whole lifetime's worth of imagination in one session. Perhaps it's not so surprising that I needed a rest afterwards.

At any rate, for a couple of days I slept, and I dreamed, and I woke, and I slept again, and when I finally came to myself I found that I knew exactly what I had to do. One of the things I like about this place is that people are allowed to do pretty well what they want. Most of the other places

I've been — my father's house, the orphanage, the Academy, the gaol and the menagerie — have been run in a pretty authoritarian sort of a way, and even when I ran the transport interchange it was all done along highly organised lines, so it's made a nice change to spend some time in such an easygoing sort of atmosphere.

What I'm getting around to saying is that, if I'd taken to my bed for a couple of days in any of those other places, if I'd neglected what I should have been doing, there would have been trouble building up for me straight away. And, as you know, when I decided to take a bit of time out from the transport interchange, things went to pieces pretty well immediately, and they never recovered. But here nobody seems too bothered if you don't turn up for something, they just muddle along without you and, when you do finally turn up, nobody's angry, they just say how nice it is to see you again.

Well, once I was up and about, I decided that there were things I had to settle with my father that couldn't be put off any longer, and that after I'd done that, it would be time for me to make my way back to the city, and to try and put things straight with my old friend Mister Brown, the publisher of charts. So I went and saw my father that night, and we had a few drinks in our usual way — yes, I know we're not supposed to, but you won't tell on me, will you, Nina?— and I finally told him what I needed to tell him, and then I showed him my chain, and he showed me his chain, and then we had a few more drinks, and eventually he fell asleep, and when I left him there and shut the door he was looking quite happy and warm and comfortable, and

I even had a moment of what might have been affection for him.

I slept well that night, for the first time in ages. Of course, I should really have set off back to the city straight away, but there was just one more thing I had to do here. I hope you won't think this is silly, Nina, but I really needed to see you for one last session, just to finish telling my story because, as you know, I'm a very meticulous sort of person, and once I start something off, I like to see it properly finished before I leave it alone.

What I hadn't counted on was that I wouldn't be able to find you! That last evening I spent with my father was a Thursday and, when I went looking for you, it turned out that you had taken a long weekend and gone away somewhere, I think someone told me that your old friends from the travelling amusements were passing close by and you'd gone off to see them for a bit. So it seemed that I would have to wait until our usual session on Tuesday afternoon before I could finish my tale. Now, in one way that was good, because we've always met on a Tuesday afternoon, and somehow it wouldn't have been right to have had our last session on a different day. But in another way it was quite nerve-racking, because I really wanted to get away as quickly as I could. I'm sorry if this isn't making sense, Nina, but I promise it'll all come clear in a minute. You see, I knew that people would start missing my father before very long, but I reassured myself that he often spent quite a bit of time on his own at the forge, and that I would probably get by for a few days before anyone started asking questions.

So, after a couple of days, I did begin to relax a bit, but then I remembered about the pies. I was standing in the queue at the Refectory, I think it was Sunday lunchtime, and I heard somebody in front of me asking the cook why there weren't any pies that day. The cook just said that they didn't necessarily have them every day, and he was sure that there would be another batch sent down before too long. Well, after that I knew that I wouldn't be safe for very much longer, but I still needed to see you, Nina, so I decided then that it would be best for me just to stay out of everyone's way and to keep my eyes open.

I got my things packed up ready, because I knew that I might have to leave in a hurry, and then I took myself off to the one place I reckoned I'd be safe, and that was the turret where the signal engine was. There was a good view of the woods from there, so I'd know straight away if anything happened. For a bit of diversion, I did try powering up the engine, but I reckon I must have exhausted its possibilities for the time being, because I didn't find anything there except darkness and silence. So, after that, I just sat, and I watched, and I waited.

Two whole days I spent up there, and I think it's fair to say that they've been the two most nerve-racking days of my life. But I'm glad that I did keep my nerve because, as it turned out, nothing happened, and all I saw was people coming and going in their usual way, so obviously nobody was missing their pies all that much. And then this morning I saw you arriving back from your vacation and, as you can see, I've turned up for our appointment in the usual way. But we're going to have to hurry things along now, Nina, because I've been watching the view through the window, and a few minutes ago I saw the old lady and her granddaughter making their way up the track that leads through the woods to the forge. And now I can see them coming back again, and they seem to be in a bit of a hurry.

So I'll have to be on my way now, Nina. I'm sorry it's all ended in such a rush. You see, I need to get off to my appointment with Mister Brown and, as you may have noticed, I've got all my stuff with me here, not that there's very much of it. Just a few spare clothes, and a few of my old charts and poems and so on. Oh yes, there is one thing I'd like you to see. Yes, that's right, my old iron chain. It's been a good friend to me, that chain, and you've heard so much about it, it would be a shame if I went without giving you a proper look at it.

No, don't get up, I'll bring it over to you. But I'm afraid I'm going to have to hurry things up a bit. No, just keep still. You don't have to do anything . . .

I'm really sorry it has to end like this, Nina but, you see, I've told you too much now. I've just gone and told you too much.

From the Keeper of the Ground, at the House of Rest: To the Council of Wise Ones (continued)

Sisters and Brothers, I wish I could say that my discovery of Geoffrey's corpse in the forge had marked the end of my troubles but, sadly, there was one more terrible event still awaiting me on that terrible day. As soon as I caught a glimpse of the square-linked chain, I knew at once who must have been responsible for what we had discovered.

'The young man?' I said to Alice.

'The young man,' she replied slowly.

'Might he still be at the House?'

Alice frowned in concentration for a moment.

'I don't think I've seen him for a few days,' she said finally. 'But it's Tuesday, isn't it? If he is here, I think he would be in the listening room with Nina.'

Panic-stricken at the thought of what might be taking place, we fled from the forge, raced off down the track towards the House, and ran pell-mell across the front lawn, scattering a circle of people who were sitting there listening to the offerings of the ballad singers. And, as we entered the House, our ears were assailed by a terrifying shriek that came from the direction of the listening room. In a second we were hammering at the door, only to discover that, as was Nina's custom, it had been bolted from the inside.

By the time we had secured the necessary assistance to effect an entry, we were too late. Nina was dead, her body slumped in her chair, the marks of the chain forming a macabre necklace about her throat. Behind her, the window of the room stood open, the curtains flapping.

Of course, we made an immediate search of the House and grounds, we even sent parties up into the hills and the fields, but it soon become apparent that our quarry had eluded us. At dusk, I called all the people together on the lawn to let them know the news, after which I asked Alice to lead them though the Sequence of Contemplation. Naturally, we have sent for the Militia but, without the aid of the signal engine, our message will be slow to reach them, so it seems unlikely that they can be of any assistance to us. We do not know where the young man was bound. We do not even know his name. Only Nina knew his story, and she, sadly, can no longer help us.

And that, Sisters and Brothers, concludes my account of the events of the past twelve months. The House of Rest is quiet again tonight, but my people go about their business with an air of numbness, and it seems to me that the vital pulse of our House, once so vibrant, is for the time being still. Some talk of quitting the House for good but perhaps, when they have had time to consider matters, a few may decide to remain here and apply themselves to the reconstruction of what once we had. But surely many will no longer wish to stay, poisoned as the air has become by what has taken place.

The ballad singers will be on their way from here in the morning, and with them goes my account, signed and sealed. As for myself, you must now understand why I no longer feel able to remain within these walls, carrying as I do the burden of responsibility upon my shoulders. I have some trifling matters still to settle but, in a few days' time, I shall be taking my place on the northbound waggon and returning to you, my kinfolk, on the Islands.

In the face of such devastating adversity, it pleases me to report one cheering piece of news. My grand-daughter Alice, for so long my mainstay in my lonely task, has intimated to me that she wishes to remain here, to begin the task of repairing the damage to our community, and to continue with the work that I began so many years ago. I therefore appoint her my successor, and I am confident that you will join your voices to mine in wishing her good fortune in the pursuance of her chosen path.

There remains no more for me to say. It is with a heavy heart that I take my leave of the House of Rest, but it is with gladness that I anticipate our reunion after so many years, my Sisters and Brothers, in our homeland.

May the Great Being grant us good guidance.

Your kinswoman, Kathleen.

Six:
THE IMP AND THE ENGINE

The Royal Digest of Affairs and Events: Volume 183 (in the Sixteenth Year of the Rule of King Matthew)

The Diary of Miss Garamond (Herald)

Greetings, Citizens!

Readers will doubtless have been shocked and saddened to learn of the unexpected death of Mister Kevin Considine, Royal Supervisor of Machinery, while in the course of carrying out his official duties at the Palace Administration Centre. The precise circumstances of Mister Considine's death are at present unclear, and are in fact currently under scrutiny by the Royal Wolf Boys Accident Investigation Department.

The known facts are as follows. Mister Considine's naked body was discovered in his laboratory by a senior member of the Administrative Staff, who was at the time engaged in the routine process of unlocking rooms in preparation for the day's business. There were extensive lacerations to the victim's throat, stomach and other parts, and the victim is in fact understood to have bled to death. In addition to the aforementioned wounds, there were some indications that the victim had also suffered molestations of a more intimate nature. The incident was at once reported to the Investigators, from whom we include a statement later in this bulletin.

At such a time of sorrow, it would in normal circumstances be appropriate to publish some personal words of tribute from King Matthew. We are given to understand, however, that although King Matthew has at long last returned to the City following his turn of duty in the Border Campaign, he remains for the time being indisposed, and has not so far been able to resume his normal duties of State. In the meantime, therefore, the author is pleased to publish the following statement of appreciation from High Master Fang, delivered in the course of his monthly Private Audience.

'Kevin Considine was one of the key members of the King's Mechanical Support Team, and has in fact occupied a leading role on that team since the very early days of its inception at the accession of King Matthew. Mister Considine's achievements include the development and implementation of the Administrative Support systems that remain in use throughout the

Royal Household. These comprise the Writing and Administrative Engines and associated equipment facilitating the production of official Memoranda and other such documents, the Illumination Devices and Window Shutters for the maintenance of a productive working environment and, of course, the Refreshment Engines for the provision of warm beverages to staff.

'Most recently, Mister Considine has devoted his energies almost exclusively to the design and installation of the Royal Signal Network. This innovative technology, now so well known to everyone, has in recent years brought about the transformation of almost every facet of the day-to-day lives of all Citizens. It is difficult at this moment to imagine how it will be possible for the development of the Network to progress further, bereft as it now is of the guiding hand of Mister Considine. But, of course, the march of progress must continue, and we remain confident that, with or without the guidance of its originator, the Network will continue to develop over the years to come, and to bring about yet more advantages and conveniences to the Citizenry.

'We pay our sincere respects to the memory of Mister Considine, and we look forward to many more years of benefit from the important work of which he was the instigator.'

A further statement follows from Master Gash, Chief Inspector of the Royal Wolf Boys Accident Investigation Branch.

'The Branch is currently pursuing a number of lines of investigation in our attempt to identify the cause of the untimely death of Mister Considine. We are particularly eager to receive any available intelligence concerning the increasingly common encounters with the creatures known as 'imps'. These 'imps' are apparently proving a great nuisance to users of the Signal Network, and we have reason to believe that Mister Considine may have been engaged in some form of congress with 'imps' during the last months of his life. We are most anxious to forestall any such incidents in the future, as we have no desire to see these 'imps' becoming a danger to the Citizenry.

'In this connection, we have received some most helpful information from a Miss Veronique Moreau, who was an early witness at the scene of Mister Considine's unfortunate demise. A brass plate discovered by Miss Moreau has been impounded for inspection, and efforts are being made as a result of this to establish contact with one Master Leonardo Pegasus, formerly a Magician in the Retinue of the Old King who, it is believed, may be able to assist us with our inquiries.

'Efforts are also being made to trace the family of Mister Considine, as his remains are currently awaiting disposal. Persons with any information are requested to come forward without delay. In the meantime, Citizens should exercise all due caution in the use of the Signal Network, and any untoward occurrences should be immediately reported to the appropriate authority.'

The author is confident that all readers will join their voices to hers in mourning the death of such a valued member of the Royal Administration. It is indeed true to say that, without the unique contribution of Mister Considine, the Kingdom would truly be a different place from the one we know today.

Sufficient space remains for the author to mention one further matter of interest.

There have been reports on a number of recent occasions of unprovoked attacks on members of the Citizenry during the hours of darkness. On all occasions, these individuals have been engaged upon their lawful business within the confines of the City walls. On one occasion, the victim was a member of the Royal Wolf Boys Militia!

According to reports from witnesses, the attackers appear to be a group of girls or young women, dressed in ragged clothes, with their faces grotesquely painted, and with their hair cropped short. These individuals are in the habit of concealing themselves on the tops of walls or buildings, and terrifying their victims by flinging themselves down upon them from above. As it happens, one of the victims of these attacks was our own Director of Iconography, Mister Norman Loxley, who was fortunately not seriously hurt. A sketch by Mister Loxley appears below, bearing his somewhat fanciful title 'Attack of the Cat Girls'. Needless to say, the Royal Wolf Boys Militia have been alerted, and the Citizenry can therefore rest assured that any further instances of such behaviour will be viewed in the most serious light, and the perpetrators apprehended and dealt with in the most severe fashion.

Finally, the author wishes King Matthew a swift recovery from his present indisposition. In the light of the many disturbing incidents of recent weeks, it is devoutly to be hoped that the Kingdom will see a speedy return to more peaceful times!

Goodbye, Citizens, and long live King Matthew!

A Visitor for Rusty

Rusty was staring glumly at the large, hand-drawn chart that was spread out on the broad table beneath the skylight in his drawing office. Across the top of it was scrawled *City Series. Sheet 5: Undertown.* Underneath this heading someone had crossed out the subtitle *Draft 14* and inserted, in pencil, *Draft 15.* Rusty rubbed the sides of his head in frustration, wondering whether the long-deferred chart of the Undertown would ever be ready for issue.

During the years following the founding of Michael Brown Publications and the release of the first five sheets of the *City Series of Charts*, a number of further series had been published at annual intervals. The first forty-eight sheets of the *Provincial Chart* had been especially successful, and the second forty-eight were now nearing the final stages of preparation. Somehow, though, the chart of the Undertown never quite seemed to be ready, and somehow it managed again and again to slip through Rusty's fingers.

Perhaps it was because the bureaucrats of the City Administration kept changing their minds about what to do with the district. They would knock down an old building here, start a new development there. Then they would change their minds, abandoning one project after another, sending away the builders, bringing back the demolition crews. Yes, perhaps it was just the prevarication of the City Authorities. But perhaps it was something less tangible, something more to do with the character of the Undertown itself. Rusty knew from his own rambles around the city just how difficult it was to maintain one's sense of direction in those convoluted networks of alleys and catwalks and derelict buildings and empty sites, and he knew also that the Undertown seemed somehow to present a different face on every visit. Sometimes he wondered whether unseen hands were at work in the hours of darkness, reconfiguring the topography, skewing the geometry, warping the compass bearings, making mischief for mischief's sake.

In his youth, Rusty recalled with contrition, he had wasted the best part of a year in the Undertown, mixing in doubtful company, cocking a snook at authority, subjecting himself and others to abuse both physical and mental. He had thought then, in his youthful arrogance, that he knew every kerbstone, every gutter, every intimate detail of its geography. Looking back now, he doubted whether he had truly done so, and he doubted too whether he ever could.

Rusty tweaked off his reading glasses and slipped them into his top pocket. Then he stood up, carefully straightened his back, and crossed over to the large, sloping, north-facing window. It had been the view from this window, he remembered, that had finally persuaded him to take out a lease on the building. The window commanded a broad northward prospect across a patch of abandoned land, taking in the tall masts of the dockside and the slablike blocks of the North Estate. Between the buildings, the sparkling surface of the river was intermittently visible, and beyond the river lay a glimpse of distant hills. In his idle moments, Rusty enjoyed watching the flock of wild goats, fourteen of them, that grazed on the rough land in the foreground. Today, they were at the far corner, almost out of sight, working their way along the tussocky grass at the foot of the high brick wall that surrounded the docks. Staring hard, Rusty could count eight white goats and five grey ones. Vaguely, he wondered what had happened to the sixth grey goat.

'Mister Brown?' Rusty's chain of thought was broken by the diffident voice of his assistant, Charlotte. Over the years, she had developed the knack of slipping gently into Rusty's office and, indeed, into his consciousness, without making any undue noise or fuss. 'Just a few minutes, if you're not busy.' He nodded, and they both seated themselves.

'So what's M. B. Pubs up to this morning?' Charlotte smiled at Rusty's customary words of introduction. They had long ago dispensed with the ritual of formal weekly meetings, and Rusty trusted Charlotte to keep everything running smoothly in the main office, and to keep him more or less in touch with what was happening there from day to day.

'Well, there's another batch of proofs ready for *Prov 2*,' Charlotte began at once, 'that's Sheets 63 to 66. And there's some stuff arrived about that conference, you know, the one about the sense of direction, or whatever it was. And the builder's men are coming later today, at least I hope they are, to patch up that wall in the basement, I really think we need to look at getting that done properly. Oh, and another pattern marker has left, so we've only got two at the moment, we ought to think about recruiting at least another one. And the signal engine's still on the blink, the kites keep blowing the wrong way.' She paused while Rusty scribbled a note. 'Oh yes, and there's a man waiting to see you downstairs. Funny-looking bloke, very tall. Long, black hair. Says his name's Tom Slater.'

'Tom Slater?'

'Tom Slater. At least, I think that's what he said.'

'Better show him in, then. Thanks, Charlotte. I knew him at the Academy.'

At home that evening, Rusty was still mulling over his meeting with his old acquaintance as he lounged in his armchair, staring out of the window of the apartment. This time, it was his wife's voice that interrupted his thoughts.

'Ashleigh, I'll want that table for supper in a minute. Can you tidy up and give it a wipe? And Rusty, if you're not too busy looking out of the window, you could come and get the knives and forks.'

Ashleigh gathered up the pages of the letter she was writing. She had been in regular correspondence with Liam Blackwood ever since her first holiday on the road with her father. The two youngsters had quickly struck up a firm friendship and, since the Wanderers' waggons did not tend to be equipped with such modern conveniences as signal engines, they had had to keep in touch by the old-fashioned method, entrusting their passionate exchanges to the rather unpredictable network of couriers and messengers that still claimed to deliver to all corners of the land.

'And where's Max?' Eileen was saying. 'Ash, can you go and look for him when you've put that stuff away? And hurry up, Rusty, the supper will be ready any second.'

'Why does it always have to be me?' Ashleigh moaned automatically as she headed for the door. 'He's probably just mucking about in the basement, as usual.'

Moments later, Rusty saw his daughter appear on the grass below. Instead of going straight to the basement where Max was expected to be playing, she paused on the lawn and spent a moment practising the flamingo kicks that she had been learning in her

Unarmed Combat class. Rusty smiled as he headed for the kitchen. When Ashleigh was younger, he had tried to interest her in some of the exercise patterns that Alice had taught him, and which he still practised intermittently. But although the girl had displayed a gratifying degree of agility, she had soon lost interest in the rather formalised sequence of attitudes, and had eventually hit upon this rather more aggressive means of dissipating her energies.

'They're so different from each other,' Rusty commented to Eileen. 'What do you reckon Maxie gets up to, playing on his own for all those hours?'

'I suppose he's more like me,' replied Eileen abstractedly, as she drained a pan of potatoes into the sink. 'I used to play on my own a lot. And at least he's not getting himself into scrapes like Ash does. She's really starting to get quite wayward. At any rate, we always know more or less where Max is.'

Rusty moved into the next room and started to arrange the cutlery on the table. He raised his voice slightly to continue the conversation.

'Oh, I meant to say. Do you remember me mentioning someone called Tom Slater? Someone I knew at the Academy?'

'I'm not sure,' Eileen's voice echoed back to him from the kitchen. 'Wasn't it someone called Slater who was involved in that transport thing all those years ago? You know, the interchange?'

'Yes, that's right. Same chap.' Rusty paused in his task, briefly uncertain about the proper way to arrange the spoons and forks for the pudding. 'He turned up at the office today. Hadn't seen him for years. I ended up offering him a job. I didn't really mean to, but I think he'll be all right.'

'Wasn't he supposed to be a bit of a dodgy character? Didn't he go to prison?'

'Oh, he's not so bad. He's had a colourful career, for sure, though – he was telling me all about it. But he knows a bit of cartography, as much as I do, anyway, and he's done a course in signal engine technology too. And one of the pattern markers left the other day, so I thought I'd give him a chance.'

'I suppose it's up to you. It's your business.' Eileen had been distracted from her preparation of the meal, and was mopping up some water that she had spilt on the floor.

'The thing is –' Rusty had now returned to the kitchen in search of place mats '– he's just come back to the city, Tom Slater, that is, and he hasn't got anywhere to live. I wondered if we could . . .' Eileen eyed him suspiciously. '. . . Well, actually, I said he could use our spare room. Just until he gets settled, of course.'

There was a short silence, during which Eileen squeezed out the mop and returned it to the broom cupboard. Finally, brushing the dust from her apron, she turned to face Rusty.

'You never learn, do you?' Her exasperation did not seem to be leavened with quite so much affection these days. 'You really must talk to me first about these daft schemes of yours. Because I've had just about enough of your batty lodgers. So this time, the answer is no. Now, is that table laid?'

Rusty knew better than to continue the argument at that moment, so he said nothing more. Seconds later, the door burst open, and Ashleigh and Max re-appeared.

'Wash your hands, Maxie, before your mother sees them,' said Rusty quickly. 'And Ash, come and get the plates.'

Later, after the washing-up had been done, and Max had gone to bed, and Ashleigh had been allowed out for one last hour to see her friend Davina from the floor below, Rusty reopened the subject of Tom Slater.

'We don't really use that room,' he said, 'apart from the signal engine. And you did say that a bit of extra money would be handy.'

'Oh, I suppose so,' Eileen conceded reluctantly. 'You say you've already told him he can come? But you make sure he understands it's only until he gets himself sorted out. Is that clear, Rusty? And next time, for heaven's sake ask me first.'

A Visitor for Leonardo

Leonardo Pegasus sometimes wondered how he had ever found the time to be a full-time magician. In his retirement, he found himself busier than he had ever been in the days when he was burdened with all the obligations of a working professional. His new employer, the landlord of the Plough, was becoming elderly, and was relying more and more on Leonardo to serve customers at the bar, to look after the cellar and to supervise deliveries. And, at the end of the day, Leonardo was expected to sweep and tidy the taproom after the last customers had departed. Granny Hopkins had finally retired from this position the previous year, at the age of a hundred and six, claiming that she needed to spend more time on her vegetable garden, and it had not proved easy to secure a full-time replacement.

And, on top of all this, Leonardo had another job as well. Every Monday he would pull on his outdoor boots and trudge off up the hill behind the village to the unmanned signal station that had appeared during the expansion of the Royal Signal Network. There, he was employed as part-time warden. Most of the time, this role required him to do little more than cut the grass and polish the brassware but, occasionally, when there was a mechanical malfunction with the kites or the signal engine, Leonardo would find himself dusting down his long-neglected technical knowledge to diagnose and correct whatever fault was giving the trouble.

All of this left little time for him to pursue his two serious interests; first, his Thursday-night drinking sessions with his friend the retired schoolmaster, and second, of course, his multiple empathy engine. This device, which after forty years was still firmly stuck at the experimental stage, now occupied most of the top floor of the outbuilding behind the inn. Leonardo still wasn't quite sure what he was going to do with the multiple empathy engine when all the fine adjustments were complete, but he knew that it was important not to let these things slide, so he tried to put in a little time on it at least once a fortnight.

One Tuesday, Leonardo was on duty behind the bar, attending to the sporadic needs of a small handful of customers and musing about the unpredictable nature of Tuesdays. Monday was all right, he thought to himself, you could always rely on a Monday to be quiet. And of course Wednesday was halfway through the week, so things were usually starting to pick up. And then, by Thursday it was almost the weekend, and of course Friday and Saturday were always busy. And Sunday would be busy at lunchtime, and then quiet again in the evening, because people would be getting ready for work again. But on a Tuesday you never quite knew where you were. It was a nebulous sort of a day. Leonardo shook his head in frustration.

Abruptly, he was jerked out of his daydream by a gruff voice that seemed to come from nowhere.

'Wotcher, Wizzy-boy! Long time, no see!'

'Veronique? What on earth are you doing here?' Directing his gaze downwards, he could just see the little clown's frizzy hair poking up above the surface of the bar.

'Never mind that now, me old Wizz-bang. Just pull your finger out and get us an ale.'

'Why don't you find yourself a stool?' said Leonardo. 'At least I could see you then.'

At that moment there was an unexpected influx of customers, so Leonardo didn't get another chance to speak to his friend until the end of the evening.

'So what's happening in the city?' he asked, by way of an ice-breaker.

'They've screwed up big-time,' Veronique replied succinctly. 'Signal Network's gone pear-shaped. Old Considine-features got himself slaughtered by imps or some such, and now nobody's got a clue what to do about any of it, so all hell's breaking loose. All running round like headless chickens, they are. But I found this.' She reached into her bag and produced the corroded brass plate that bore Leonardo's name. 'Seems like little Kevvy had been a bit of a bad boy. They reckon he must have nicked some old bit of your kit and changed its name. And now they want you to go back and sort it out for them.' She paused to ignite one of her short, vile-smelling cigars. 'And they thought I might be able to persuade you.'

'Well, who'd have thought it!' Leonardo finished polishing a flask and returned it to its proper place on the shelf. 'It must be ten, no, more like fifteen years since that young whippersnapper of a King kicked me out. And now he wants me back again. I hope they can make it worth my while.'

Veronique raised her eyebrows, impressed by her friend's new-found commercial acumen.

'I'm sure they can,' she replied. 'Thing is, they want you on the next coach. Is there one tonight?'

Leonardo smiled wanly. Veronique was very much

an urban clown. She clearly had a lot to learn about the ways of the countryside.

'Not tonight, old friend. Nor tomorrow. Actually, not until Monday. So I'm afraid we'll have to endure a little delay. Of course, I will need a day or so to make the arrangements for this place before we go. But, mainly, I reckon we're just going to have to spend –' he counted on his fingers '– six days catching up on old times.'

A conspiratorial grin stole over the clown's face.

'So we're stranded here for six days?'

Leonardo nodded inscrutably.

'Time for another one of the same, then?'

Leonardo reached for a couple of flasks.

The Perfect Lodger

Rusty was halfway through his Wednesday-morning shave when he heard the rasping honk of the courier's horn echoing up from the courtyard.

'Can you go, Eileen?' he shouted. 'I need another few minutes in here.'

'I can't hear you,' came the muffled reply. 'What did you say?'

'Can you go down for the courier?' Rusty repeated. 'I'm shaving. It won't take you a minute.'

'I'm still doing the dishes,' Eileen shouted from the kitchen, 'and the kids aren't ready for school. Can't we leave him until tomorrow?'

'Oh, Mum –' it was Ashleigh's voice this time '–

I'm expecting something from Liam. It nearly always comes on a Wednesday.'

'You go, then, if it's so important,' Rusty shouted back to her. 'Damn it, you've made me cut myself. Do I have to do everything in this house?'

'But I haven't finished my hair,' wailed Ashleigh. 'It's a mess, a vile mess. I can't go down looking like this. Mum, tell Max to go!'

'I can't find my homework,' shrilled Max. Rusty could hear the noises of objects being frantically over-turned as his son rummaged randomly for his missing exercise books. After a few moments of this, there came a distinctive creak from the door of the spare bedroom.

'Why don't I go down?' Tom's voice joined the commotion now. 'I'm ready for work, and it sounds like you're all busy.'

Rusty emerged from the bathroom, mopping blood and foam from his face.

'Thanks, Tom. It would really help. Maxie? What colour is your homework book today?'

By the time Tom returned with the letters, Rusty had managed to patch up his face, Ashleigh was almost satisfied with her hair, and Eileen was on her hands and knees removing invisible specks of dirt from the kitchen floor. Only Max remained in a state of panic, crawling under armchairs in search of the missing books. As Tom manoeuvred his lanky frame through the doorway to the sitting room, Ashleigh began hopping from one foot to the other in a state of frenzied anticipation.

'Just two letters,' said Tom, teasingly, holding the

envelopes aloft. 'One in a cream envelope for Mr and
Mrs M. Brown. That one looks interesting.' He handed
the letter to Rusty. 'And this other one's in a white
envelope. But I don't think it looks very interesting.
Shall I throw it away?'

'TOM!' howled Ashleigh, precariously balanced
between laughter and tears.

'Oh look, it says Miss Ashleigh Brown,' Tom
laughed. 'I suppose you'd better open it, then.'

Ashleigh seized the letter and withdrew to her
bedroom to examine it. Meanwhile, Rusty had opened
the other envelope.

'It's an invitation to a housewarming,' he called to
Eileen. 'Charles and Sally. Do you remember them?
Seems they're moving into one of those new devel-
opments in the Undertown.'

'A party?' Eileen, flustered, appeared at the kitchen
door. 'When is it? Charles and Sally who? And who's
going to babysit for us? Oh, look at the time! I just
can't think about it at the moment. Ash, Maxie, are
you ready?'

'Yeah.' Ashleigh presented herself in the hallway, still
engrossed in the letter from Liam.

'I still can't find my books!' came Max's voice from
somewhere under the sofa.

Tom reached behind a cushion.

'Max,' he said quietly, 'is this what you're looking for?'

Later that morning, at the offices of Michael Brown
Publications, Charlotte finally persuaded Rusty to

make a personal inspection of the wall in the basement storeroom.

'See, Mister Brown, it's just been patched up with
bits of old plank. And it's all damp earth on the other
side, so the planks have started to rot, see, here, and
here as well. I got them to put new planks in before,
but they just went like the old ones, so I asked the
builder to come back, but he never turned up last
time, I ended up having to wait in for him and it was
Maisie's birthday and all, so now he's saying he'll definitely come today, only he thinks it'll be later rather
than earlier, but he can't say exactly when.'

While Charlotte paused for breath, Rusty poked a
tentative finger at the damaged area. The rotten timber
gave way at his touch and, when he withdrew his
hand, he found a crescent of dark soil under his fingernail.

'Yes, all right, I suppose we'd better get it bricked
up properly. We'll need to move all that stuff out of
the way, of course.' Indicating a stack of cardboard
boxes packed with newly copied charts ready for
dispatch, Rusty paused vaguely, seemingly losing his
thread. Charlotte waited politely while he recovered
command of his thoughts. 'The storeroom really ought
to have decent walls,' Rusty continued more deci-
sively. 'Can you ask Mister Slater to talk to the builders
when they come?'

Charlotte appeared taken aback at this.

'Oh, yes. All right, then.'

*   *   *

Staring out of his window during the midday rest period, Rusty noticed that Charlotte had wandered into the field and was feeding her sandwich crusts to the goats. From years of working with her, he knew that this was something she did only when she was feeling upset or slighted.

Halfway through the afternoon, she came back into his office to collect some proofs.

'*Prov 2* ready?' she asked shortly.

'I've done Sheet 63,' he replied. 'Over there. And I've nearly finished 64. Should be done by the end of today. And 65 and 66 should be ready early next week.'

Charlotte remained where she was, making no move to collect the finished work.

'Something wrong?'

'No, not really . . .' Rusty could tell at once that this was not the case. '. . . Well, oh, I don't know, it's just that . . .' The words came in a rush now. '. . . Well, you've always asked me to look after builders and things like that, it's always been me that's done it, but now all of a sudden it's Mister Slater will see the builders and Mister Slater this and Mister Slater that . . .' She produced a surprisingly large handkerchief and started dabbing at her eyes. 'I don't feel like I matter to you any more.'

'Oh, Charlotte, it's all right, don't be silly.' He crossed over to her and put his arms round her. 'No one could ever replace you. You've been here as long as I have. But I know how busy you are, I'm sure you've got plenty of other important things to do. But if you want to talk to the builders . . .'

They clung to each other for a moment longer, until they were interrupted by a discreet cough.

'I'm sorry,' said Tom. 'I thought you heard me knock. It's just that I've finally got the signal engine sorted out. I thought you'd like to see it.'

When the builders eventually did arrive, it was just a few minutes before the end of the work period, and it turned out that Charlotte needed to leave in a hurry to meet her sister. Tom, however, was quick to sense his friend's dilemma.

'It's all right, Rusty,' he said. 'I don't mind stopping on to explain things to the chaps. Why don't you give yourself an early night?'

'Thanks,' replied Rusty. 'I'd really appreciate that.'

As he made his way through the main door, Tom was already leading the two men down the steps to the basement.

'Goodnight, Charles. Goodnight, Sally,' Rusty called back up the path to his hosts. 'It's been really good seeing you again.'

'Yes, thanks for a lovely evening, it's been nice meeting you,' added Eileen. 'You'll have to come and see us soon.'

'Definitely,' replied Charles and Sally in unison. 'Mind how you go.'

The door closed softly. Rusty and Eileen could still hear the muted sounds of music and chatter as they made their way up the street.

'Thank heaven that's over,' Eileen commented

sourly, as soon as they were out of earshot. 'Bloody boring people. When did you say you last saw them?'

'Not since the Academy, I don't think,' mused Rusty. 'But come on, Charles is all right. I think he was just a bit preoccupied tonight. It can't be easy for him, what with all his responsibilities. And heaven knows what Sally was on about, but her heart's in the right place. But I do think we could have stopped a bit longer. It's not as if I had to go to work tomorrow.'

'Oh, bugger them,' snapped Eileen, clearly unconvinced of Charles and Sally's virtues. 'Let's look for a hackney coach.'

'Why don't we walk?' suggested Rusty. 'The rain's cleared up. And it'll only take half an hour or so. We could go up the North Way and pick up a coffee at the stall.'

Not touching each other, they walked in silence along the Eastern Boulevard and turned right onto the Ring Road. The Palace towered above them, its windows dark, its crenellated outline cutting a jagged hole in the moonlit cloudscape. There were no signs of life in Beggars' Row, and even the North Way seemed deserted. When they arrived at the coffee stall, the waiter was wiping the tables and inverting the chairs.

'Sorry, sir, ma'am. Quiet night. I'd let you have a freebie, only I've just tipped the last of it away.'

As they walked on, Rusty made another attempt to communicate.

'All right, I suppose it was a bit of a crappy party,'

he conceded. 'But at least we can have the odd night out, now that we've got Tom.'

'I suppose so.' After a moment's thought, Eileen seemed to brighten up. 'Yes, all right. Maybe I was wrong about Tom. And he does seem to get on with the kids.'

'He's like one of the family.' Rusty tried to encourage her. 'He really does do his bit. Go on, admit it. He's a really good lodger.'

'Yes, all right. But it does take ages to get in the bathroom.'

When they arrived home, the apartment was silent. The children were in their rooms, and they found Tom stretched out on the sofa in front of the fire, browsing through a copy of the *Royal Digest*.

While Eileen straightened Max's blankets, Rusty joined Tom by the fire.

'Everything all right?'

'Yes, good as gold,' replied Tom, folding the *Digest* away. 'We went out and got some pies for supper. Oh, and then there was a shower, so they couldn't go out again to play. So I let them have a go on the signal engine, just for half an hour, I hope that's all right. And, after that, they went to bed without a murmur. I could get used to being an uncle.'

'The signal engine?' Eileen had returned from her bedroom inspection. 'Are you sure that's a good idea?'

'Come on, darling,' Rusty reassured her. 'Tom's the world expert. He's got his certificate and everything.'

★   ★   ★

Both the children slept late the next morning, and Rusty eventually had to haul them from their beds for breakfast.

'Did you have a nice time with Tom last night?' Eileen asked.

'Tom's all right,' said Max. From the taciturn Max, this was praise indeed.

'He showed us the signal engine,' gushed Ashleigh. 'I saw an imp, at least I think I did. It was fearsome! Can we do it again today?'

Rusty and Eileen looked at each other.

'Maybe for a quarter of an hour, if you're good,' said Rusty cautiously.

'Ten minutes, and no more,' said Eileen. 'We're not made of money.'

The Magician's Return

As the carriage clattered down the hill towards the city, Veronique tossed the last empty flask through the window.

'One thing I always said about you, Vero,' Leonardo observed groggily, 'you know how to pace your drinking. How many flasks did you say we'd need for the journey?'

'Eleven.'

'And how many have we got through?'

'Eleven. Well, ten, actually. Put one up my sleeve to take home. Hope you don't mind.'

The magician found this very funny.

'One up your sleeve, I like that. Just like the old Veronique. One up your sleeve . . .' It was several moments before he managed to collect himself. 'Look, we're nearly there. We'd better try and make ourselves presentable.'

'Fat chance,' replied the clown. 'How come no one ever saw through us in the old days?'

'Actually, I think they did see through me,' replied Leonardo, and they were both helpless with laughter again for several minutes. They were finally jolted back to sobriety when the waggon came to a sudden, unheralded halt.

'Whassat?' Leonardo poked his head out of the window, and was able to discern that their conveyance had taken its place in a long line of vehicles that seemingly extended further than the eye could see. 'What's going on?'

'Transport interchange,' Veronique explained. 'Have to queue to get in there these days. Ever since the, whatjacallem, efficiency measures. You know, the reorganisation thingy. Stupid load of pillocks, couldn't reorganise their way into a whore's knickers.'

'Have there been a lot of, what do you call them, efficiency measures, then?' queried Leonardo.

'Never stops. Soon as they've changed something one way, they change it back the other. And it got even worse when that High Master Fang came in. And then when the King became indisposed . . .'

'Indisposed?'

'That's what they call it. But no one's seen him for years. I reckon that Fang's got him locked up somewhere. But mum's the word, me old sorcerer. Can't be saying things like that in public, not these days.'

'Sounds like I've got a lot to catch up on,' Leonardo pondered. 'But that transport interchange always was a bit of a shambles. You just had to get used to it, I suppose.'

'I reckon they should bring Tom Slater back,' said the clown. 'Dodgy geezer, maybe, but at least he had the waggons running on time . . .'

'Tom Slater?' Leonardo broke in. 'I know that name, don't I? Tom Slater, you say . . .'

But at that moment their conversation was interrupted by two Wolf Boys, leering in through the carriage window, brandishing clipboards in a rather aggressive fashion.

'Your papers, sir, madam? Identity papers, travel warrants, transfer dockets, insurance certificates, notices of destination, luggage inventories, green tickets, yellow folders . . . I'm sorry, sir, have I said something funny?'

It took the rest of that day for the carriage to reach the front of the queue, for Leonardo to persuade the Wolf Boys that he was able to satisfy all the administrative requirements of the new and efficient transport interchange, and for Veronique to persuade a deputation of striking waggon drivers that they had no intention of offering their services to the Wolf Boys as blacklegs.

As night fell, they lapsed into an uneasy doze but, after a couple of hours, they were unceremoniously awoken by an aggressive hammering at the carriage door. Leonardo was startled to find himself confronted by a gang of five or six young girls. Their fierce, juvenile faces were crudely painted with the pert noses and whiskers of small mammals, their cropped hair stood up in spikes, and their ragged clothes barely covered their pubescent figures. A couple of them were clutching wicked-looking knives in their bony hands.

'Hands in the air!' demanded the leader in a strident voice. Terrified, Leonardo was quick to comply, but Veronique had other ideas. Reaching into the depths of her handbag, she produced a heavy black revolver and fired a couple of warning shots over their assailants' heads.

'Sling yer hook, you little gits!' she growled. Without delay, the startled girls obeyed her command, and a moment later they had vanished without trace. Slowly, Leonardo allowed his hands to return to their normal position.

'Who were they?' he gasped, mightily impressed by his friend's display of sang-froid.

'Cat Girls.' Veronique, seemingly unperturbed by the incident, was wiping her gun with a large pocket handkerchief.

'In my day, we used to get attacked by the Wolf Boys,' Leonardo reminisced. 'They knew how to give you a good kicking.'

'Wolf Boys have gone respectable now,' replied Veronique. 'Well, sort of, anyway. But these girls can do a tidy job. They're pretty nimble, I can tell you. And quite cute as well, some of them.'

'Veronique, I despair of you,' moaned Leonardo. 'Have you ever thought of getting yourself a gentleman friend?'

The next morning, there remained the final hurdle of the ferry terminal before the two friends were eventually able to flag down a hackney coach and make their entry to the city along the North Way.

Rather than dismounting at the end of Beggars' Row, Veronique called up to the driver to take them around the Ring Road to the front gate of the Palace.

'Didn't think you'd fancy the rear passage.' She leered smuttily. 'More's the pity.'

'Quite,' replied Leonardo primly. 'If one is to return in triumph after one's years in the wilderness, one may as well do it in the proper style.'

Veronique had secured a spare token for the security engine at the front gate and, having gained entry for the two of them, she conducted Leonardo across the courtyard, through the small door, along the familiar passages, past his old workshop – now converted into a lavatory, he noted wryly – and, eventually, up the staircase to the throne room. An administrator acknowledged their arrival with a minimal inclination of the head.

'Master Leonardo Pegasus and Miss Veronique

Moreau,' Veronique intoned pompously. 'We have an appointment with the King.'

The administrator eyed them suspiciously.

'King Matthew remains indisposed,' she said finally. 'But High Master Fang is expecting you. Please take a seat for a few moments.'

An hour passed. Other visitors arrived, and were admitted to the throne room, but no further attention was paid to Leonardo and Veronique. Eventually, Veronique roused her friend with a poke in the ribs.

'Reckon I ought to be back at my post, Wizzy-boy,' she said. 'Will you be all right on your own?'

'Don't worry, Vero,' replied the magician, who was an old hand at being kept waiting. 'You get back to your admin. Maybe we can have a drink later.'

'Right you are, mage-face,' croaked the clown. A moment later, she was gone, and Leonardo was left to his own devices. After another hour, he had a gentle word with the administrator, extracting from her a grudging promise that she would try and have a word on his behalf with High Master Fang. Eventually, after ushering in yet another more fortunate guest, she approached Leonardo, stony-faced.

'Administrative error,' she said, without a hint of apology. 'It's Accident Investigation you should be seeing. East Wing, third floor. Can you find it?'

Wearily, Leonardo headed off down the long corridor.

The Numbered Tags

The lighting on the staircase at Tower Mansions was, as usual, not working. Rusty groped his way up the steps in semi-darkness, let himself into the apartment, hung up his overcoat on the row of overloaded hooks next to the front door, and stooped down to ease himself out of his shoes. He was just straightening up his thick, grey socks, which had as usual become twisted contrarily round his ankles, when he heard Eileen's voice calling out to him from the sitting room.

'You're too late for supper, we've had ours.' Her tone had an unmistakably hostile edge. 'And I didn't know what time you were coming back. You never tell me. You might find a bit left over in the oven if you still want it.'

Inside the apartment, Rusty found Eileen, armed with a yellow duster, furiously polishing the mantel-piece. He found this an odd choice of occupation for the time of day, but chose prudently not to remark on it. The clatter of crockery told him that Tom was at the kitchen sink washing dishes. The children were nowhere in sight.

Eileen carefully adjusted the position of her father's portrait, then turned around to face Rusty. From her expression, he could see at once that an explanation was required.

'Sorry,' he said haltingly. 'I didn't realise how late it was. The thing is, I really needed to stop on at the office, just to finish off *Prov 2*. I told you about the deadline, didn't I . . .'

'I know all about your deadlines,' snapped Eileen. 'Were you on your own?'

'Charlotte was helping me,' Rusty admitted reluctantly. 'It would have taken even longer otherwise.'

'Why have I never met this Charlotte? Doesn't she have a home to go to? I don't even know whether she's married.'

'Married? I'm not sure. I think she used to be. Her husband left her, that's it, or did he die? Oh, I remember now, she's got a son, and her sister—'

'Yes, well, I think you're spending too much time at the office and not enough time with your children. I don't know what they're up to half the time. I can hardly control them any more. They seem to spend more time with Tom than they do with me.'

Rusty was about to say something that he would certainly have regretted, but at that moment Tom entered the room bearing a tray with three steaming mugs of cocoa.

'Sorry, I'm not interrupting, am I?' said the lodger with a rather ostentatious display of tact. 'Why don't we all sit down and have a drink?'

This timely interjection temporarily mitigated the tension in the atmosphere, and Rusty and Eileen followed his suggestion, lowering themselves into the two armchairs.

'Sorry,' said Tom, motioning towards the coffee table

with his foot. 'Could you just clear that stuff out of the way?'

Rusty half-rose to rearrange the items on the table.

'What are these?' he asked Eileen. Among the usual litter on the cluttered surface was a collection of small, numbered tags, attached to short pieces of string.

'Something of Maxie's, I think. He never tells me what he's up to.'

'A school project,' supplied Tom. 'He was talking to me about it.' Eileen shot him a suspicious glance. 'Oh, and I let him use the signal engine to check up on something. Just for a few minutes before he went to bed. I hope that's all right?'

Rusty and Eileen frowned at each other but neither chose to pursue the matter.

'Where's Ash?' asked Rusty after a while. 'She hasn't gone to bed already, has she?'

'I think she's on the engine now,' said Tom. 'I think it was something to do with her Unarmed Combat classes. I can go and ask her, if you like.'

But when they looked in the spare room, there was no sign of Ashleigh. A hurried inspection of her bedroom yielded no results either.

'Oh no, not again,' said Eileen. 'I don't think I can put up with much more of this.'

'She probably just popped out to see Davina,' suggested Rusty. 'She doesn't always say when she's going down there.'

But, an hour later, there was still no sign of the girl.

'I'll wait up for her if you want to go to bed,' Rusty offered, anxious to forestall the recriminations that he suspected were awaiting him. 'Just to make sure she's all right.'

But Rusty must have dozed off in front of the fire, for it was not until after midnight that he was suddenly awoken by the sound of the front door. He caught the briefest glimpse of his daughter but, rather than coming into the sitting room, Ashleigh disappeared straight into the bathroom. Rusty tapped gently on the door.

'Ash?' he called anxiously. 'Ash, are you all right?' But he could hear only the sound of running water.

When Ashleigh finally emerged, she was wrapped in a large bath towel and had a smaller towel knotted damply around her head. Finding herself confronted by her father, she appeared momentarily flustered.

'Sorry, Dad,' she apologised, once she had collected her wits. 'I was with people . . . with friends. And I didn't notice the time. And then I needed to wash my hair. Look, I'm really tired now.'

'Best get to bed, then,' replied Rusty, half relieved and half concerned. 'How about a kiss for your dad? But, Ashleigh, you and I will need to have words about this in the morning.'

'Yeah. Whatever.'

But when Rusty arose the next day, his daughter was already on her way out of the front door, looking extremely demure in her school blazer and beret.

'Got to dash,' she called to him over her shoulder. 'School trip. Didn't Mum tell you? Have to be early for the coaches.'

And Rusty and Eileen had to be content with that for the time being.

Later the same morning, sitting alone in his drawing office, Rusty was finding it difficult to concentrate on the affairs of Michael Brown Publications, burdened as he was with uncertainty over how best to deal with Ashleigh's increasingly wayward behaviour. He supposed that either he or Eileen would need to have stern words with the girl, warn her of the dangers that the night-time streets posed to a vulnerable young woman. He was not looking forward to the confrontation. And what about Max? Were they paying him enough attention? Although Max never appeared to get himself into any trouble, he seemed to be living increasingly in his own self-contained world.

It occurred to Rusty then that neither he nor Eileen was really any longer in touch with how Ashleigh and Max were spending their free time. He realised that he had no idea who they were seeing, what they were doing, what they were thinking. The only adult they seemed prepared to talk to was Tom. Rusty furrowed his brow, his work lying unnoticed in front of him. Painfully, he admitted to himself that he did not even have any real idea of what they talked about with Tom. He wondered whether it would be a good move to have a word with Tom about the whole business, but then decided that it might be wise to speak to Eileen before he did so. Although he was not greatly concerned about Tom's presence in the family home, he could sense in Eileen a growing feeling of unease.

'Mister Brown?'

It was Charlotte's voice.

'Have you got *Prov 69* there? Is it nearly ready? Sorry, I can see you're busy, but it's just that the builders still haven't come back to do the wall, and Mister Slater wants to know whether to send someone round to see them. Oh, and the courier brought this, I thought it might be important.' Realising, belatedly, that her boss was not that morning in a conversational mood, Charlotte deposited the document on his desk in front of him and withdrew.

Rusty stared for some moments at the medium-sized sheet of vellum before he managed to take in what it was. Oh yes, that conference on, what was it? *The Sense of Direction*. It had come around sooner than he had been expecting. He had been looking forward to it, actually, a few days in a pleasant little market town, a few days away from the city. Direction-finding had always been one of his pet subjects. He had always relished the opportunity to listen to different theories about it, and to compare notes with people working in areas related to his own. But now Rusty was beginning to doubt whether he would be able to spare the time to attend this year's sessions. There was just too much else going on, not just at the office, but at home as well. Wistfully, he ran his eye down the list of subjects and speakers.

Traditional Methods of Direction-Finding: Are They Still Valid in the World of the Signal Engine?
(Professor Ernest Octavian, Academy of Cartography)

Well, he would probably have given that one a miss. He had dozed through enough of old Octavian's lectures at the Academy to have a fair idea what he would be saying.

New Degrees of Accuracy in the Measurement of Compass Bearings
(Doctor K.R.G. de Voonik, Institute of Calibration)
That would be as dry as dust, of course, and about as lively as an elderly tortoise, but he had to admit to a sneaking enjoyment of de Voonik's almost otherworldly precision.

Explaining Cartographic Principles to the Ordinary Reader
(Mister Michael Brown, Michael Brown Publications)

With a hollow feeling in his stomach, Rusty registered the presence of his own name, down there in brown and white, on the list of speakers! Now it came back to him that, months ago, in a moment of weakness, he had indeed agreed to make a presentation at this year's conference. In an agony of uncertainty, he weighed up the likely professional consequences of a cancellation at this late stage against all the problems and inconveniences of having to attend at a time when he was really too busy to do so. Still uncertain, Rusty turned the document over.

Never the Same Road Twice: Towards a Theory of How the Wanderers Find Their Way
(Professor Laurel Greening, University of the Lanes and Byways)

For a moment, Rusty felt as though his heart had stopped. Laurel, the wandering girl! How long was it since he had seen her? Ten years, fifteen? Sightlessly, he started at the other names on the list. The last time he had seen Laurel, he calculated, had been at least fifteen years ago, at his mother's funeral, and, the time before that, maybe ten years earlier, she had been in a circus, and then, earlier still, the two of them had been, briefly, at the village school together. He had often wondered what Laurel had been getting up to more recently, and now here was the answer. Laurel had decided to make a career in the academic world! Rusty imagined her sitting in a futuristic-looking office in her strange, modern university, studying the thoughts and deeds of the Wanderers, delivering lectures to ranks of respectful undergraduates, writing books. He wondered whether his old friend Gideon Blackwood knew anything about the University of the Lanes and Byways. He had certainly never mentioned it . . .

Once again, Rusty weighed up the factors for and against attending the conference. This time, it didn't take him long. He could cobble a paper together in a couple of days . . .

'Charlotte!' he called. 'I want to book a room for that conference! Ask Mister Slater to get the signal engine powered up.'

'I think it's on the blink again,' Charlotte called back to him.

At the end of the work period, the builders still hadn't arrived, and the signal engine still wasn't working properly. Rusty found Tom rummaging under the open lid of the cabinet, screwdriver in hand.

'I really want to get moving on that booking,' Rusty said. 'Do you think there's any chance of getting the engine working tonight?'

'Shouldn't take too much longer,' Tom muttered abstractedly. Rusty waited for a few more moments while Tom completed whatever operation he was engaged in. Eventually he sat up and turned to face his colleague. 'Well, probably another couple of hours, actually. I don't mind staying on to get it done, if you want to go home. Just give me the keys, and I'll lock up when I'm sorted.'

'Thanks, mate,' replied Rusty. 'I reckon I really ought to have an early night tonight.' He dropped Tom a wink. 'I'll see you later, then.'

'Yeah, see you later,' said Tom, and disappeared back under the lid of the cabinet.

★   ★   ★

When Rusty arrived home, Ashleigh still hadn't returned from her school trip and Max had gone out to do whatever it was that he spent so much time doing in the old stables and outbuildings. Rusty found Eileen in the hallway. She was on her knees again, attacking the carpet with a dustpan and brush.

'This place is filthy,' she complained. 'I'm going round every day, but it never seems to get any better. I don't think it would make any difference if I did it twice a day.'

'I think we ought to have a word with Ashleigh when she gets in,' said Rusty tentatively.

'You can talk to her,' snapped Eileen. 'She never pays any attention to me.'

'She doesn't take much notice of me, either. Do you think she'd listen to Tom?'

'Tom? Are you mad? I'm sure it's only because of Tom and that stupid signal engine that any of this has happened. Putting all his crazy ideas into her head.' Bewildered, Rusty stared at her.

'You don't mean that,' he said finally. 'What's Tom got to do with it? She's just growing up, that's all it is. You can hardly blame Tom for that. She probably just needs a few firm words.'

At that moment, they were interrupted by the sound of the front door opening. Ashleigh tiptoed furtively along the hallway and vanished into her room.

'Well, now's your chance,' said Eileen. 'I'll leave you to it. I've got the supper to do.' She turned smartly and went into the kitchen, slamming the door behind her.

Rusty paused for a moment to collect his wits. Then he went to the end of the corridor and tapped on his daughter's door.

'Ashleigh,' he called. 'Could you come out here, please.'

'I'm busy.'

'Now, please. I don't want to have to drag you out.'

After a few moments, Ashleigh appeared. She had changed out of her school uniform, apart from the beret, which she was still wearing.

'Sit down at the table.'

Father and daughter took up opposing positions across the dining table, which was littered with another batch of Max's numbered tags. After a short silence, Ashleigh picked up one of the tags and started to fiddle with it.

'Ashleigh, will you look at me? And take your beret off, for heaven's sake. You're not at school now.'

'Don't want to,' Ashleigh replied sulkily. Rusty decided, for the moment, not to make an issue of the beret.

'Where were you last night? Your mother and I were worried.'

'I told you. I was with some friends. I didn't notice the time. Sorry.'

'What friends?' Rusty was becoming exasperated. 'And will you stop playing with those stupid tags?' Suddenly, Ashleigh looked up, her youthful features blazing with defiance.

'Just friends,' she repeated. 'From school. From

Unarmed Combat. I don't know. What does it matter to you?'

'I'm your father. It matters to me who you spend your time with. And it matters to me if you're out late and I don't know what you're getting up to.'

'Don't get so excited, Dad. You wouldn't understand, anyway. And I've got homework to do. Can I go now?'

They were both on their feet by now. Intending to make a dramatic exit, Ashleigh spun around, only to collide violently with Eileen, who was at that moment emerging from the kitchen carrying a tray loaded with plates and glasses. There was a crash of breaking crockery, and mother and daughter collapsed in a heap on the floor.

Ashleigh was the first to rise. Too late, she realised that her beret had become dislodged in the collision. And then, to his horror, Rusty saw that her long, thick, red locks had vanished from her head. What remained of her hair she wore instead in an ugly, jagged crop.

'Ashleigh,' gasped Rusty, stunned. 'Who did this to you?'

'I did it myself!' bawled the girl, clutching her hat to her chest. 'I'm old enough to cut my own hair, aren't I? I'm old enough to do lots of things that you don't want me to do! Anyway, I like it like this! What do you care?' And she stormed into her room and slammed the door behind her.

Eileen was still picking herself up from the floor.

'It's horrible,' she said finally, and Rusty noticed that there were tears in her eyes. 'What have we done wrong? I can't bear to think what Paul will say. No, leave me, I need to clear this mess up. Go and look for Max, if you want to be useful.'

Eileen clearly did not want to be comforted, so Rusty left the apartment and started out on a tour of the various outbuildings where Max was likely to be playing. Walking quickly down the eight flights of steps, he tried the doors of the old elevator shaft on each landing, but each one remained firmly locked. When he got to the ground floor, however, he discovered to his surprise that the final door was standing ajar. Inside, he found a shapeless mound covered with an old tarpaulin but, when he looked underneath, there was only a stack of gardening equipment, stored there, presumably, by the caretaker.

Rusty closed the door of the shaft and made his way around to the rear of the building, where there was a row of outhouses that had once served as stables for the elevator captain's ponies. The first one contained a wheelbarrow, piled high with more gardening tools, and the second appeared at first glance to be empty. But, as his eyes became accustomed to the gloom, Rusty noticed something lying close to the centre of the floor. He knelt down, squinting in the half-light to examine the small object. When he saw what it was, his heart began to pound.

The object was a dead rat. And around its neck was tied a small tag, bearing the number 376.

'Hi, Dad.' Rusty was startled to hear his son's light voice at his side. 'Oh, great, you've found 376. I wondered where he'd got to. Is he dead? That's a shame.'

Involuntarily, Rusty put his hands to his head.

'Maxie, what in the world have you been up to?' He seized the boy by the arm. 'Come upstairs. We're going to have to discuss this with your mother.'

'Rats?' Eileen was aghast. 'You've been putting numbers on rats? You stupid boy! Don't you realise, they carry all sorts of diseases? What were you thinking of?'

Max seemed unconcerned.

'It's all right, Mum, you needn't worry, they're all quite clean round here, the ones in the Undertown were the only ones that ever carried any infection. And they mostly got killed in the clearances. But it's really interesting, we give them numbers, these other kids and me, and then we can track them all over the city, they use the drains and sewers, some of them go really long distances.' Rusty and Eileen listened in horrified fascination. They had never heard Max so animated.

'Who are these other kids?' Eileen asked, faintly, after a moment.

'Well, I've never actually met them, you see, but I get in touch with them on the signal engine, Tom showed me how. There's a sort of club, we swap numbers, and there are prizes for finding the rats that go the longest distances . . .'

'You're not to do any more of this, do you hear me?' Eileen shouted. 'Not ever, do you understand? Do you understand? Go and wash your hands. No, go and have a bath. Wash everywhere. And come and see me when you're clean.' She waited until Max had gone into the bathroom. 'I've got a good mind to bath him myself,' she raved, 'even if he is twelve! Rats in the stables! I don't see how we can live here any more!' Unexpectedly, she rounded on Rusty. 'And you've brought in this so-called friend of yours, this criminal, this madman, and he's taught my children these horrible habits, playing with rats, going out who knows where, and all you can think about is your conference and your stupid charts . . .'

'I could go and have a word with the caretaker,' Rusty suggested. 'About the rats.'

'What can he do? You heard Max! They crawl all over the city!'

'We had them in the country as well,' Rusty reminded her.

'I've got a good mind to go back and live in the country!' snapped Eileen. 'Back in the village! Go back and stay with Daddy. He needs me there with him, anyway. And the children, too. He never sees them. And at least they'd be safe from lunatics like Tom!'

'You can't blame Tom—'

'But I *do* blame Tom! I blame Tom for all of this! And I'll tell you what you can do! You can tell him to get out of our house! I won't have him under my roof for one more night!'

At that moment, they were interrupted by the sound of the front door. Tom Slater had returned from the office.

'You tell him,' said Eileen, her tone icy now. 'Tell him now. I'm going to bed. And if he's still here in the morning . . .'

Hastily, Rusty headed for the hallway to intercept his guest.

'Would you like to come out for a beer?' he suggested wearily. 'We're going to have to have words.'

Mister Considine's Reports

Master Gash occupied a stuffy, windowless office that appeared to be at least twice as high as it was wide. This impression was enhanced by the tall, grey metal filing cabinets that surrounded his small desk on three sides, and by the hard, vertical shaft of light cast by the single overhead bulb. When Leonardo was eventually admitted, towards the end of the afternoon work period, Gash, who was short and rather on the stout side, was in the process of descending a rickety wooden ladder that was propped against the right-hand stack of cabinets. Under one arm he carried a bundle of scruffy-looking documents, which he deposited on the desk with a loud slap before depositing himself heavily in his wooden revolving chair.

'Have a pew,' he wheezed, breathing heavily. 'I used to be quite an athlete once, though you'd never think it now. I could outrun any villain on the patch. Could jump over walls. Used to tear beggars in two with my bare hands. But of course all that went out the window when they stuck me behind here. Want some coffee? Cocoa? Anything?'

'No, thanks,' said Leonardo. During a long day of being kept waiting in one office after another, he had been consuming cups of this and mugs of that more or less non-stop. 'Nice thought, though.'

'I suppose you'll want to take a look at these,' said Gash, indicating the stack of papers. 'Can't make head or tail of them myself. Bog off, can't you see I'm busy!' This last was to an unfortunate colleague who happened to open the door at that moment. 'Sorry about that. But I'll tell you what I can.'

'About the imps?' inquired Leonardo hesitantly.

'Imps? Yes, that was what he used to call them. It wasn't really my sort of thing,' Gash explained, 'but Kevin Considine really had a bee in his bonnet about them. But then, of course, he had his little accident, so muggins here got lumbered with all the reports. You can keep them, as far as I'm concerned.'

'What's in them?' Leonardo fingered the top sheet doubtfully.

'Well, all sorts, really. Nobody really knew much about imps, apart from young Considine that is, but I don't suppose he'll be able to help you much. They reckon it was imps that saw him off, although I'm not so certain myself. Anyway, he'd asked us to put out a call to the citizenry, we put it in the *Royal Digest*, actually, and this little lot was the result. Like I said, none of it makes any sense to me, but you're welcome to have a crack at it. Anything else I can tell you?'

'Is there anywhere I can . . . ?'

'Oh sorry, yes, of course. They've cleared out a little office for you to use. Just along the corridor. Right next to the coffee engine.'

The office to which Master Gash had directed Leonardo was pleasantly spacious and had a medium-sized lattice window that overlooked the main court-yard of the Palace. The room had been cleared of furniture, apart from a single table and chair. From time to time, as Leonardo set to work, people would poke their heads around the door and ask for some-thing called a 422/f, or occasionally for something else called a B19. Naturally, Leonardo was unable to offer them any assistance with either of these things. He wondered for what purpose the room had previ-ously been used.

The daylight soon began to fade. There was appar-ently no electricity at this end of the corridor, but Gash had thoughtfully provided Leonardo with a couple of oil lamps, and it was by their flickering yellow light that the magician began his inspection of the bundle of documents. Starting at the top of the pile, he began to read.

A Miss Davina Wright, aged thirteen years, had, it seemed, been in the habit of conversing with an unknown, possibly imaginary, friend by means of her father's signal engine. Two months ago, she had left the apartment and had not, so far, returned . . .

A Mister Norman Loxley had been experiencing headaches and sleeplessness, which he believed were connected with his use of a signal engine in the course of his employment as Director of Iconography at the Herald's Office. In an outburst of rage, he had one day hurled the signal engine from his office window, after which his ailments had promptly ceased . . .

A Miss Maisie Rowland had been making excessive and inconsiderate use of a signal engine owned by her sister Charlotte. Her conduct had become 'unruly and unseemly', although the precise nature of this misbehaviour was not specified by the author of the report. Upon disconnection of the engine, Miss Rowland had taken to her bed, where she had remained for several weeks . . .

A Mrs Paola Mezzoforte had become enraged with her husband, after the former had spent a continuous period of seven hours in communication with an unknown individual by means of his signal engine. When challenged by her, Mr Mezzoforte had turned on his wife and beaten her violently to death . . .

After reading ten or twelve reports of a more or less similar nature to these, Leonardo began to conclude that there must indeed be some connection between these people's use of the signal engines and their various behavioural irregularities, whether these were merely bizarre or irrational or, as in the case of Mr Mezzoforte, downright criminal. But what, Leonardo wondered, was actually taking place? If these people had indeed been receiving messages that encouraged them in their various forms of odd behaviour, who or what was transmitting the messages? And why were they doing it? He started to read the next report.

A Mrs Eileen Brown, after being in touch with her father by means of a signal engine installed by her husband Michael, had developed an obsession with domestic hygiene, and could not be stopped from cleaning her apartment, even at the most inappropriate times of day. When questioned, Mrs Brown said that she had been encouraged in this by an acquaintance named Leah or Leigh . . .

Leonardo sat bolt upright in his chair. It was dark outside now, and the flickering pool of light cast by the pungent-smelling oil lamp provided his only illumination.

'Leigh?' he fretted. 'Leah? Now where have I come across a name like that before?'

But, at that moment, he was interrupted in his speculation by the unmistakable sound of a heavily booted foot kicking open the office door. It was Veronique.

'So this is where they've put the old genius,' she croaked. 'Look at you, with your nose in those papers. I bet you haven't had a thing to eat! And where are you staying tonight? You haven't even thought about that, have you, you daft old sod!'

Shamefaced, Leonardo peered mutely at her over his spectacles.

'Come on, put that old junk down now,' said his

friend with some exasperation. 'Let's take you off and get you sorted out.'

'I used to go to the Crier's Rest when I lived here last,' Leonardo remembered.

'The Crier's Rest?' chortled Veronique. 'Yes, it's still there, just about the same as ever. Are you ready?'

'Can I just finish this . . . ?'

'No,' Veronique interrupted him. 'Put it down. Start again tomorrow. They close in an hour.'

Getting Ready to Go

'Charlotte?' Rusty called. 'Can you spare a minute? I've got the speech ready for the conference.'

As he had estimated, it had taken almost two days to rough out his notes and prepare a draft text. This meant, of course, that the drawings for the long-awaited *Prov 69* still weren't quite ready, but Rusty reckoned that he would still have time to get them done in the few days before his departure. He turned the stack of papers from side to side in his hands, squaring the edges against the battered oak surface of his table. There always seemed to be one sheet that insisted on sticking out from the pile . . .

'Mister Brown?' Charlotte had, as always, insinuated herself unheard into his presence. 'If you let me have them now, I can get the copies done before you go, and, oh yes, if you could manage to finish off *Prov 69* . . .'

'It will be done, Charlotte, I promise you.'

'Yes, of course. Oh, the builders have turned up, by the way. I think Mister Slater's sorting them out. Is there anything else?'

'No, I don't think so, Charlotte.' Rusty noticed that she did not seem keen to hang around. 'Can you ask Mister Slater to pop up? When he's finished with the builders?'

He turned his attention to his next task, the final alterations to the master copy for the long-awaited *Prov 69*, and he did not notice her leaving the room. As always, when Rusty was concentrating on preparing a chart, he became totally engrossed in his work, now adding a small detail here or there, now standing back from the table to assess the overall impact of the design. It might have been an hour, or it might have been two hours, before he became aware that Tom was standing at the door, looking about as diffident as it was possible for a man of his height to look.

'Oh, hello, Tom, sorry, I didn't hear you. Come in. Have a chair.' He put the work aside and turned to face his visitor.

'Look,' said Tom quickly. 'Before you ask, I've found somewhere else to live. So you don't have to worry about that. Actually, I'd been making plans for a while.'

Rusty managed to contain a sigh of relief.

'I'm sorry about the other night,' he offered ruefully. 'I mean, it was kind of embarrassing, but you know how Eileen gets these odd ideas sometimes. You just can't reason with her. Well, I can't, anyway.'

'No harm done,' replied Tom. 'And I guess it was sort of time for me to move on, anyway. Is everything all right at home now?'

Rusty pressed his lips together and wriggled to adjust his position in his chair.

'Well, sort of. Eileen's still in a bit of a state about the kids. And I don't think she really wants me to go to the conference. But I keep telling her, it's only for a few days. And I'm taking that little portable signal engine, in case she needs to get in touch. Is it ready, by the way?'

Tom leaned back, stretching his long legs.

'Yes, all done. And I'll get the accumulator charged up, in case there's no electricity there. Makes it a bit bulky, but I reckon it'll be worth it.'

'Thanks,' replied Rusty. 'Look, I'm sorry I can't ask you to join me. I think you would have enjoyed it. But I need you to look after the office while I'm away. I've never really been completely happy leaving everything to Charlotte. Maybe you can come along next time.'

'Don't give it a thought,' said Tom, relaxed as ever. 'And I'd have to stick around here anyway. Make sure the builders don't destroy the place.'

'Great. Thanks, mate.' Rusty turned back to his work, indicating that their conversation was over, and Tom took himself off to attend to the signalling apparatus.

There were no further interruptions until the bells of the Institute of Calibration announced the end of the morning work period. A few minutes later, when Rusty strolled across to the window, he noticed that Charlotte was standing outside on the grass. In front of her, the goats were ranged in a ragged semicircle, their vapid faces chewing contentedly on the scraps that she was throwing.

Since his parents had forbidden him to play in the elevator shaft and the outbuildings, Max had taken up his flute practice again. Through the door of his bedroom, a single, unvarying phrase echoed repetitively around the apartment. Each time, the boy made exactly the same mistake in exactly the same place and, each time, he started again at the beginning, presumably hoping that, with enough repetitions, the fault would eventually correct itself.

'Can you give the music a rest for a few minutes, Maxie?' called Rusty. His son's efforts were beginning to grate on his nerves. The shrill warbling ceased abruptly, and Max's head emerged from his room.

'What can I do, then?' the boy complained. 'You won't let me play outside. And now you won't let me practise. What am I supposed to do?'

'What about something quiet?' suggested Rusty. 'Can't you see I'm trying to concentrate? Haven't you got any homework?'

'I suppose so.' The door slammed shut again. Rusty resettled himself in his armchair and turned his attention back to the text of his speech. He was leaving the next day for the conference, and was struggling to memorise what he had to say.

'Can I borrow your leather jacket, Dad?' Ashleigh had been confined to her room for some days, and was now being allowed out again, on the strict understanding that she was back home at a reasonable time.

Rusty sighed. The hour before supper, once a quiet interlude of domestic peace, had in recent weeks degenerated into a fractious and unsettling succession of family skirmishes. He was looking forward to getting away from it all for a few days.

'Let's have a look at you. Isn't it a bit big across the shoulders?'

'Oh, Dad. All the kids are wearing them like this. Don't you know anything?'

'Probably quite a few things,' Rusty responded sarcastically. 'But not much to interest you, apparently.' As Ashleigh pirouetted in front of him, the kitchen door opened and Eileen appeared carrying the tray of supper things. This time, she just managed to avoid dropping it.

'Ash! What do you think you look like?' she scolded her daughter. 'I've always hated that jacket. And haven't you got a better skirt? That one's practically in ribbons. And you're surely not going to go out without any stockings?'

'Whatever.' Sulkily, the girl vanished back into her room.

A little later, Ashleigh's friends called for her and, following another inspection by Eileen, she was eventually deemed fit to accompany them, with a final warning about the necessity of a punctual return. Max was packed off to bed at his usual time, and Rusty and Eileen sat up with mugs of cocoa, waiting for their daughter.

'Will you be all right while I'm away?' Rusty asked.

'Oh, come on, Rusty,' came the sharp retort. 'We both know damn well that you'll go to your stupid conference whatever I say. I suppose Charlotte's going with you?'

'Charlotte?' Rusty was taken aback. 'No, she's not. Charlotte's looking after the office with Tom.' He noticed his wife wincing at the mention of the name. 'Things have to carry on, you know. Even when I'm away.'

At that moment, the front door opened and Ashleigh reappeared, excited and out of breath, but on time as promised.

'Did you have a good time?' queried Rusty. But as the girl stepped into the pool of light in the centre of the room, his jaw dropped. It wasn't the first time he had seen Ashleigh with her face painted, but it was the first time he had seen her looking anything like this. The jagged red hair framed a dead white foundation, against which an inexpertly wielded black pencil had created on the juvenile features the clumsy illusion of slanting almond eyes, thin black lips, and the unmistakable button nose and whiskers of a cat.

Confronted by the accusing stares of her parents, Ashleigh averted her eyes.

'What's the matter?' she mumbled in embarrassed defiance. 'It's just face paint, that's all. It's only a bit of fun.'

'Get in the bathroom this minute,' said Eileen, her voice trembling. 'You're not coming back in here until it's washed off. And get those horrible clothes off, as well. I can't bear to see you like that. I just can't bear it. Do you understand?'

Without another word, Ashleigh fled.

Eileen stared at Rusty with something akin to hatred.

'So go to your bloody conference,' she hissed. 'Do what you like. But the way I'm feeling right now, you'll be lucky to find me here when you get back.'

That night, Rusty slept badly, dozing and waking and dozing again. Dimly, he was aware of Eileen turning to and fro beside him but, more vividly, he found himself enmeshed in interlocking strands of dream-stuff that wove their webs about him both when he slept and when he woke. The truncated, obsessive phrases of Max's flute threaded their way in and out of the paragraphs of his conference speech, half remembered and half elusive, and the harsh grit of Eileen's savage words supplied a peppering of punc-tuation.

And, at the centre of the web, shimmered the frail figure of Ashleigh.

For, more than anything else, it was Ashleigh's star-tling metamorphosis that had robbed him of his sleep that night. Ashleigh, with her grotesque make-up and her savagely cropped hair. Ashleigh, with the old leather jacket draped carelessly around her narrow shoulders. Ashleigh, with her long schoolgirl legs barely covered by the ragged skirt and the torn stockings. Ashleigh, he realised, was no longer his little girl. Because that night, for the first time, Rusty had discerned in his daughter the fragile prototype of a woman.

For the rest of the night, he twisted restlessly from side to side in the bed while, beside him, Eileen also twisted restlessly, enmeshed perhaps in some nightmare of her own. But, at the other end of the apartment, peaceful in their narrow beds, the two children slept soundly.

Seven:
THE ELEVATOR SHAFT

The Royal Digest of Affairs and Events: Volume 191 (in the Sixteenth Year of the Rule of King Matthew)

The Diary of Miss Garamond (Herald)

Greetings, Citizens!

As the reader will doubtless be aware, Citizens intent upon the conduct of their day-to-day affairs continue to be confronted by an endless succession of frustrating obstacles. The unwary pedestrian finds himself in constant danger of attack from the savage gangs of young women who have come popularly to be known as 'Cat Girls'. Users of the Royal Signal Network suffer persistent harassment from the mysterious entities known as 'imps'. Travellers who wish to avail themselves of the facilities of the Transport Interchange are, despite the unremitting efforts of the City Authorities, still subject to interminable delays and difficulties.

Sadly, following his long-postponed return from the Borders, King Matthew remains indisposed. However, the affairs of the Kingdom remain for the time being in the capable hands of High Master Fang, Director of Internal Affairs, and the author is glad to be able to reassure the reader that all due attention is, as ever, being paid to the safety and security of the Citizenry. At his monthly Private Audience, the High Master graciously saw fit to enumerate the many and varied initiatives that are at this moment being pursued with the purpose of restoring daily life in the City to its accustomed state of order and decorum.

Firstly, concerning the matter of the 'Cat Girl' attacks, the High Master vouchsafed his personal guarantee that immediate and decisive steps are being taken to eradicate this menace from our streets for ever. The frequency of foot patrols of the Royal Wolf Boys Militia has been doubled, and a number of arrests have already been made. A report from Master Gash, Chief Inspector of the Royal Wolf Boys Investigation Branch, reads as follows:

> *Following the increase in the number of patrols as a consequence of the 'Cat Girl' attacks, a number of persons have now been apprehended and the individuals in question subjected to vigorous interrogation. Following these interrogations, the Branch has made the remarkable discovery that the perpetrators of the attacks are not, as had been popularly supposed,*

vagrants or beggars, but young women and girls of good family and character who appear to have adopted ragged clothing and an unruly style of behaviour in a deliberate and contemptuous attempt to disparage the forces of authority. The intention behind this wayward conduct has proved difficult to determine, but the foot patrols have been instructed to continue their pre-emptive work for the time being, and Citizens may rest assured that order will very soon be fully restored.

High Master Fang stated further that, in addition to these measures by the Investigation Branch, he has personally invited a number of the young women to his private quarters for interview, and, after thorough and extensive exploration of their feelings and motivations, has come to the conclusion that their behaviour has its origin in the frustration or repression of the natural impulses of a healthy young female. In other words, these individuals, although already in possession of a considerable degree of physical and intellectual maturity, feel themselves disregarded and undervalued by the Authorities and thereby excluded from taking any significant part in public affairs. They thus find themselves driven to fulfil their potential through what they have come to see as the only means available to them, namely that of motiveless violence. After much consideration, therefore, High Master Fang has ordered the following promulgation to be issued.

It is apparent that the girls and young women of this City are possessed of an abundant reserve of youthful energy and vitality which, lacking a proper outlet, has regrettably found its expression in the outbreaks of distressing misbehaviour of recent times. It being our heartfelt desire to ensure that these lively and talented young persons should be availed of the opportunity to play a positive and useful role in public affairs, we are therefore pleased and proud to announce the formation of a new branch of the Royal Wolf Boys Militia, which shall henceforth be known as the Royal Cat Girls Cadets. The Cadets will in the first instance be trained and overseen by experienced members of the Militia, but it is our intention in the long term that the Cat Girls shall operate as a sister division to the Wolf Boys, playing a full part in all law enforcement and emergency services. The Cadets will welcome applications from any young woman aged fourteen years or more. We are confident that this initiative will, within a few months, once more eradicate the threat of unmotivated attack from our streets.

The author, too, wishes to express her confidence that the young women of the City, their families, and the Citizenry at large, are certain to enjoy countless benefits from this redirection of energies that have, until now, sadly gone to waste.

Secondly, concerning the matter of the Royal Signal Network, it remains a matter of grave public concern that users continue to be faced with the nuisance of 'imps'. Numerous reports of disturbing incidents have been gathered and collated by Master Gash, and steps have been taken to secure the services of an acknowledged expert in this field who, it is devoutly hoped, will prove instrumental in addressing the problem. High Master Fang has therefore issued the following statement.

> *We have become increasingly concerned about the mysterious and troubling activities of the 'imps' that are infesting the Royal Signal Network, and the consequent bizarre and irrational behaviour that has been observed on the part of many users of the Network. We have, regrettably, been hindered in confronting this nuisance by the untimely death of Mister Considine, former Supervisor of Machinery. It is therefore with some relief that we have succeeded in engaging the exclusive services of Master Leonardo Pegasus, who some Citizens may recall in his former position of Chief Magician during the reign of King Roderick. Master Pegasus is entitled to much credit as the inventor of many of the fundamental components now incorporated into the Royal Signal Network, and Citizens may rest assured that no one is better qualified for the task of investigating and dealing with this nuisance.*
>
> *Citizens will doubtless be aware that a successor to Mister Considine has not thus far been appointed. Recognising as we do the need for a comprehensive and trustworthy signalling network in the operation of any modern system of government, we are therefore*

pleased to announce our intention of taking personal command of the Royal Signal Network with immediate effect.

The author looks forward to significant improvements in the Signal Network in the capable hands of High Master Fang and Master Pegasus. At the time of publication of this issue, the whereabouts of Master Pegasus could not be determined, but the author is eager to secure an interview with him with the utmost urgency. In addition (and on a personal note!) she can assure the Citizens (from her own experience!) that no better, kinder, more dedicated man walks the surface of this Land.

Thirdly, concerning the matter of the Transport Interchange, the High Master was regrettably unable to report any further developments in the resolution either of the strike by waggon drivers or of the ever-lengthening queues of vehicles on the approach roads. This lack of progress is thought to result from the temporary redeployment of Wolf Boy patrols to deal with the Cat Girl attacks. In the light of the foregoing, however, it is hoped that the author will be in a position to report some progress in the next issue of *The Royal Digest.*

Goodbye, Citizens, and long live King Matthew!

The Dance of the Ladders

Rusty pulled off his socks and tossed them into the far corner of his bedroom at the inn. Then he stretched out contentedly on the big brass bed and started gently to massage his toes on the two ornamental knobs at the ends of the foot-rail.

It was the final night of the conference, and his speech had gone well, arousing considerable interest from the delegates. The other presentations, as he had expected, had offered a wide and sometimes surprising variety of viewpoints on the general theme of the sense of direction. Doctor de Voonik, of the Institute of Calibration, discoursing upon the accuracy of compass bearings, had delighted and exasperated him in equal measure with his meticulous dissection of the fine gradations of measurement. Joanna Peterson, a young ornithologist, had intrigued him with her novel theory concerning the apparent disturbance in the sense of direction displayed by the flocks of seagulls that had recently forsaken the coast and started to venture inland. Rusty had, however, found himself utterly baffled by the impenetrable mumblings from the meteorologist who was apparently seeking to explain changes in the prevailing winds, and had soon found himself staring out of the window at the town square, wondering what lay beyond the neat rows of shopfronts. Professor Octavian's session he had skipped altogether, making use of the time to refresh his own navigational skills in some of the tempting backstreets, passages and alleyways of the little market town.

Of Laurel Greening, there had been no sign until the final afternoon, when she had arrived in some haste at the lecture theatre, just in time to mount the podium and deliver her presentation. Rusty realised afterwards that he had taken in nothing of what she had been saying, captivated as he had been by the sheer magnetism of her presence. In the years since their last meeting, she had matured into an elegant and confident woman, her long, dark hair now fastened on top of her head in startlingly insouciant fashion, her sober costume betraying only the subtlest hints of her origin as a child of the Wanderers. She had been mobbed by admirers as soon as she had finished speaking, and Rusty had not so far had a chance to talk to her. To his mild annoyance, he remembered that he had made a dinner date with de Voonik for that evening, but he was still hoping for an opportunity to speak to Laurel before travelling home on the morrow.

It had been an exhausting few days, and Rusty allowed himself to drift into a doze but, after a few minutes, he was awoken again by a commotion from below. Crossing to the window, he gazed down at the narrow cobbled street. Directly beneath him, four lads were dragging a heavy cart laden with wooden ladders, each one festooned with flowers and ribbons in a different permutation of colours. The party was working its way along the row of houses, fastening a ladder under each of the upstairs windows, presumably in preparation for the Ladder Dance which was to take place that evening. The organisers of the conference always took care to ensure the provision of some entertainment on the final night, and this popular local festival was to be the offering at this year's venue. Rusty watched the boys as they manhandled one of the gaily decorated ladders from the cart, propped it under his window, and secured it to a pair of brackets that had apparently been attached there for the purpose.

'Evening,' he called down to them. 'Nice night for it.'

'Evening, master,' came the reply. 'Just make sure and leave the window open tonight. For the dancers, like. But best carry your money with you. You know, just in case.'

'Can't be too careful, I suppose,' replied Rusty. 'But I'm looking forward to it.'

Their task completed, the lads made their way along the street to the next house. As he turned back to face into the room, Rusty's gaze was caught by the portable signal engine, which stood on the table at the foot of the bed with its leads trailing, still disconnected. He realised, to his annoyance, that he still hadn't found the time to get in touch with Eileen. For some reason, he hadn't been able to get the device working properly, although he was sure that he had understood Tom's instructions. Oh well, he thought, there was probably time to have another go at it before he went out.

★　　★　　★

Doctor de Voonik carefully decanted his brandy into the precisely graduated crystal cylinder from which he always drank, and squinted critically at the scale. He was a very thin, bald-headed man in late middle age, who wore tight-fitting dark clothes and had a small, meticulously trimmed beard.

'Spot on,' he said finally. 'Or, at any rate, within an acceptable degree of accuracy given the, er, somewhat less than conducive circumstances. Oh, I'm sorry.' He turned to Rusty, as if noticing him for the first time. 'Would you like me to measure yours? I can't recommend it too highly. Speaking personally, I find it essential to monitor my intake with the maximum practicable degree of precision these days.'

'It's all right, thanks, Doctor,' replied Rusty, who considered himself still young enough to adopt a less structured approach to such things. 'Nice brandy, though.'

They sipped in reflective silence for a few moments. The two of them were seated at a corner table in the crowded upstairs dining room of one of the more select restaurants in the town. Faintly, through the open windows, they could hear the distant music of the ladder dancers. Earlier, Professor Octavian had joined them for their meal, but he had departed after the cheese, excusing himself with the wish for an early night.

'You can call me Wazzo,' said de Voonik after a while. 'All my friends do, although I really can't think why. I have to say, by the way, that I was most intrigued by your little talk yesterday, most intrigued indeed. Most refreshing to hear a word from our, er, commercial brethren. But I have to confess that one small matter has continued to prey upon my mind. Perhaps you might be able to enlighten me . . .'

While he spoke, the music outside the restaurant had started to get louder, and a number of the other diners were craning their necks towards the windows, anxious to get a good view of whatever was about to happen. Rusty, too, would have liked to investigate, but did not want to appear rude to his companion, who continued to speak at the same volume as before, apparently unaffected by the disturbance.

'. . . Something which you could perhaps spare a moment to explain,' de Voonik was saying. 'How exactly do you calculate the precise number of copies to be made of each chart? Surely the level of, er, demand cannot be accurately ascertained until such time as the product is on sale to the citizenry? At which point, surely, it is too late—'

At this point, however, there occurred a disturbance that even de Voonik could not ignore. There was a sudden clatter of footsteps from outside the windows, and all at once the ladder dancers burst into the room and proceeded to caper around the tables in boisterous procession. They were mostly young men and women, their smocks and bonnets festooned with multicoloured ribbons and tinkling bells. Some of them were carrying mouth organs and tambourines, on which they were playing a rumbustious, if somewhat disjointed, melody. As the dancers wove in and out of the tables, some of the less inhibited diners arose and joined themselves on to the end of the line, which eventually returned the way it had come, the participants hurling themselves through the windows and sliding back down the ladders to the street.

The music could be heard fading into the distance as the somewhat stunned restaurant cautiously began to restore itself to its former state of decorum. De Voonik gulped the last of his brandy and called out for more.

'Four measures, please,' he instructed the waiter. 'No, could you make that four and a quarter? Wazzo de Voonik has decided to enjoy himself tonight.'

Rusty wondered what form his colleague's enjoyment was about to take. With some curiosity, he surveyed de Voonik as the latter produced a much larger measuring cylinder from his briefcase and proceeded once again to decant his liquor.

'Acceptable. Most acceptable.' De Voonik finally appeared satisfied with his calibration. 'But, of course, we are now left with something of a problem.'

Rusty raised an eyebrow.

'The apportionment of the account, Mister Brown, the apportionment of the account.'

Rusty raised his other eyebrow.

'You see, young colleague,' de Voonik continued, 'you and I have eaten four courses, although, in fact, my choice of soup was slightly more costly than yours. But that old skinflint Octavian, always a difficult character in my experience, he chose to spurn the meat, and instead elected to take only soup, fish and cheese. And while you and I divided between us a bottle of wine . . .'

'Two bottles, actually,' Rusty interjected. He noticed that de Voonik's speech had started to become slightly slurred.

'Yes, two bottles, quite so, most remiss of me. While you and I shared between us two bottles of wine, the division being in surprisingly equal measure, Octavian elected to order only the very smallest flask of sour ale. And now, of course, you and I are quaffing brandy, yourself with some restraint, myself with little if any restraint, but with meticulous scrutiny of the precise quantity ingested. And, according to my initial calculations, the niggardly financial contribution deposited by our colleague on his departure is insufficient to make good his liability. So you see . . .'

'Why don't we just take the difference and split it two ways?' proposed Rusty.

'Split it two ways?' De Voonik seemed taken aback by this notion. 'A most interesting suggestion – perhaps I ought to give it some consideration. However, there is a further complication. An immediate complication, in fact.' He took another large draught of brandy, allowed the remaining liquid to stabilise in the cylinder, and squinted again at the scale. 'We have ordered coffee, for two persons. But, you see, I have taken the liberty of inviting Professor Greening to join us. Which should, of course, have necessitated the ordering of coffee for three persons. I hope you don't mind.'

'No,' Rusty laughed. 'I don't mind.'

As it happened, Laurel chose that very moment to make her entrance, sweeping towards them between the tables in a long red-and-gold evening dress that showed none of the restraint of her daytime outfit. As she arrived at the table, the two men arose to greet her, Rusty's heart pounding with sudden apprehension. Laurel kissed them both warmly.

'Wazzo, how lovely to see you again.' With maturity, her voice had acquired a creamy evenness. 'And Rusty! What a marvellous surprise! I'd no idea you'd done so well for yourself. I haven't seen you since — how long has it been?'

They seated themselves around the table. De Voonik beckoned a waiter over, increased the coffee order, and requested another three-quarter measure of brandy for himself. While they waited for it to arrive, the three of them made tentative efforts to strike a conversational balance between Laurel's smooth poise, Rusty's boyish nervousness, and de Voonik's increasingly manic state of intoxication. However, polite etiquette continued, just about, to hold sway, and the two men allowed Laurel to set the pace. For a while they exchanged moderately decorous gossip concerning their colleagues and peers in the world of direction-finding, Rusty noticing, with some interest, that the Doctor had begun to display a hitherto unsuspected anarchic streak in his character. After a while, the atmosphere between them began to relax, and

Rusty became aware that Laurel's knee was pressing against his under the table.

Eventually the bill arrived, and they persuaded de Voonik that it was time to move on. He turned out to be somewhat unsteady on his feet, and Rusty and Laurel had some difficulty in helping him down the stairs.

'I think we're going to have to take him to his hotel,' said Laurel with some amusement.

As they frogmarched de Voonik back up the main street, threading their way to and fro between the feet of the ladders, they could once again hear the music of the dancers close at hand and, all at once, a group of about twenty people precipitated themselves from the windows of a nearby building, skidding down several adjacent ladders, and almost knocking the three of them from their feet.

'Yes!' roared de Voonik, awakening suddenly from his torpor. 'The ladder dance! Wazzo's weekend starts here!'

Abruptly he tore himself free from the supporting grip of his companions, and lurched off in pursuit of the dancers, his spindly arms and legs gyrating in the manner of some monstrous, uncoordinated insect. Rusty and Laurel gaped at each other.

'Let's not spoil his fun,' said Laurel finally.

'I take it you've met him before?' queried Rusty.

'Wazzo? Yes, he quite often tips up at these things. He usually disgraces himself in some way or other. Actually, I thought he seemed quite restrained this year, compared to his usual.' In the distance, they caught a last glimpse of de Voonik, pursuing the dancers up a ladder, his agility apparently fully restored.

'Why don't I walk you back to your inn?' suggested Rusty. 'Where are you stopping?'

'Same place as you, actually,' said Laurel, smiling as she slipped her arms around his waist. 'I'm quite well-organised over things like that.'

Suddenly, Rusty realised that their faces were very close together, quite a lot closer than one would normally consider acceptable with a professional associate, close enough, in fact, for him to feel the warm whisper of her breath across his cheek.

And then, just for an instant, he caught a glimpse of the hard fires that had once burned behind her dark eyes, a glimpse of the magic and the mystery and the mischief she had once brought into his life, a glimpse of the secret she had passed to him so many years ago, a glimpse of so many things that had lain dormant for so long that he had almost, but not quite, come to forget their baleful presence. Almost, but not quite. For a moment, he nearly felt tempted . . .

'Shame on you,' Rusty scolded her resolutely. 'I'm a respectably married man these days.'

'The married ones are always the worst,' said Laurel. 'Come on. Nobody will know.'

Several hours passed. The town was quiet at last. The dance of the ladders was over for another year, the ladders themselves abandoned against the walls, the dancers returned to their homes and their warm beds. Even Doctor de Voonik had finally found his unsteady way back to the inn where he was staying, had finally crawled, on hands and knees, up the stairs to his room.

And at the other end of the town, in another upstairs room, the two secret lovers, exhausted and replete, slept their guilty sleep.

So nobody saw the gaunt, silent figure that made its ascent, rung by careful rung, of the ladder beneath their window. Nobody heard the stealthy hands that softly explored the controls of the signal engine at the foot of the bed. And nobody felt the snaking wires that connected the terminals of the engine to the two brass knobs at the end of the bedstead.

At least, nobody in that quiet little market town saw or heard or felt anything. But, when the two people who slumbered in the brass bed awoke in the small hours of the morning and reached out again for each other, the invisible web of the signal network began, very gently, to oscillate in cold, merciless empathy.

The Three Windows

'Mum, the buzzer's going on the signal engine!'

Eileen was awake at once. In the half-light she could just make out Max's sturdy figure hovering nervously at the door of her bedroom.

'It's probably your dad, Maxie, at his conference. He said he'd be in touch. I'll go and see. You take yourself back to bed.'

Sleepily, she groped her way along the corridor to the spare bedroom, the room that until recently had been occupied by Tom Slater. Sleepily, she seated herself at the signal engine, sleepily she fitted the headphones over her ears, sleepily she adjusted the controls and peered into the eyepieces. Gradually, the scene came into focus.

She was standing in a small, empty, six-sided room with no windows and no doors. The walls, ceiling, and floor were an uneven pale grey in colour, and the dim light seemed to emanate, directionless and bland, from the eight surfaces that enclosed her.

Eileen recognised the room at once. She had been in this room before. She had been here many times. And she knew that the surfaces were supposed to be pure white, and she knew too that, with constant use of the signal engine, a deposit of dust or dirt had built up on the surfaces and gradually discoloured them. And she knew that, if she failed to carry out her daily cleaning routine, the walls and ceiling and floor would slowly darken until, inexorably, they would turn an opaque black and exclude the light entirely. And, without fully understanding the reason, Eileen knew that this must never be allowed to happen. Wearily, she gave the controls of the signal engine a half-twist, and a little metal scraper appeared as usual in the air in front of her. Resignedly, she grasped hold of the small, inadequate tool and once again set about removing the deposit from the walls.

'Eileen?' A hoarse voice broke in upon her thoughts. Startled by the sudden interruption, Eileen let the scraper slip from her fingers. 'Who's that?' Kneeling, she started to search in the dust for the dropped tool.

'Never mind the scraper, Eileen,' said the voice. 'Just look at what's in front of you.'

'Don't I know that voice? Who are you?'

'Never mind who I am. Just look at what's in front of you.'

Eileen looked. At the edge of her field of vision, an insubstantial form hovered, but she found that her eyes were somehow reluctant to focus on it. Because in front of her stood a tall wooden ladder, a ladder decorated with dry, withered flowers and ragged, filthy shreds of ribbon. And Eileen could see now that she was kneeling, not in a room, but at the base of a deep, six-sided shaft, a shaft that rose above her for ever, a shaft whose walls tapered away to infinity.

'Climb, Eileen,' said the voice. 'Climb the ladder, and see what you will see.'

'What's going on? Where's Rusty? Where's my husband?'

'Just climb.' The voice was firmer now, and deeper. The tone was commanding. There was no possibility of disobedience.

So Eileen climbed. Step by painful step, she hauled herself up the ladder, the dead flowers crackling against her cotton nightdress, the grimy rungs blackening the palms of her hands and the bare soles of her feet.

Then, in the wall in front of her, a window appeared.

Pausing, she peered through the smeared glass, trying to make sense of the scene within. She could make out a small figure, facing away from her, kneeling . . . the figure of a boy . . . surely it was Max, her own precious boy . . . But wasn't there something else in the room with him . . . ? Yes, there in front of the boy, lined up like soldiers, were row upon row of little animals, their upturned faces expectant, their eyes glowing red in the gloom . . . And around their necks were little tags, each tag bearing a number . . .

'Max!' she screamed. 'Max! How many times must I tell you? Get away from those rats! You'll catch all sorts of diseases! Come here, Maxie, come to Mummy . . .'

But the boy did not respond. Perhaps he could not hear her. Frantically, Eileen reached out to tap on the glass, but the window was just too far away, just beyond her reach . . .

'Climb the ladder, Eileen.'

And now she was climbing again, her arms and legs aching, her breath rasping in her throat. And then, in the wall in front of her, another window appeared.

Again Eileen peered through the glass.

This time, it was a girl. Again, she had her back to Eileen. She was seated at her dressing table, draped in a bathrobe, studying her face in the mirror, carefully applying black and white face paint to her cheeks . . .

Despite the macabre white foundation, despite the slanting cat's eyes and the grotesque button nose, despite the mockingly jaunty whiskers, there was no mistaking the face in the mirror . . . Suddenly, the features contorted themselves into a savage snarl, teeth bared, eyes blazing . . .

'Ashleigh!' howled Eileen. 'What have they done to you?'

But again there was no response. Desperately, Eileen reached out to tap on the glass but, once again, she found it just beyond her reach.

'Climb the ladder, Eileen.'

And now she was climbing once more, her soft body sagging with fatigue, her face streaked with tears of rage and frustration and exhaustion. And then, in the wall in front of her, a third window appeared.

Again Eileen peered through the glass. This time, there was a big brass bed in the room, its foot towards the window, a brass knob at either end of the rail. In the bed were two people, a man and a woman. They were both naked, and there could be no mistaking what they were doing. The woman had her back to Eileen. She was squatting astride the man's body, her head flung back, her long, dark hair swishing from side to side as she rotated her pelvis . . . The man was stretched out flat, his face hidden from her, his head twisting spasmodically one way and another . . .

And then, as the pair reached their climax, he raised his head for a moment. Even with his eyelids screwed shut, even with his mouth gaping open, Eileen knew him at once.

'Rusty!'

But, once again, it seemed that her grief-stricken howl went unheeded.

'Rusty!' The furious pounding of her heart seemed to engorge her whole body until, suddenly, Eileen knew that she could endure it no longer. Bit by bit, she could feel her feet losing their purchase on the ladder, could feel her blistered hands relinquishing their grip on the uprights, and suddenly she was skidding and clutching and bumping her way downwards, torn ribbons snagging in her hair, brittle flower stalks ripping at her nightdress, until finally she hit the ground with an ungainly thud, her strength exhausted, her breath dashed from her body.

And there, standing over her, at the foot of the ladder, was the gaunt figure of her tormentor. And, at last, she could see his face.

'Tom Slater,' she sobbed. 'What's happening? Why are you doing this?'

'Why am I doing this? But I have done nothing, Eileen. I have done none of these things. All of the things you have seen, your family have done to themselves. All I have done is to allow you to see things as they really are.'

'You're mad! I'm going to kill you! Where are you?'

'Where am I? Don't you know where I am? Do you not know this place? Do you really not know?'

And Tom Slater began to laugh, a harsh, vicious, demoniacal laugh that echoed from wall to wall, and from floor to ceiling, and from deep past to distant, unknown future.

And then, abruptly, the scene faded from Eileen's view, and she found herself sprawled on the floor of the spare bedroom, the signal engine towering above her, the headphones tangled about her neck, her night-dress torn and her hands and feet blackened.

'Ashleigh! Max!' In an instant, she was on her feet. Ashleigh's room was the nearest. Eileen pounded at the door. It wouldn't move. Something was jammed up against it on the inside. Again and again, she hurled herself at the door until finally it yielded. Bursting into the room, Eileen could see that a chest of draw-ers had been wedged up against the door. The narrow bed was empty, and a length of rope, tied to the bedpost, dangled through the open window.

'Ashleigh?' Desperately, Eileen heaved pieces of furniture aside, unable to comprehend what was happening. Helplessly, she stared around the empty room. And then, silently, silhouetted against the night sky, a figure appeared at the window and stepped lightly inside.

'Ashleigh? Ashleigh, darling? What have you been doing?'

Eileen snapped on the light. The startled creature that stood before her in the flat glare of the overhead bulb was hardly recognisable as her daughter. Her feet were bare, her long legs soiled with mud and grime. Her thin shift, torn into jagged ribbons, barely concealed the raw lines of her adolescent frame. Her short, red hair was sticking out in irregular spikes, and her unformed features were caked with smeared make-up. And from her parted lips, dribbling down her chin, streaking her neck and throat, there bubbled a stream of frothing, crimson blood.

For a moment, mother and daughter faced each other in mute incomprehension. Then, with a furious hiss, Ashleigh spun around and vanished again through the window. By the time Eileen had stumbled across the obstacle course of overturned furniture, her daughter had disappeared from view.

Terror-stricken, Eileen dashed to Max's room. Her son was curled up in bed, fast asleep. Roughly, she shook him by the shoulder.

'Max! Max! Wake up! Get your things!'

'What's happening?' the boy murmured drowsily. 'Was it Dad on the engine?'

'Never mind that now!' In her panic, immediate flight presented itself to Eileen as the only conceivable option. 'We're leaving! We're going to stay at Grandad's! We can't stop in this place a moment longer!'

'Is Dad coming? And Ashleigh?'

'I don't know. I don't think so. Maybe later.'

'And what about Tom?'

'Tom?' For a moment, Eileen's crazed momentum was broken. 'Tom?'

'Yes. Can't Tom come? I like doing things with Tom. He lives in the elevator shaft now. Didn't I tell you?'

Eileen stared in horrified disbelief at her son's open, upturned face. Then, heart thumping, she ran to her bedroom, climbed up on a chair and started to drag the suitcases down from the top of the wardrobe.

The Magician and the Herald

'This way, Pegasus! You'll never find me if you keep stopping for rests!'

Leonardo Pegasus had never been much of an athlete, and the unremitting pursuit of his quarry through the tangled maze of the Signal Network was proving more than his ageing body could bear. Wearily he hauled himself yet again to his feet, blankly he peered this way and that, finally he selected the most likely of several directions and set off again at an unsteady shamble.

'That's better! You'll soon catch me now! Can you see me yet?'

In the far distance, silhouetted against the faint light at the end of the corridor, a dark, spindly figure was hopping mockingly from one skinny leg to the other. For a moment, Leonardo forced himself to believe that he was starting to gain ground but then, with a sneering laugh, his adversary leaped in the air and cartwheeled away down a side turning. Panting, the magician continued his dogged pursuit until it seemed that his legs could no longer support his sagging weight. Gasping for breath, he propped himself against the nearest wall. It was no good. If his search were ever to prove successful, he would have to devise some other method of pursuit . . .

'Master Pegasus?' It was Gash's voice, clumsily breaking in on Leonardo's vision. His concentration destroyed, the magician irritably pulled off his headphones and shut off the power supply to the signal engine.

'What is it now? Can't you see I'm busy?'

'Sorry, Master. You know I try not to interrupt you. But it's just that the person from the *Digest* is here to conduct an interview. She says would you mind sparing her a few minutes?'

'I suppose so,' Leonardo agreed reluctantly. 'Show her in. And see if you can get the coffee engine working.'

It was some weeks since the magician had been engaged to tackle the problem of the imps. After some days of protracted negotiation with caretakers and storemen, he had managed to get a filing cabinet and a couple of battered armchairs delivered to his temporary office and, after still more complex negotiations with Veronique's department, a spare signal engine had been installed for his personal use, and a temporary supply of electricity made available to power it. But, although Leonardo had been spending the greater part of each working day hunched over the apparatus, he had made no significant progress in his task, and the imps continued to run amok over the network with as much abandon as ever. Even the coffee engine was proving unreliable. And now he was faced with a further unwelcome interruption. Wearily, he resigned himself to yet another unproductive day.

'Hello. I suppose we'd better make ourselves comfortable, then.' He managed a half-hearted smile of welcome. His guest turned out to be a tall, big-boned woman of about his own age, untidily dressed and wearing a large pair of dark-rimmed spectacles. She looked slightly uneasy.

'Hello, Master Pegasus. It's not a bad time, is it? Thought I'd better come along in person for this one. I'm the Herald, by the way. Funny to think we're still using the old-fashioned title, isn't it?' They seated themselves in the two armchairs. The Herald prattled nervously on. 'The Department doesn't actually use Criers any more. Nearly all my work is for the *Royal Digest* these days. Anyway, I'm doing a piece about the imps for the next issue. Perhaps we could start . . .'

'I don't really know where to start,' Leonardo began, staring forlornly out of the window. 'You see, I'm supposed to be investigating this problem with the Signal Network, but of course I didn't have anything to do the original design of the Network. That was Kevin, er, what was his name . . . ?'

'Kevin Considine,' supplied his guest.

'Considine, that's right. Actually, he was one of the people who got me kicked out of here, years ago. He ended up completely out of his depth, didn't he? Just between ourselves, I think he probably deserved every-thing he got. Don't print that, will you? But it's ironic, isn't it, that they decided to call me back after all this time to sort out the mess he left.'

'Ironic, yes. So what have you done up to now?' the Herald prompted him.

Leonardo frowned. Outside the window, circumscribed by its mullioned frame, he could see one of the turrets of the Palace, outlined against the overcast sky. Incongruously, a small flock of seagulls was circling around it.

'What have I done?' he replied at length, sighing. 'It doesn't feel like much, really. Trouble is, the engine they've given me isn't really powerful enough. And there don't seem to be any charts or diagrams of the Network, so I'm getting pretty confused about the geography of it all. But I suppose there is one thing I've begun to understand a bit about the imps, at any rate.'

'That's interesting.' Leonardo noticed vaguely that the woman had produced a writing tablet and was starting to make notes. 'What have you found out?'

'Well, I got my first clue when I started reading those reports, the ones Gash collected. You see, some of the imps had names. But the odd thing was, they all seemed to have very similar names. Lee, or Leigh, or Leah. Sometimes Leroy or Levi. But all more or less the same, in the end. So I started to think that perhaps all the imps were actually the same imp, maybe appearing in different guises to different people, but in essence all the same. So I've more or less come to the conclusion that there's just one creature behind

all this.' He frowned. 'And, of course, it's a very mischievous creature. Worse than mischievous, I suppose.
Malicious, perhaps that's it. Maybe even evil, although
I don't like that word. And very powerful as well, of
course.'

For a few minutes, the magician seemed sunk in
thought. Eventually, his visitor prompted him again.

'So do you know anything else about Lee?'

There was another long silence.

'Just one other thing,' said the magician finally. 'It
may not be anything, But, on the other hand, it may
be quite important. Because, you see, Lee was my own
creation. Years ago. So, in a way, I suppose all this must
be my fault.' He noticed that the Herald was scrib-
bling busily on her tablet. He took a long breath, and
then continued. 'It all started way back in the time of
the old King. I was a very young magician in those
days. I devised a piece of equipment called the
Empathy Engine. It was quite famous in its day, but
I don't suppose you're old enough to remember it.'

The Herald smiled at Leonardo's feeble attempt at
gallantry.

'Actually, I do remember. Quite well, actually. But
go on. You were saying that you created Lee?'

'Yes. I was using the Engine to help the King with
some of his decision-making but, in between doing
that, I was also using it for a private project of my
own. I was quite curious in those days about the workings of the human mind, so I was using the Engine
to carry out some little investigations. And, mostly,

I used my own mind to experiment upon. Some of the things I found there were pretty interesting, I can tell you. There were actually people in there, like the characters in a marionette show perhaps, characters who each seemed to embody a different aspect of my nature. And I suppose you could say that Lee was the character who sort of represented my, er, my secret side, I suppose you could call it. Lee embodied all the hidden bits of me, the bits that nobody knew about, the bits that I didn't *want* anyone to know about. I didn't even know about some of them myself. Not to begin with, anyway. But it was only ever intended to be a private experiment. It was just for my own amusement. I never meant anyone else to get involved in it.' The magician was staring at the floor now, his hands knotting and unknotting themselves like two hesitant wrestlers.

'So this creature, this Lee, sort of represented the dark side of your nature?'

'I suppose you could call it that, yes. But it was all quite safe, or at least I thought it was safe, because it was all locked away inside my Empathy Engine. I thought I was the only one who could get in there. But then I lost the Engine, and someone else got their hands on it.'

'That sounds a bit careless of you. How did it happen?'

'Well, my Empathy Engine was stolen. I don't really want to talk about how it happened, but I suppose it was my fault, really. An error of judgement, anyway.

Let's just say I trusted someone I should never have trusted. And then, after that, other people seem to have used the Engine as well, without any of them really understanding the true power of it. And, all the time, Lee was there, collecting up all their dark stuff, and growing bigger, more powerful. And then Kevin, er . . .'

'Considine.'

'Yes, Kevin Considine, thank you. He managed to get hold of the Engine, and it seems that he somehow built it into this Signal Network of his. And then he let Lee escape on to the Network. So now the whole of the Kingdom is at risk.'

'And you've got the job of tracking Lee down?'

'Yes, that's right. But, at the moment, I really haven't any idea how I'm going to do it. Lee is stronger than me, and faster than me. And I'm getting so tired.'

Drained of energy after unburdening himself in this way, Leonardo slumped back in his armchair and, for the first time, looked his visitor full in the face. His visitor looked back at him in inscrutable silence.

'Don't I know you from somewhere?' said Leonardo finally.

'I'm sorry,' replied the Herald. 'Terribly rude of me. I never really introduced myself. I'm Ruth Garamond. And of course you know me. We used to work together, oh, it must have been about forty years ago.' They stared at each other, temporarily speechless.

'Ruthie,' said the magician eventually. 'Ruthie Garamond. Well, bless my soul. My very first apprentice. No, wait a minute, there were two of you, weren't there? What was the lad called?'

'Geoffrey. Geoffrey Slater.' Miss Garamond was smiling faintly.

'Yes, Geoffrey, that's it. Used to be very fond of mutton and parsnip pies. It's all coming back now. And the two of you had to be sent away, because . . .' Leonardo blushed.

'It's all right. It was because I was going to have a baby, so I couldn't stay in my job any more. Because of the celibacy rule.' Leonardo nodded. 'We went to live by the sea. And the baby was born there, we called him Tom. Tom Slater. He did all right for himself later on. But then I did a terrible thing.' For a long moment, the Herald hesitated. Then, suddenly, she abandoned her professional poise. Her writing tablet slid unheeded to the floor. There were tears in her eyes. 'I ran away. I left Geoffrey with the baby. And I never went back.'

'So Tom never knew his mother?'

'That's right.' Ruth sniffed. 'And he never knew his father, either.'

'But didn't Geoffrey bring him up?'

'Oh yes. Geoffrey brought him up all right. But Geoffrey wasn't his father, was he?'

'I don't understand.'

'*You* were his father, Leo. You were Tom Slater's father. Only I pretended it was Geoffrey, because . . .'

Leonardo was staring at her, open-mouthed.

'Because I wanted to protect you. I was in love

with you, Leo. And I think I still am. There's never been anyone else. Even after all this time.'

There was quite a bit of catching-up to be done after that. Outside the window, the light grew dim, the seagulls flew away, and the pointed outline of the turret gradually merged with the darkness beyond. One by one, the yellow lights at its windows were extinguished, until finally the window frame presented a perfectly featureless black rectangle.

'I wonder what became of Tom?' said Leonardo eventually. He was on his feet now, lighting the oil lamps. 'I kept track of him for a while. He was studying for a degree in Cartography. But that was at least fifteen years ago, maybe even twenty. I don't know what he did after that.'

'Oh, that's easy,' replied Ruth. 'He came here, to the city. He was looking after the transport interchange for a while, didn't you know? He became a bit of a local celebrity, actually. But I never got in touch with him. There didn't seem to be any point. Because it wasn't him I wanted to see. It was you, Leo, and I couldn't see you because of the stupid celibacy rule. So I never tried to see Tom, I suppose I resented him really, because he was the one who had kept me away from you in the first place. And then there was that bit of a scandal, I wrote about it in the *Digest*. I think I said some pretty mean things about him, actually. Anyway, he ended up in prison for a few years. But he's back in the city now, sort of lying low for the time being. He got a job with someone I know, Michael Brown, the chap who publishes the charts. As a matter of fact, he was renting a room from him. Somewhere in the Western Suburb. A place called Tower Mansions.'

'Tower Mansions?' said Leonardo. 'That's extraordinary. That's where I used to live. Why don't we go round there and see him one day? If you want to, that is.'

'That would be a surprise for him, wouldn't it?' mused Ruth. 'His old mum and dad popping round for tea. What do you think?'

'I'm not sure,' replied Leonardo. 'I suppose we could take some cakes, biscuits maybe. But listen, I haven't had anything to eat today. Would you fancy dropping round to the Crier's Rest? They should be open by now.'

The Empty Space

When Rusty awoke, he was relieved, although not very surprised, to find himself alone. His head was throbbing from the previous night's intake of brandy but, even after he had bathed, dressed and breakfasted, he still found himself feeling dazed and bewildered and disorientated. He tried once again to get in touch with Eileen, but with no more success than before, so he dismantled the signal engine and the accumulator and stowed them away in his luggage. Having done this, he made his way down to the town square, where the carriages were waiting to take the conference delegates back to their various destinations. He noticed that the ladders had been taken down from the house fronts and, as his conveyance bumped along the road that led back to the Royal Highway, his nostrils caught the unmistakable whiff of burning timber. In a field at the edge of the town, the ladders had been roughly stacked and made into a huge pyre, the smoke from which had started to drift into the carriage. With a glance at his fellow passengers, Rusty pulled the window shut. Then he rested his head against the back of his seat, closed his eyes and allowed himself to drift off into uneasy slumber.

Some hours later, at the outskirts of the city, the carriage bumped to a halt in the long queue for the transport interchange. Wishing to circumvent the inevitable delays and chaos there, Rusty decided to alight prematurely and finish his journey on foot. It would be a good opportunity to call in at the offices of Michael Brown Publications and check that all was well before returning home to Tower Mansions. He crossed the river by ferry and strode down the North Way, attempting to put his thoughts in order.

Arriving at the office, he was annoyed to find the building deserted. There were no signs of Tom or Charlotte, and it appeared that the rest of his staff had also awarded themselves an unofficial holiday. The copying engines and drawing boards were abandoned, and the room, normally buzzing with noise and talk, was silent. Making up his mind to administer some stern words the next day, Rusty prepared himself for the journey home. But, just as he was reaching for his keys, his ears caught the sound of distant weeping. He stood still for a moment, attempting to locate the source of the noise. It seemed to be coming from the basement. Alarmed now, he ran down the stairs, three at a time.

The scene that greeted his eyes was one of utter devastation. The cartons that had contained the newly copied charts had been ripped open, and the floor was knee-deep in shredded paper and cardboard. The planks that had covered the gap in the wall had been torn aside, the builders' tarpaulin tossed into a corner, and the soil shovelled away, allowing unrestricted entry to the goats from the neighbouring field, half a dozen of whom were munching contentedly at what remained of his stock-in-trade. And, in the far corner, he found Charlotte, slumped alone on the floor, weeping inconsolably. Pausing only to shoo away the animals, Rusty struggled across the room, kicking away the litter as he went, and knelt at her side.

'Charlotte, what's happened? Was it the builders?' For a moment, she did not reply. Carefully, he slipped a finger under her chin and tilted her tear-stained face up towards his.

'Oh, Mister Brown, I'm so sorry,' she gasped between sobs. 'But it wasn't the builders. It was Mister Slater, he promised it would be all right, he said I could take a few days off because of Maisie, he said he'd look after the office while you were away, I didn't like to, but he swore everything would be safe . . .'

'Mister Slater? Tom sent you away? Tom did this?'

Charlotte nodded miserably, then burst into tears again.

Eventually, between the two of them, they managed to evict the remaining goats and make yet another temporary repair to the wall.

'Best get home,' said Rusty gently. 'It's all right, Charlotte. None of this is your fault. I'll see you in the morning, and we can start working out what to do.'

Charlotte lived somewhere in the North Estates, in the opposite direction from Rusty's apartment, so the two of them parted company at the office door. A faint drizzle was dampening the air. Stunned, scarcely able to comprehend what had happened, Rusty picked his way along the line of the old city wall, stumbling over glistening chunks of fallen masonry, staring with unseeing eyes across the rippling surface of the river towards the distant rooftops of the Western Suburb. Tom did this, he thought. Perhaps Eileen had been right about Tom after all. But why would he do such a thing? What was he planning? And would he ever dare to reappear at the office? Rusty realised that he no longer even knew where his former friend was living.

Dusk was approaching as he arrived at the bridge by the West Gate, and the lights of the evening traf-fic were reflected in the water, their images fragmented and softened by the ripples of its surface and by the light rain that had now started to fall. As Rusty entered the apartment building, he noticed that the door of the old elevator shaft was hanging open again. Reflexively, he kicked it shut, reminding himself to speak to the caretaker about it in the morning. As he climbed the eight flights of stairs, he started to rack his brains, wondering what on earth he was going to say to Eileen.

But, when he arrived at the apartment, a final surprise awaited him. Pushing open the front door, he found the hallway dark.

'Eileen,' he called, 'I'm back. What's for supper?' There was no reply.

'Maxie? Ash? Where's your mum?' Still there was silence. Puzzled, he pushed open the bedroom door. Sitting down on the bed to take off his shoes in the half-light, he had his back to the wardrobe, and he did not at once notice that the suitcases were missing. In fact it was not until he had made himself a cup of tea and sat down in front of the empty grate that the truth finally struck him. Staring at the mantelpiece, Rusty realised that the engraved portrait of Eileen's father, the portrait that he had always hated, no longer occupied its customary position.

Slumped in the sagging armchair, exhausted and bewildered, long after it became too dark to see, Rusty continued to stare at the empty space. Beside him, forgotten in its flower-patterned cup, his tea grew cold.

★   ★   ★

Rusty didn't go back to the office the next day, or the day after that. In fact, he didn't get beyond his own front door for some time afterwards. Aimlessly, he wandered around the apartment, not bothering to get dressed, picking at scraps from the larder, dumping cups and dishes unwashed in the sink. After a while, it occurred to him to that it might be worth trying to power up the signal engine and get in touch with Eileen, but it seemed that the engine at her father's house had been disconnected, and he could not think of anywhere else she might be. Next, he attempted to contact the Royal Wolf Boys Investigations Branch to report three missing persons, but the administrator who eventually spoke to him was unhelpful.

'We're very busy at the moment, sir, what with the transport strike and the imps and what-have-you. Of course, I can fill out a search docket, and we'll try and send someone round to you when we can. But I expect they'll all turn up sooner or later. They usually do.'

From time to time, he was startled out of his reverie by the jangle of the doorbell. There was a visit from Charlotte, who wanted to know when he was coming back to the office. She told him that the rest of the staff, scenting disaster, had already deserted, and she was now the only one left. Ashamed of the state of the apartment, Rusty kept her on the doorstep and finally sent her away with a month's wages, promising to contact her when he had decided what to do.

A man from the transport interchange arrived after

a few days to deliver the luggage that Rusty had abandoned on his return from the conference, and presented him with an invoice.

But of Eileen and Ashleigh and Max, there was no sign. So Rusty stayed in the apartment, not knowing what else he could do. Sometimes he languished on the sofa, facing away from the rain-spattered window, staring at the ceiling. Sometimes he lay in the bath, forgetting to wash himself, his fingers clenched around the flannel, until the chilling water puckered his flesh and seeped away through the leaky plug. But for most of the time he sat in Ashleigh's room, or in Max's room, inhaling the fading aroma of their presence, ceaselessly smoothing the covers of their cold, empty beds.

And then, one afternoon, the signal engine started buzzing again.

'So how did you finally take your revenge?'

That's probably the question Nina would have asked me, if she had still been here. I must say, I've been missing my little chats with Nina, and sometimes I still like to imagine that I'm talking to her. I don't suppose she would really have approved of the notion of revenge, though. She would probably have encouraged me to come to terms with things as they were, or perhaps to acknowledge my negative feelings and begin the process of moving on. So perhaps it's just as well that she'll never know what I finally did. I'm truly sorry about what happened to her, though. None of this was her fault, but I'm sure she would understand that I wasn't left with any choice. And, of course, I never actually did tell her what became of my father. But I certainly told her what sort of father he was. Because, if I'd had a proper father and a proper family, maybe none of this would have happened.

But I can't say anything to Nina any more, so instead, I'll say it to you, Michael Brown. Yes, you, the little red-haired kid who thought he was such a clever boy all those years ago at the Academy. Of course, by the time I finally caught up with you, here at Tower Mansions, you weren't a kid any more, and your pretty red hair had started to go grey here and there, it had even started to fall out in places. But you were the one who lost me my degree. You were the one who had all those things I could never have. And you were the one who started me on the path that led me to where I am now. So you were always the one that was going to have to suffer.

When my punishment was over, when I came back to the city, it wasn't too difficult to track you down. Your charts were at the front of every bookstall, and your address was on the front of every chart, so all I needed to do was to turn up at your office one day and ask you for a job. And you had always been a soft-hearted fellow, so you couldn't do enough to help an old friend who had fallen on hard times.

Once I was in that office, I just did what I have always been best at. I watched, and I listened, and I made myself useful and, after a while, people started to believe that they could trust me. So I had plenty of time to find out about your business, plenty of time to study your correspondence, and of course I also had plenty of time to tinker with the *signal engines and to make a few modifications. And then, of course, I had the chance to befriend a few imps and to encourage them to give me a helping hand.*

When I learned about the conference, I knew that my moment had finally come. It wasn't too hard to persuade the builders to stay away when it suited me, and it wasn't too hard to do a few little building modifications of my own. That girl Charlotte was my only problem, the only one who was really difficult to deal with. She was the only one among your staff who was really loyal to you, but when I found out about her sister and all her problems, I found that I could use her to keep Charlotte out of the way when I needed to.

So in the end it wasn't too hard to destroy your business. But, while all that was going on, I was also making myself busy working on your family. It was a real stroke of luck that you had a spare room to rent, and even more of a stroke of luck when I discovered that that was where you kept your signal engine. I don't think your wife ever really trusted me, though, so I had to tread carefully there, really make an effort to be the perfect lodger, but it certainly paid off handsomely. And the boy and the girl were no trouble at all. They loved playing with that engine, once I'd shown them how to work it, and it didn't take any time at all for my imps to set them off on the road to mischief. I hardly needed to do anything, really, once I had discovered their little weaknesses. Once I had done that, they did all the rest for themselves.

And, after all that, my little stunt at the conference was all that was needed to finish things off. Once I had found out about the good Professor Greening, it wasn't too hard for my friendly imps to persuade her to do a bit of renewing of old acquaintance. The only other thing that was necessary was my modification to the portable signal engine. But by then I had your complete trust. You followed my instructions to the letter, and all I had to do was to arrange for the machinery to be connected up at the critical moment. And, when I made contact with your wife that night, things just couldn't have worked out better.

Of course, I had to move out of the apartment after that business with the girl and her late nights. I found myself a place to sleep in the old elevator shaft after that, and I've been living here quite comfortably these past few weeks, with just the rats for company. I've rather enjoyed it, sleeping on a hard floor again, it puts me in mind of my old billet at the Academy, at the feet of Roger the Blind. Oh yes, I managed to hook into the signal apparatus on the roof of the building, so that I could keep an eye on how things have been going, and that's all been really interesting.

So I destroyed your livelihood, Michael Brown, and now I've destroyed your family too. I had been considering whether to take the final step and destroy you as well, but I'm not really sure that I need to do that. I think I might just prefer to leave you to suffer.

I envied you once, Michael, for all the things you had that I didn't have, but now, at last, I've taken every single one of them away from you. You're not even good to look at any more. You've lost your nice loose-limbed figure, you're losing your nice red hair, and now you're well on the way to losing your nice orderly mind as well.

So perhaps it's time to call it a day. This afternoon, I've been looking through some of the old things in my pack. The old poems and crosswords are still there, although they're all looking a bit dog-eared now. It seemed so fascinating once, learning to play with words and letters, learning to make them do things, but in the end it didn't add up to more than a bunch of silly tricks, just like that girl at the House of Rest who used to walk on her hands. Looking at it all today, I can see it for what it is, just a pile of litter.

Oh yes, I've still got those old charts of yours, those childish scribbles that you probably forgot about years ago. It makes me a bit sad, though, looking at the charts, imagining the boy who drew them, wondering what might have happened if things had been different.

Last of all, of course, there's the old iron chain, the chain that my father made. That chain is the oldest thing I've got and, as I let the links run through my fingers, it almost seems to me that I can still feel a ripple of its old power. That chain has always stopped with me. The chain has always reminded me where I came from. And it's the chain that's speaking to me now, reminding me of the final thing I have to do.

And when I have done that, Michael Brown, you and I will truly be even.

The Litter Patrol

'I think he lives on the fourth floor, Leo,' Miss Garamond panted. 'Do you need a rest before we try the stairs?'

After a few rather tantalising weeks of indecision, Leonardo and Ruth had finally decided to pay an unannounced visit to Tower Mansions, to surprise their long-lost son. The magician, clutching a crumpled bag of biscuits, had wanted to retrace the steps of his old route between the Palace and the apartment building, and the elderly pair were now both feeling rather short of breath.

'No need for stairs,' replied the magician. 'There's an elevator. Or, at any rate, there used to be. A pony-driven one. I used to have little chats with the Elevator Captain. It was all rather splendid.' He started to rummage in the pockets of his robe. 'I've probably still got the key somewhere. Good heavens, whatever's this?' He hastily discarded the unwanted object. 'Ah, yes, I think this is the one.'

But, when he finally succeeded in unlocking the door to the shaft, the elevator was not there. In fact, there was nothing at all to be seen, except for a scattered mess of dog-eared parchment that looked as if it had been nibbled by rats.

'Looks like poetry,' commented Ruth, squinting down into the pit. 'I wish people weren't so bloody untidy. Anyway, where's this elevator? Is there some way to call it down?'

'The call buttons never really worked properly,' Leonardo admitted. 'In the end, I usually had to go looking for it. Come on, let's walk up. It's probably on the next floor.'

But, when they arrived at the first landing, there

was still no sign of the elevator, nor, when they had dragged themselves up the next two flights, did they fare any better on the second.

'It's hardly worth bothering now,' panted Ruth. 'Shall we just keep going?'

But Leonardo was nothing if not methodical and, by the time his companion had finished speaking, he was already turning the key in the lock.

However, when the door swung open, it was not the sight of the hoped-for elevator that greeted their eyes. Instead, they were startled to be confronted by a pair of legs, suspended in space at such a height that the large, heavily booted feet hung level with their eyes. Slowly, the legs were rotating, first to the left, then back again to the right. Accompanying each movement, a dry, grinding, squeaking noise was audible from above.

They gaped at each other in alarm. Then, pushing rudely past someone who was hurrying downstairs, they made their way, with as much haste as they could muster, up the last two flights of steps to the fourth floor.

But, just as they arrived at the door to the shaft, another door burst open in the adjoining corridor and a dishevelled man blundered out. He was clad in a grubby-looking nightshirt, and his thinning hair looked as if it might once have been dark red.

'Michael!' exclaimed Ruth. 'Michael Brown! What's happened? You look terrible! What's going on?'

'I've just had a really peculiar message on the signal engine,' replied Rusty, who appeared somewhat dazed.

'I think we need to look in the elevator shaft.' As he said this, he found himself sidetracked by the sight of Miss Garamond's companion. 'Master Pegasus!' he said, baffled. 'What are *you* doing here?'

'It's rather a long story,' said Leonardo. 'I'll explain later. Damn, I've dropped the biscuits.' By now, he had inserted his key in the lock. As the door swung open, all three of them stared.

Framed in the lower half of the opening, they could see the upper half of a man's body, presumably attached to the legs that had been visible from the floor below. It was the body of a tall, long-boned man, with gaunt features and lank, black hair. Tightly encircling the twisted neck was a corroded iron collar, fastened at the front with a large, rusty padlock. And, attached to a ring at the side of the collar, extending upwards into the gloom at the top of the shaft, stretched a long, square-linked, black iron chain. The chain was making a slight squeaking noise as the body rotated placidly from side to side.

Along the corridor, apartment doors opened and neighbours wandered out to investigate the commotion. And, below them, unnoticed by anyone, the biscuits rattled merrily down the stairs.

'I don't think I want to stay in the city any longer. Not after all that. It's not the same place it used to be.' Leonardo shook his head slowly.

It was evening now. Rusty had finally persuaded his two guests that he had no further desire for company and, promising to return the next day, Leonardo and Ruth had left him to deal with the situation at Tower Mansions. They were now installed in their usual corner booth at the Crier's Rest, mulling over the events of the past few hours.

'Poor Tom,' said Ruth. There was a silence between them as they considered the fate of their son. Tentatively, their hands sought each other's across the table top. 'I agree with you about the city, though,' Ruth continued finally. 'I don't blame you for wanting to get out. But what about your job with the imps? Won't you need to finish that off somehow?'

'I've been giving it a bit of thought,' replied Leonardo, taking a long pull at his flask. 'Once we've buried Tom, I think I'd like to get back to my village. Because I don't see why I shouldn't do the job from home, as long as Master Gash is happy. You see, I've got my Multiple Empathy Engine there, I've spent years developing it, and it's far more powerful than any of the gear they've got at the Palace. If I can use that, I might just be in with a chance. And, of course, there's the signal station, just up there on the hill.'

'So you could connect your engine up to the network from there?'

Both of them were discovering some relief from this return to practical matters.

'Exactly.' The magician was warming to his theme now. 'And, of course, they tell me that all the smartest people are working from home these days. But there is just one snag . . .'

Ruth reached into her bag, found a cigarette, lit it and inhaled.

'Sorry,' she said after a moment. 'You don't, do you?'

'No,' said Leonardo. 'It's one vice I never got round to trying. What was I saying?'

'You said there was a snag.'

'Yes, that's it.' He hesitated for a moment, unsure how to continue. 'The thing is . . . you see . . . Well, it's just that I don't really want to go back to the village on my own. Not after what's happened. And now that I've met you again . . .'

Ruth had begun to smile.

'Does that constitute some kind of an offer?'

'Yes,' replied Leonardo slowly. 'Yes, I suppose it does.'

'So, after forty years, you finally want to make an honest woman of me?'

After a moment, the two of them burst into relieved laughter.

Tom Slater's body remained in the elevator shaft for several days, after which time a detachment finally arrived from the Royal Wolf Boys Litter Division to remove it.

Rusty paid them little attention. Still in a state of shock, he continued to haunt the apartment, bathing himself, smoothing the beds, fending off the occasional visitor. As he carried out these tasks, he slowly came to understand that it was Tom Slater who had brought about everything that had happened to his family and to his business over the past few weeks. Sometimes he wondered why his old friend had set out with such determination to ruin his life, but sometimes he just stared at the wall and didn't wonder about anything.

After a few days of this, Rusty was aroused from his torpor one afternoon by a sudden outburst of buzzing from the signal engine in the spare room. The communication turned out to be from the unhelpful administrator at the Royal Wolf Boys Investigation Division.

'Mister Brown? Regarding your Missing Persons Search Docket? Can I confirm that one of the persons listed was a Miss Ashleigh Brown, aged fifteen years?'

'Ashleigh? My daughter? Yes?' Suddenly, Rusty's palms were perspiring. He struggled to maintain his grip on the controls of the engine.

'There has been a development. I believe we may have some news for you.'

'Can you tell me . . . ?'

'We'll send someone round. Sorry, that's Branch policy, nothing to do with me. And we're still short-handed, of course, so it'll probably just have to be someone from the Cadets.'

And then the connection was broken. For what seemed like hours, Rusty paced restlessly up and down the living room, staring out of the window, awaiting the jangle of the doorbell, the endless stretch of time punctuated only by the distant chimes from the Institute of Calibration. Finally, he spied someone below him, someone wearing the blue outfit of the Cat Girls, someone making their way across the lawn to the main entrance of the building. When the messenger arrived on the fourth floor, Rusty was waiting impatiently at the threshold.

'Yes?'

Before him stood a slight figure, clad in a stiff-looking new uniform that was slightly too large, and boots that were slightly too shiny. The hair that framed the immature features beneath the forage cap was short and spiky and dark red in colour.

'Hello, Dad,' said Ashleigh sheepishly. 'I thought I'd better do the decent thing.'

'Ash!' Rusty could not stop his tears. 'Come here!'

And they collapsed into each other's arms.

The Royal Digest of Affairs and Events: Volume 193 (in the Seventeenth Year of the Rule of King Matthew)

The Diary of Miss Garamond (Herald)

Greetings, Citizens!

The author begs the reader's indulgence in respect of the extreme brevity of this entry; the reasons for this will shortly become apparent.

At the command of High Master Fang, *The Digest* will, after this issue, cease to appear in its present form. It is the wish of the High Master that, following the considerable advances over recent years in the various technologies of communication, the Royal Signal Network, under his personal direction, will in future constitute the principal vehicle for the promulgation of all information that is expected to be of interest to the Citizenry. Citizens may look forward to receiving *The Network Update* in the safety of their own homes and offices, and the author has been assured that this publication, its novel form notwithstanding, will continue to offer all the advantages of the old *Royal Digest*, with the additional benefit of many new features, the nature of which the High Master has not, thus far, seen fit to reveal.

Readers may be surprised to be reminded that the present author has occupied her current position as Herald for some sixteen years, and has therefore decided that the impending reorganisation of her Department will provide a suitable pretext for the relinquishment of her duties and her consequent retirement from public office. She is no longer a young woman (as her staff are constantly at pains to remind her!) and she therefore proposes to bid farewell to the City and to pass her remaining years in the tranquillity of the countryside where, the reader may rest assured, challenges and opportunities of a very different nature await her.

It is, then, the author's desire:

Firstly, to express her heartfelt thanks to her readers for their patronage;

Secondly, to express her appreciation to her staff for their years of unswerving loyalty;

Thirdly, to wish all Citizens many years of continued pleasure and enlightenment as recipients of *The Network Update.* Without our readers, there could have been no *Royal Digest,* and, without the *Royal Digest,* life in our Kingdom would not be the life that we enjoy today.

Last of all, the author wishes to express her most sincere assurance that, in the hands of High Master Fang, each and every Citizen may be confident of a happy, prosperous and secure future.

Goodbye, Citizens, and long live King Matthew!